MW01137399

WAR PAINT

BRIAN LEHMAN

ISBN: 978-1-6847-0398-2 (sc)
ISBN: 978-1-6847-0399-9 (hc)
ISBN: 978-1-6847-0400-2 (e)

Library of Congress Control Number: 2019907091

Lulu Publishing Services rev. date: 07/22/2019

DEDICATION

This book is dedicated to the following groups and individuals

WO1 Charles A. Richardson, United States Army.
Killed in action in Thua Thien Province, South Vietnam June 5, 1970

Signalman Arly Thomsen (1952-2000) United States Navy

Every United States Navy sailor who ever served
aboard the *USS Rupertus* DD-851

Every United States Navy sailor who served
aboard a ship in the Vietnam War

Dava Parks

My Anh Nguyen

Julie, my wife and best friend, for her love, her inspiration
and for putting up with my consumption of vast amounts
of time and energy to complete this book.

Colby, my son, who has always been encouraging and
supportive of my writing endeavors and aspirations.

PROLOGUE

October 1967—The Eastern Mediterranean, near Port Said, Egypt

This would be the last day, the last hours, of the Israeli destroyer *Eilat*. She had started out her life in Britain in 1944 as *H.M.S. Zealous*. Sold to her new country in 1955, she had now just passed her 23rd birthday. At 363 feet and armed with four 4.5 inch guns, six 40mm anti-aircraft guns and torpedoes, the *Eilat* was not a particularly impressive vessel among the world's navies, but she was the pride of her country and crew.

Many thought it laughable that the war that had begun in June had become known as the "Six Day War." It was now October 21st and the captain felt very much that he had been at war for more than four months. Three months earlier the *Eilat* had blown an Egyptian torpedo boat out of the water and ever since he had wondered when the retaliation would come. Being a knowledgeable electronics officer, he worried that the destroyer had no reliable means for defending against an attack from the missiles that were carried by some Egyptian patrol boats, though not much was known about them. It was commonly believed that Isreal's air superiority and ability to retaliate would prevent the missiles from being used. After all, even during those first six days of more intense warfare not one had been fired.

The *Eilat* and other naval units had been patrolling the Sinai coast in the eastern Mediterranean for four months. The captain confirmed they were not only outside the twelve mile territorial limit but another mile and a half just for good measure. To the east was Port Said, the northern entrance to the Suez Canal. It was late afternoon, coming up on 1730 hours and the sun would be setting in a few minutes. The crew of just over two-hundred men would complete their assigned patrol in a few hours and set a course for their homeport in Israel.

In Port Said, someone in the Egyptian navy had decided enough was enough. They knew there would be consequences to suffer for what they were about to do, but they had held their Komar missile boats and their Styx missiles at bay long enough. As the *Eilat* took up its patrol position, two missile boats just at the entrance to Port Said finished their launch preparations. They motored slowly out to sea toward the destroyer that was now silhouetted so well against the setting sun, their small low profiles not yet attracting any radar attention.

As they neared a ten mile distance they targeted the *Eilat* with their radar and fired their first missile—the first one in history ever fired on an enemy ship from another surface craft.

Aboard the *Eilat* the flash of the launching attracted a great deal of attention. Most of the crew, including the gunners, having never seen such a thing did not fully recognize the danger, even though they were at battle stations and watching the approaching threat.

The smoking, lumbering missile with its bulbous fuselage and stubby wings looked more like a plane in some sort of trouble. The captain watched as the sub-sonic missile showed no signs of slowing or falling short. Too late, he ordered the destroyer into a turn that would present her narrow beam as a small target, but the missile kept coming. The gunners seemed to finally realize what they were seeing as it came closer, but by then they had only seconds. A frantic sailor began firing a machine gun at the approaching Styx, but the missile was keeping its appointment with history.

The destroyer reeled from the huge explosion just above the water line. A boiler room and engine room were incinerated by the thousand pounds of explosive. All power was out, many of the life rafts had been disintegrated, several gun positions were gone and a fire was spreading.

Moments later a lookout reported, "Missile to port!"

The stricken warship was slowly circling, powerless, with its port side coming around full profile for the second missile. Several men began firing machine guns sooner this time, but their ineffective weapons were no match. The missile struck the port side, peeling back the main deck amidships and toppling one of the stacks. The basic structure of the hull was now buckled out of shape. There were no radios and no power to fight the spreading fires.

The ship was listing fifteen degrees to port and taking on massive amounts of water. Many of the crew had been killed or wounded. It was nearly dark now. They had dropped anchor to stop their slow drift closer to Port Said. After jury-rigging a transmitter, a radioman was finally able to contact an army unit inland to relay their distress message. The wounded were put into rafts so the rest of the crew could depart faster if the order was given.

Key bulkheads were giving way and the destroyer was beginning to settle at the stern and listing more. The captain gave the order to abandon ship. Many of the crew were still clinging to the hull as the floatables were thrown overboard and the crew was warned to move farther away from the sinking ship.

A man in the water shouted, "Missile!" They all watched as this one made its fiery low approach from the darkness and hit at the stern, staggering the ship with a needless final, mortal blow. Scattered in the darkness, the captain and his surviving men struggled to put distance between themselves and their former ship. It was bow up now and slipping beneath the sea. Groups of men did their best to stay together and find others in the pitching darkness.

Unbelievably, a fourth missile was fired. There was no ship left to hit, but more men were killed by the force of the explosion in their midst as the missile struck where the *Eilat* had been.

The survivors were rescued a short time later. Of the crew of more than 200, forty-seven were killed and more than a hundred wounded. For the first time in history a ship had been hit and sunk by missiles fired from another vessel.

ONE

Present day—Santa Cruz, California

"Grandpa, you ever kill anyone in the war?"

Across the room, Jeffs Ryder looked up from the magazine he was reading. His thirteen-year-old grandson, Mav, was standing looking at the living room wall crowded with family photographs.

His son, Cruz, who was leaning against the door frame chewing something from the kitchen and sipping from a bottle of beer, shrugged and gestured at the wall. "Navy pictures."

"Yeah, I did," Jeffs said.

"Really?" Mav pointed up at a ship photograph. "Were you in the war on this ship? Is that a battleship?"

"It's a destroyer," Jeffs explained. "It was the Vietnam War."

"This the ship I heard you call a rat before?" Mav said.

Jeffs smiled a little. "It is."

"Grandpa means his ship killed people in the war," Cruz said, then he saw the peculiar look his father gave him and knew right away that was the wrong explanation.

Mav turned and caught a glimpse of the unspoken exchange between the two men. "The ship killed a lot of people?"

Jeffs nodded.

"Wow!" Mav looked at his father for a moment then repeated his first question. "You ever kill anyone yourself, Grandpa?"

Jeffs thought back more than forty-five years to days he thought of

1

often but rarely talked about, mostly because nobody ever asked him, but also because he knew most people who weren't there just didn't get it.

"Yeah, I did," he repeated.

"Did you shoot him?" Mav asked.

"Yup."

"Where was he?"

Jeffs pointed. "On that ship, the destroyer."

Mav turned and looked at the photo again then turned back. "Why'd you shoot him?"

"It was a war. He was an enemy soldier and he was shooting at me and my friends," Jeffs said.

"Grandma Cathy said you were a big war hero and I should ask you about it."

Jeffs glanced over at his son, whose mouth was hanging open. "Maybe that day I was. It was a very interesting day."

"I've heard some navy stories from you but, you shot a guy? On the ship? How come I never heard about this before?" Cruz asked indignantly.

Jeffs cocked his head and a grin took over his face that made him look years younger. "I guess I should tell you all about it sometime."

TWO

The long war in Vietnam, after winding down the last couple of years, appears to have reawakened in the form of a large scale invasion by North Vietnam across the DMZ—the area separating North and South Vietnam. On March 30th, a massive attack by thousands of North Vietnam Army (NVA) troops, accompanied by hundreds of tanks and preceded by what may have been the largest artillery barrage of the conflict, overran forward bases all along the DMZ and miles into South Vietnam's northernmost provinces.

In a hotel room at the edge of downtown San Diego, Jeffs Ryder and Cathy Stone were lying in bed, her head resting on his chest.

A short drive away, the destroyer *USS Rattano* rested pier side at the 32nd Street Naval Station waiting for him.

"It was bad enough when we thought it would be weeks away," Cathy said.

Jeffs glanced at the alarm clock and sighed. "Seven hours."

She kept telling him she didn't want to waste the time they had left with crying, but he could feel tears tickling their way down the side of his chest.

"How much time will we have on the ship in the morning?" she asked shakily. They had already talked about this, but she needed to hear it again.

"Family and visitors get to come onboard and hang around for thirty, forty minutes or so before the ship gets ready to get underway."

"My mom told me the other day that she thinks it's a good thing that all this delayed our wedding plans," Cathy said. "She said the seven months that you're gone will be a good test for us. She thought it would especially be good for you to have a chance to do some growing up."

"No guarantee about the seven months." Jeffs scowled then let out a quick sneering laugh. "Yeah, my mom and dad said almost the exact same thing. They said something about you being more mature than me and that I had a lot of partying to still get out of my system before I had any business getting married. They said twenty and nineteen is way too young. I told them we'd both have birthdays before I came, back and I asked them how old they were when they got married. They told me I was being a smart-ass. I don't think they expect us to stay together through all this."

She raised up on one elbow, wiping away her tears and looking into his eyes. "What do you think?" she asked.

"Well, I think I was being a smart-ass."

She made a face and waited.

"Hey, even after we're married can't I still surf, party on the beach, hang out with our friends, all the usual stuff?"

Cathy stared at him as she slowly shook her head. "Well, no, Mister Smart-Ass, not all the usual stuff."

She quickly rolled away from him and stood. More tears were coming now, and she angrily wiped them away with both hands as her voice rose. "Have you forgotten how the hell you ended up in the navy? If it weren't for Judge Crawford, you'd be sitting in jail! We've been talking and planning about building a life together and now you say this bullshit. Is that what you think that you're just going to go back to your life of partying and getting arrested for stupid shit?"

He sighed. "I'm sorry I said that. I want you more than I want my old life back."

He knew it sounded like the thing he should say, but he wasn't so sure it felt true. Some days he almost liked the navy and other days he hated it. Some days he felt like marrying her and some days he thought it would all just be easier if he did go back to his life of partying and not giving a damn. But he knew she loved him, and he thought he loved her. And he sure as hell knew he didn't want to be taking off in the morning to go to a far-off war.

A grin came to his face. "You know you're cute when you're mad and naked."

She looked down at herself and grabbed a pillow, hugging it in front of her. She wanted to stay angry, but she couldn't help smiling. Her voice calmed and returned to a softer level. "Dammit, Jeffs. Are they right? Are you still too immature? Are we both too young to get married?"

"Honestly, I'm not sure, but we are getting older every minute." He held open the sheet and motioned her back into the bed.

She hesitated a few moments then shoved the pillow into his face and hurried back under the sheet beside him.

He wrapped his arms around her, and they were quiet for a long time. "You promise to be safe over there?"

It was the same thing she had said every few hours for the last two days. They both knew it was a senseless, desperate question.

As he always did, he answered, "It's a war."

She nodded and said, "I know," like she did every time.

"I promise," he said as usual.

But neither of them had any idea what any of that meant, or what to expect or how to act or what to think or how to feel or how to just be normal in this situation.

Cathy rolled away from him, then turned back and straddled him giving him a shy half smile. "You recovered yet?"

"Let's find out," he said.

"Wait. How old were they when they got married?" He reached for her breasts and she slapped his hands away. "Really, how old were they?"

Jeffs grinned up at her. "Nineteen and twenty."

THREE

War News – April 1972

It has become apparent after the initial hours of confusion following the so-called Easter Offensive which began on March 30th that it is indeed, according to American military spokesmen, a massive attack and an all-out effort designed to bring South Vietnam to its knees. Because of the "Vietnamization" process there are now fewer than 70,000 American troops left in South Vietnam, a steep decline from the 1968 peak of over a half million. The bulk of the fighting has now fallen to the ARVN, the Army of the Republic of Vietnam.

For too many people in too many ways, life had been askew for quite some time. Napalm, Hueys, Viet Cong, KIA, body counts, Tet, doves, hawks, DMZ, fragging, the Ho Chi Minh Trail, Agent Orange. Names and words largely unknown just a few years before were now common knowledge. Children had grown up hearing them, teenagers had come of age along with them, adults engaged in everyday conversation about them. For years the television war news, rather than being simply delivered, had intruded into homes with the droning background *whop, whop, whop* of helicopter rotors. That noise was now firmly entrenched in the American psyche as the signature sound of the Vietnam War.

During the peak years of the war, the national television news had routinely and unemotionally reported weekly and monthly combat deaths in the hundreds, week after week, month after month. Those numbers were also announced in cities and towns where they became names of sons, brothers, friends, neighbors, and former classmates, and the reaction was anything but unemotional. The number of Americans killed had passed an inexcusable 55,000, and there were few people left who had not known, or known of, at least one of them.

For a couple of years the war had been going through something called Vietnamization. This was President Nixon's dubious scheme to "end the war with honor" that would gradually hand over the unwinnable war to South Vietnam to fight. In truth it was nothing more than giving up a little at a time while piling up the number of killed and wounded in the process of rolling along to eventual sure defeat for South Vietnam.

Many in the Pentagon knew some kind of attack by North Vietnam was inevitable as American military strength in the country steadily dropped. Most of these experts had concluded that it would be a while longer before the North would be able to mount much of an attack. The inevitable came on March 30th, sooner than thought and on a massive scale which caught everyone by surprise. Americans called it the Easter Offensive and if it wasn't stopped, South Vietnam would be overrun and fall in a matter of weeks. Letting that happen now would put responsibility for such a swift defeat on the United States and would tarnish the "honorable" process of gradual withdrawal from the war.

The next day all pending leaves were cancelled for sailors stationed aboard many west coast warships, including the crew of the destroyer *Rattano*, a ship known to many as the *Rat*. Crew members were given seventy-two hours to get their affairs in order and prepare for immediate deployment to the Western Pacific. The same was happening all over the fleet. Carriers, cruisers, destroyers and support ships on their way home were ordered back and most ships scheduled to return soon to the States had their deployments extended.

Crewmembers and families were talking and milling about the *Rattano*. Most of the conversations were bland small talk or sailors pointing out features of the destroyer to their families and friends. But the tension in the air was palpable and everyone was feeling the time slipping away. Their parents were there, but Jeffs and Cathy were nearly oblivious to those around them. They could not hold hands any tighter and the two lovers' eyes kept trying to reach into each other but what they saw gazing back was mostly profound apprehension.

At 0845, the announcement was made throughout the ship. "Now hear this. At this time all civilians and non crew-members are requested to make their way off the ship. On the *Rattano*, make all preparations for getting underway. Set the special sea and anchor detail. Duty officer set the bridge watch. Line handlers stand by."

A crowd of wives, girlfriends, parents, grandparents, siblings and friends stood waving and cheering. Some just stared, and many of them struggled through tightened throats and tear-blurred vision, as the *USS Rattano* pulled away painfully slowly from pier three at the San Diego Naval Station at 0900 hours the morning of April 7, 1972, to begin the first day of what would be her final deployment. She would soon became part of the largest U.S. Naval force to be assembled since World War II.

FOUR

War News – April 1972

This week in the war:

April 2nd – President Nixon authorized U.S. vessels offshore to strike at the enemy forces with carrier launched warplanes and naval gunfire.
April 4th – President Nixon authorized increased bombing of NVA troops in South Vietnam and B-52 strikes against North Vietnam. A Pentagon spokesman said these missions will be flown out of Thailand and Guam.
April 10th – For the first time since November 1967, U.S. B-52s bombed North Vietnam. To protect upcoming U.S. air attacks, their priority targets were surface to air missile (SAM) sites.

Four days after leaving San Diego, the *Rattano* sailed into Pearl Harbor, Hawaii with her 268 enlisted crew and twenty-one officers aboard. The haze grey warship penetrated its 390 foot length into the seductive clear waters of the island paradise with the swagger of an aging but still dangerous gunslinger. Just a few hundred yards behind sailed the two other destroyers that made their way across the Pacific from San Diego with her. The day before, two others had come and gone. The next day a cruiser and three more destroyers would pass through.

Destroyers were the predators of the navy. Long, narrow, low, fast, with sleek upswept bows and, like that aging gunslinger, they wore their guns out where everyone could see them. Their lean, menacing form cut through the sea with a certain attitude and the men who served on them knew it.

One of those men was Signalman Seaman Jeffs Ryder. His route into the navy had been an uncommon one, and the rowdy, smirking, tall, blonde California beach kid was unlikely to ever be transformed into a proper navy man, but he was learning to adapt. He had been aboard barely two months, but long enough that he was gaining some appreciation for just what it meant to be a destroyer sailor.

When he let himself think about it, his heart ached for Cathy and he couldn't fathom how he could possibly be apart from her for what was scheduled to be seven months. Even so, there was a youthful, naive part of him feeling restless, maybe even a little eager, to get on with the adventure of going off to war halfway around the world. Right now though, he had a more immediate concern that was keeping his mind less on Cathy and the war. He had been to Hawaii before and he'd been grumbling the entire way across the Pacific that this visit would be just twenty-four hours long, restricted to the base and include no surfing.

The next morning, Commander James "Mac" McHenry, Captain of the *Rattano* strolled out onto the port bridge wing holding an after-breakfast mug of coffee. At forty-seven he was the oldest man aboard the ship and he was coming up on his thirtieth year in the navy. He had thought the last deployment would be it for him with the war winding down for the United States, but his ship and a host of other warships were now on station or advancing toward the waters off Vietnam. So this one was a bonus—one more chance to do what he did best, and this time around he planned to do some things differently.

He knew most of the obsolete gun destroyers like this one would be scrapped or sold off to foreign navies as soon as this obsolete war was over. He wasn't shooting for a promotion or a new command and there was no one to please but himself.

Taking a minute to enjoy the rest of his coffee he gazed around the historic harbor, absently rubbing his graying stubble with his free hand.

Downing the last swallow he turned and shouted up toward the signal bridge just one deck above. "Any signalmen up there?"

Jeffs' head appeared over the railing. "Yes, sir."

"How ya doing, Ryder? Want to get off the ship for a while?"

"Sure, Captain. We hitting the waves for a little surfing?"

McHenry shook his head. "No such luck. Find out if Radio has any traffic to send or pick up and meet me out by the truck."

Two minutes later, Jeffs and Leon Thomsen, a radioman and one of Jeffs' best friends, made their way across the pier. Both were dressed in the standard enlisted working uniform—blue chambray shirt, denim bell bottoms, and dark blue ball cap. McHenry was waiting by the bulky, drab-gray four-door pickup the base had provided, holding the refilled mug, dressed in the normal officer khaki trousers and shirt.

Leon held up a manila envelope. "Classified traffic I gotta take myself, sir."

They both saluted, but McHenry casually waved them off and opened the passenger door himself.

"Radio just about back in action?" McHenry asked.

Leon nodded. "Yes, sir. Chief Ross says they'll be done with the transmitters in a couple of hours then we'll be back to sending our own message traffic."

Jeffs started the truck. "Where you headed, Captain?"

"The *Holliner*, a couple of piers over." He pointed out the direction. "You guys drop me off, go on over to the message center then come back. I can walk back when I'm done."

He dug his wallet out of his pocket and handed Jeffs a five. "Here, grab yourself some doughnuts from that little place right next to the club. Get a couple dozen, enough for the signal and radio gang. Get me a couple of maple bars. It shouldn't be too long, but I have to meet with that bastard DeMoorts, so it might take longer than I want."

Jeffs held up the five. "Thanks, Captain. Isn't DeMoorts the skipper of the *Holliner*?"

McHenry turned so he could talk to them both. "We were Lieutenant J.G.'s aboard a destroyer on a training cruise. On his turn at berthing the ship, he was screwing it up. I jumped in, gave new orders to the helmsman and engine room, and saved some of the pier, at least"

Jeffs laughed. "Some of it?"

McHenry was grinning at the memory. "Yeah, we still tore up about fifty feet of it. It wasn't much of a pier. More like a rotting boat dock. It was old and I don't even think it was being used for anything, but still..."

"So Captain DeMoorts thinks you made him look bad?" Leon asked.

McHenry nodded. "He made himself look bad. The training officers spent half a day dissecting his mistakes for the rest of us. He's hated me ever since."

"Everyone says you never use help from tugs when you berth the ship." Jeffs said. "Just to keep showing Captain DeMoorts you can do it?"

McHenry chuckled. "I don't need the help but some ports make you use tugs. We're all good at something. Me, I can thread one of these cans anywhere, forward or backward."

"Backward?" Jeffs asked.

McHenry nodded. "You never know."

Leon was nodding emphatically in the back seat. "Well, Captain, I wasn't there, but I'll bet you were right on."

"Thanks, Thomsen. Pull up right here, Ryder."

Jeffs stopped the truck at the head of the pier. The *Holliner* was the first ship in line.

McHenry stepped out, closed the door and leaned back in the open window. "By the way, Ryder, who was that good-looking brunette I saw you saying goodbye to when we left San Diego?"

"That was Cathy, my fiancée. We were going to get married in a few months, maybe, but I guess it's going to be a little longer now."

McHenry nodded. "Maybe, huh? Well, if you're worth waiting for she'll be waiting."

"Hope so," Jeffs said. "You have somebody waiting, Captain?"

McHenry nodded slowly. "I do, Ryder, my third wife. And the other two always waited for me to come back before they divorced me."

Leon laughed out loud from the back seat and Jeffs stifled his own response.

"Something else I need to ask you about," McHenry said. "I heard somewhere you do a dead on impression of Lieutenant Wiffler. I had a conversation with Mr. Simons this morning. It seems someone called down to the quarter deck last night, said they were Lieutenant Wiffler and ordered him off watch to come personally to the wardroom to get something. You wouldn't know anything about that, would you?" McHenry gave him an unflinching stare.

Jeffs thought over his answer for a few moments. "Well, sir, I might be able to tell you something about that."

McHenry nodded, and with a dead serious look pointed his index finger inches from Jeffs. "Seaman Ryder, you don't want to end up standing before me at a Captain's Mast, so watch yourself. I'll let this one slide, but don't pull that shit anymore. I'll tell Mr. Simons to be expecting an apology from you today. Got it?"

Jeffs nodded and cleared his throat. "Yes, sir."

McHenry started to turn to leave, then put his head back in the window. "Also, don't take this as a compliment, Surfer Joe, but you're starting to look like a beach bum again. Hit the barbershop before the end of the day." He turned to Leon. "And you, I'm not absolutely clear on what the regs are right now, but I know an Afro is too fuckin' big when half your hat disappears down inside it."

McHenry eyed them both for a few more seconds then turned and walked away.

Jeffs put the truck in gear and pulled away from the pier as Leon climbed over into the front seat and began a low chuckle that grew into a high pitched giggle. "You stupid honky!" He started punching Jeffs in the arm. "You knew Simons would give you a bad time about your hair and you wanted him out of the way so you could head over to the club."

Jeffs grinned, then in a perfect imitation of the pompous and widely hated Lieutenant Wiffler, said, "That young Seaman Ryder is just such a clever son-of-a-bitch, isn't he?"

✦
FIVE

Dear Jeffs,

…After your ship pulled away from the pier I hurried to the car and drove as fast as I could around the bay and out to Cabrillo Point at the entrance to the harbor. I told your parents and mine that I just wanted to go by myself. I beat the ship! I wanted a last look. It was too far to tell from up on the hill, but when the ship sailed by I imagined the men I saw on the ship included you. I stayed there for a long time until your ship disappeared far out in the sea. I love you Jeffs. Please stay safe.

Love,
Cathy

McHenry was the last of the four men to enter the wardroom of the *Holliner*, another destroyer of the same class as the *Rattano*. In addition to McHenry and DeMoorts, also present was the captain of the *Wilson*, a newer guided missile destroyer. The three ships had sailed together from San Diego. Joining the three skippers was Captain William Gordan, McHenry's long-time friend. As commander of Destroyer Squadron Seventeen, which included the three destroyers and three others currently operating in the Vietnam area, Gordan was referred to as commodore though his actual rank was still Captain.

When McHenry and DeMoorts shook hands there were no greetings or smiles exchanged as with the other two men. In his mind, the fact that McHenry's first command came several years earlier than his own, was due to that training incident. Occasionally he still ran into men who would make some joke about it, and he hated it.

The meeting lasted just fifteen minutes, ironing out details about the formations and drills they would run on the way across the Pacific. Their orders were to make best possible speed and they were planning to leave in the early afternoon in just a few hours. They all had healthy power plants and the weather forecast looked good so the decision was made to continue pushing across the rest of the Pacific at a fuel-gulping twenty-six knots rather than a more leisurely pace they might have maintained during peace time exercises. That would gain them almost a day.

McHenry and Gordan lingered for a while after the captain of the *Wilson* excused himself to other duties. A couple of minutes later DeMoorts awkwardly excused himself and left his own wardroom to the two friends, knowing they would now be talking about him.

The two men exchanged grins as DeMoorts' footsteps retreated. Gordan shook his head. "I should move my flag to the *Rat*."

"Anytime, Commodore" McHenry said with a sarcastic chuckle. "Hell, it'd serve DeMoorts right if you moved. He just gets some kind of ass-kissing charge out of being the squadron flag ship."

McHenry walked to the other end of the conference table to fetch the iced tea pitcher. "Speaking of ass kissers, I saw Admiral Loflin waking around earlier with his usual entourage of them."

Gordan gave a disgusted look. "He's here on some kind of bullshit inspection visit. I get to be at a dinner with him tonight. You know, sometimes I think he's seriously off. You would think they'd want someone a little bit more rational in charge of the whole fucking 7th Fleet."

"You'd think," McHenry said. "Probably the secret to making flag rank."

"I'm going to be in a briefing with him and some brass from intelligence sometime next week," Gordan said. "I haven't heard the details yet, but I guess the North Vietnamese may have some new toys. Styx missile boats."

McHenry raised his eyebrows. "They've been saying that might happen for years. For real this time?

"Sounds like it, but I'll know more after this briefing.

"Hey, how's that kid Ryder doing? I got a call from the judge just before we left San Diego. He's concerned."

"Concerned, huh?" McHenry said. "He did offer to drop all Ryder's legal shit if he enlisted. Now that this damn war has heated up again for us maybe he's feeling a little guilty."

Gordan nodded. "He's worried the kid might be causing problems because of what he calls his rebellious nature. I was looking over Ryder's paperwork. He'd already been put on probation twice in the space of a year or so and then he was arrested a third fucking time and it's all the same bullshit."

McHenry laughed. "I know. It's all stupid shit like disturbing the peace, illegal partying on the beach, some minor destruction of public property, and the thing that always makes me laugh, nude surfing. I'm gonna ask him about that one someday. He's a pain in the ass sometimes, but he's not really a trouble maker. Does his job, gets along well enough, pretty sharp kid. But he likes to get around every rule that doesn't suit him and sometimes he has this idea that he can do whatever the hell he wants. And he never gets a fucking haircut without being told to."

Gordan grinned. "Hell, he sounds just like you!"

McHenry made a face. "Maybe that's why I think he's okay. Anyway, you can tell Hizzoner he's doing fine."

"Good." Gordan stepped to the air conditioning vent and held his hand up to it. "They gotta get this AC working better." He walked back to the table and took a long swallow of tea. "So here's a strange one. You heard anything about bounties over there?"

"I heard something awhile back about bounties on our snipers," McHenry said.

Gordan shook his head. "Ships. There's some story going around that certain ships have a price on them. A pilot, gun crew or whatever who scores a hit on one gets money and time off."

"Any truth to it?"

"Sounds screwy," Gordan said, "but CINCPAC is sounding like they're at least wondering if there's something to it."

McHenry stood, checked his watch and finished his tea. "Well, that's just dandy! Ship bounties and missile boats. You've really made my day, Commodore."

"I try my best," Gordan said. "Maybe this will make you feel better." He pointed to a tall narrow cardboard box with a large red bow on top, leaning against the corner. "New breakaway flag. Just flew in from Yokosuka yesterday. Your whole crew pitched in. Ryder was one of the ones who helped design it. Damnedest one I've ever seen. It's got a pirate and some kind of fucking crazy looking surfer rat. You'll love it."

SIX

Dear Cathy,

…You said you were going to write every day and number the envelopes because we knew the mail delivery would be messed up. Today I got number 1, 2, 6, 7 and 9. I think I've mailed three so far.

Love,
Jeffs

Shortly before sunset on April 19, nine days after departing Hawaii, following quick refueling stops at Midway and Guam, the *Rattano* was just tying up at the pier upon arriving in Subic Bay, the Philippines. She was scheduled for three days in port loading ammunition and other supplies and taking care of a few small maintenance items before steaming west to join the fight. The crew was looking forward to liberty in the sin city of the western Pacific. In fact, many of the men in the night's liberty section had passed up evening chow aboard ship in anticipation of going ashore within the next hour or so and treating themselves to a meal on the base or in town.

In Radio, Leon Thomsen uttered a soft, "Whoa" to himself. He tore the flash message, the highest priority, off the fleet broadcast Teletype and walked it a few feet to a desk where Radioman Chief Frank Ross was seated. Ross was the Chief Petty Officer of OC Division which consisted of radiomen and signalmen. That message was immediately followed by another flash which Leon also set in front of him.

Ross set the messages down on the open dictionary he'd been studying and read them both silently. "Son of a bitch," he said. Raising his voice to the other three radiomen on duty he called out, "Looks like we're getting into the war a little quicker than we planned on, boys."

He shook his head, chuckled nervously and handed the papers back to Leon. "Take them to the captain right now." Then raising his voice to carry through the open doorway to where Teletypes were clattering away, "Omata, Shakes, watch the broadcast!"

Captain McHenry was out on the port bridge wing looking forward and aft down the length of the destroyer barking commands to the helmsman and the officer of the deck as he maneuvered the ship closer in against the pier.

"Message, Captain," Leon said.

"Now, Thomsen?" He looked aft again. "All engines stop!"

"It's a flash, sir. Actually, two of them."

"Flashes? Shit, did the war end or something?"

"Kind of the opposite I think, sir."

McHenry felt his shirt pocket for his glasses, then checked fore and aft again along the ship as it slowly drifted into position. "I don't know where my damn glasses are. Give me the highlights."

"Okay, sir, let's see. The guided missile cruiser *Oklahoma City*, destroyer *Lloyd Thomas*, the Guided Missile Frigate *Sterett* and the destroyer *Higbee* came under enemy fire from shore batteries during an attack at Dong Hoi yesterday. *Oklahoma City* took some minor shrapnel damage. A MIG hit the *Higbee* with a bomb."

McHenry turned and looked at Leon. "Jesus! Casualties?"

Leon looked down at the paper. "A few, all minor it looks like. Uh, the bomb hit near the aft gun mount, set off some of the ready ammunition and blew apart the gun mount. There were no personnel inside the gun mount."

McHenry had returned to watching the side of the destroyer just reaching the bumpers on the pier. "Damn, what else?"

"Something about tracking surface targets and the *Sterett* was fired on by a Styx anti-ship missile."

McHenry whipped his head around and grabbed the papers from Leon's hand. He silently moved his lips as he struggled to read through squinted eyes. "Son of a bitch," he whispered. "Says they downed the MIG and the missile."

He shoved the papers back into Leon's hand. "Thanks Thomsen. Make me a couple dozen copies and bring them back to me either here or in the wardroom."

"Captain, the other message says our three day stay here is cancelled and we are not reporting directly to the gun line. We're meeting up with some other ships in forty-eight hours and attacking Dong Hoi soon after. We're taking on food, fuel and ammo and getting underway at 2100."

"2100 today?"

"Yes, sir."

McHenry looked at his watch. "Jesus that's just four hours. Well, now I know why we've got ammo trucks and couriers and a bunch of staff officer cars waiting all over the pier. Goddamn, Thomsen, you got any good news there?"

Leon looked down at the papers in his hand then back up with a grin. "Guess not sir."

McHenry shook his head, his mind already racing ahead to try to think of everything he needed to do. "Make copies of all that shit for me."

By the time Leon returned to Radio to make copies, two more flash priority messages had come through with more details to follow up the first two. All over the fleet, these messages were being read with growing alarm. It would soon come to be known as the Battle of Dong Hoi and was a turning point in the war for the navy. This was the first time North Vietnamese MIGS had directly attacked U.S. warships and the first time a Styx missile had been fired at a U.S. ship.

After quickly delivering copies of the four messages to the captain, Leon took the long way back to Radio, scampering up two decks to the signal bridge. Jeffs and George had just finished the normal routine of pulling down the steaming ensign and running up the pennant to indicate the captain was aboard. Jeffs was inside the signal shack leaning out the open window talking to George.

"Got news," Leon said as he approached.

He stepped closer and spoke softly as he motioned toward the port bridge wing which was down a ladder just out of their sight. "You can forget liberty. We're leaving later tonight."

"Tonight?" Jeffs said.

George shook his head, pulled the unlit cigarette out of his mouth and looked suspiciously at Leon. "You're fucking with us."

Leon motioned to keep their voices down. "Listen, I just took some messages to the captain. They dropped a damn bomb on the *Higbee* yesterday and another ship shot down a Styx missile. We ain't heading right to the gun line. We get to join some other cans in an attack in North Vietnam at Dong Hoi."

Jeffs glanced at George, who was staring at Leon in disbelief.

"Okay, white boys, I gotta go before the chief starts wondering where I went and hits me with some big-ass words. Later." He walked aft and disappeared down a ladder.

George Hays was a first-class signalman, three notches above Jeffs, an eight-year veteran of the navy and the lead petty officer of the division. The two got along well and had developed a friendship while standing many two-man signal watches together which consisted of mostly several hours of talking about everything and anything.

"So, you did this before?" Jeffs asked.

"A few times. In fact the last time they landed a small shell on the fantail just aft of the gun mount. Punched a hole right through the main deck into the aft sleeping compartment. Shrapnel everywhere. Lucky nobody was in there."

Jeffs nodded. "So what's a Styx missile?"

"Some serious shit," George said. "The navy's been worried about North Vietnam getting them. It's an anti-ship missile fired from patrol boats. Knock the shit out of a destroyer, sink her maybe, especially an old one like us. They call it a ship killer."

Jeffs was silent for several seconds. "Ship killer. Great. So where are we when we attack this Dong Hoi place?"

George draped his arm over Jeffs' shoulders and gestured sweepingly with the other. "Right up here, buddy, watching all the action."

SEVEN

Dear Jeffs,

…I found a job! It's at a hospital in Chula Vista just south of San Diego. I'm going to be a ward clerk. It's full time and after a couple weeks of on the job training I get a small raise. My cousin Betty lives in San Diego and she said I could stay with her for a while. How is it going over there? Is it scary? I'm sure you have seen there are a lot of demonstrations against the war going on. I love you, Jeffs. Please be careful. I miss you. I love you.

Love,
Cathy

Thirteen hundred miles across the South China Sea from Subic, a young man named Tran Dinh Quan scooped the last few grains of rice from his bowl into his mouth. He glanced around quickly at his five companions and saw the same hunger on their faces.

One of the men stood, muttered "Du ma," threw his empty bowl to the ground and stomped around the corner. They all wanted more, needed more, but that was the end of this meal.

Quan was twenty years old, but an American might guess his short stature and slight build at closer to fifteen. They were just outside of Dong Hoi, forty-five miles north of the DMZ that divided North and South Vietnam. His duty at the coastal defense site had begun just two months before, but it was already beginning to feel to him like it had been a long time.

On either side of where he and the others in his crew slept, ate and lived were openings that led into two larger tunnels. These two tunnels each concealed a powerful artillery piece--a French-made, World War II vintage 155mm howitzer. They were barely used, but they were not new.

The French army had brought them to Vietnam in 1954. Two weeks later they had been captured by Viet Minh forces. Over the years they had spent some time hidden away and also in action in various locations. Now they were each mounted on a rolling wooden platform, concealed behind twenty feet of concrete and earth, with a hundred feet of earth above them to the top of the bluff.

There were many other gun emplacements of various sizes and design spread along the expanse of the hilly terrain, but these two guns were the pride of the NVA commander in charge of the coastal defense installation. The crews who manned these two pieces were looked upon as somewhat elite. Quan did not understand why he had been assigned here, but guessed that one of the elders from his village must have known someone who owed them a favor. It seemed to be very good duty compared to others he had heard about.

For two months his days had been filled with firing drills, cleaning and maintaining the guns and other equipment. During the time he had been stationed here, there had been no attacks from the sea, until yesterday. Over the span of just a few minutes his quiet duty station had been transformed into a pandemonium of artillery firing, explosions and fear.

Two nearby positions had been destroyed as the naval gunfire punch in all along and above their hillside. They and the other gun positions had fired on four ships that had made a daring daytime attack on the area. Their gun crew commander thought they had hit very close to two of the ships, but the ships had not come in very close to the shore and in the humid haze it was difficult to know if they had scored any direct hits.

They had all watched afterward as a MIG attacked one of the ships, hitting it with a bomb and they had seen the plane shot from the sky by a missile fired from another ship. There had been more missiles fired and more gunfire from the ships, but Quan and the others did not know what the ships were firing at.

The men he had eaten the evening meal with had talked for a while after their meager rations, mostly about the lack of food and the action of the day before. They had been told that the war was going through another change and the Americans were sending even more bombers and more ships. They were told this evening to expect more attacks soon, probably at night.

After a bit the gathering broke up as men reported to their duties or to bed if they had a watch coming up. Quan stood and started toward the sleeping area at the rear of the cavern.

"Hey soldier." The young man was one of his superiors and enjoyed keeping that superiority as visible as possible. "Don't forget you have a lookout watch at 0100 hours."

Quan turned toward him and forced himself to remain composed. "How could I forget with you reminding me every few minutes?"

The young officer looked at his companion and they both laughed. His companion said, "See, you are a shit! Even Quan thinks so and he barely knows you."

Quan smiled, pleased the man agreed with him, but said nothing as he continued along to the sleeping area. The tunnel widened here and the floor was covered with various kinds of mats. In the corner was a pile of grey, wool blankets with U.S. stenciled on them. A candle in a niche above him provided a dim glow as he spread one of the blankets over a straw mat and eased his weary body down onto it.

He had never met an American, yet here he was manning a weapon for killing them. He did not understand much of the politics or military strategy involved and most often what he wished for, longed for, was to just go home and have his life return to as close as possible to whatever normal was these days.

He turned onto his side. He did not feel elite, just hungry, tired, lonely and a little fearful of what the next days or nights would bring. In another minute, sleep began to dissolve his restless pondering, and his thoughts evolved into dreamlike simplicity. He imagined floating many miles to the north, to the Village by the Lone Hill, to Lam, his young wife of just three months.

❧
EIGHT

War News – April 21

Protests escalating

On a growing number of campuses across the nation the renewed bombing and escalating naval bombardment in North Vietnam has triggered a variety of student protests. At Columbia University in New York City, eight large windows in the School for International Affairs were broken as 1000 people marched through the campus late Wednesday night. Four days ago at the University of Maryland a huge demonstration took place to protest the ROTC program on campus. Hundreds of students were arrested and 800 Maryland National Guardsmen were ordered onto campus.

After a hectic all-hands working party that topped off the *Rattano* with fuel, food and ammo, the warship was just clearing Subic Bay and beginning to make good speed into the South China Sea due east, ever closer to the crew's first taste of war.

Jeffs found himself in his rack with a decent amount of hours to get some sleep before his morning watch just after breakfast. He turned his head and looked at Cathy's photo. Someone turned out the rest of the lights, but enough light from the mess deck came through the open hatch that he could still see the photograph, her eyes seeming to stare back at him. Turning onto his side he continued to study her face. The crew was being told they were scheduled to return in November, but that schedule meant nothing now in the face of the Easter Offensive. Wars didn't follow schedules. Back in the real world, seven months was a relatable amount of time, but in his present situation, even if seven months turned out to be true, it seemed like too long to even think about.

He could hear the sea rushing by just a couple of feet from his head. As the continuous rolling of the ship slowly rocked him closer to sleep he wondered, as he did from time to time, just how little steel was between himself and the salty darkness. He thought back to February, just a few days after reporting aboard. He had been required to attend an orientation session for new crew members. He and ten other men had assembled as instructed on the torpedo deck just below the front of the bridge.

A tall, black, muscular first class petty officer had stood before the group of new sailors who had reported aboard during the last few weeks. He was wearing the expression that he liked to think of as his grim smile. His teeth clamped the remaining half of a dead cigar.

"Good morning, gentlemen. I'm Hull Technician First Class Jones. My job today is to teach you everything there is to know about this tin can in the next hour. Your job is to pretend you're listening and remember it."

He was well-spoken with just a hint of a Louisiana accent, and he filled his work dungarees with a style and authority suitable for a recruiting poster. Reading from the list on his clipboard, he called out last names and each man answered.

Looking up from the list, Jones asked, "Which one of you is Ryder?"

Jeffs raised his hand.

"What's your first name?"

"It's Jeffs."

"Not Jeff?" Jones asked.

"No, sir, it's Jeffs."

Jones nodded. "Save your sirs for the officers. Okay, Jeffs, let's get this session started."

Jones turned and walked a few steps to set his clipboard down, when the man standing next to Jeffs, a quartermaster by the name of Mike Gonzales, said, "How many names you need, ass hole? You look like just one guy to me, Jeffy."

This wasn't the first time he'd had to defend his name and he quickly gauged the source and decided the best course of action. Before Jones could turn to see, Jeffs pushed the man hard in the chest with both hands, sending him stumbling backward where he tripped over a mop left leaning against a railing, skidded on a wet spot and sat down hard on the deck, knocking over a bucket of water."

The group erupted into laughter just as Jones turned back to them. Jeffs hurried to the shocked and still seated man, leaned down over him and said, "Hi, I'm Jeffs, Mikey. Then he offered his hand and helped him up off the deck.

Jones said, "Goddamn, Gonzales, what're you gonna do in a storm, fall overboard?"

Everyone laughed some more while the two men stared each other down. "You two done dancing or am I gonna have to escort you back to your divisions for some additional instruction?"

"No, we're done," Jeffs said. "Right?"

The other man looked Jeffs up and down then back at Jones. "Yeah, we're done. And the rest of you, I wouldn't recommend giving Jeffs any shit about his name."

A friendship was born.

Jones sighed and started his session. "In case any of you are lost, this is the *USS Rattano*, DD-856. That's Rat-uh-no, with the accent on the first syllable. Most of us just call her the *Rat*. Now that's for us, you understand, the crew. We call her the *Rat* out of fuckin' affection. Those other bastards out there can call her by her proper name, and you can tell 'em I said so."

He paced back and forth as he spoke. "This ship is a Gearing class or 710 class destroyer, the first one being the USS Gearing, DD-710. A total of ninety-eight Gearings were commissioned, all during the last months of World War II and the next year or two. The *Rat* was commissioned in 1946. That's right, boys and girls, she's just celebrated her 26th birthday. In dog years that's 182. In ship years you can bet your ass it's way more than the navy ever intended. She just missed World War II but she saw plenty of action in Korea."

He stopped, pulled a lighter from his pocket and re-lit his cigar. After a few puffs and a swirl of smoke, he continued. "This vessel is 390 feet in length, give or take, and carries a crew of right around 270, plus fifteen or twenty officers. Her primary mission is anti-submarine warfare. Her secondary mission is to provide gunfire support, and that's just what all of these old cans have been doing in this war. She's got two gun mounts, one forward and one aft. Each of those houses two, five-inch .38 caliber guns. In navy gun lingo that means the inside diameter of the gun barrel is five inches and the barrel is 38 times longer than the five inches which comes to how much? Time's up, 190 inches. Which equals how many feet? Time's up, a little less than sixteen feet. So these gun barrels are just under sixteen feet long. They fire a projectile that weighs around fifty-five pounds, give or take and a range of twelve miles, give or take. If you've never heard a five-incher fired then you're in for a hell of a treat sometime."

He took the cigar from his smiling lips and chuckled softly. "First time or the thousandth, scare the shit out of you *every* time. Make you mad, make you cuss! If we head back over to Nam then you're gonna hear them plenty."

He pointed up above from where they were standing. "The bridge wings are these outside extensions of the pilot house or bridge on each side here. While we're in Nam there will also be a .50 caliber machine gun mounted along the walk aft of each bridge wing. Here where we're standing is called the torpedo deck. As you can see there are six tubes, three starboard and three to port, for surface targets."

At this point, Jones started the group on their walk around the ship. "During the early to mid-60s most of these old cans went through some major changes. FRAM they called it—Fleet Rehabilitation and Modernization. Depth charges and anti-aircraft guns are gone. An all new aluminum superstructure. Larger bridge, CIC, communication spaces, better radar, new sonar. A hangar and chopper landing deck were added as part of the aft superstructure. The chopper was experimental and isn't in use anymore, but the hangar makes good storage and the landing deck is a good drop point for deliveries by chopper. It's also good for barbecues."

Looking down into engine room from the main deck passageway. "The boilers run on fuel oil and she's got completely refurbished steam turbine engines that put out sixty-thousand shaft horsepower. I don't know exactly what that means, but it's way more than a GTO and on a good day she'll push thirty-four knots. That's pretty fast. Just a touch under forty miles per hour, and it feels like you're on a damn speed boat! Some snipes swear she'll do thirty-five knots, but they're probably lyin'." He eyed a couple of men from engineering.

Standing one deck above the main deck, amidships between the stacks. "This is the ASROC deck and that big ugly box is the ASROC launcher. Stands for Anti-Submarine Rocket. Launches a rocket out a few miles that drops a submarine hunting torpedo."

Pointing to the aft end of the forward superstructure. "Right inside here is Radio Central. One deck up is electronics shops and the back side of CIC or Combat Information Center. Radar, sonar, charting surface and air contacts, stuff like that."

Pointing up another deck to the top of the superstructure. "Up there is the signal bridge. Signalman send and receive messages by flag and flashing light. Tucked in underneath the mast there is a little square hut with big windows. That's the signal shack." He gave Jeffs a look. "The signalmen like to hang out in there and pretend they're workin'."

He neared the dramatic ending of his well-rehearsed lecture as he led the group back to the torpedo deck where they had begun. "Some of these old cans break down a lot, but not this one. Keeps on chuggin' along, especially the guns. Best damn destroyer guns in the fleet. She may be getting' old but she's still a mean bitch in the right kind of fight."

He walked through the group, reached into a life jacket locker and returned to his position at the front. His right hand held a large box of saltine crackers. It was getting toward lunch and it occurred to a couple of the younger men in the group that maybe this was snack time. They were wrong.

"The hull of a destroyer ain't very thick and no armor. She's built for speed. It might interest some of you to know that after all these years of chipping paint, pressure blasting, repainting and salt water corrosion, they say there are some places in the hull that are just an eighth of an inch thick, maybe less. So, what we haven't covered are the procedures in the event of a direct hit by a large bomb or missile, or an explosion below the water line from a mine or torpedo. You see, gentlemen, we really don't have any special procedures for those events, and we really don't need any, because here's what will happen."

The box of crackers dropped to the deck in front of the men and a second later a size thirteen, steel-toed navy work shoe slammed down onto the box with an explosive crunch. The group of new crewmen stood silently staring.

Petty Officer Jones stared back, holding the extinguished stub of his cigar and smiling amid the destruction of cardboard and enriched whole wheat flour. "We're done boys and girls. Clean up this mess before you report back to your divisions." He turned, walked a few steps and disappeared down a ladder.

The silence lasted for a while as each man imagined himself aboard that box of crackers when the big bang came.

NINE

Dear Jeffs,

…I think my parents are kind of proud of me about making some solid plans and being brave (my dad's word) about starting out a life of my own. They gave me some money when I left and made me promise to call at least every other day. I love you. Stay safe.

Love,
Cathy

Around the same time the *Rattano* was leaving Subic Bay to join the war, seven men gathered for a late night meeting forty miles north of Dong Hoi, near a place called Hon La in North Vietnam. This was a group that many did not believe even existed, and had achieved a sort of legendary mythical status among their countrymen. Exactly who they were and how they accomplished their work was known to only themselves and a few trusted accomplices. They called themselves Bay—Seven in English.

The members included six military men who held various positions in the Viet Cong, the North Vietnamese Army and Navy, and a civilian who served as their leader. None of them were high level officers, but they were high enough to have access to the right information and the right people. They had all grown up in or nearby the same village in North Vietnam, or were relatives of those who had. It was an unimportant place known to the locals as The Village by the Lone Hill.

So far their efforts had resulted in the assassinations of several American military officers, a dozen South Vietnamese military or government officials, the downing of a few specific American fighter pilots, and the murder of two navy officers who had the misfortune to be from aircraft carriers that had been singled out for retribution for their supposed bombing of civilians.

The war-torn chaotic conditions of their country made it both more difficult for all seven of them to meet regularly and easier for them to work without others taking any particular notice. Most people around them had more important things to worry about and they were all in positions which allowed them to travel without the need for much in the way of explanations.

They had been lucky at first, back in 1967, when they were less careful, not to have been found out. Now, though, they went to great lengths to keep their identities secret. Meeting face to face was their preferred routine and this day they had all managed to gather together. They were in a celebratory mood over their latest success.

Chu Minh Chien, their leader, raised his glass of rice wine, a gesture he had learned from the French years ago. "To the *Higbee*."

The others raised their glasses in return and drank.

Chien was by far the oldest and they treated him with the respect an elder commanded. But it was more than his age that made him their leader. He had served in the Viet Minh, the forerunner of the Viet Cong, and fought alongside Ho Chi Minh against the Japanese in World War II, then later against the French. He had been a squad leader at Diem Ben Phu in 1954, where the French suffered their final crushing defeat at the hands of the Viet Minh forces. Yes, he knew a thing or two about handing out defeat to a supposedly superior Western military. He was a knowledgeable man, shrewd and patient, and his counsel had helped Seven become successful.

"Do you have the name of the MIG pilot?" Chien looked at the Air Force officer.

The man nodded. "Yes, his family lives just outside Than Hoa. Wife, five young children, mother, father, grandmother."

Chien nodded. "See to it that his family receives the bounty. Make sure it's someone you can trust who delivers it."

Bao, one of the Viet Cong, reached into his khaki jacket. "I have

photos of the ship they call the *Rat* entering Subic Bay a few days ago."
He handed them across the table to Chien.

He looked at them silently, one by one, and passed them around the
table. "Yes, the *Rattano*, eight-fifty-six. That is the one. They are back
soon." He stopped on the close-up shot of the outside bridge and signal
bridge. "That is the captain. His name is McHenry. The same man who
has commanded her for several years now. Who is this young one?"

Bao looked across at the photo and chuckled. "One of the signalmen.
His white blond hair stands out, even at a distance. A group of us were
looking at the photos and someone called him Beach Boy."

Chien leaned closer and pointed to the background of the photo.
"What is that?"

Bao smiled and shuffled through the remaining photos finding the
same view from farther back. Behind Jeffs, lashed at an angle to the side
of the signal shack, was the object Chien was wondering about. "It's a surf
board. You know, they ride waves..."

"I know what a surfboard is," Chien said testily, then, stopped himself
and smiled briefly at the silliness. "That's good to know. There may come
a time when we need to find Beach Boy. His blond hair and surfboard
should be easy to spot."

His serious expression returned quickly. He turned to Tai, the navy
officer. "What about the Styx boats?"

"The Soviets are still holding back on delivering any additional units,
but we do have the original two and I have a very reliable contact to the
two boat captains."

"And the Hai Kich?" Chien asked, using the Vietnamese term for what
the Americans called SEALS.

"Our own Hai Kich are ready," Tai responded confidently. "Khiem has
direct communications arranged to divert actual Hai Kich assignments.
Key people are in place. We still need to recruit some additional boarding
troops for the final mission, but all the technical positions are filled."

Their leader looked pleased. "When the time is right, when our plans
are fully ripened, we will use this *Rat* to teach the Americans a lesson."

None of the others had asked him why the obvious contempt crept
into his voice whenever he spoke of this ship. They had heard partial

stories and conflicting rumors. They hoped he would choose to tell them at some point.

"We have to make sure everyone knows there is no bounty," Chien reaffirmed, "but make certain than Khiem passes along to Admiral Loflin that there is such a bounty. He is our key to the success of this operation."

He picked up the photographs again and shuffled through them, stopping on the one of Jeffs. "Beach Boy is a signalman?"

Bao nodded. "That is what our sources say."

"Check for yourself and make sure those sources are correct," Chien ordered. "He looks so American, doesn't he? Contact our people in Subic Bay. Find out the ship's schedule there and send them his picture. I want him followed and watched the next time the *Rat* is in port there. I have some ideas concerning our young signalman that may prove useful."

Chien stroked his "Uncle Ho" goatee. He was pleased their scheme seemed to be progressing well so far. Known to no one but himself, he would be leaving the country in a few months. Once the success of this mission seemed assured it would proceed on its own without him. He had done his patriotic duty for a long, long time and now he had arranged for the last few years of his life to be just for himself.

It would be, quite literally for him, a parting shot. If all went as planned he would achieve his long awaited revenge by destroying the *Rattano* and at the same time they would stun the Americans with a blow of such magnitude that it would rank right alongside December 7, 1941 in the history of spectacular surprise naval attacks.

TEN

War Protests Continue

At the University of Wisconsin in Madison, 2,000 anti-war protesters marched several blocks to the state capitol. A group of demonstrators carrying wooden crosses and the intestines of a dead sheep disrupted an ROTC class at Iowa State University in Ames. In North Hollywood, California, police smashed through a door with an ax and arrested 19 demonstrators who had barricaded themselves for eight hours Wednesday inside a Naval Reserve training center.

Less than forty-eight hours out of Subic, there was another briefing in the wardroom of the *Rattano*. Crowded into the room were Captain McHenry, Gil Smith the executive officer or XO, and several department heads, division officers and chiefs from Operations, Engineering, Weapons, CIC and Navigation.

McHenry walked to the opposite side of the table and faced the assembled group. A large map hung behind him. "Okay, listen up. This so-called storage and assembly area is spread out all along from here to here. It's taken some air strikes before, but the terrain's a problem and there's more SAM sites surrounding it than ever. Word is there's a hell of a big backlog of stuff, so it's the gun navy's turn again. Plus we need to show them we weren't scared off by that little action the other day. *Rat's* job will be riding shotgun, as they call it. We'll be operating with the *Parks* and the *Sarsfield*. The three of us will angle in toward the beach in a line.

They have designated targets just behind the beach. Our job is to pour as many shells as we can into these gun sites plus any others we can spot and cause as much mayhem as we can all around them all along the hillsides. Our attack angle should allow us to train both gun mounts at the enemy through most of our run. Some of these emplacements are tunneled into the sides of the hills, others are just sitting on top or on terraces cut into the hillsides. We'll be the last in line so we can hit 'em hard on the way out too. In case there are any MIGs the missile cruiser *Chicago* will be standing off shore a few miles for air defense."

Chief Neal raised his hand. "We up against anything new we should be worried about?"

"You mean besides fucking MIGS and missile boats?" A few men chuckled nervously. "Looks like the usual mix, Chief. Lots of three-inch type stuff and some 105's, but they may have something bigger now.' He gestured to his XO.

"Unconfirmed," Smith said, "But there's some intelligence, or maybe just a story, floating around that there's a couple of 155mm pieces dug into the bluffs up there. That's a little over six inches. A tad bigger than we're packing with some decent range. Big enough to cause real damage with a direct hit."

McHenry placed his hands on the edge of the table and leaned in with a serious look. "Listen, most of you know we got a shell dropped on us last time. We were just lucky it was small and hit where it did. We've got a lot of new guys onboard who haven't been through this before. I want those damage control parties on their toes. Flak jackets for all bridge and outside personnel are mandatory and tell 'em to keep their damn helmets on. The *Okie City* and the *Higbee* were never closer in than five miles when they got hit and shot all around the other day. We're going in at night, but we'll be coming within twenty-five hundred yards, less than a mile and a half. This attack is going in closer to see what they've really got and to give us a better look. Let's all keep in mind this is the real deal. This ain't watching the news, gentlemen. This is war and the *Rat* is going to show her teeth tonight."

Smith handed out copies of the battle plan as he spoke. "So, we'll be going in hard and fast. It'll be over in a matter of minutes. For Weapons and CIC there are target coordinates and firing sequences. They think they've got a lot of those guns spotted from the recent missions, but as usual, they've probably moved some around and added a few."

McHenry spoke up again, directing his comments to Warrant Officer Michaels. "Harry, I want CIC plotting all surface craft within twenty miles and keeping me apprised. We've been advised, again, by Com 7th Fleet to assume that small surface craft could be missile boats. That's all for now. We'll be going to general quarters thirty minutes before the first firing."

"Captain?" It was Ensign Carter, the very young assistant engineering officer. "Those Styx missile boats, how big a bang they got?"

McHenry knew the answer, but he gestured toward the Weapons Department head Lieutenant Owens.

"The Styx warhead is around a thousand pounds," Owens answered. "If one of those hits a destroyer like this it might break her in half. Even if it didn't sink her, it would blow the living shit out of her. Lots of dead sailors."

McHenry let that settle in for a bit, then uttered a quiet, "Dismissed."

He watched them all go except for his XO. "Drink?"

Smith nodded. The two men had been together almost three years and this was their third deployment to Vietnam. At thirty-five, Smith was twelve years younger than McHenry and fully expected to receive his own command after leaving as the second in command of the *Rattano*.

McHenry reached into the bottom drawer of his desk and pulled out a half-full fifth of Jack Daniel's. In the center of the table, as usual, sat a tray with several glasses and a full ice bucket. He poured two short whiskeys and the two men sat in silence, sipping and studying the map on the wall.

McHenry said, "I'm going to call up and get those two down here."

"You sure you want Ryder on this?"

McHenry took a sip. "Don't trust him?"

"Maybe," Smith answered. "He doesn't seem to take anything too seriously. Always trying to get away with as much as he can."

McHenry nodded. "That's true, but there's something about him in spite of all his bullshit. He's okay, he's smart. He just needs to grow up a little."

"I guess so, Mac," Smith said. He took another sip. "We do too, probably."

McHenry stood and walked to the phone and picked up the handset.

"Surfer Joe, this is the captain. I need you and Hays to come down to the wardroom right now. I'll let the bridge know."

He smiled at his XO. "They'll be worrying all the way down here about what kind of trouble they must be in." He reached up to the intercom. "Bridge, this is the captain. The signal bridge is unmanned for the next twenty minutes or so. My orders."

It took less than a minute to make the trip down to the wardroom, and the entire way Jeffs and George were speculating about what kind of trouble they were walking into. Their job provided them with plenty of contact with the captain and other officers, but neither of them had ever been summoned to the wardroom quite like this.

"Hey, I'm new at this shit," Jeffs said. "This usually happen?"

"Never," George said, walking briskly. "It has to be something you did."

"Oh, fuck it," Jeffs said softly. "Whatever it is, at least it's something different." He was using both hands in a futile attempt to flatten his straight blond hair back behind his ears before they knocked.

"Come in," McHenry called out. George walked in first, followed by Jeffs. "Have a seat, relax, you're not in trouble for anything that I know of. There's ice, there's tea. If you want any Jack Daniel's, half of one of those short glasses is all you get."

The two men looked at each other, then back at the table, wary of the circumstances. Smith stifled a grin as he watched the scene unfold.

McHenry stood, smiling. "I'm not kidding, guys. It's your lucky night. I want to talk over some stuff and I want you to just relax."

"Thanks, Captain," George said finally. They both half-filled a glass with ice and whiskey and seated themselves where McHenry indicated on the side of the table facing the map.

McHenry pointed to the map. "That's where we're headed in a few hours. Do you think you two will be very busy sending or receiving any messages during this attack?"

They looked at each other, then laughed. "I hope not, sir," George answered. "Unless the NVA wants to send greetings."

"Exactly," McHenry said. "I'd like the two of you to try something new for us. We're going to set up some night vision gear for the starboard big eyes. I want you two to watch for gun flashes, or even actual visuals of gun emplacements at our closest point."

He unrolled a photo that was about thirty inches long and a foot tall. A thin, white-lined grid of one inch squares had been printed on the picture. "I'll get this mounted on a piece of cardboard and brought up to you. Use a grease pencil and just mark gun locations right on it."

"Weather is clear with a low half moon behind the beach," McHenry explained. "Should show up the hilltop against a lighter sky."

George studied the photo for a few moments. "If we can spot this rounded top here and this point off to the left, it shouldn't be too hard. Beats sitting around wondering if we're going to get hit."

Jeffs nodded and took a sip from his glass.

"Good," McHenry said. "It's going to be windy and hectic and louder than hell, but you might pick up something new that will help out next time. You two are used to viewing things from up there and using the big eyes, so I think you're the guys for the job. We'll be using the gun director to guide the guns to some of the flashes and we've got comm techs who'll be listening for fire control radar signals we can lock onto. The *Sarsfield* says they're trying out some camera thing, but I figured some real eyes might be a good idea. They tell me there's more guns than ever returning fire so I think the more ways we can spot them the better."

McHenry motioned everyone to chairs and for just a few minutes the four men took a rare break from the customary situation and just talked as equals, about the war and life, and a bit about their wives, girlfriends and families.

McHenry looked at his watch. "Well, we've got a lot to get ready. Thanks for taking this on. Before you leave, remember, United States Navy personnel are not allowed to consume alcohol aboard ship, except as prescribed by a doctor or other medical personnel, or unless the captain says so." He flashed a grin, raised his glass and downed the contents.

"I'm sure Doc would approve," George said.

"Okay, that's it," McHenry said. "Back on watch."

They stood and stepped to the door to leave.

"Remember," McHenry added, "keep those helmets and flak jackets on and watch your ass."

✦
ELEVEN

War Protest Continue

At many campuses there is a growing movement to call a nationwide anti-war strike today. Student protest coordinators from coast to coast have organized teach-ins, workshops, rallies and class boycotts as well as plans for an upcoming march on Washington D.C.

Jeffs stood against the starboard railing of the signal bridge, straining through the darkness trying to see some land or something—anything. A half moon hung low in the sky behind the coastline, but it seemed to him that the night swallowed up its light. He thought he could just make out the white water in the wake of the ship several hundred yards in front of them. Beyond that was only darkness, but he knew there was another destroyer farther ahead. In the last fifteen minutes he had sensed the ship's increase in speed. They were now doing twenty-five knots

The crew had gone to general quarters, or battle stations, over half an hour earlier. The men with outside duty stations had donned their required flak jackets and helmets. Most of them had also donned a different attitude, a serious sense of purpose. In their battle dress the young crew looked older, their hearts pumped just a bit faster, their eyes kept a sharper watch. This was much closer to their movie-fed expectations of what war was supposed to be than all the drills across the seven thousand miles of the Pacific.

It had been just sixteen days ago that they had pulled out of San Diego Harbor. Sailing off across the sea to war, even this war, held a certain measure of glorified seductiveness for young men who largely felt invincible and were ignorant of the hazards of combat. Facing off against an enemy from a distance did not often carry the same immediate peril as slogging through jungles and rice paddies as an infantry soldier, but war often displayed a surprising reach that could lash out into places naively judged safer.

George finished adjusting the night vision equipment. "There, that's better."

Jeffs stepped up to the powerful mounted binoculars, often called big eyes, and looked through the lenses. His vision pierced the night and he could see land, hilly and bleak, silently peaceful just four miles away. Turning, he could clearly see the ship in front of them and the lead ship beyond, all in a ghostly, bleached-out greenish white.

Seconds later, the ship leaned into a wide sweeping turn and came alive with surprising acceleration. Around the ship men's eyes shifted as they exchanged uneasy looks. The low pitched whine of machinery and deep vibrations from the bowels of the destroyer accompanied the increased effort as the powerful engines fought to turn the twin screws faster and bring the warship to near flank speed.

George tightened his helmet strap. "This is it, man." He reached over and slapped down the front of Jeffs' helmet. "Keep it lower."

All three destroyers were soon headed at an angle toward the coast at better than thirty knots. The *Rattano* began with synchronized firings of all four guns simultaneously for maximum damage to the targets. This was not routinely done due to the injury it usually caused to the ship itself.

As the first two salvos hammered the ship, half the fluorescent lights in the aft crew's head exploded into tiny fragments. The fourth firing cracked a tightly closed window on the bridge. The next two firings started small leaks in the fresh water piping in the galley and mess deck. At each firing, the men on the bridge grimaced and flinched as the double barrels discharged just a few yards forward of their position.

By the time the other two destroyers moved their targeting from enemy gun positions to their assigned inland targets, the three ships together had already hurled over six tons of high explosive projectiles at the North Vietnamese gun batteries. Each four-gun volley delivered two-hundred twenty pounds of high explosive shells to its destination from each of the three destroyers.

Almost immediately two enemy gun positions were completely destroyed and three others damaged. Several others, though not hit directly, were disrupted and silenced by the sheer aggressive enormity of the barrage of naval gunfire punching into their hillside.

Jeffs was standing next to George, waiting to mark X's where he pointed to on the grid photo. "Christ!" he hollered between two of the first few blasts. "It sounds like a war!"

"They're shooting back!" George yelled, pointing.

Unlike the destroyers, the coastal batteries were not using flashless powder and gun flashes were blinking all across the hillsides. Jeffs' immediate thought was that it seemed impossible to miss with so many guns firing. His next thought was hoping he was wrong.

The ship was making better than thirty-two knots now and they were being whipped by the wind. George pointed quickly to two places on the photo and Jeffs marked them. They had a dim red-lensed flashlight mounted on the railing, shielded behind a small metal shroud, to faintly illuminate the photograph.

Quan could not believe the awful bedlam of destruction was happening again all around him as the projectiles slammed into the hillside. He had been lying near the mouth of the tunnel when the attack began. From there he could see some of the other gun positions on the curved face of the hill. He watched and felt the concussion as a salvo walloped directly into the mouth of a tunnel just forty yards away. The gun and its crew had tumbled wildly out of their lair and plunged down the mountain in a flash of flaming debris.

Now he stood behind the gun, opening the breech after each firing and ramming in a new projectile when it was passed to him. Another man rammed the powder bags in behind the shell. As the breech was closed each time, the gun crew would quickly bring their hands to their ears just a fraction of a second before the gun fired. With each convulsive firing, dirt sifted down from the roof of the tunnel and each opening of the breech added more noxious fumes to the already contaminated air.

Quan peered around the gun and wished the moon was brighter so he could see the ships. Instead, there was just darkness sending forth fear and death. Explosions were still slamming parts of the hill and occasionally he could hear the hollow buzz of shells passing over them to their destinations inland.

As the ships began their curve away from the beach, still firing, the spotters at the gun emplacements equipped with night vision equipment stared hard through their viewers, barking settings faster and louder. They wanted a ship, and a few of the more knowledgeable men cursed the lack of modern fire-control radar and computers that would make the difficult job of hitting a moving destroyer at least more of a possibility. All of them hoped that what they lacked in accuracy would be overcome by overpowering numbers creating some lucky shots.

Suddenly, the gun captain in Quan's tunnel threw up his arms in a sign of triumph. He had seen their last round splash just a few yards starboard and behind the last destroyer. He estimated their range and present course, barked a few changes and ordered a rapid succession of firing.

The gun crew worked furiously behind the gun and got off three rounds in ten seconds. Now the gun captain watched intently, hoping the last of the three destroyers was headed straight for where the 155mm shells were going to end their journey. He was sure that the first or second shell would land on the ship and depending on the ship's speed, the next one or two, would fall in line behind the first, somewhere along its length.

Captain McHenry stormed into the bridge from the port wing, "Jesus, there's splashes everywhere! We can't run a straight line out of here. Hard left rudder, sailor, now!"

For a moment the helmsman did not realize the yelling had suddenly been directed at him. He turned the wheel and the warship leaned over hard, but gracefully, her throbbing engines powering her through the dark water at thirty-two knots, the twin rudders and twin screws straining against the sea.

Both gun mounts were now firing two guns at once every few seconds, and the forward guns were turned back at the farthest angle at which they could still be fired, just missing the superstructure. Two of the eleven windows that ran across the front of the bridge were cracked. The men on the bridge still grimaced with each firing, flinching in spite of their best efforts. It was an impossible thing to become accustomed to.

One deck above the bridge and just slightly farther aft from the forward gun mount, Jeffs steadied himself against the railing just beside George, who was still watching through the lenses, although they were no longer marking gun flashes on the grid. He had shoved the front of his helmet up again so he could see down at the photo and out to the water. Between the deafening blasts, in spite of the whipping thirty-two knot wind, they both could feel the deep vibrations from the powerful engines and the rumble of the screws churning up piles of white water behind the ship.

There was just enough moonlight for Jeffs to see a plume of water shoot up just off the starboard bow and slightly ahead as the first shell exploded where the ship would have been. He reached out to tap George to point out the splash and the second shell hit less than ten yards from the starboard side amidships.

A spray of sea water and shrapnel slapped into the hull and up the superstructure. George jerked his head back as several jagged fragments struck the powerful binoculars. The ship began its turn in the opposite direction and the third shell hit near the stern, but not as close, sending up another blossom of sea water. One last parting shot was fired from the *Rattano* as she continued to speed through the calm sea for a time, even after the return fire had died out.

"Look at this!" George yelled above the buffeting of the wind. He was inspecting the casing of the big eyes in the dim moonlight. One lens, along with its plastic shroud, was shattered and the metal casing had a star shaped cut through it. A piece of the night vision equipment was hanging by one strap, with most of the viewer missing.

"Hey!" Jeffs shouted. He opened his hand and the moonlight showed two small pieces of jagged metal. "It hit my helmet. I picked these up. It's all over the deck!"

Jeffs walked inside to ask the phone talker if anyone reported any other hits, while George returned to the big eyes to study the damage.

Inside the signal shack, Jeffs wiped his hand across a tickle on his forehead and felt slick wetness. He looked at the smear on his hand in the dim light. "What the..." He wiped his forehead again and more blood ran into his left eye.

Villegas, the signalman phone talker who was stationed inside the shack, stood suddenly. "What's going on, Ryder? You okay?" He grabbed the flashlight from the desktop next to him and shined it on his face. "Damn!" He stepped outside. "George, get in here! Ryder's hurt!

Jeffs felt pain now as he wiped his forehead again and tried to sweep the blood from his eye with his finger. He unstrapped his helmet and took it off.

George appeared in the doorway. "Man, I think some of that shit hit me." Jeffs told him.

George came closer with concern on his face. He took Jeffs by the arm and sat him down on the stool and flipped on the bright fluorescent desk lamp even though they were officially still under darkened ship conditions. "You sure that's it?"

An increasing flow of blood was now running down both sides of his nose and right eye dripping onto the front of his shirt. While Villegas directed the flashlight on him George began checking around Jeff's neck, in his eyes, under his shirt and the back of his head. He knew from his Riverine Force experience the weird ways of bullets and shrapnel.

George grabbed a rag from the hook in the corner and pushed it against Jeffs' forehead. "Here, hold this. Shit, you're making a mess." He reached up to the intercom, widely known to sailors as the "bitch box." and held down the talk lever. "Bridge, sigs. This is Hays. Ryder's been hit. I don't think it's too bad, but he's bleeding like hell from a couple of shrapnel wounds on his forehead. We better get a corpsman up here to check him out."

Villegas was talking into his sound powered phone to Radio. "Hey, Ryder's bleeding all over the place up here. Hit in the head by some shrapnel or something. Hays called a corpsmen to check him out."

Jeffs was holding the rag himself now. George let go of the lever, leaned back against the small desk and lit a cigarette. "Well, you dumb bastard, you're a certified war hero how. You might get another medal just for getting your fat head in the way. I told you to keep that helmet down."

Jeffs smiled weakly. "Chief will be glad I'm using my head."

"No, he won't," Villegas corrected. "You bled all over the papers on the message log clipboard."

In the tunnel, the gun captain watched as the last shell splashed into the water behind the retreating ship. He slammed the top of his viewer with both fists, then just stared out into the night before he turned and walked quickly back into the darkness of the tunnel.

Quan watched him go, then jumped over to look through the viewer. He saw a strange, dimly lit colorless sea, but no ships. He pulled away and looked out into the darkness again, wondering at the strangeness of fighting an enemy he could not see.

Loud voices from deeper in the tunnel ordered the crew to roll the gun back into its position and to report quickly to the hilltop. The two lead ships had poured ten tons of shells into the area inland from the gun positions and there was plenty of clean up and salvage work to be done.

❧ TWELVE

Dear Cathy,

Hi baby. I miss you. We arrived off the coast of Vietnam last night. We attacked a place in North Vietnam and did a bunch of shooting. Anyway, it all went fine and I have no idea what we blew up but it was loud on this end! One guy was hit by some shrapnel from shells hitting near the ship but it was just minor skin wounds. A couple of stitches and he will be fine. I love you. I miss you. I can hardly wait for you know what with you!!

Love,
Jeffs

The Operations compartment was the living and sleeping space for more than fifty men of that department. Normally all the men not on duty would be sleeping until their next watch but it was full of young men who were wide awake and talkative, even though it was just coming up on 0200 hours. The adrenaline overload that came as part of the attack on Dong Hoi was another step in the crew's bonding that would carry them through the next few months. Several conversations were going at the same time and nobody felt much like going to sleep. It was the same all around the ship in the other compartments.

Another milestone had been reached that most of them hadn't thought of yet. On their way across the Pacific, some of the crew had been concerned that they would not get any shooting in until May, but it was still April so they would get their sixty-five dollars extra combat pay for the month plus, for as long as they were operating in a war zone, their income was tax-free. None of them thought of it as an extra incentive for risking their lives, but more like a bonus for the inconvenience of being stuck into the war. They were young men, after all, in the prime of their lives, invincible. If pressed on the matter they might have admitted that what they were doing had its dangers and that something could happen, probably not to them but maybe to someone else.

Jeffs came down the ladder into the compartment, returning from being treated in sick bay and grabbing a quick snack from the mess deck. Several men applauded and cheered as he made his way to his rack. He smiled, a little embarrassed by all the attention. All he had to show for his wounds was a four inch white bandage from the middle of his forehead to his right temple, held down by a couple of strips of tape. Underneath were six stitches on one of the wounds. The other was taped together.

He boosted himself up onto his top rack and lit a cigarette. He was one of the handful of the crew who had viewed all the action topside, as well as the only casualty.

A large group of the men in the compartment crowded around him or positioned themselves nearby. "What was it like out there?" two of them asked at once.

Jeffs shook his head, searching for the words he wanted. "When they hit right next to us it was all so fast that I wasn't sure what happened at first." He reached up and felt the bandage on his head. "Really, though, I think they were aiming at George."

Several men laughed and someone slapped George on the back.

"Does it hurt?" someone else asked.

George answered the question for him. "Hell, it only hurts when he thinks, so not very fucking much!"

One of the radarmen said, "If that place is so damn important, why just three destroyers? Why not send a bunch of destroyers or something like the *Newport News* and really wipe it out?"

George agreed. "The *News* could sit there and do a hell of a lot more damage with those eight-inchers."

"Shakes did a lot of damage last year in Subic and I hear he only has a six-incher!" Leon said.

Everyone broke into laughter, including Shakes, one of the radiomen, who was lying in his own rack just one row over.

This shifted the whole conversation over to Subic Bay exploits for the next few minutes.

Finally, Jeffs interrupted. "Guys, I think it's time for my beauty sleep. Us wounded war heroes need our rest, you know." He put his hand to his bandaged forehead and fell back, groaning, onto his pillow.

"Yeah, you need your beauty sleep all right!" Hughes, a radarman called out.

Mike Gonzales leaned in close and punched his shoulder. "Night-night Jeffy."

Everyone had learned that Gonzales was the only one allowed to call him that. Nobody else ever tried it.

"Sweet dreams, Mikey," Jeffs answered.

With laughter and more parting comments the men began to go their separate ways. Most of their extra adrenaline was used up by now and the late hour was catching up with them. Some went to their own racks and others, still too wound up to sleep, formed new groups to retell the stories of the day's events.

Jeffs stretched out on his back staring up at the pipes and wires, wondering once again how in the hell that great life he had going, the one he had taken for granted for so many years, could have put him into this war. He was also still trying to figure out if he should be hating it or not. Someone switched off the lights on his half of the compartment. He reached up and touched his bandage again and smiled a little at the fuss that was made over it. Some adventure, he thought.

THIRTEEN

In war, truth is the first casualty.—Archelys.

At 0900 the next morning, while the crew of the *Rattano* was enhancing the reputation of her guns just off of Quang Tri, a briefing was taking place at 7th Fleet Headquarters in Yokosuka, Japan. Vice Admiral Tillman Loflin, Commander 7th Fleet, was seated at the head of a massive mahogany conference table.

At 52, he looked a leathery, sun-dried ten years older. He was one of the most powerful men in the United States military. His realm, the U.S. 7th Fleet, consisted of nearly everything afloat between Hawaii and the eastern shores of Asia. During a successful and decorated naval career he had commanded several cruisers, destroyers and an aircraft carrier. Some of his predecessors, men like Nimitz and Kinkaid, were legendary figures in naval history. Now he was building a legend of his own, but so far it seemed that he would be best known for his unreasonable temper, his swearing and for being what many people considered a raving tyrannical nut case.

Seated around the table were three members of his staff, an officer from Naval Intelligence, a CIA analyst, and a liaison officer from the staff of Commander in Chief Pacific Fleet (CINCPACFLT). Also present were three captains who headed cruiser-destroyer squadrons in the Pacific. Wil Gordan was one of them.

The briefing had been scheduled for some time, but after the recent action at Dong Hoi, it had taken on new urgency and significance. A young CIA analyst standing at the opposite end of the table from Admiral Loflin had just begun the prepared part of his slide presentation.

"Here's a photo of one of these boats. This particular one is Egyptian, but the configuration of the North Vietnamese boats would be identical. They are Soviet "Komar" class patrol boats. Overall length is eighty-two feet and they have a top speed of about forty knots. The two large covered pods on each side aft are the missile launchers. Each boat is armed with two P-15 Termit missiles. Radar acquisition and launching is all forward. They have to be facing their target. The NATO designation for these missiles is the SS-N-2 Styx, so the short hand usually used to refer to them is simply Styx."

He clicked to the next slide which showed one of the missiles. "As you can see it has a markedly unstreamlined bulging shape. Styx is a twenty foot ship to ship missile with an effective range of range of maybe twenty miles or so, but we think that may be a stretch. Probably twelve or less is more realistic. There are updated versions with better homing radar but we think these Komar boats are carrying the older version. It carries an eleven-hundred pound warhead. It's not the newest technology but we all know about the *Eilat* in 1967. Also as I'm sure you know, just last year India took out a Pakistani destroyer and minesweeper at sea and some smaller vessels in port. Different patrol boats but the same Styx missiles. It's cheap muscle for a country that doesn't have much of a navy."

"Does anyone know how many of these boats North Vietnam has?" Loflin asked.

"Well, Admiral, it has not been confirmed they have any."

Loflin glanced quickly at the others around the room then returned his attention to the CIA officer. "Are you fucking kidding? Then why in the hell are we here talking about the goddamn things?"

"Because they may have them," the CIA officer said. "CNO and our office thought it would be wise to bring everyone concerned up to speed. There is some second hand and unconfirmed hearsay evidence they may have acquired some. The Soviet Union still denies having provided them with any. We have no photographic intelligence proving they have them. However, considering our huge naval presence now in the gulf and the region, they may feel the need to counter that by acquiring these boats and missiles."

Loflin was slowly shaking his head in disgust. "All right, Mr. CIA, has it been confirmed that the boats that attacked the *Sterett* and those other ships at Dong Hoi actually fired a Styx missile? And did the *Sterett* take it out with one of their missiles? I've been hearing some doubting opinions."

The young analyst nervously cleared his throat and shrugged. "No, that has not been definitely confirmed. The *Sterett* thinks they did but weather conditions were very hazy and clear visibility was only a couple miles or so. Between MIGS, patrol boats, missile launches and gun targeting, the electronic signatures and radar environment was complex and changing fast. There was no visual confirmation."

Loflin just stared for several moments, then sighed. "Does your fucking agency know anything for sure? If they get them or already have them, are they going to use them?"

The young officer looked around the table at the faces staring at him waiting for an answer. "Admiral, assuming they have them, some of our analysts think they will still try to keep them mostly out of sight because they're afraid of losing them. We've also discussed the scenario where even if it wasn't sanctioned by the North Vietnamese leadership, a rogue boat captain or two could conceivably take it upon themselves to attack one of our ships."

"On another topic, does the agency have any information about bounties being put on certain ships?" Loflin asked.

"We've heard rumors of that from time to time," the CIA officer said. "We've been unable to confirm the existence of bounties on any navy ships. For that matter, we're not sure just who would set these bounties or how they would be paid. Seems to be one of those stories that just circulates around and gets repeated as the truth."

The CIA officer knew better. He knew there was a group calling itself Seven and several sources had reported hearing of bounties being set. They suspected the group's reach was quite limited but they knew almost nothing about it. Better not to ratchet up the tension when they didn't yet know enough to do anything about it.

A grim-faced Admiral Loflin nodded and sighed. The response to his questions just confirmed his already diminished opinion of the CIA's expertise. He knew from his own source that North Vietnam did indeed have the missile boats and he knew there were bounties being arranged.

"And, by the way, Admiral, there's no firm confirmation that any of the boats the other day were destroyed by the *Sterett*. They may have just shut down their electronics and run off into the haze or some cove."

Loflin had reached his limit. He stood now and everyone in the room braced themselves. "Young man, all you intelligence types guess too goddamn much. The rest of us are left to sort through the "intellishit" to figure out what the hell to do. I can't have these goddamn boats cruising around over there with fucking ship-killing missiles! It pisses me off that we can't just bomb the shit out of the sons-a-bitches right where they are right now, wherever the goddamn hell that is! Of course according to you, nobody knows for sure if they even have these boats and nobody would know for sure even if they did. And if you did know they had the boats you wouldn't know if they had any missiles on them. Jesus Christ almighty!"

The volume of his voice was rising with every sentence. "The *Sterett* got damn lucky knocking down that missile. The next time it's going to be some gun destroyer and the crew is going to have to watch that goddamn Styx coming straight at them, and there won't be a goddamn thing they can do about it except stick their fingers in their goddamn ears just before the fucking kaboom!"

He snapped his fingers, the signal to his staff that his stay at the briefing was over. They stood and began shuffling papers back into neat piles. Loflin pointed across the table at the CIA man. "If those little slant-eyed gooks want one of my ships, then I'll find a way to take a bunch of those fucking boats down with her!"

He turned and stormed out of the conference room followed by his staff.

Nobody in the meeting was very surprised. Such displays of anger were vintage Admiral Loflin. What was not so obvious to everyone was what was going on in his mind these days. Even beyond how he had always felt, he believed more and more that he was the only one who knew how to do anything right. He laid awake at night thinking about how incompetent and stupid everyone around him was. On top of that he was having other obsessive thoughts that seemed to be filling up his head. Most of these had to do with Styx missile boats.

He couldn't stop envisioning them attacking his ships and destroying them in great flashes of destruction and death. He thought about them when he was watching television, eating meals, or enduring his wife's incessant talking. Some nights, when he wasn't lying awake pondering the idiocy of everyone around him, he had dreams about swarms of the missile boats. Often he would awaken suddenly, sweating and his heart pounding as though it was going to break out of his chest. When this happened he felt very afraid of them and completely fixated on their destruction, and he knew he could trust nobody but himself to find a way to take care of the problem. Now validating his feelings even further, he just found out that he knew things even the CIA apparently didn't know.

Admiral Loflin was shrewd and deceptive enough to know that he had to keep such thoughts to himself. He knew that others did not have the deep understanding of the situation or the private information sources that he did. And he understood he would be labeled as some kind of overblown crackpot if he openly persisted with pushing the idea that he knew better than everyone else.

FOURTEEN

My Dear Lam,

…I miss you so much and it is even worse knowing you are not that many miles away. I hope our village continues to be lucky and the war stays away. I am still at the coastal defense site near Dong Hoi. Most of the time it is just boring practice drills and cleaning. The place has a very nice ocean view and I wish you were here to enjoy it with me. You probably know there is a lot more bombing going on but there hasn't been much right around here. I hope you are safe. I want us to be together soon. I love you and miss you.

Love,
Quan

Jeffs found himself with wide open eyes out of a deep sleep. He listened for a few seconds and heard nothing out of the ordinary. The compartment was dark but he could see the light from the mess deck showing through the open hatch. After a while he realized he had awakened because the ship was not rolling or pitching and there was no longer the sound of the sea rushing by just a few feet from his head. It was difficult to tell if they were moving at all, but he thought he could feel just a bit of a roll.

He turned on his rack light and looked at his watch. It was 0600. Seeing Leon's empty rack, he clicked off the light, dropped to the deck, dressed in the dark and headed topside. The sun had not yet broken the horizon, but the night was falling away quickly as he stepped out onto the main deck and lit a cigarette.

As he had thought, the ship was moving slowly, about eight knots, parallel to the beach toward their assigned waiting position. They had pushed hard south after the raid on Dong Hoi to get the *Rattano* to her gun line station. It was only about eighty miles, but he knew the captain had wanted to arrive well before daybreak and have plenty of time to assess the situation. It looked to Jeffs as though they had made it.

The dark line of the beach was just four miles away and the water, as advertised by men who had been here before, was indeed calm. Except for the ripples the ship created, there was no apparent texture to it at all, and the surface of the water seemed to softly blend into the air above it.

He made his way up the three ladders to the signal bridge for a better view and found Leon leaning on the railing looking out toward the open ocean. "You couldn't sleep either, huh?" He handed Leon a cigarette, then he stepped over to the starboard big eyes to get a closer look.

"They already replace the wrecked eyes from last night," Leon noted. "I guess they have extras stored somewhere. How's your head?"

Jeffs reached up and pushed on the bandage. "A little sore. Kind of a headache. Not bad."

Leon pointed. "Here comes the sun."

As the light grew, the dark line showed itself as the trees along the water's edge, and as the sun broke the horizon, the sandy beach gave off a silvery gleam. Jeffs was getting his first real look at Vietnam.

They were just off of the city of Quang Tri. The surrounding area had been the site of some of the most intense fighting and bombing to repulse the invasion. As Jeffs trained the eyes toward the coast he could make out individual trees and the abrupt dense line they formed behind the sand. The ground sloped gently upward beyond the trees and he aimed up higher to see further inland.

He watched a pair of Cobra helicopters darting back and forth producing quick puffs of smoke when they fired their rockets, all in silence from this distance. Here and there he could see the jagged rooflines of shattered buildings. The formerly charming city of Quang Tri was in the process of being completely digested by the war.

He strolled around the signal bridge checking out the surrounding glassy calm waters to see just what the gun line was all about. He counted six other destroyers, two of them in the distance to the north, four others spread out from what looked to be three to six miles away to the south and he knew there were several more ships in both directions just over the horizon and farther.

He grabbed the hand grips of the port eyes and swung them around to get a better look at a much larger ship just two miles off. "That's the ship Lacy and Schultz went to," he said, referring to two men who had hitched a ride across the Pacific aboard the *Rattano* on temporary duty.

Leon let out a laugh. "I'd like to see those two again. Yeah, it's the *Newport News*. Chief Ogden and some snipe chief were up here a few minutes ago talking about it. They were saying she's the last all-gun cruiser left in the navy. Mean lookin' bitch, huh? Looks like a battleship."

"No shit," Jeffs agreed, still watching through the big eyes. "Damn, there's guns everywhere on that thing."

She was indeed a unique ship and the last of her breed. All the others had either had some or all of their guns replaced by missile launchers or had been scrapped or moth balled. The new cruisers being built and those still on the drawing board were all missile ships. Built and launched in the years just after World War II, at 716 feet with a crew of more than twelve-hundred, she was one of just three of the largest, most heavily-armed cruisers ever built. Her two sister ships were no longer in the active fleet. In a war increasingly in need of naval firepower, the *News* had plenty. Nine, eight-inch, rapid-fire guns in three triple mounts, and twelve, five-inch guns in six double mounts. She could throw up more than twenty thousand pounds of extremely accurate, high explosive projectiles in just one minute.

As Jeffs stood watching the hulking cruiser, three sudden eruptions of smoke in quick succession issued from the barrels of one of her eight-inch turrets. Ten seconds of silence followed as the sound rolled across two miles of smooth tranquil sea between the ships. When it reached them, every man felt the concussions slam into the ship along with three sharp blasts that sounded like sonic booms.

Several curses sounded from the bridge just below them while others clapped and hollered encouragement. More of the same could be heard from around the ship from other men who were topside.

"Jesus!" Jeffs uttered, after a moment's silence.

Leon started laughing. "Brother, if we get to see Lacy and Schultz I'm gonna ask them what the hell it sounds like over there!"

At 0800 the 1MC, the ship's PA system, clicked to life.

"Good morning men, this is the captain speaking. Welcome to the gun line. In a few minutes the *Rat* will fire on several enemy positions around Quang Tri in support of an operation being conducted by South Vietnamese Marines. Down here on the southern gun line we will not be going to battle stations during routine firing missions, but keep in mind the main deck forward and aft in the vicinity of the gun mounts are off limits to non-essential personnel. Announcements will advise you shortly before firing missions begin. You have all done a fine job getting us here and you did an outstanding job last night in your quick introduction to this chapter of the war. Fortunately, or maybe unfortunately, down here on the gun line it will be a lot less exciting than last night, but still plenty busy. The *Rat* and all the other destroyers in the vicinity have so many firing missions we will probably be rearming every few days. The XO or I will be making announcements from time to time to keep you informed of our situation. Good luck and good shooting."

McHenry gave the proper orders to the engine room and the helmsman, and the destroyer swung around and headed toward the beach then turned away and stopped a little more than two miles off shore, the stern of the ship facing the beach to bring the aft gun mount into action. The voice from the spotter plane crackled over the radio speaker on the bridge, giving the coordinates of the first target. A group of trucks had gathered under some trees on the west edge of the city.

A mixed group of young and older Vietnamese men were gathered around the lead truck laughing and talking. They had successfully brought their fifteen trucks together under cover of night and had parked them in a long line, hidden under some tattered camouflage nets between two rows of withered rubber trees, the remnants of a formerly thriving plantation that existed before the war.

The area around them was held by the Viet Cong along with some regular North Vietnam Army units, and all the drivers would have to do now was wait until nightfall when they would receive their orders and move. The majority of the fighting was on the other end of the city now, and even most of that had moved further away in the last couple of days. Most of the drivers were not even soldiers. They were being paid only in food, often the most desirable medium of exchange in their war-ravaged country.

For many of them it did not matter anymore if they were working for the North, the South or the Americans. Some of the older men had even worked for the French. It all turned out the same—fighting and destruction and continued disruption of life's routines. What mattered was their stomachs, and their families and staying alive until someday when things would have to be better.

They could not see the ocean from their location. They knew that the American ships were out there, but they were nearly four miles from the beach and the ships were out another mile or more. Too far away to worry about, they reasoned. They felt safe enough hidden by the trees from the constant air surveillance and the deadly helicopters.

But on a small rise two miles farther inland, a team of five South Vietnamese Marines, along with two Americans who were training them, had set up an observation post. Hidden by the dense growth and haphazard piles of debris around their position, equipped with high-powered binoculars and infrared viewers they had watched the night's activities. Now they were in radio contact with air spotters.

The first round, because of an error in the coordinates, was over two-hundred yards wide. The men looked around and a few halfheartedly began to head for cover, but after a several seconds of silence they wrote it off as a stray shot from somewhere and returned to their storytelling.

Thirty seconds later, after the settings aboard the *Rattano* were adjusted, a fifty-five pound high-explosive shell completed its six mile journey and disintegrated the truck at the opposite end of the line from where the drivers were gathered. A couple of them ran away, farther into the remains of the plantation's groves, but most of them crawled and took cover underneath the first two or three trucks.

Jeffs was standing on the forward starboard edge of the signal bridge, just above the open door that led out onto the bridge wing. He could hear the excited voice of the spotter yelling from the loudspeaker inside the bridge. The ship began firing in earnest, alternating the two aft guns, launching a shell every four seconds.

As the *Rattano* slowly drifted in toward the beach, the explosions walked perfectly down the line of trucks destroying all of them and the men under them.

The pilot of the small Cessna two-seater had been crisscrossing high above the general area for a half hour. He had been careful to not attract attention by circling too near the area of the assembled trucks. He was now beside himself with disbelieving laughter. He had been hoping for a few of the trucks before the rest went driving away wildly, but the drift of the currents and a little luck had provided him with a story he would be repeating for the rest of his life.

Another chapter had just been written in the legend of the *Rattano's* infallible guns and talented gunners.

❦ FIFTEEN

War News - April 27, 1972
The Paris Peace Talks have resumed.

Commander Nguyen Chi Khiem was the South Vietnamese Naval Liaison stationed in Yokosuka, Japan. Such a position had only existed since mid-1968 and Khiem was just the second person to have filled it. He had a small office, a personal aide who came with him from Vietnam and two part-time secretaries provided by the U.S. Navy. His position was viewed as nothing more than a courtesy extended to an ally. He was invited to certain briefings and provided with selected reports concerning the operations of the U.S. and South Vietnam navies.

But he was not included in most truly important meetings or provided with too much information, and he knew that. He knew the Americans didn't trust the South Vietnamese government or military leaders and they knew that he didn't trust them.

In spite of the lack of trust, his position was of little importance to anyone on the American base and there was no real attention paid to anything he did.

The arrangement suited his goals just fine and he kept a low profile. It allowed him to live in Japan with very few official duties and plenty of time to enjoy himself in a much freer and more interesting society than Vietnam, and as an Asian he was able to blend in quite easily. No one seriously considered him of being worthy of any important mistrust.

He was, of course, working in intelligence. But if anyone did suspect this, they would have been quite surprised at his assignment. He wasn't gathering information in the way most people thought of spies doing. In fact, his assignment was very specific and involved giving information more than taking it, and he was doing none of it for either of the governments in Vietnam.

For nearly a year he had been spending nearly all of his time and energy feeding specific pieces of information to Vice Admiral Loflin from Seven, and to keep them informed of the Admiral's actions concerning missions and activities of the destroyer *Rattano*.

Khiem grabbed his hat from the hook by the door as he left his office. He walked toward the corner at the end of the block where he would meet Admiral Loflin for one of their periodic conversations. Today, as he often did, he had information from Seven that he knew the admiral would be interested in. But today's particular conversation was definitely designed to up the ante and move their conspiracy forward.

Admiral Loflin relished the attention his command car received as he was driven around the base. The flags on the fenders of the black Cadillac let everyone know that riding in the back seat was a three-star admiral and Commander of the 7th Fleet. Every sailor knew to salute the car when the flags were flying just as they would salute the man if he walked by. Loflin never tired of seeing them, especially the officers, saluting his vehicle as he watched from behind the dark tinted windows. He especially enjoyed seeing the salutes from the commanders and captains with their "scrambled eggs" on the bills of their hats signifying that they were, oh so important.

But that was on most days. On his little outings to meet with Khiem, he ordered the driver to put the flags down, to show that he was not in the vehicle. He missed the recognition, but he didn't have to endure the lack of it very often.

The car stopped for just a couple of moments on the narrow side street at the end of the block and Khiem stepped in as the door opened. As usual, the driver was ordered to take a leisurely drive around the huge base, with the partition window up and the radio on in the front seat.

It was not a limousine, but Cadillac's slightly longer "Sixty Special" version of the Sedan Deville with a roomier back seat and, in this one, the partition window. Loflin had ordered the vehicle delivered for him to Japan because, as usual, he generally figured he could do whatever the hell he wanted as Commander of the 7th Fleet.

"Commander Khiem, how are you?" Loflin greeted.

"Good, Admiral. Yourself?" Khiem spoke English well, with a slight French accent.

The mini bar in the center of the back seat was already swung down and Loflin was mixing two martinis. "Never better, commander. Here you go."

Khiem took his usual vodka martini and Loflin lifted his traditional gin.

"To victory," Loflin offered.

Khiem just smiled coldly and said nothing.

Their liaisons had developed a routine than now involved several minutes of silence as they enjoyed their drinks and watched the scenery go by.

Finally Loflin broke that silence. "So, what's the latest on these bounties?"

Khiem took the last sip from his glass and slid the olive off the toothpick into his mouth. "There is now talk of the *Rattano*."

"So they've put a price on her?"

"Yes, but not like the *Higbee*," Khiem explained. "That one was for any kind of hit. This one is a little different. I don't know why, but this *Rat* seems to be a special case. Something must have happened to anger someone. This one is much larger and it's only for destroying or sinking it."

Loflin had to restrain himself from attempting to throw his companion out of the moving car. "Sinking? Goddamn, Khiem, you're friends over there are getting a little carried away, aren't they?"

Khiem smiled and shrugged. "Admiral, in this war would anything surprise you?"

"Anything new about those Styx missile boats?" Loflin asked.

Khiem lifted his glass. "Another for the road?" Loflin obliged, pouring it while Khiem held the glass. "Save the vermouth, Admiral, but I'll take another olive."

"There you go," Loflin said as he speared an olive and dropped it into Khiem's glass. "Now, what about those boats? I just recently found out that our own CIA doesn't know for sure if you even have them."

Khiem took a sip. "I know that some in my navy have been afraid to use them to their full potential for fear of awakening the true wrath of your country in retaliation for destroying a ship."

"Really?" Loflin said, sarcastically. "Well, then why have them at all? Just trying to scare us?"

"I think that some of my colleagues have thought exactly that. It has worked, hasn't it?"

Loflin considered how to answer that. He decided to repeat something the CIA officer had said in the briefing. "They're cheap muscle for a country without much of a navy."

"True enough," Khiem answered. "There is something else I know about these boats. You now have a destroyer out there with a price on her head. Your constant air patrols would make it very difficult to use MIGS to go after a ship, but you have been wanting to use your fleet to go after these boats. Now you have a bounty on one of your destroyers. Such an incentive might bring them out of hiding. After all, Styx missiles are called ship killers."

Loflin said nothing as he reached into his coat and handed Khiem an envelope containing the usual five-hundred dollars. He gazed out the window while he pondered all he had learned. The information he had been collecting from Khiem to develop a strategy to draw the missile boats into a fight now seemed clear. He had a sudden thought that he knew was so completely immoral that he would never remotely think of sharing it with anyone. Maybe, he reasoned, he could risk the possible sacrifice of one ship to save all the others from potential disaster.

Khiem transferred the envelope into his own inside coat pocket and hoped, as he had many times before, that the war would not end too soon. He knew, though, that his assignment would be coming to an end even if the war never did. He felt sure that Loflin had taken all the bait exactly as planned, which meant then at some point in the next few months or weeks he would be leaving his position as naval liaison and participating in the final phase of Seven's magnificent conspiracy.

He was always amused by Loflin's superior attitude. It had been so easy over their last few visits to maneuver him into helping Seven to carry out their treachery. Khiem smiled just a little as he considered the irony of what was going to happen. The very boats Loflin was so worried about would not only be attacking his ships but they would be doing so with his approval. Khiem sometimes contemplated if it would be more satisfying to kill Loflin or to leave him alive to witness the carnage as they lay waste to his precious destroyers.

SIXTEEN

The military don't start wars. Politicians start wars.
William Westmoreland

The *Rattano* fired 218 high explosive rounds that first day—just about six tons of destruction. The other ships were busy too, and by late afternoon a second observation post had been set up near Quang Tri and several more spotter planes were operating north and south of there. The ships on the gun line had firing missions keeping them busy around the clock.

"So, isn't it kind of weird that we don't even know what we're shooting at?" Jeffs asked during a short lull in the shooting.

George nodded as he concentrated on sewing a button back onto the shirt he was wearing. "I've thought that before, especially like now when we're not even at battle stations or anything. We just go on about our work and the gunners do their job. The captain announces stuff sometimes, or the next day the Plan of the Day will have a report from the day or two before. It's probably some poor bastards just sitting around bored, like us."

"So, why don't they fire back at us?" Jeffs continued. He was watching for signals from nearby destroyers.

George looked up from his button sewing. "Christ, Ryder, didn't you get enough of that shit last night?"

He touched the bandage on his head. "Sure, but a war is supposed to be a two-sided thing, right?"

"We've got all the air power," George explained, returning to his sewing. "So if they did set up something and start firing at us, the air spotters would get on it and one of us would wipe it out in a few minutes.

I guess somebody gets a wild hair up their ass once in a while and fires a few rounds from the beach on close-in cans, but pretty much it's a one way thing down here. Not like up north. But we're not that far south around here and with the *Higbee* getting bombed everyone's a little jumpy about any air traffic." He returned to struggling with his button.

"I've heard North Vietnam called Indian Country. What's that all about?"

George chuckled. "I think it started with pilots, but it's kind of caught on with other guys too. I don't know why they call it that. When I was in the Riverine Force some of the guys called the north that too. Probably 'cause we've been fighting this war like a bunch of fucking cowboys."

"You know what else?" Jeffs added as he watched George struggle clumsily with the button on his shirt. "I think that button would be a lot easier to sew if you took off the damn shirt!"

A deafening discharge from the forward gun mount interrupted and both men jumped.

"Shit!" Jeffs yelled.

George laughed. "I know it would be easier to take my shirt off to do this, but I started doing it this way and now it's a matter of principle to finish it. If I took it off now it would be like the shirt winning, you know?"

Jeffs shrugged and nodded.

One of the forward guns fired again, then again. A few seconds later the aft gun mount came to life with twenty firings one after the other. Then a minute passed with nothing from the guns.

Jeffs sighed. "Maybe there gonna take…"

A blast from the forward mount cut his sentence short, followed by three more in quick succession.

"Dammit! I guess not!" he shouted.

George chuckled again.

Unknown to them, Chief Ross had come up the ladder and was standing and staring at the signal shack. As usual, his red, faded, hard cover Webster's dictionary was under his left arm.

"Ryder!" Both men jumped and whirled around. Ross pushed up his black rimmed glasses. "A surfboard was bad enough. What's with these?"

On each side of the door into the shack stood a six foot tall pole with a torch sitting on top.

"They're tiki torches," Jeffs explained. He walked over to admire them alongside Ross. "I got the good ones instead of those cheap bamboo ones they use for backyard parties. The pole and the torch on top are metal. You like them, Chief?"

Ross turned his head and stared in answer.

"Don't worry, we're not going to light 'em," Jeffs continued, "unless you think we should."

"We put a bolt through the top and bottom of each one," George explained. "They're not going anywhere."

Ross stepped closer to examine the job. "Jesus! You drilled holes through the shack?"

"We figured it was safer that way," Jeffs said.

"We can take them down if there's an inspection," George said. "A little dab of gray paint on the bolts and nobody will even notice. It worked so well we attached the surfboard with a couple of bolts too and got rid of the line it was tied with. Looks a lot better. Safer too."

Ross stepped around the corner to look at the surfboard. He removed his black rimmed glasses for a closer, incredulous look. "So you drilled four holes clean through the shack to bolt down this crap?"

Jeffs followed him. "You know a couple of small holes like that won't even hurt the board. I can always patch them up later if I want. I might not even keep it to surf on."

Ross turned to him and stepped closer. He opened his mouth to yell, but realized he didn't know quite what he wanted to say. Instead, he sighed. Then speaking softly, he said, "The captain was just saying again the other day that he likes the surfboard. Thinks it adds a little character to the place. Maybe he'll like this too. He still wants to know one thing though. How did you get a surf board onto the ship?"

Jeffs smiled. "I told you, Chief, I just walked on board with it. The torches too. Got them from someone I know in Hawaii. The guys on watch saw me."

"What did they say?" Ross asked.

Jeffs shrugged. "Leon was helping me carry it. Nobody said a thing."

Ross was nodding and thinking. "You know what this is? It's an unvarnished affront to the naval canon."

George turned and walked to the aft railing to put some distance between his laughing and the chief.

Jeffs was still staring at Ross, trying hard to decipher the latest high level vocabulary utterance from his boss. Ross routinely enjoyed instructing his men to enhance their vocabulary understanding. Sometimes he dared them with it. This was a dare. Jeffs didn't know the precise meaning of what Ross had just spoken, but he knew that it meant he didn't like the whole idea of his signal shack being decorated with surf boards and tiki torches.

Jeffs was well aware of his ability to be annoying as hell while feigning ignorance. "Of course it's unvarnished, Chief." He reached over and rubbed his hand on the surf board. "Fiberglass."

Ross looked over at George, whose shoulders were convulsing as he leaned over the railing ten feet away from them, his hands holding his head. To Jeffs he said, "Look, the captain is allowing a lot of individual freedom with dress and hair to help crew morale. He likes his men to do a good job, but he doesn't want to be a hard ass about it. He thinks the surf board idea is cool so that's fine. But don't push it and get yourself in a bind."

"If the captain wants them down, I'll take them down," Jeffs said.

"Damn right you will." Ross cocked his head leaning in closer to Jeffs and sneered, "What if I want them down?"

"Then I'll take them down," Jeffs said. He stepped closer to him and lowered his voice a bit. "I'm not trying to be an asshole. I'm just trying to have a little fun. Chief, in spite of my beautiful blonde locks I'm part Cheyenne and I've studied our history some. You're big on teaching us new words. Well, look, maybe I can teach you something here."

He gestured at the surfboard. "This shit is kind of like our war paint. You know, some of the Plains Indian tribes used war paint on their faces and bodies. They had certain designs that were just for them. Some were to protect them in battle. Others were to show their bravery. We're the signalmen and we're sending a signal. We're telling them we are not just another destroyer out here. We're special. We're better. We want people to notice us. This beach stuff is the *Rat's* war paint."

Ross folded his arms and took a step back. He surveyed the shack again. "Make sure those bolts stay tight. I don't want this shit flying around when were in heavy seas."

He turned and headed toward the ladder. "Hays!"

George swallowed his laughter and turned back around, tears streaming down his face. "Yes, Chief?"

One of the forward guns fired and all three men flinched.

"Shut the fuck up!" Ross ordered, without even looking at him, then disappeared down the ladder.

The last couple of hours of their watch were busy with receiving greetings and congratulations on the "fine shooting" from the captains of several of the other nearby ships. Jeffs brought the first batch that had come in one after the other down to the bridge.

At both forward corners of the bridge was a tall padded chair, captain's chairs, with a good view out to that side of the ship and the row of windows that ran across the forward face of the bridge. Captain McHenry was leaned back comfortably in the starboard chair with his feet up resting on the ledge under the window. He was watching with interest out over the bow to where another destroyer, about a mile away, was firing at targets inland.

Jeffs walked to his side and cleared his throat. "I've got some messages for you, sir."

McHenry turned and flashed a quick smile. "How you doing, Ryder?"

"Fine, sir."

Just then another round was fired from the *Rat's* forward mount shaking the ship and causing every man on the bridge to flinch.

McHenry took the clip board and flipped through the three brief messages, shaking his head as he did so. All were full of standard navy rhetoric like "outstanding shooting" and "excellent gunfire support." Predictably, one even made reference to the line of trucks being totally destroyed, and the number had already grown to twenty.

"These guys just love kissing each other's asses and they want me to join the party." He took a pen from Jeffs' pocket and scribbled something on the back of one of the papers and gave the clipboard back to him. "Here, I imagine there will be more of this useless shit coming your way. Just send that reply to all of them. Hopefully you have better things to do than run down here all day with their crap."

Jeffs looked down at the brief two sentence generic reply. "Thanks, Captain."

McHenry leaned in and lowered his voice. "There's a second class boatswain's mate they call Sonny. He's pretty handy. I was talking to him about the torches. How about if I have him modify them to have a bigger flame? Might be a nice touch for our unreps."

Jeffs was smiling. "Sounds good to me, sir."

"I'm sending somebody up there to get them in a few minutes," McHenry said. "Be good if Sonny can get them ready for our first unrep. Probably just a day or two off."

"I'll have them ready to go," Jeffs said. "I think they use kerosene but other stuff might work too."

"He'll figure it out," McHenry said. He leaned back in his chair again. "How's your head feeling?"

"A little sore, but not bad."

"Good. You and Hays were lucky. It could've been a lot worse. By the way, I know you did hit the barbershop the other day after we talked in Pearl, but not much, huh?" He reached out and flicked the blond curls at the back of his neck.

A couple of the men nearby were snickering.

Jeffs cleared his throat. "Just a quick trim, sir. Smitty said he had a lot of people waiting and I didn't want to hold him up too long. I know some of them were anxious to get their hair cut."

McHenry motioned for Jeffs to lean in closer. In a voice just above a whisper he said, "I saw in your paper work that one of your charges was nude surfing. What's with that?"

Jeffs checked how close the men behind him were. "Well, sir, it's not really too safe but the idea is to encourage any girls with you to join in, you know?"

McHenry smiled a little. "I figured." Then raising his voice again he added, "Okay, Surfer Joe, see you later."

Jeffs was smiling too as he walked away amid stifled laughter from the other men on the bridge.

The day went on, the air grew hotter, the ships juggled positions and the guns hammered away. The young men on the warships did their jobs well, sending shell after shell far away to kill an unseen enemy, and the captains sat in their tall chairs, sipping iced tea and wondering, now and again, if they were doing anything that would make any difference in what they figured must be the waning months of this long, tired war.

SEVENTEEN

Dear Jeffs,

I found an apartment in Chula Vista. It will be perfect for us! $150 a month including utilities and it's furnished. It's a complex with about forty apartments. Nice landscaping, nice pool and a nice old couple are the managers. It's a one bedroom, everything seems clean and pretty new. It's close to the freeway and just a quick drive to the naval station. I'm moving in next week. My dad even said he would buy a portable TV for us. I love you and can't wait for you to come home. I love you I love you I love you. Stay safe.

Love,
Cathy

The navy had a long, unofficial tradition of relaxed uniform and hair rules when operating at sea for extended periods. Some captains were always more lenient than others, but it was common, especially in warmer climates, for men to work without shirts and even short pants. Overdue haircuts sometimes got taken care of just before entering port. Lately, though, things had gone somewhat beyond "relaxed."

Just like the rest of American society since the mid-1960s, even the tradition-rich and doctrine-bound United States Navy was going through some upheaval. The navy's top ranking officer, Admiral Elmo Zumwalt, Chief of Naval Operations, CNO, had issued a series of directives over the last couple of years known as Z-Grams. His aim was to break the navy's entrenched racial discrimination as well as bring some of the navy's policies more in line with the current conditions in the civilian world, hopefully making navy life less harsh and increasing reenlistments in the face of an unpopular contentious war. Haircuts were no longer required to be quite so short. Afros were allowed to be fuller. Beards and mustaches were being allowed and overnight liberty was sometimes permissible. Sailors were now authorized to wear civilian clothes on base if they were off duty. In fact, due to the rising anti-American sentiment in much of the world because of the war, sailors on liberty were now required to wear civilian clothes in many ports.

There was a widespread, but unofficial, policy that allowed enlisted men bound for the western Pacific to wear cutoffs and white T-shirts once they were passed Hawaii. Some captains kept a tight rein on any change, but many, including James McHenry, had given in to the pressures of a new society. He demanded that his men know their jobs and do them well, but he had taught himself to be less concerned about their looks over the past few years. As long as they were out to sea he would be allowing a great deal of latitude on individuality.

Leon proudly held up an ancient pair of faded cutoff jeans that he'd been laboring over. "There, that ought to work. Fifty pound test fishing line!"

Jeffs had been watching for messages from two nearby destroyers. He turned and grabbed the shorts, smiling as he examined the fishing line that crisscrossed up the length of the formerly torn side seams. "It'll hold unless a fifty-one pound fish jumps up here and grabs your balls!"

Leon laughed. "Yeah! Those big fish better lay off!"

Jeffs was wearing a similar pair of faded cut-offs, black work shoes with no socks, a black and blue tie-dyed sleeveless tee shirt and a white head band tied at the back with the ends hanging down past his shoulders. He tossed the cut-offs back to him. "So, when do you go on watch?"

Leon stood and slipped them on. "Never, man. I'm just going to stroll around the ship modeling my handiwork and this magnificent physique."

George looked over from the opposite railing and slowly shook his head. He took the unlit cigarette from his lips. "I can hardly wait to hear you tell the chief."

Being a first class, George was not able to stray quite as far from accepted dress. He too wore cut-off jeans, but with an untucked regulation work shirt and his work hat turned backwards. He sometimes wore a camouflage bush hat from his Riverine days.

"You going to smoke that thing or what?" Jeffs asked. "It's been just hanging out of your mouth for an hour."

George nodded. "Pretty soon. I read about this somewhere as a way to quit smoking, or at least cut down. Sometimes I forget it's not lit and just let it go for a while."

Just then the 1MC came to life. "Now hear this. We will be departing the gun line in a few minutes to refuel from the *Mispillion*. Be ready to turn-to when called to your station."

This would be the *Rattano's* first unrep since arriving off Vietnam. Underway replenishment, unrep, meant maybe no sleep and probably a lot of work. The oilers, ammunition ships, food and supply ships ran regular routes miles off the coast, sometimes servicing twenty or more ships in a day. This service fleet was a strong point of the United States Navy and no other navy in the world had one that came close in size or proficiency.

The *Rattano* wheeled southeast and headed toward the open sea of the Tonkin Gulf, increasing her speed to twenty-seven knots. After nearly thirty minutes, the *Mispillion* came into view. CIC had been tracking her on radar for some time.

McHenry began barking a series of instructions to the helmsman and the engine room, lining up the ship for the approach. The sun shined brightly over a calm sea with just two to three foot swells. The oiler, riding full and low in the water, held her course and steadied her speed at fourteen knots. McHenry skillfully slid his destroyer alongside the larger ship and now the two captains made their ships sail as one, a hundred twenty feet apart moving in unison at fourteen knots.

Two crews of thirty-five men each, one for the aft refueling hose and one for the forward hose, were needed to pull the lines to bring those hoses over to the destroyer. This day Jeffs and Leon had the good fortune of being on the aft refueling crew. Unlike the crew working on the opposite side of the ship, they had only boredom to look forward to instead of occasionally being washed over by a freak wave from between the two ships.

The slick, grimy lines were pulled hand over hand by the sailors until the heavy refueling hose reached the connection, where it was attached and thousands of gallons of fuel oil was transferred from one ship to the other. The men on the crews had no job other than to wait while the fuel was being pumped, just in case there was some problem that required them to go through their routine a second time.

Jeffs, Leon and the rest of the group were sitting on the main deck, their backs against the dull gray of the superstructure.

"How many times you think we'll have to do this?" Jeffs asked.

Leon let out a long sigh. "Millions! If it ain't fuel it'll be ammo, food or some damn thing. They just don't want us to sleep. I think it's some kind of fucking plot from the white folks!"

Jeffs laughed. "So why am I on this duty?"

"It don't matter! You're a nobody. Now if you were some kind of uppity white guy, well, you wouldn't be here. You'd be sittin' by a pool somewhere sippin' on margaritas. But you're just a regular fucking peon. So the white folks that make all this shit happen don't really care about you either. In fact, you might as well face up to it, you're just a white, black guy."

The other men on the crew, white, black, Asian, Latino and all, were laughing now too as they listened to Leon's ranting, glad for something to pass the time while they waited on station.

Jeffs was nodding thoughtfully. "You're right, you're right."

Leon responded with a tired chuckle and leaned his head back wearily against the bulkhead.

Jeffs leaned over close to Leon and lowered his voice. "I spent some time hanging out with Esparza last night."

Leon squinted. "Esparza, the gunner?"

Jeffs nodded.

"I barely know the guy," Leon said. "What's up with him?"

"Not much." Jeffs dropped his voice further. "I don't know him much either. Nice guy. He's the one who's going to be starting the tape for the breakaway music. We discussed some options," Jeffs said, then just stared back at Leon with a widening grin.

Leon looked around then turned to face Jeffs. "What did you do now?"

"I don't want to ruin the surprise for you. I have a feeling the captain might even like it."

Leon was staring at him trying to decide if it was something funny or something he wanted nothing to do with.

"Okay, here's a hint," Jeffs said, trying to contain his laughter. "Give me an 'F'. You've seen that performance from Woodstock?"

Leon squinted, thinking. "Yeah, that guy does that chant then goes into that Vietnam song. That's what we're going to…? Well, it's been nice knowing you dumb ass." He shook his head then started softly laughing. "This really gonna happen?"

Fifteen minutes later, all the hoses were disconnected, lines pulled back and the *Rattano* was prepared to speed back to her gun line position. The crews were dismissed from their unrep stations and Jeffs hurried back up to the signal bridge.

Since sometime in the 1950s, the United States Navy and navies of several other countries had developed a tradition of playing a "breakaway song" over the receiving ship's PA system and running up a special flag as a kind of parting salute to the service ship. The *Rattano* would unveil her new breakaway flag today—the gift that Wil Gordan had passed along to McHenry in Hawaii. It had been on display for several days on the mess deck on their way across the Pacific. Custom-made in Taiwan, it had a crimson background and gold lettering arched across the top that read "McHenry's Marauders" and across the bottom "DD-856 The Rat". In the center was the head of a shaggy-haired, bearded, sneering pirate. Crawling over his shoulder was a large, snarling, salivating brown rat wearing a sailor hat and a surfboard strapped to his back. Jeffs thought it fit well into the war paint concept.

The weapons department had received approval from McHenry to play the theme from "The Good the Bad and the Ugly" for the breakaway music. The officer of the deck had just inquired and been assured that the tape deck in gun plot was cued and ready to go.

"Light 'em up!" McHenry announced over the 1MC and Jeff's lit the tiki torches as George ran up the new flag.

Sonny had done a great job on the torches. They only held enough fuel for about fifteen minutes on high, but the flames were about two feet tall.

"Officer of the deck, let's breakaway," he ordered to Lieutenant Wiffler.

Lieutenant Wiffler gave the proper orders to the engine room and helmsman and the destroyer began to smoothly increase her speed to pull away. Then, to the joy of many, to the dismay of some and to the amazement of everyone, booming out over the speakers came "I-Feel-Like-I'm-Fixin'-To-Die Rag," the song by Country Joe and the Fish that had become the anthem of the anti-war movement.

The clear, loud music echoed off the side of the oiler and men on both ships cheered, whooped and waved and many were singing along with the chorus. On the bridge of the destroyer, by-the-book and despised Lieutenant Wiffler flew into a tantrum of swearing just as McHenry stormed in from his parting salute to the captain of the oiler that had suddenly gone awry.

Wiffler reached up, punched the button for gun plot, and held down the switch on the intercom. "Who the hell am I speaking to?"

"Seaman Esparza, sir," a decidedly meek, shaky voice answered for all on the bridge to hear. "Uh, sir, uh, they told me to just press the button on the tape deck when we broke away, sir."

The music was still blaring, and outside the oiler was slipping past as they pulled away. The cheering and whistling from the crews of both ships could be heard over the music and Wiffler had worked himself into a spit-foaming fit. "We're going to press your button, sailor! Turn off that fucking hippie music!"

The helmsman, quartermaster, both lookouts, the phone talkers and other personnel on the bridge watch were turning their backs, grunting and wheezing, shoulders shaking.

McHenry was watching the reaction of the men on both ships and thinking that in light of how this war had gone over the years he had started to like the song more than a navy destroyer skipper probably should.

He took another look at the cheering from the sailors on the other ship, then reached up to the intercom and gave Lieutenant Wiffler a silencing look. "Esparza, this is the captain. Leave the music playing. That's not the song I approved, but I've decided it's going to be our new breakaway music. Is that understood?"

After a few seconds of silence, "Yes, sir!" came the reply.

McHenry turned and without looking at Wiffler, walked back out to the bridge wing with the beginnings of a smile on his face and a quick wink for the starboard lookout.

Captain McHenry's already high approval rating with the crew had just gone up a few points. It wouldn't be a popular decision with most of the other skippers, but the *Rattano* soon became the most popular ship, by far, with the crews of the replenishment ships.

EIGHTEEN

What is absurd and monstrous about war is that men who have no personal quarrel should be trained to murder one another in cold blood.
- Aldous Huxley

Even within the usually cooler tunnel it was smotheringly humid and hot. Quan sat cross-legged at the mouth of one of the gun tunnels hoping for a breeze as he gazed out over the peaceful rim of the Pacific known as the South China Sea. Even the ocean seemed to be lying still under the oppressiveness of the two-day-old heat wave. His thoughts were far north to Lam and home and how he had ended up here.

There had always been distant rumblings of the war in his village, but for many years, quite remarkably, it never came near enough to change much for them. Occasionally an American fighter or a North Vietnamese MIG would streak over, and at quiet times they could hear the distant thunder of bombs, but most of their knowledge of the war came by way of soldiers passing through and rumors. In spite of being surrounded relatively closely by the war, for many years, for the inhabitants of the hamlet known as "The Village by the Lone Hill" life went on largely as it had for hundreds of years.

Eventually changes came. In January there had been talk of a new offensive and more men would be needed. One day a group of government and military officials came and picked those who would go into the service of their country, including Quan. He was assigned to a regular NVA unit. It was an honor to be chosen, or at least it was supposed to be, but there was much sorrow mixed with the patriotic pride among his family and friends.

Finally, after he and the others from the area had trained for several days with various men in the different aspects of military discipline, an officer came and led them away as they bid farewell to their families.

That had been less than three months ago, and now here he sat looking out over the ocean wishing he could be somewhere else. The damage from the attack of a few nights ago had been cleared. Some gun positions had been rebuilt and some new ones had been tunneled into the hillside.

There had been no new attacks, but they had been told that the next one could be any time, because the war was changing and there wouldn't be much slack time. They were told that the American navy was trying to wipe them out and stop their invasion and win the war. Almost every night they could hear and feel the deep rumble of B-52 strikes, some just a few miles away.

So, Quan thought that he had gotten into the war and an interesting time, an important time, maybe a time that mattered. The war was changing. But the evening meal had been just a short while ago, and they had been rationed even more during the last few days. He was still hungry, and hunger had a way of eating away at the importance of the cause

Along a river a hundred miles north of Hon La, Captain Denis Anasov strolled along the pier with his aide, Lieutenant Yegor Koshkin, admiring the two Soviet Komar missile boats from twenty yards away. His Soviet contingent of eight naval advisors was nearing the completion of the training of the North Vietnamese crews.

"I can't believe we're standing here in this God-forsaken country. I'm expecting an American bomb to fall on my head any minute."

Anasov laughed. "We leave tomorrow, just keep moving."

They both stood in silence for a bit watching the North Vietnamese crews practicing, once again, getting underway from the docks. They would be circling out a hundred yards then pulling back in again to practice their approach to the docks. "You know, these boats are still good. New or not, in the right hands they can do the job," Koshkin said.

"You're right," Anasov said. "But are these the right hands?"

Koshkin shrugged. "The crews are learning fast, but I don't know if *they* are in the right hands. Using them in pairs to go after ships is a good strategy. Three would be even better, but you heard that Commander

Ngo. If we send them more than these two he wants to have them operate singly. He wants to spread them out all over hell and gone. He's afraid to commit them to battle two or three at a time. He's also afraid of having them attacked if they are sitting here in port."

Koshkin glanced upwards. "He may be right about that. You know, his second in command, Commander Nguyen, seems a bit more creative. His idea is to make several runs at various ships or groups of ships to see how they react. Then after doing that for awhile he wants to send two against a cruiser or destroyer group and fire all four missiles."

Anasov nodded. "I think he may be onto something there, especially if the Americans think them to be false alarms and let down their guard a bit."

Koshkin cursed under his breath. "If you and I could operate these boats with our own crews, the U.S Navy would move far off shore."

Anasov was nodding agreement. "We should've taken Ngo and some of the other high command out to some target firings with the Styx. The boat captains too. Hearing what these boats and missiles can do and seeing it is two different things. Remember that one that peeled the main deck of the target ship right up over the stern like a can of fish?"

Koshkin nodded and chuckled softly. "Having them see that would have been a good thing, all right."

The first boat was heading back into the docks.

"Maybe they will end up doing the right thing, and maybe they will get a little lucky. If not they will end up just a small footnote in the history of this Godless mess." He looked around and up at the sky again.

What the Soviet training officers could not know, of course, was that these two boat captains had no plans to follow through with whatever their North Vietnamese government or military had in mind. They were well aware of how the Egyptians sank the Israeli destroyer *Eilat.* They had studied Operation Trident, the daring attack by Indian Navy missile boats on the Pakistani navy in Karachi less than a year ago, destroying a number of ships. Both of these attacks used the same Styx missiles that their boats were armed with and these boat captains were firmly committed to the plan that Seven had laid out for them. They had every intention of using their boats and missiles for the destruction of as many American navy ships as possible.

NINETEEN

More War Protests

With crowds of marchers, window breaking, and sit-ins which disrupted life for many as highways and public buildings were blocked, thousands of protesters around the nation took action yesterday in response to President Nixon's decision to mine North Vietnamese ports. Many were peaceful but as often happens these days, several also turned into chaotic clashes with the police.

After five days of nearly continual but uneventful fire support missions in and around the Quang Tri City area, the *Rattano* was again in need of replenishment.

"Good morning, this is the captain speaking. There have been some changes in our plans that I want to pass along to you. The South Vietnamese Marines will begin another operation late this afternoon to retake a sector of Quang Tri City. The *Rat*, along with several other units on the line and planes from the *America* will assist in this effort. We're a little low on everything right now so about 1000 hours we'll be leaving the line and starting a series of three unreps to take on food, ammo and fuel--beans, bullets and black oil. I'm going to try to get us some fresh water too. I expect this will take a good part of the morning and early afternoon. So stand by and turn to when you're called upon."

Leon folded his arms and leaned back. "This is bullshit, man. We get to sleep for a couple of hours, then carry bullets and shit all day, then go back on watch after supper until midnight."

"Captain said we might get water," George said. "That might be nice since this is the sixth damn day with no showers. You guys are starting to stink."

Jeffs leaned toward him and sniffed. "Don't worry, you're right there with us. And why is it we are always short of water? Is this a Viking ship?"

"Happens to most of these old cans," George explained. "Something to do with the evaporators not working right with all this slow barely moving stuff we do here on the gun line. When we're steaming across the Pacific or to and from Subic there's fresh water."

They had long since finished their breakfast and were the last ones left on the mess deck. Fake Eggs, the first class cook, had already walked through once and directed them to leave and had now returned to chase them out for good. He was Filipino and spoke barely understandable English, especially when angry. Nobody could ever get his lengthy name right, but a couple of years ago someone had remarked that it sounded like Fake Eggs and the name stuck.

"Come on, Fake Eggs," Jeffs teased, "we always leave a good tip."

The cook glared at Jeffs, but the humor was not completely lost on him and for just a second he showed a small smile. "You goddamn guys don't tip shit! Get out so they can clean up!" He waved a metal spatula at them as he spoke and continued on by and through the opposite doorway.

Leon leaned over the table and lowered his voice to nearly a whisper. "Check this out. You know that Radarman, Hughes? Third class, scraggly beard."

Jeffs and George nodded.

He looked at George. "You can't go all First Class Petty Officer on us here, okay?

George chuckled. "Don't worry."

Leon lowered his voice even more. "He's taking the ship apart!"

Leon snorted into laughter on the last word and Jeffs wasn't sure he had heard him correctly. "Taking the ship apart?"

The look on both their faces just made Leon laugh more and it took him several seconds to recover so he could continue his explanation. "He's carrying around a screwdriver and a pair of vice-grips with him all the time. Whenever he has a few minutes he takes out a screw, a bolt, a sheet metal rivet, whatever. Says he does a lot of his work while he's sitting on the can. He said he figures if he does it just right, he can have the whole ship fall apart just as we pull into San Diego at the end of the cruise." He barely finished before breaking into more laughter.

George was still staring, then he too broke into disbelieving giggling. "Jesus, there's always somebody, huh?"

"He did mention that he didn't want to kill us," Leon explained. "Said he wasn't going to mess with any weapons or navigation stuff."

They were suddenly interrupted by a jumble of English and Filipino swearing from the food serving line. Chief Ross came running wildly through the doorway, stumbling onto the mess deck holding a piece of bacon he had snatched from the serving line leftovers. With a look of genuine fear he turned just in time to duck as the spatula came flying. It hit the paneled bulkhead behind him with a loud pop, leaving a greasy splatter behind as it dropped to the seat below.

"Now just a damn minute, Fake Eggs! Don't you throw shit at me!" His pitch and volume were both on the rise.

"Hi Chief!" Leon greeted cheerfully.

Ross turned to their table and saw Leon waving like a little kid with a dopey grin on his face. "Shut the fuck up, Thomsen! Can't you see I've got a problem here?"

The cook appeared in the doorway. "You goddamn guys! You fucking think you can act smart to me and steal food. You just like the goddamn Japs!" Fake Eggs had been born in 1937 and carried vivid childhood memories of the Japanese occupation of his homeland, but he had never before referred to anyone aboard the ship as a Jap.

"I think he's upset, Chief, 'cause we didn't leave him a tip," Jeffs explained. He and George were both struggling to keep their laughter in. Finally, George put his head down on the table.

Ross was still standing in the same spot and the bacon in his hand had not come near his mouth. He turned his head and looked at it as though he had forgotten it was there. Then he took a bite while he looked straight at the crazed cook, pointing what remained of the bacon at him. "This isn't your food, you just serve it! Now knock this shit off!" As he said the last word he defiantly stuffed the last of the bacon into his mouth, looked over at his men and without meaning to, began to chuckle.

"You goddamn Japs, that's what you are!" Fake Eggs yelled again.

Leon stood suddenly. "Hey, these dumb honkies may be Japs, but I'm no Jap you dummy!"

Fake Eggs stared for a few seconds then turned and stomped back through the doorway and began yelling at the two mess cooks who were just beginning to clean up. Utensils and trays clanged and bounced loudly.

Chief Ross walked to their table. "Damn, Thomsen, didn't you think he was pissed off enough already? I grab one little piece of bacon and he goes ape shit. What's wrong with him?"

"He does get awfully angry lately," George said. "A couple of days ago Tinsley complained about sticky spaghetti or something and he went nuts then too. He's always easy to get a rise out of, but not like this!"

"Did you guys give him a bad time?" Ross asked.

"Not really," Jeffs said. "We were hanging on here just talking and he told us a couple of times to leave. We barely talked to him. It's all your fault, Chief."

"You should tell him some big words to help him out," Leon said sarcastically.

Ross narrowed his eyes and gave Leon a long look. "You are an obtuse simpleton."

All three of them broke into laughter.

"You can't get that one by us," Jeffs said. "It just means he's a fucking idiot."

Ross nodded and smiled. "Good enough for now."

George stood suddenly and began moving away from the table. "I'm turning in. Maybe they'll start late and we'll get a few hours sleep out of this deal after all."

Heeding George's suggestion, the three of them left Ross on the mess deck still wondering about the cook, hurried down into the Ops compartment, stripped down to their underwear and climbed into their racks.

At 0900 everyone was awakened, although as it turned out, the first unrep was delayed by more than an hour.

Leon walked into the signal shack with a broad grin on his face. "Guess what, honky types? I just came up from Radio. We've been talking to the *Haleakala* on the Teletype. They've got four-hundred pounds of mail for us and they're going to give us ten-thousand gallons of water. I just took a copy to the captain."

Jeffs folded his arms. "Bullshit! We haven't gotten mail since we left Hawaii and we don't get showers either, remember? Something will happen. The *Haleakala* will probably blow up with all our mail and water still on board. What do think, George?"

George reached into his shirt pocket and pulled out a ten-dollar bill. "I think we're going to get the mail but not the water. If we get both I owe you ten. If we don't get any of it you owe me ten."

Leon laughed and rubbed his hands together. "Well, this makes it a little more interesting. I say put up or shut up."

"You're on," Jeffs said. He shook hands with George. Then to Leon he said, "You don't get anything either way. What do you care?"

"True, but I don't lose anything either, man, and I get to give a bunch of shit to whoever does."

After getting off to a late start, it all went very smoothly and the replenishment ships were in reasonably close proximity to each other.

At 1010 they pulled alongside the *Haleakala* and took on ammunition. It was an extra-large order and there was no room to store all of it properly. After all the racks in the magazines were full, shells and powder canisters were stacked wherever there was extra space in the cramped magazines and inside the gun mounts themselves. Several pallets were left intact and shoved into the hanger. The *Rattano's* magazines could store about nine-hundred shells and their accompanying powder canisters. On board this day were over fourteen hundred. It would be used up in just a few days.

Before lunch they refueled from the *Wabash* and by 1400 hours they completed taking on food and other consumables from the *Niagara Falls*.

His hands and arms were grimy and achy from pulling refueling lines, carrying more than forty of the fifty-five pound shells, then carrying several cases of food down to cold storage. But Jeffs now found himself, unbelievably, back in his rack again with a couple of hours before his evening watch, plus George's ten dollar bill in his pocket. He and the rest of the crew were hoping the water they received from the ammo ship might provide them quick showers for at least the next day or two.

As he drifted off to sleep he could hear the aft guns come to life, sounding very distant as they began to hurl round after round across the peaceful sea into the southern outskirts of what was left of the city.

TWENTY

War News - May 4, 1972

The U.S. and South Vietnam have suspended participation in the Paris Peace Talks indefinitely.

During the first part of May, President Nixon ordered North Vietnam's ports mined to prevent military deliveries from supporting their efforts to sustain the war. This halted nearly all shipping in and out of Haiphong, North Vietnam's chief port, as well as many smaller harbors.

The *Rattano* spent most of the month on the gun line in a grinding routine of nearly round the clock firing and rearming every four to five days. Finally, on the first of June, they were detached from the gun line and headed to Subic Bay for regularly scheduled maintenance and liberty for the crew.

"Good morning, this is the captain speaking. I guess word has gotten around the fleet about how beautiful some of you are looking topside during unreps. Also, some humorless bastards out there just don't appreciate our breakaway music. On the positive side, our new flag seems to be catching its share of attention along with the flaming torches. I've heard the crew of this vessel referred to more than once lately, with some envy I might add, as McHenry's Marauders. The signalmen and radiomen tell me most of the unrep ships have been sending friendly 'surf's up' greetings. You're a damn fine crew, one of the best I've had the pleasure of serving with, although honestly not one of the best looking I've ever laid eyes on."

He paused, knowing there would be some laughter around the ship.

"Here are some policies I want followed from here on. Any personnel topside during unreps are required to wear shirts, and no headbands. If you have to wear a headband to keep your hair out of the way, then wear a hat. Also, you might want to consider an appointment at the barber shop. Work with me on this and maybe I won't get as many judgmental messages from my superiors. As long as we're away from the unrep ships, you can go back to being the Marauders. We've been out to sea for over a month and you're going to have to get yourself cleaned up a little so we don't catch it from the base command in Subic Bay. Uniform of the day is the normal working uniform, regular dungarees and shirts. Off the base it's civvies only. You can comb and plaster down the hair on top, but if it's too long down the back of your neck or if your beard is getting too scroungy you're going to get nailed by the Marines at the gate on your way into town. That is all, carry on."

McHenry flipped the off the switch and leaned back in his desk chair in his cabin. He turned to his executive officer and grinned. "Nothing like a little team building, huh?"

Smith chuckled. "Man, someday I'm going to be answering a shit pile of questions about you. Chief Ross is waiting outside to see you."

"Oh, that's right. We began a little conversation earlier. Send him in, and stick around if you want."

Smith opened the door and Chief Ross stepped in, stiffly holding his hat under his left arm. "Relax, Frank. Have a seat, have some tea."

"Thank you, sir," Ross replied. He poured himself some iced tea, sat at the table, but still seemed reluctant to relax. "Captain, we've served together for over two years now. I feel like we can discuss things with no problem. I want to talk about Seaman Ryder." His tone was conversational, but it had just an edge of formality and he sounded ready to argue if he needed to.

McHenry looked at Smith, smiled, and then to Ross. "Chief, we were just talking about this very subject. Listen, I know where you're coming from. Hell, you and I have been in the navy a long time. You're over twenty, I'm looking at thirty."

"Yes, sir," Ross interrupted, "which is why I'm a little surprised by the surfboard and now the tiki torches." He leaned back and sighed. His tone softened and sounded friendlier. "Captain, some of the chiefs are wondering about you. I mean, we'd do anything for you, sir, but the surfing shit and the breakaway song? A lot of us are already rubbed the wrong way with some of Zumwalt's new leniency with hair and everything. We're just..." he threw up his hands, uncharacteristically unable to find the right word.

"Pissed!" McHenry offered. "You are pissed off. You think two hundred years of fine navy tradition are being thrown down the toilet and you think discipline has gone to hell!" He stopped and stared at the chief.

Ross was taken aback by the sudden agreement with what he was saying. "Yes, sir...I guess that's it. Well put."

"Believe me, Chief, I understand how you and some others feel, but hear me out here. More than half the crew is under the age of twenty-five. This damn war is in its eighth year if you count it from the Tonkin Gulf incident. They've grown up with this war and seen it get nowhere and kill fifty-thousand guys. At the same time look what's happened to American society—long hair, hippies, pot smoking, everyone protests everything. I could go on and on. Think of 1962 compared to now, Chief. That's just ten years ago and look how much has changed."

He'd been pacing the length of the table but now he sat down across from Ross. "Everything!" He pounded his fist on the table and the ice bucket jumped. "Every fucking thing you and I grew up thinking was right and normal has changed in that short time."

Ross was nodding agreement. "Then shouldn't the navy hold out against all that change? Shouldn't we be an example of decent standards and discipline?"

"Don't confuse discipline with all this surface bullshit. Hair and clothes and radical music don't undo discipline unless you let them. It's still the navy and we still have a job to do. Zumwalt understands that. He knows he's catching hell for allowing the beards and all that other crap. All the flag officers are ready to mutiny! We just happen to be living through a time of widespread social change and if there's one thing people our age don't like, it's change. And we all know that the slowest changing thing in the whole damn universe is the United States Navy. I'm surprised we aren't still firing cannon balls at the beach!"

Ross and Smith both chuckled. Ross took a gulp of tea. "I guess I agree with all that, but I'm not so sure that appearance and discipline aren't part of the same thing."

"I'm not so sure sometimes myself," McHenry agreed. "But I'm an optimist at heart. I'm hoping things probably aren't really going to hell as bad as we think. I'd like to think that no matter how much people's looks change, what's in here doesn't change all that much." He pointed against his own chest. "So, I've got a bunch of kids who are from that real world, Chief. They're out here fighting in that war they hate. But I haven't just given in. I'm using it to my advantage. All this bullshit with the shorts and T-shirts, the beards, the bandannas, the goddamn turned around and cut off hats and all the rest of it."

He gestured to Smith. "Gil, what do I call this wonderful new look?"

Smith cleared his throat. "Well, let's see. I think the one I've heard the most lately is the Fuckin' Hell's Angel Hippy Pirate Surfer Look."

Ross smiled and nodded. "I think you're on to something there, sir."

McHenry was grinning at his own creativity. "The old Esprit de corps is a pretty rare find after being eaten away by this war, but this crew has it. This war may be going to hell in a hand basket, but this crew, McHenry's Marauders, is feeling like they're doing a good job for their skipper, for their ship, for each other. In spite of how I let them look out at sea or how they feel about the war, the snipes are proud of how this ship runs. The gunners think they're the best. And you can go all around to every division on the ship and say the same thing. And up on the signal bridge, Ryder and the rest of those guys think they're showing us off to the whole goddamn fleet. He's proud of all that surfing crap because to him it's become a part of the personality of the ship and we've got the crew buying into the whole cool surfing idea. I want this crew feeling like it's us against them, Chief, and "them" is not just the North Vietnamese. It's all the other ships and the whole goddamn navy."

McHenry stood and stretched, shaking his head slowly. "Between McHenry's Marauders, the surf shack and the Country Joe break-away music, the brass is going to think I've lost my fucking mind! But, hell, I figure this is my last cruise. I'll do a shore rotation somewhere and then I'll retire, so I might as well go out in a blaze of glory."

He pointed at Smith. "You were just saying how they are going to be asking you a lot of questions about me someday. Tell them whatever you want and just blame it all on me."

The XO was smiling. "Thanks, Mac. You know, for this war, it all just seems to fit though."

McHenry said, "Well, Chief, have I made any sense here?"

Ross stood. "You've given me a lot to think over, Captain. Thanks for the time."

They shook hands and Smith opened the door to let him out.

On the way down to the chief's quarters Ross tried to sort out how he felt about what McHenry had said. He understood his ideas and they mostly made sense to him, but he was having a difficult time getting his navy-trained mind around it all. Still, the motives were good, so he hoped it would work like the captain wanted it to.

He made his way down to the mess deck, then forward to the chief's quarters. Chief Neal, the gunnery chief, was sitting on the edge of his rack tying his shoes. Sitting across from him on another rack was Chief Garcia, a boiler technician.

"Hey, Ross," Neal called out, "the signal bridge just called down. The Beach Boys are flying in this afternoon to give a concert."

Both men giggled and stood, obviously begging a response from Ross.

"I wrote up your boy Ryder," Garcia said. "He needs a haircut."

Ross tossed his hat on his own rack and walked up to Neal. "Very humorous." He forced a smile to stay on his face. "If the Beach Boys were playing you'd be up there to see them and so would I."

He and Neal got along well enough, but Ross regarded Garcia as an overweight Neanderthal. He took a step closer and planted his face just inches from Garcia's. "You have a problem with any of my guys you talk to me. I don't go crawling down into the engine room to shake down those fucking snipes of yours and write 'em all up for being out of uniform for those dumb-ass hats of theirs, do I?"

The two men glared at each other, inches separating their noses. "Take it easy, Frank. I didn't turn in the paperwork on him, but he needs a haircut."

"Half the fucking crew needs a haircut," Ross replied. "You would too, you bald bastard, if you had any hair left."

This sent Neal into a high pitched shriek of a laughing fit that helped diffuse the situation.

"I'll see to Ryder's hair," Ross said, then turned and flopped down on his rack and pulled a paperback book from under his pillow.

Garcia shook his head and smiled in spite of himself then shoved Neal for his continued laughing.

TWENTY-ONE

Now hear this. During our transit to Subic Bay we will be encountering some rough weather due to a typhoon now located two hundred miles north of the Philippines. The forecast for tomorrow calls for increasing winds with six to ten foot seas and swells to twelve feet. This is a big change from the calm conditions we have experienced lately. All personnel are ordered to recheck and secure items in all work spaces to avoid breakage and injury. That is all.

Two days later they entered Subic Bay, the Philippines, one of the largest military complexes in the world. Although this was their second time here for this deployment, this stay would be for several days rather than the hurried few hours on their first arrival.

For years Subic Bay had been the foremost United States Navy base in the Western Pacific. Over the years, U.S. ships had regularly made port calls in Japan, Taiwan, Singapore and Australia during their western Pacific deployments. For the last few months, though, the pace of the war had severely curtailed visits to these extra liberty ports. Seeing the world for many navy personnel lately meant seeing mostly Vietnam, Subic and the business district of Olongapo City.

The once clean waters of the bay had long ago turned a drab non-color, only partially from years of fuel leaks, sewage releases, rust, paint, cleaners, and the other varied detritus that a large navy produces. Mostly it was due to a massive outpouring of waste from the densely packed civilian population, which some had pointed out, was also a result of the navy's presence.

The navy base cut into the big island of Luzon at the southwest corner of the province of Zambales, taking in just the tip of the infamous province of Bataan, encircling the bay and extending several miles inland at some points.

It was the height of the rainy season and the islands were awash from a disastrous, record-breaking month of rainfall compounded by the effects of two typhoons which had skirted the archipelago just weeks apart. Around the inland perimeter of the base, standing a defiant watch over the continuous activities of humans and modern machines of war, rose lush, green hills standing as a reminder that any intrusion, however long and extensive, was only temporary. The rain forest, alive and steaming, was patiently waiting to someday regain its lost territory.

The *Rattano* knifed slowly through the bay toward its berth. The crew was again in their whites, manning the rail and standing proudly. Their uniforms were a little more wrinkled, a little more soiled than they had been in Hawaii, but they still stood out impressively against the haze gray of the destroyer.

Jeffs was working the signal light, sending the routine arrival message to the base headquarters as George dictated.

Shakes, a radioman, was standing with Chief Ross watching the scenery slide by under the low, grey, overcast sky. "How come they're sticking us way down at the southern end of the base?" he asked.

Bobby Dexter, known simply as Shakes to most of the crew, was regarded as a likable but somewhat strange individual. Almost completely bald with hands that constantly trembled, he evaded all questions about his physical condition, but always hinted that the navy had something to do with it. He refused to discuss his age, and most of the men he worked with guessed it to be somewhere around thirty-five or forty instead of his actual twenty-eight.

"We have to get some work done by the tender," Ross explained, "and that's where the tender is tied up."

Shakes continued his complaining. "But it's too far from everything and we'll have to take taxis everywhere."

Ross gave a dramatic look over to Jeffs and George and then back to Shakes. "Goddamn, Dexter, you sure do bitch a lot! So you gotta take taxis. They're probably the cheapest damn taxis in the whole world, you tight bastard!"

Shakes was smiling broadly. The chief knew that in a strange sort of way Shakes enjoyed this, and he sometimes thought he complained just to get him to yell.

Leon came up the ladder and walked up to Jeffs and George. Ross immediately threw him a scolding look. "I know, Chief. I'm going right back down to Radio in just a minute. It's real slow right now and there's two other guys in there."

"Okay, Thomsen," Ross replied in a measured tone. "That's okay. I'm writing all this down. When it comes time for you to get out of this navy you're going to owe me another two months just from all your malingering, which in simple navy terms is known as fucking off!"

"All right Chief, I understand," Leon answered. "I just wanted to malinger a little to see where we were tying up."

Jeffs picked up on the conversation he had just witnessed between Ross and Shakes. In the official tone of a tour guide for a harbor cruise he said, "We're going to be way down at the southern end of the base because that's where the tender is tied up and we need to get some work done by the tender. We'll have to take taxis everywhere, but they're very inexpensive."

Leon looked at him with raised eyebrows, while George stifled a giggle.

Jeffs turned to the chief. "Ain't that right, Chief?"

Ross shook his head slowly while he decided whether to laugh or yell. "Yes, Ryder, that's right," he said calmly. "He knows exactly what he's talking about, Thomsen. He listens and learns. There's a good example for you." But he knew there was more coming.

Jeffs was nodding with mock seriousness and giving Leon an unflinching look. Still nodding, he turned back to Ross. "By the way, Chief, what in the hell is a tender?"

Leon knew perfectly well that a destroyer tender was a large ship where destroyers could get repairs and maintenance done. He raised his hand high and waved it like an over-enthusiastic school kid dying to answer a question in class. "I know, Chief, I know. That's when you cook those steaks just right. Charred on the outside with just a little pink on the inside and they end up really tender."

George walked away snorting and Shakes was giggling and staring at Ross waiting for his reaction. Jeffs and Leon were managing to keep perfectly straight faces.

Ross thought it was worth a laugh too, but he didn't want to give in to them this time, plus it was an opportunity for another vocabulary lesson using some of those words he was always looking up and memorizing. "You guys think you're funny, huh? Well, you're just a couple of goddamn asinine loonies!"

George was gasping over the rail and Shakes was now doubled over, braying while he slapped both thighs.

Ross added, "Deficient, dim-witted, fucking loonies!"

Jeffs and Leon were very pleased that they had generated such a marvelously entertaining reaction from their chief. Leon quickly disappeared back down the ladder heading toward Radio while Jeffs followed George around to the other side of the signal shack.

Shakes was standing next to Ross, just beginning to control his laughter. When Ross turned to him, Shakes burst into renewed gasping and choking and he too walked away and down from the signal bridge.

That left Ross standing alone talking aloud to himself. "Hm, I'd say I handled that rather well. I think my vocabulary is really improving!"

Later that afternoon, Jeffs, Leon and Shakes were headed off the ship to do some laundry. The laundry service aboard the ship was available, but it had a curious habit of returning clothes that looked dirtier than before they were "washed" with new permanent wrinkles added.

They took a taxi from the ship and were dropped off just a block from the laundromat. It was on the base and was rumored to have a beer vending machine, which made the prospect of a dull afternoon of doing laundry a little more appealing.

"You get mail this morning?" Leon asked as they walked down the road.

Jeffs nodded. "One from my mom, and fourteen from Cathy. She said she was going to write every day. I guess she meant it!"

"How the hell could anyone have that much to write about in less than a month?" Shakes complained

"You're just jealous," Jeffs answered.

Shakes shot one of his over-serious looks at Jeffs. "I got mail, you dumb, horny bastard."

"I saw your mail," Jeffs countered. "A newspaper and a letter from your mother. What happened to that girl you're always bragging about with the big knockers back in San Diego? Does she write?"

Shakes sounded disgusted. Hell, I had to break it off with her. She didn't believe in oral sex."

The comment brought both other men to a halt. With a straight face Shakes continued his explanation. "It was some religious thing. She wouldn't try it, talk about it, nothing." He threw his hands up. "So I finally just said 'fuck it' but, of course, she wouldn't let me!"

Jeffs had to set down his laundry bag until he could stop laughing enough to get some oxygen again. Leon just dropped his bag and walked away shaking his head and howling.

Shakes was smiling now too, obviously proud of himself for disabling Leon.

Bobby Dexter, aka Shakes, was a loner who was never alone. On and off the ship his companions were just as likely to be gunners or machinists or supply clerks or radiomen. He floated easily from one group to another, but never seemed to develop any lasting friendships. A good deal of his popularity stemmed from his sense of humor, which was generally considered to be uninhibitedly vulgar, but entertaining.

Jeffs, and finally Leon, managed to gather their composure and their breathing after a bit and the three of them continued on.

As soon as they started their laundry they made their purchases from the San Miguel machine and sat down to wait. Jeffs wiped his wet forehead and took a long drink. "I think they bought a beer machine for this place instead of an air conditioner."

Leon was just finishing a beer and already opening another. "Well, priorities, you know." Then he wandered back across the room to marvel at the first beer vending machine he had ever seen.

Jeffs boosted himself onto one of the folding tables and pulled an envelope from his back pocket, opened it and began reading the letter.

Shakes was leaning against the table across from him. "So, you really a surfer?"

Jeffs nodded and smiled. "Where you from?"

"Minnesota," Shakes said glumly. "Nobody's a surfer there."

Jeffs looked him over for a few moments. "Ever see a surf movie called *Endless Summer*?"

Shakes shrugged. "I've heard about it. I think I've seen some scenes from it. It's got some guys surfing on some gigantic waves in Hawaii, doesn't it?"

"Some other places too," Jeffs said. "My father knows the guys that made it. He's in a couple of the shots. I learned how to surf from my dad and some of his friends. He's pretty damn good."

Shakes looked impressed. "That's pretty cool."

"I've spent at least a couple of days a week for the past ten years out on the waves," he continued. "Sometimes every day during the summer. Last summer, just before I joined the navy, I finished third in a big national meet at Santa Cruz. It's a pretty popular surfing spot. Ever hear of Santa Cruz?"

"I saw stuff in San Diego about it," Shakes said. "That the place with the boardwalk?"

Jeffs nodded. "That's where I grew up. Still live there."

"So I've wanted to ask you about your name but didn't know if I should. What's the deal with your name?" Shakes asked. "Why Jeffs and not Jeff?"

"There's a surfing place in South Africa called Jeffreys Bay," he explained. "Never been there, but my dad really likes the place. In fact it's in a scene in that surfing movie. I'm named after that place, so my real name is Jeffreys and my parents just called me Jeffs from as far back as I can remember. Some people would call me Jeff and they would always correct them. They made sure everyone called me Jeffs."

Shakes smiled. "It sounds like there's two of you."

"Funny story about that," he said. "Fourth grade, the first day of school. New teacher. She's calling off the names and she gets to mine and she asks if my name is Jeff."

"I tell her my name is Jeffs and she starts in with some shit about there are only one of me and Jeffs is plural and she's just going to call me Jeff. I got home that day and told my parents. My dad didn't like that at all. He drove me back to school and told that teacher that my name was Jeffs and that's what she was going to call me."

"I bet she never called you Jeff again," Shakes said, laughing.

"No she didn't. It would be like calling you Shake. It just doesn't sound right."

"Absolutely," he said, nodding his agreement. "So how did you end up in the navy?"

"Well, to make a long story short, my draft number was twenty-eight, I lost my student deferment for not taking enough units at the local junior college, and hardly ever going to class, then a judge put some pressure on me."

Shakes leaned forward. "A judge?"

"There were a couple of minor things over the last couple of years. Trivial stuff like partying on the beach, contributing to the delinquency of minors, disturbing the peace, naked surfing, you know. I was on probation and I got nailed for some more of the same stuff."

Shakes was clapping his hands now while he laughed. "Naked surfing?"

"So, I was on probation for that stuff and then a few other things happened. This judge told me if I didn't enlist in the service I'd probably end up in jail. If I did enlist he'd drop all the charges and the probation."

"I thought they couldn't do that anymore," Shakes said.

"Yeah, but this was unofficial in a private session in his chambers. He said he couldn't make me, but he was giving me a way out of all the legal shit. So I took him up on his offer."

Shakes headed for the beer machine. "Pretty interesting, Ryder. Hey, you want a beer?"

"Sure."

Leon returned from marveling at the beer vending machine. "How many cans you suppose are in that thing?"

Later in the afternoon, Shakes headed back to the ship with some other crewmembers who had come in, leaving Jeffs and Leon working on lightening the load of the vending machine. They were seated on top of a short wall outside the laundromat drinking what they had vowed was going to be the last beer, for now.

Jeffs let out with a snorting laugh. "Hey, when you first came aboard the ship did you go through an orientation lecture with Jones?"

Leon nodded. "He do his trick with the box of crackers for you?"

"Yeah," Jeffs said. "Ever think about that?"

Leon took the last swallow of his beer and crushed the empty can. "Every once in a while when it's quiet and I'm lying there in my rack listening to the ocean go by." He held up the crushed beer can and looked directly at his companion. "Yeah, once in a while."

"Me too," Jeffs said. He reached out and took the crushed can from Leon and held it out for both of them to ponder. "Me too."

TWENTY-TWO

Dear Cathy,

...We got a bunch of mail today from an unrep ship. I FINALLY got letters 3, 4 and 5! I also got 29, 31, 32, 35 and 36. I don't know exactly how the navy mail delivery system works but not very good huh? Smitty, who is the barber, runs the ship's store and helps sort mail says your perfumed letters smell great. They smell up the whole mail bag so everybody's mail kind of smells good. They are pretty great. Can't wait to smell it on you. When I get home you can just wear perfume. It will save on doing laundry. HA HA!! I love you.

Love,
Jeffs

Early in the evening, Jeffs and several of his companions, made their way off the base into Olongapo City to the Cave, a club with walls that looked like rock, to begin their evening's activities. Shakes was anxious to resume a relationship with a girl he had met there on their last deployment.

Upon arriving in Subic, they and every member of the crew received the usual cautions from their chiefs or division officers. These included being careful of pickpockets, not wandering off the main street, not starting any trouble with the locals and the fact that Olongapo had a population of prostitutes that numbered between five and ten-thousand. As with most of the world cross roads down through history, venereal disease was rampant and the Navy systematically issued these warnings to every arriving ship.

They exchanged some dollars for pesos on the base before walking out the gate into town. On base the official exchange rate was followed-currently seven and a half pesos to the dollar. In the bars in town the rate was usually six or whatever they could take a confused drunken sailor for. They gladly accepted dollars, but being billed correctly or receiving the right change was a hit and miss proposition.

The typhoon that had skirted the area had left behind some damage in Olongapo but repairs had begun before the wind had even died down. This was, after all, the lifeblood of the area and one way or the other, materials and manpower were always found to repair at least the facades and the neon signs to keep the bars and clubs in business. They knew that as long as the beer kept flowing, the music kept playing and the money kept moving the right direction, nobody would know or care that the broken storage room window was covered with cardboard or that the roof leaked in the back bathroom or that sea birds were nesting in the attic.

Dusk was deepening, the multi-hued neon signs and lights were popping on and the real crowds were just building. About thirty round tables, half of them still empty, were arranged down both long rooms of the L-shaped club. A rock band, whose members spoke almost no English, had just begun the evening set of hits from the 50's and 60's. In a far corner away from the blaring band sat Leon, Shakes and Jeffs along with three girls who worked in the bar.

Jeffs and Leon had bought a round of beers so a couple of the girls were hanging around hoping to sell more drinks. The girl Shakes had been hoping to reconnect with was sitting on his lap. Jeffs and Leon both thought she was one of the ugliest girls they had ever seen and they had spent the past fifteen minutes making faces and remarks to make sure Shakes knew what they thought of her. Apparently she had talents only Shakes was aware of.

"You guys want another round?" Shakes asked testily. Much to their enjoyment, they had succeeded in aggravating him

"Nah, we don't drink," Jeffs said.

"You guys funny!" the girl on Shakes' lap said in an unbelievably raspy and deep voice.

Jeffs' and Leon's eyes met and they burst into laughter. Shakes reached into his shirt pocket and threw a twenty peso note onto the table. "Okay, ya dumb asses, I'll pay!"

Their laughter increased, incited by his annoyed attitude and the girl's laughter, which was punctuated by loud snorting. Shakes turned and watched her as she laughed, looked back at Jeffs and Leon and finally began laughing himself.

Leon leaned close to Jeffs' left ear. "How about that voice? Man, I hope she's really a chick."

Jeffs answered with a laugh, but then seriously turned to studying her conversation and gestures for several minutes. Finally he turned to Leon and said, "I wouldn't bet my life either way. We'll just have to ask Shakes later."

"What's with George?" Leon brought up. "He's the one who's always saying we should stick together and he's been off at that damn casino for an hour."

Jeffs shrugged. "He says it's his one vice, but man, you ever noticed he'll bet on anything?"

Leon grinned. "Hell, he even bet you on that damn load of mail and water the other day."

"That was a weird thing to bet on," Jeffs answered. "You know he's into that endless pinochle game that supply is running for over two hundred dollars. He's probably trying to win some money to pay off his poker debt."

Leon shook his head, then started to laugh. "That dumb honky. Does he think they're running some kind of honest games over here?"

"Tell you what," Shakes said to Jeffs, "I'll bet you twenty pesos he comes back here at least fifty pesos in the hole."

"You're on," Jeffs said.

George returned a half hour later, a hundred pesos lighter. After another round of beers, Jeffs and Leon stood to announce they were going to hit a few bars on their way back to the base. George decided to join them, which was no problem at all for Shakes. He happily waved them good-bye with a beer in one hand, his girl in the other, and moved a few tables over to a group of fire control techs from the ship.

Just across the narrow street from the club, three young Filipino men were waiting. Other than a few watchful pickpockets and pimps who regularly worked this section, their presence was noticed by nobody on the crowded, noisy street. As soon as Jeffs and his companions walked outside, the three men began following them, one of them crossing over and closing in behind the three unsuspecting sailors.

They had no knowledge of the real source of their assignment, but their orders were very simple. They were to snatch the blond American sailor known to them only as "Beach Boy." Physical force was to be kept to a minimum. If they had to hurt his companions to accomplish this, that was okay, but Beach Boy had better be delivered with nothing more than superficial bumps and bruises.

The three young men had decided that they could easily handle a group of three. The element of surprise was on their side plus all were experienced street fighters. They had chosen several locations along the street where they could strike and then sweep their victim away down one of the dark side streets in a matter of seconds. Less than one short block to either side of the main street the illusion ended and the real Olongapo City materialized. They knew this territory well and no Americans would be able to pursue them for long through the dark, dangerous, unfamiliar streets and alleys.

Before Jeffs, Leon and George had ventured very far up the street they came upon the brightly lit, toothed doorway of the Godzilla Club. On the way by, Jeffs stopped and peered through the brightness into the dimmed space beyond. "Hey, isn't that Schultz?"

"It is," George said. "Lacy is there too."

Leon pushed by them both. "Good, I need to talk to that boy. He's must have a friend in Radio on the *News*. He got the guy to send out a page full of dirty limericks over the Teletype circuit. I know it was him 'cause his name was in a couple of them."

Schultz and Lacy had spent two weeks on temporary duty aboard the *Rattano* before her departure from San Diego and had ridden along as far as Guam. From there they had flown to the Philippines to report aboard their ship, the *Newport News*. During their stay aboard the destroyer they had spent much of their time hanging around on the signal bridge where they had become friends with the whole signal gang as well as Leon and some of the radiomen.

They walked in and found Schultz, Lacy and six of their shipmates crowded around a small round table. The base of a massive pyramid-to-be of empty San Miguel beer bottles took up most of the center of the table. Work on the second level had just begun. Nearby, the management was keeping a suspicious eye on the noisy young Americans.

Outside, the three men again took up their waiting stations. This time just one of them waited across the street while the other two hung around on either side of the toothed entrance. One of their prime spots was just a short distance down the street where it narrowed in a slightly dimmer area between clubs. If Beach Boy and his two companions emerged and continued on toward the base unaccompanied, they would hit them there.

"So, how are you cruiser jockeys doing?" Jeffs greeted.

Lacy looked up and a smile spread across his face. "Hey, surf's up! How you guys been?"

"Lousy," George returned. "You?"

Schultz held up an almost empty beer bottle. "Kinda drunk, but good!"

Lacy reached out and grabbed a handful of Jeffs' hair. "Damn, boy, you still in the navy?"

"Hey, this is as good as we get," he answered. "You should see us out at sea!"

Schultz was nodding. "Yeah, we've heard a few things about McHenry's Marauders."

They were sent to the bar before they even had a chance to sit and returned carrying eighteen bottles of beer in their hands and hugged against their bodies. Three more chairs were found and introductions were made all around.

Leon tapped Lacy on the arm. "So how you doing you honky, perverted poet?"

Lacy and Schultz looked at each other and laughed. "So you saw my limericks," Lacy answered. "Good ones, weren't they? I've got some more too, but I've got to wait awhile. Some chief from the *Shields* bitched out everybody on the circuit so we had to lay off for awhile."

"But they were never sure it came from the *News*," Schultz added. "A successful mission."

"So how did you get access to Radio?" Leon asked.

"I'm one of those non-rated seaman types, but I'm striking for radioman."

"I've heard of guys doing that in the past," Leon said, "but I thought the only way now was going to radio school."

Lacy shrugged. "I know, but I made a lot of noise about it and kept bugging the chief. When they found out I could type they gave in, got me a security clearance and started me training on the job. They're talking about sending me to school and then bringing me back to the *News*."

"That's cool," Jeffs said. "So, Schultzy, what are you up to?"

"I don't know if I can explain it after this much beer," Schultz said, "but I'll try. I'm actually a third class supply clerk, but for some reason there are too many supply clerks on board. The ship's office is short of personnelmen. I can type and I've had a little college, so I'm on loan to the ship's office. They think I'm a fucking genius, and they might be right 'because sometimes when we have quarters, both divisions think I'm with the other one, so I just sleep."

"But!" Lacy interjected, "on the *News* there are a whole bunch of damn gun mounts and a lot of the jobs that don't really require gunners, so guess which two divisions get to help man gun turrets and do the shit jobs?"

Jeffs was shaking his head. "Supply and ships office?"

"Bingo!" Schultz yelled. "And, all non-rated seaman are right there in the pool too!"

"Let me get this straight," Leon said, pointing at them in turn as he spoke. "You are supposed to be learning to be a radioman, and you are a supply clerk, but you're on loan to the office because they need you, and they've got both of you working in gun turrets?"

Lacy and Schultz looked at each other with brows furrowed. "I think that's right," Schultz slurred.

Leon slapped Jeffs on the arm. "That's the damn navy for ya, huh?"

"So, how long are you in port?" George asked.

"We've been here two days," Lacy said. "I think we leave day after tomorrow. Just long enough for a few repairs and to load up on some more of those eight inchers."

"You ever find out why they didn't just fly you guys over to the ship right away?" George asked.

Both men shrugged. "Too sensible," Schultz offered. "Something about the *News* having a couple of extra guys who were getting out in a couple of weeks and you guys needing a couple of know-nothing office seamen."

"It's all fucked up," Lacy added. "We were both scheduled to report to her in Norfolk when we got out of boot camp. But about three weeks before that, they sent the *News* and some other east coast ships over to Nam for this big build up that's going on. So all of a sudden they fly us to San Diego and tell us we're hitching a ride on some damn destroyer we can't even pronounce! I think they didn't want to spring for an airline ticket to the Philippines."

Shultz gave a disgusted look and a wave of his hand. "You guys and your shitty war over here. Remember I told you we were scheduled for a Mediterranean cruise? Man, we could be in Italy or Spain right now sipping wine at a street cafe and flirting with the locals. Instead we're here with you bastards."

"You love us and you know it," Jeffs said. "Hey, I've gotten a look at the *News* a few times. Looks like a damn battleship!"

"Lots of guns," Lacy said. "I'm sure we can win the war all by ourselves." He emptied his beer and slammed the bottle down on the table with a large, drunken grin. "We probably won't need any fucking destroyer help."

"Good!" Leon answered. "We're tired of helping you dummies."

By midnight they were all several beers beyond what a reasonable young man might consume in an evening. The top of the pyramid stood almost five feet above the table with only three bottles to go to complete it. The conversation had just moved from sex to surfing.

"Here, I'll show you," Jeffs announced, and he hopped onto the empty table next to theirs. He planted both feet, spread his arms out wide and bent deep at the knees to demonstrate the position for "shooting the curl." He was doing fine, but not the table. There was a loud crack as the top separated from the base and he fell toward the beer bottle pyramid.

Shultz, Leon and another man jumped up to catch him, which they did, but they all bumped hard into the table and 113 bottles came crashing down. It was astoundingly loud and seemed to take a very long time to finally finish. After several seconds of stunned silence, Jeffs and his companions burst into unstoppable laughter and applause. At the same time, several employees began yelling at the sailors in an agitated mix of Filipino and English.

The sound of the falling bottles was loud enough that it attracted the attention of the two shore patrol duos out on the street. Three of them were first and second class petty officers from the *Newport News*, filling shore patrol positions for the night. The fourth was their supervisor, a marine staff sergeant attached to base security. They came striding into the Godzilla Club with nightsticks drawn, prepared to quell whatever the situation was.

They were met with a dozen people all yelling at once. After several minutes the shore patrol managed to get most of the story straight. Fortunately for the nine sailors, six were shipmates of the three shore patrol petty officers. Since there had been no fighting involved, they were all made to clean up the mess and then taken back to their ships in two shore patrol pickups rather than being processed through base security and having them picked up there.

The three would-be attackers standing together now near the entrance to the club were disappointed and angry as the shore patrol escorted the group away. They were looking forward to splitting the five-hundred pesos they would earn for delivering Beach Boy, but they knew the *Rattano* was scheduled to be in port for a few more days and they would probably get another chance to collect their fee.

The next morning, Jeffs and the others appeared before Captain McHenry at an informal Captain's Mast. Even though they had been brought back to the ship as a favor instead of being officially processed, there had still been an oral report made to the officer of the deck. Unfortunately that duty officer had been Lieutenant Wiffler who smilingly made as big a deal as he could out of it and went out of his way to formally relate the whole incident to the captain.

Fortunately for Jeffs, his table surfing escapade earned him ten hours extra duty and cancellation of his liberty for the remainder of their stay in Subic. Beach Boy's capture would have to wait.

TWENTY-THREE

Summary of psychiatric evaluation, Admiral Tillman J. Loflin, Jan. 31, 1972

...Based on three interviews with the subject as well as anecdotal evidence from a number of his colleagues, my findings are as follows:

Admiral Loflin displays a range of behaviors suggesting mild paranoid personality disorder as well as some inconsistent sociopathic tendencies. However I do not consider him to be a danger to himself or others. He continues to fill his command position adequately and carries out his duties satisfactorily. In light of this, although others often find him a difficult person to work with, these findings will be kept confidential and a recommendation of fit for continued command duties will be passed on to his superiors.

Two days after the *Rattano* left Subic and headed back to the gun line, the *Holliner* arrived for a similar four-day stay. Early that evening, a visitor came aboard to see the captain. He had called just that afternoon to say he would be coming, causing Captain DeMoorts some frustration due to canceled dinner plans as well as some apprehension about the reason for the visit.

The men on watch on the quarter deck, the area where the gangway came aboard from the pier, were shocked when alerted to the fact that such a high level visitor would be arriving during their watch. Upon his arrival, in keeping with the standard navy tradition of the time, a bell was sounded over the PA system followed by the announcement, "Commander 7th Fleet, arriving."

DeMoorts hurried to greet him while the officer of the day escorted his driver and aide to the mess deck to wait.

As they walked into the wardroom, Loflin said, "Franklin, I wanted a chance for just the two of us to talk." He seated himself with a groan at the table. "You're a good skipper and you know these old destroyers. These damn missile boats the gooks have gotten hold of are a genuine threat, and I plan to kick their ass."

Part of forward "officers country" aboard this type of destroyer was just off the wardroom, and DeMoorts quickly checked the nearby compartments, located just a few feet down a passageway, to make sure they were unoccupied as he had requested.

He returned to the table. "Thank you, Admiral. I hope I can be of some help to you."

He poured two glasses of iced tea and seated himself across the table. Loflin had specifically asked for the two of them to meet alone. DeMoorts was curious, but wary. Loflin had never been particularly friendly with him. In fact, this was the first time he had spoken more than a passing sentence or two with him.

"I got Wil Gordan out of your hair for a couple of days," Loflin said. "He's in Yokosuka attending some diplomatic bullshit thing with the Japanese government." He took a long drink from his glass. "The intellishit on these boats says they aren't going to take on anything very far from shore. Staying close in gives them lots of inlets, rivers and such to hide in. It seems that their favorite target is going to be something like an old gun destroyer operating alone near the coast. You never know, though. If they can get off a long shot they might go after something we don't expect."

DeMoorts nodded. "An old can does give them something they might be able go up against and have a fair chance of taking out."

"That's right," Loflin agreed. "And even if they don't sink one, a solid hit will blow the fucking hell out her and get the bastards in the news all over the world. That's never happened to any ship in this damn war. Everything's been relatively small and very few casualties."

"So have they got these things in the area and ready to go?"

Loflin spread his hands. "Good fucking question. I think they're shuffling them around. They say there is some evidence that they are building some facilities for them at the southern end of the Haiphong area, but nothing real complicated."

"Can't we bomb those facilities?" DeMoorts asked. "That would at least make it a little more difficult for them."

"Not yet," Loflin said, wagging his index finger. He leaned closer over the table. "I want *us* to hit them. They're after my damn ships so we ought to be the ones to take them out and not some air force or carrier fly boy. When that time comes, I don't want to just hit those facilities and scare off the rest of the boats. I want to hit them at the same time in all the other rivers and inlets around where they're hiding them. We might be onto a couple of them already."

DeMoorts nodded slowly, thinking. "Do we know they're all Styx boats? Could be some of their regular fast attack boats. Lot less dangerous."

Loflin sighed. "I don't give a fuck which ones are which, they're all made for attacking my ships! The more I can take out the better chance I get any Styx boats in the mix."

"So, how far south of Haiphong do we think they might operate them? They'd have to come down around Dong Hoi or Hon La. That's the only area they're going to find any destroyers operating solo or in pairs."

"Yes, one would think so." Loflin answered. He was impressed with the captain's thinking. "We don't think they will bring them very far south at all. For one thing, they're too scared of our air superiority." He waited to see where DeMoort's thinking processes would lead him now. He had to admit to himself that he was having a bit of fun.

"I'm not sure I understand, sir." Actually, he was afraid he was beginning to understand very well. He took another sip of his tea for his suddenly drying mouth. "If they won't bring the boats to the south and we don't have any ships operating very far north on their own, then where's the threat?"

Loflin put on an annoyed look. "I've heard that plenty. I say as long as they are out there, they're a threat. They could come farther south. They could make some kind of kamikaze attack on the northern end of the gun line, or at Hon La where we commonly have just two destroyers operating. I say the fact that they're so unpredictable is the real problem."

DeMoorts cleared his throat. "So, you want to send a destroyer north to tempt one of these missile boats into attacking her."

Loflin almost smiled, and spoke just above a whisper. "To be honest, Captain, I'm hoping for two or three of the bastards."

DeMoorts straightened visibly. "*Holliner* stands ready to take on any mission, Admiral."

A low chuckle escaped Loflin, but he stifled more laughter. "No offense, Captain, but if I'm going to send one of these shit cans into harm's way, I want the best. Hell, you're good. All you destroyer skippers are good, but we need an edge on this one. There's one man over here that has quite a reputation. Some people call him a genius, for Christ's sake! It just so happens that his ship has one of the best reliability records going. She never breaks down and I don't know if it's her guns or her gunners, but her shooting has gotten to be downright legendary. Guys who've never even seen her are telling stories about her."

DeMoorts could feel his sudden sense of dedication sink a bit, but mostly he felt relief. "The *Rat*."

Loflin nodded and watched him intently. He knew all about the long standing grudge between the two men, which suited his needs just fine.

"How far north?" DeMoorts asked.

The admiral broke into a genuine grin, leaned forward and lowered his voice to just above a whisper. "So damn far north it'll make the hair on back of your neck stand straight up and your balls pull in just hearing about it. I'm not going to just send a ship up there to hang around waiting for them to fire some damn missile at them. I've got my staff looking into a choice spot to run the *Rat* up a river and take out some shit while she's up there. That'll attract some attention even if we don't see any boats."

"Admiral, why are you telling me this?"

Loflin stood and began to slowly pace his side of the table. "I'm going to be very blunt about what I want from you. Whether you can help me or not, this conversation never happened."

"Understood, sir."

Loflin grasped the back of his chair and focused intently across the table. "I know there's no love lost between you and Mac. The mission I have in mind is right on the edge. A lot could go wrong. I need two things from you, Captain. One, support the feasibility of the mission even if you think it's a little too dicey. As a fellow destroyer skipper and a member of the same squadron, you can go on about what a great idea it is, how it will be a real feather in the cap of the destroyer force, what a good use of the firepower and capabilities of the *Rat* it is, how Mac is the perfect man for the job, and all that great shit. Two, don't say anything about the real intent of the mission having to do with those goddamn missile boats. Remember, nothing ever gets accomplished without taking some chances."

DeMoorts held his poker face. "Suppose Mac gets himself blown out of the water? We might not look so smart then."

Loflin spread his arms wide. "That's the beauty of this whole thing. If the *Rat* takes on a missile boat and beats it, then I've got one boat destroyed and a reason to go after the others. If, God forbid, he gets his ass kicked by one of those boats, then I'll still have a reason to go after the rest of them. Either way, those boats were never supposed to be a part of the mission and it'll just be another damn sneaky gook trick."

He paused for a bit. "Franklin, if I wanted to get one of our ships sunk, I wouldn't send the *Rat*, I'd send some broken down piece of shit. The whole point of sending Mac up there is to give us the best chance possible."

He seated himself again and waited for a response.

"Can't you just do more air reconnaissance and go after the boats anyway?" DeMoorts asked.

"Hell, they're making me be real careful about it," Loflin said angrily. "If I come right out and tell them I want to put together a mission to go after the boats they're going to tell me to go to hell and send the fly boys after them."

"Would that be so bad?" DeMoorts asked.

Loflin continued to fume his voice grew louder. "Shit! First it's a bombing halt, then it's a partial lifting with all kinds of rules to protect the civilians. Now there's talk of further bombing halts if the Paris Peace Talks start making progress. It's all political. Those damn peace talks are fucking up everything! If I don't do it myself it might not get done at all. If I can get those boats to attack a ship, then the rules are off. I can go after those damn boat facilities and every fucking thing even remotely connected with them and it won't matter if the goddamn Queen of Hanoi is sitting right there on the pier!"

DeMoorts smiled, then leaned back in his chair and folded his arms. He wondered if maybe Loflin was crazier than anyone really knew. As a destroyer captain, the idea of sending a crew into unnecessary danger left a feeling in his gut that he didn't like, but his long seething hatred for McHenry made it a little more attractive. "Any air cover?"

Loflin nodded emphatically. "That's part of the finesse of this plan. I want to keep the fighter cover as far off as possible, probably too far to help them for several minutes, but that way the boats won't get spooked. That's where you can help. Support the idea that McHenry can handle this mission and that whatever happens, air support is just minutes away. You might even push the idea that keeping air cover away doesn't attract any attention to the area and maintains the secrecy of the mission. It might be a few more minutes away than he wants, but it'll be there. He's getting the Red Eye before the mission in case any MIGs show up."

"Is CNO and CINCPAC going to go for this?"

"Well…" Loflin hesitated for a bit. "I might have to tell a few white lies to get it green lighted. What they don't know won't hurt them. Besides, three star admirals get whatever the fuck they want most of the time."

"Okay, I guess I can go along with all this," DeMoorts said. "You're not hanging him out to dry, your just hanging him out. So, that brings us to what's in it for me?"

Loflin nodded slowly and allowed himself a small satisfied smile. He appreciated the direct approach. "Always good to know where everyone stands. Wil Gordan will be rotating out of his squadron commander position in a few months and I think I could lean heavily toward choosing someone like you. How do like the idea of eagles on your collar and that squadron commander title, Commodore DeMoorts?"

DeMoorts stood and extended his right hand across the table. "You know, Mac and Commodore Gordan are buddies. He might have something to say about a mission like this."

Loflin firmly grasped the captain's hand and stood as well. "Already thought of that. Our good commodore is being left completely out of the loop on this one until it's all planned. Thank you, Captain. It might take a while to put this together. I'll be in touch."

Loflin reached for his hat and prepared to leave. "Oh, by the way, I was contacted earlier by the South Vietnamese Navy SEAL Commandant. My people will be getting a message out to you tomorrow. When you leave Subic Friday you're heading down to Da Nang before you head back to the line. They want to use the *Holliner* for some kind of exercise. Something about staging a boarding and then you can give them a tour of the ship and make 'em feel important. It's a half day thing and then you're back to the usual gun line shit."

"Okay, Admiral. Thanks for the warning."

Loflin left the wardroom to fetch his two aides from the mess deck.

DeMoorts stared at the door as it closed and called the quarter deck to let them know Loflin was leaving. He knew the man was lying and that McHenry would get squadron commander, if he was still alive. Either way, he now had an IOU to cash in sometime.

TWENTY-FOUR

War News - July 13, 1972
The Paris peace talks have once again resumed.

After fourteen days and three unreps, the South Vietnamese had gained back some territory and the *Rattano* had used up another thirty tons of destruction. That night they took on fuel and ammunition, and headed for a new assignment.

Jeffs and George were standing outside the signal shack watching the sea in the approaching dawn. The ship was cruising north at only fifteen knots, but even that small breeze was welcome. The weather had been the same for several days—unceasingly hot, and so humid that at times it felt like breathing water.

"You finally finish the last of your extra duty?" George asked.

Jeffs smiled and pushed his hair off his wet forehead. "Yeah, I'm done and I'm sick of chipping paint. The captain was pissed this time, wasn't he?"

George nodded and chuckled at the memory of that night in Subic and of their appearance before Captain McHenry the next morning. "Man, you looked bad that morning." He laughed more while he shook his head. "Really bad."

"I think it was the table surfing that really got him, but he almost smiled for a second there," Jeffs said. "Too bad about the pyramid. Only three bottles to go."

He stopped talking and lit a cigarette. "So what's the name of this place again?"

"Hon La Anchorage," George answered. "From what Chief said, there's been some Chinese merchant ship there unloading for a few weeks. Hon La is an island right up against the mainland. The freighter is anchored kind of between the island and the mainland. We can't shoot at a Chinese ship but we do shoot at the boats that take the stuff to the beach. The anchorage has been mined, so the freighter is stuck there. I guess the other destroyer on station and us just cruise back and forth a few miles off shore and take pot shots at the boats and the road up the hill out of there. Chief said the Marines have been hitting the boats with Cobra attack choppers too."

"This is not what war movies used to show us. It sounds stupid."

"Boring too," George agreed. "I guess we'll hear more about it at quarters tomorrow."

"Yeah, what's with that? We haven't had quarters except in port since we've been over here."

George shrugged. "Maybe so we don't forget we're in the navy."

While they were talking, the sun had neared the horizon and it was now light enough to begin making out some details of the land. It was a considerable change of scenery from the flat beaches and low-lying inland areas of Quang Tri. Six miles away, the rugged, mountainous coastline, stood thick with greenery. Here and there an outcropping of rock or earth lay bare and a few rocky cliffs were visible down near the water.

They began receiving a flashing light from the destroyer they were relieving when they had approached to within two miles. Jeffs manned the light and grabbed a pad from inside the shack to record. It was a routine message welcoming them to the Hon La station and instructing the captain to contact their captain via voice circuit.

Chief Ross, carrying his dictionary, reported for quarters at exactly 0800 hours. OC division, Operations Communications, consisting of radiomen and signalmen, was assembled topside on the ASROC deck just outside Radio. At various locations around the ship, the other divisions were assembled as well.

In port in San Diego, quarters was an every-morning ritual that began each workday. There, back in the real world, every sailor came to at least somewhat reasonable attention and a passerby would see orderly groups of men in full working uniform standing in straight rows saluting toward the stern where the American flag flew while the national anthem played over the PA system. Then the various chiefs or lead petty officers would give out the important information from the Plan of the Day, along with any other details concerning the day's work routine.

This day, however, was something altogether different. Since they had not had quarters at sea since arriving in Vietnam the crew had taken it upon themselves to make it a particularly memorable event. This was prime McHenry's Marauders in all their blasphemous splendor. All of the officers were in their regulation khakis, but of the entire enlisted crew of 269 men, just forty-eight were in full regulation working uniforms with hats, and most of them were Chiefs or First Class Petty Officers. Many were wearing shorts or dungaree pants with white T-shirts. Some were even wearing their regular work shirts, but most of them were being worn with shorts. In addition, only about half of the shorts being worn were the "allowed" neatly hemmed denim. The rest were everything from Bermuda shorts with splashy prints to swimming trunks to incredibly ancient, ragged, frayed denim cutoffs. One machinist mate's cutoffs included only the waistband and the front pockets.

More than two dozen men sported various styles of headbands, nine had donned cowboy hats for the occasion and many crewmen were wearing a blue navy work shirt with the sleeves cut off. Some of the crew were wearing shirts other than the regulation work shirts or white t-shirts, a sampling of which included: a solid red t-shirt with Animal from the Muppets with the declaration Me Want Woman, a black shirt with a picture of Janis Joplin on the back and a print of a poster on the front advertising Big Brother and the Holding Company at the Fillmore in San Francisco, a long sleeve sport shirt seemingly made from pieces of an American flag, and one that depicted a silhouetted couple entwined in a different sexual position for each sign of the Zodiac.

The entire B Division, made up of boiler technicians, were attired in their swankiest finery for the occasion—bare chests, work caps with the bills cut off, frayed shorts, and work shoes with no socks. One of the supply clerks was wearing several leis he had been saving since Pearl Harbor. Incredibly, two of the electronics technicians were wearing black tuxedos with frayed denim shorts and shined dress shoes. Even more incredibly, Mike Gonzales was wearing a gray zoot suit.

OC Division were all wearing denim cutoffs, brightly colored Hawaiian print shirts and baseball caps with various team logos or other designs such as bare breasts, bare butts or a hand with the middle finger extended. Jeffs had the tails of a red headband hanging down a foot below the back edge of his hat. The front of his cap showed the figure of a topless girl surfing.

The one real standout was Signalman Seaman Carlos Villegas. He had been cursing and swearing all morning about not being able to get to his clothes because he had somehow lost his locker key. In his ranting anger he had turned down all offers of clothing and he had refused to call for bolt cutters to get his locker open. He was dressed in light blue boxers, black work shoes and an oversized helmet made for wearing over headphones that he had found in the signal shack.

Jeffs was deciding whether to laugh, feel sorry for him, or both. "What the hell you wearing the helmet for?"

Villegas was just beginning to think that maybe he wouldn't get written up after all when he saw how the rest of the division was dressed. "I don't know," he said apprehensively. "It just seemed like I was wearing more this way."

As Ross unsmilingly eyed his division he was thankful that of the eight radiomen and five signalmen assembled, at least they were all wearing some kind of shirts and socks, except for Villegas, of course.

The men in every division turned toward the forward mast where the steaming ensign flew and saluted while the Star Spangled Banner blared from the ship's PA system. The boatswain's whistle sounded again and everyone dropped their salute and again faced their division leaders.

Ross stared a while longer, deciding what, if anything, he should say about uniforms. "Hays, is everyone present and accounted for?"

"Yes, sir," George replied. "Omata and Shakes are in Radio, Pruett is up on the signal bridge, everyone else is here. Including you, Chief, that's seventeen."

Ross sighed and managed a weak smile. "You know, after passing some of the other divisions on the way up here, you guys look pretty fucking good, I guess." He massaged his forehead, hoping to fend off the stress headache he felt coming on.

In the back row, on either side of Villegas, stood Leon and Jeffs. They had scooted inward and partially in front of him in a vain effort to keep Ross from noticing him.

"Villegas," Ross said calmly, "are you expecting some sort of attack the rest of us don't know about?"

Jeffs and Leon, along with the rest of the division, were struggling to at least partially control their laughter, but they stood their ground. Villegas, with his face lost inside the oversized helmet, looked beyond ridiculous. "Uh, well, Chief, I've been reading about a new environmental problem called acid rain and I didn't want to be exposed to it, or expose my uniform."

Jeffs and Leon both stopped snickering and turned to look at him at the exact same time, eyebrows raised, impressed with the creative impromptu response.

"Wow," Jeffs whispered, "I couldn't have done better myself."

Ross was still staring, expressionless, but he too was struck with the unexpected answer. Quickly bringing into play the people managing skills that had gotten him this far in the navy, he decided to cut his losses and give no further attention for now to whatever in the hell was going on with Villegas.

Leon decided to try a diversion. "Chief, why are we having quarters? We haven't since we left Subic and some of us just got off a mid-watch. We should've been in our racks an hour ago."

The beginnings of a smile came to the chief's face. "Thomsen, this is the goddamn navy, you know, not the Holiday Inn. Now listen up, you guys. We're having quarters today because our operations are going to finally slow down a little and the captain figured it would be a chance to get our shit together again. By the way, that also includes getting caught up on preventative maintenance items. There are a few things in the POD to go over, then we can all go back to whatever it is we'll be doing." He pointed a look in Leon's direction.

Ross was holding a copy of the Plan of the Day, reading over it as he began his announcements. "Okay, the following personnel are to report to the mess deck at 0830 tomorrow to take the test for petty officer third class. Ryder, you're one of them. You got all your paper work squared away for that?"

"All set, Chief."

Ross nodded and returned to reading from the Plan of the Day. "Next item. Our mission here off the coast of North Vietnam at Hon La is primarily one of surveillance, as well as harassment and interdiction firing at various target areas. We will be observing activities of the Chinese Communist merchant ship at anchor near the shore and firing at off-loading boats when feasible. The freighter itself will be staying, as the harbor has been mined. Additionally, we, along with the guided missile destroyer *Buchanan*, will be keeping the road leading up out of the area closed as much as possible. Traffic on the road is an authorized part of our mission. We are in North Vietnam territorial waters and are more vulnerable to enemy attack than we were down on the gun line. The surface-to-air capability of the *Buchanan* will take care of any threat from MIGs."

"How long are we going to be here, Chief?" George asked.

"A couple of weeks, at least," Ross answered. "After we leave here we'll be heading back to Subic for a few days. Now, before we get on with the rest of the POD..." He held up his dictionary. "The word for today is 'maladroit'. Anybody know what it means?"

They all looked around at each other shrugging, scratching their heads and repeating the word to themselves, but nobody seemed to have heard the word before.

Ross was getting the smug little smile that always came to him when he stumped his men with a new word. "It means inept or awkward. A maladroit doesn't handle a situation or problem well. You could use it in the sentence, 'The shy man was a maladroit when it came to talking to women.'"

Now everyone was nodding and quickly figuring how they could use the word in the most annoying or obscene way possible.

"Just another example of continuing education at work," Ross said. "Okay, guys, listen up. Just a couple more items. Laundry...let's see... Tuesday is CPO, OPS, cooks and stewards. All laundry must be in the ship's laundry by 0830 to insure pick up the following morning. Laundry will only be accepted from divisions or departments on their assigned days."

Ross stopped and read silently for a few seconds and scratched his head. "Now, under that it says that due to severe water shortage problems the ship's laundry will only be operating on Monday, Wednesday and Friday." His voice trailed off and he stared down at the paper as he read it over to himself.

"Great, Chief," George said. "We're part of OPS department, you just said OPS is Tuesday, so when do we..?"

"How the fuck do I know?" he hissed. "Look, anybody here got a friend in the laundry?"

Jeffs raised his hand. "I do, Chief. I'll go talk to him as soon as we're done here and see what they're doing with this."

Ross nodded with relief. "Thanks, Ryder."

"I wouldn't get my hopes up though," Jeffs continued. "He's probably the one who gave out that information. He's kind of a maladroit"

Everyone laughed while Ross gave one of his famous looks. "Okay, Ryder. Maybe you can get him straightened out."

"All right, last item," Ross said, returning his attention to reading from the POD. "Report of our activities yesterday before we left the gun line to head up here. This is a quote from the gun line report received early this morning. The destroyer *Rattano* caused one secondary explosion while firing against enemy positions five miles north of Quang Tri City and three secondary explosions in a shelling mission six miles northwest of the city. During the afternoon, the *Rattano* fired on troops with mortars in a bunker, an AA site, and an AA/mortar site. Late report on the previous day's activities for the *Rattano*: Two artillery sites silenced, six structures destroyed, a large secondary explosion in a staging area, eight water buffalo destroyed and the person tending them."

All thirteen men erupted into laughter at the same instant.

Ross looked disgusted with his navy for a second or two as he reread the passage silently, then he dropped the paper, placed his hands on his hips, and slowly shook his head while he looked out toward the land. "Dismissed!"

TWENTY-FIVE

War News - July 25

It is being reported that when Jane Fonda visited Hanoi a week ago that not only did she speak out against the war but took part in broadcasts of anti-war messages on Hanoi Radio. She was also photographed sitting on a North Vietnamese anti-aircraft gun. War protesters are celebrating her actions while some government spokesmen and military officials are calling for investigations into weather she committed treason.

Commander Lieu Hung Dao stepped out of the boat, along with his two aides, and onto the lowered gangway of the *Holliner* while it rested at anchor in Da Nang Harbor. He climbed the few steps up to the main deck of the destroyer and was greeted by Captain DeMoorts.

"Good afternoon, Captain. Permission to come aboard?"

"By all means," DeMoorts said, returning the salute.

Commander Dao and his aides exchanged salutes and handshakes with DeMoorts and his executive officer before they all made their way to the wardroom.

The stewards had set out pitchers of iced tea, pots of hot tea and coffee and a plate of pastries on the wardroom table. Captain DeMoorts, the XO, Dao and his two officers were joined by the Operations Officer and Chief Quartermaster of the *Holliner*.

After all the men were seated, with glasses or cups filled, Demoorts turned the conversation to the business at hand. "So, commander, I understand that your team will be staging a mock boarding of the *Holliner*. The original message said that it would be some sort of navigation exercise and we would be taking you out a couple of miles. Are we on the right page here?"

Dao took a sip of tea from his cup. "Yes, Captain, that is quite right. But just two weeks ago we had a chance to go through that exercise on another ship, so we decided to move ahead to our next training exercise. I hope that is not a problem for you."

"No, it's not a problem at all, Commander," DeMoorts assured him. "I've been instructed to extend any assistance you might need and I look forward to putting *Holliner* at your disposal. The only limitation is we must get underway in the morning for our return to the gun line by 0800.

Commander Dao smiled politely. "I thank you very much for affording us this opportunity, Captain. We will not keep you waiting nearly that long. I think we will be completed well before midnight. Just outside the harbor to the south are some boat docks. The area is quite secure and is actually on a little used corner of the base property. We will show your quartermaster on the charts where to proceed to. You will be anchoring just off shore, about three-hundred yards, I believe. We have scheduled the exercise to begin at 2100 hours if that is okay with you."

DeMoorts and his XO looked at each other and shrugged. "I think that will be fine, commander."

Dao nodded. "Good. I would like your crew to go to general quarters and to follow the standard procedures you would for a firing mission in hostile waters. We will be approaching the vessel in several small motorized rafts and boarding from both sides of the ship near the fantail. From there we will proceed as though we are taking over the ship. It should be completed in a matter of fifteen minutes."

"Sounds interesting," DeMoorts said. "Are we supposed to offer any resistance, do anything to stop you?"

Dao chuckled. "No, Captain. This is a training opportunity for us and we don't want any casualties to our personnel or your crew. We will be armed, but with weapons unloaded. When we encounter members of your crew, our procedure will be to say, "Bang, you're dead."

Everyone around the table laughed. "Is this practice for something you intend to do in the future?" DeMoorts asked.

Dao opened his hands palms up. "Who knows? Just like your SEALS, the Hai Kich need to be ready for anything and that includes the most unexpected things. This type of destroyer is very common and several have been transferred to the navies of other countries as well. Someday it may be to our advantage to better know our way around one."

"True enough," DeMoorts said. "I understand your team would like a bit of a calmer tour after the exercise is completed."

"Yes, that would be appreciated. Please make sure that your crew understands what is happening and offers no resistance. We don't want anyone hurt."

"No 'Bang your dead' back?" the XO said.

Everyone laughed at this remark as well. The mood around the table was relaxed and friendly. It was common for U.S. naval units to be involved in various sorts of joint training and public relations events with their South Vietnamese allies.

The men of the *Holliner* had no way of knowing that the mock attackers were not a South Vietnamese SEAL team, but rather a group of North Vietnamese that Seven had gone to great trouble and expense to assemble and infiltrate into this setting. Most of them were former NVA regulars or members of special police forces.

By 2030 hours, the *Holliner* was anchored at the designated location. At 2100 they went to general quarters with a full complement on the bridge, as instructed by Dao and his team, just as though they were actually underway.

A few minutes later four motorized rafts with five men each pulled up along the port and starboard side of the destroyer in the area of the aft gun mount and the hangar deck. Here the main deck was just eight feet above the water. The team did their job well as the rafts were quickly lashed alongside and the men from each raft clambered aboard. Each team had a destination. One went to the bridge, the other to CIC just aft of the bridge. Another split into two parts and made their way to the signal bridge and Radio to secure communications. A fourth made their way below decks to the engine rooms. From the time the first man stepped aboard the warship, just six minutes passed until they declared the ship secured and the exercise terminated. Thirty-nine crew members received a "Bang, you're dead" in the process.

When it was over, the crew went off of general quarters and the team was escorted to the mess deck where they were served refreshments and visited with many members of the crew who were off duty at the time.

Later, they were given a tour of the ship by a team made up of the XO, operations officer, lead weapons chief and the engineering chief. By 2300 hours, the team had said their good-byes and left in their rafts. A few minutes later, *Holliner* weighed anchor and headed north to the gun line.

The boarding team headed due east where they met with three Vietnamese fishing boats. The men were taken aboard and their rafts sunk on the spot. Dao would be reporting within hours to his superiors that the training exercise was a complete success.

On the real mission when they would be boarding and taking control of the *Rattano*, there would be ten men in each raft with additional teams to secure the gun mounts, magazines and weather decks. These additional personnel were still being recruited, but the twenty men who participated in the exercise this night would serve as the nucleus to train the remainder of the boarding party. Thanks to their practice this night aboard the *Holliner*, there would now be several men in each raft who had already practiced aboard a destroyer just like the *Rattano*. At that time, of course, there would be no need for any "Bang, you're dead."

TWENTY-SIX

Now hear this. Due to a mix up in our food stores order from yesterday's unrep we received several cases of steaks and several more of lobster instead of our order of hamburger. For the next several days the crew's mess and the ward room will be serving steak and lobster at some dinner times. Lieutenant Stewart, our supply officer, wants the crew to know that in the unlikely event he covertly had any part in the scheme to bring about this mix up, no thanks is necessary. Bon appetite.

After three uneventful weeks of operations at Hon La the *Rattano* again returned to Subic Bay for the usual maintenance, resupply and, this time, some special training. The navy brass had come up with a cheap fix to enhance the air defenses of the non-missile ships on the gun line. Each gun destroyer would be given the Red Eye shoulder fired anti-aircraft weapon. The signalmen on each ship, because they worked in a raised topside area of the ship with good visibility that could serve as a launch platform, would be trained in the use of the weapon.

"Here it is gentlemen, the Red Eye. The marine captain opened a long metal case that rested on the table in front of him. Inside, set into molded foam rubber, was the weapon that was going to protect the *Rattano* and the other gun line destroyers from MIGs.

"As you can see, it looks a little like what some of you would probably call a bazooka from old war movies. The Corps has had them for several years now. The word is they are developing a new and improved replacement for this weapon called the Stinger, but that's still a few years off, I guess. The Red Eye is easy to use and reliable. This baby's got a decent success rate. They were designed to provide troops on the ground with some capability against enemy aircraft. Unfortunately the gooks have been successful with a similar weapon the last couple of years against our choppers and other aircraft. Always something to keep things fuckin' interesting around here, huh?"

Jeffs sat and watched the training lecture along with George and signalmen from six other destroyers. They were inside the hanger deck of the *Guam*, an amphibious assault carrier, sometimes referred to as a "baby aircraft carrier." Instead of jets she carried thirty helicopters and their accompanying complement of marine pilots, mechanics and assault troops. The Red Eye training was being conducted weekly during a six-week period. That would take care of all the 7th Fleet destroyers in action in Vietnam as well as new arrivals. Some were receiving training before they left the States.

"The Red Eye is a heat-seeking missile with a range of up to three miles" the trainer continued, "but you'll have better success closer in. This is a shoulder launched, optically sighted weapon. We like to call stuff like this "fire and forget." Once you pull the trigger you're all done. It's the missile's job to go after the target."

An hour later, Jeffs and George left the training session all checked out and certified as Red Eye missile operators and began the long walk back to the ship.

"Damn, it's hot! I'm sweating my ass off."

George just grunted and nodded. For a while there was just the sound of their footsteps in the gravel along the shoulder of the road.

"So, how come so quiet?" Jeffs asked.

George looked over at his companion. "Just thinking."

Some questions had come to Jeffs' mind too during the training session. "So, you're thinking about stuff like, if the Red Eye is so damn good then why didn't we get them until now?"

George smiled. "Partly."

"Or about the rules of engagement he laid on us," Jeffs continued. "How we can't fire unless the ship has been fired upon?"

George nodded, then added in an official tone, "Or vessels in the immediate vicinity."

Jeffs laughed. "Like hell! As far as I'm concerned, immediate vicinity means the same damn hemisphere. Hey, here's what I've been thinking. Why do all these old cans on the gun line need more protection against planes all of a sudden when we've got missile cruisers and destroyers around that are supposed to take care of that?

"I don't know," George muttered. "Something's up. I can feel it. Now all of a sudden signalmen are in charge of shooting down MIGs *after* they shoot at the ship. I tell you, Jeffs, I swear the navy is trying to kill me with this Nam shit. First it was the Riverine Force on the Mekong and now they want me to stand up on the damn signal bridge with a missile launcher on my shoulder and wait for MIGs to shoot at us!"

Jeffs took off his work ballcap and used it to wipe the sweat from is neck. "Damn it's hot!" Across the road stood a sign that showed the enlisted club was just a quarter mile to the left.

"Nobody knew this morning how long this training session was supposed to be," Jeffs observed.

"Right," George answered.

"And it's about a mile back to the ship."

"Right."

"A taxi from the club back to the ship would be quick and cheap."

"Right."

Jeffs folded his arms and squinted as he tried to make out where the club was down the street, "Okay, George, as the petty officer in charge here, it's your duty to declare a medical emergency due to the heat and get us some fluids."

George considered this for a moment. "Let's go." They began walking. "If they catch us we'll just get chewed out."

"Sounds worth it to me," Jeffs replied.

"You never know," George added. "He might be itching to give you some more extra duty. Just stay off the tables, okay?"

Jeffs lifted his hat and gathered his hair back under it. "It's still worth it." Hell, what are they going to do to us? We're the Red Eye experts now. We're protecting the ship!"

TWENTY-SEVEN

My Dearest Lam,

...I don't know for sure that my letters are even reaching you. With all the bombing there does not seem to be any system in place anymore for mail to be moved. I try to send them with men who I know are traveling that way. Someday this war will end and we will be together again.

Love,
Quan

Quan was lying on his back feeling very awake, his thoughts on Lam, as they often were. He wondered what she was doing right that minute, and whatever it was he wanted to run away and be with her. He wanted to climb out of his dirty hole in the ground and run outside in the fresh air all the way to his home.

He could picture the village, his parents, his friends, their families. He had grown up there and as far as he could remember it had changed little during his lifetime. A few groups of huts had been added here and there. The arrangement of some of the rice paddies and tea plots had changed some, but little else. Even the war, with all if its renewed intensity, had barely touched the area.

There was a legend that went back several generations that told how The Village by the Lone Hill was protected by various spirits that supposedly resided in the surrounding countryside. The near isolation of the village from most of the hardships of the war fueled the belief in this myth. Quan never thought much about if he actually believed the story, but he never denounced it either. Right now he was longing for the protection that his home might provide, and more than ever he wanted the legend to be true.

He rolled to his side and felt the rough earth pressing into his ribs. His stomach growled at the fading memory of the small evening meal. He heard footsteps approaching and someone pushed on his shoulder. "Quan, you awake?"

He rolled back and looked up into the face of one of the men on the crew of the other gun. "I am now," he lied.

"Captain Nguyen wants to see you, right now."

He sat up and reached for his sandals. "Do you know why?"

The man shook his head. "No, but he didn't seem upset or anything. He sounded very routine. Maybe you're not in trouble. Maybe they want to give you more money or make you a general. Maybe they decided to send you home." The man laughed out loud as he turned to return to his post.

Quan made his way out of the gun tunnel to the top of the hill and walked the short distance to the bunker-like low building that served as his command headquarters. A sentry was seated at a small table just inside the door. "Captain Nguyen sent for me."

The sentry stood and motioned him toward an open doorway.

Captain Nguyen was standing behind his desk. Quan had never seen him in anything other than full and proper uniform before. Now, though, he was wearing sandals, his uniform trousers and an untucked, baggy, white shirt.

"Relax, young man," he said as Quan began to plant himself at rigid attention before his desk. Then he laughed as he saw his young recruit relax just a little as a questioning look came over his face. "It's late and I just want to talk. Sit and have some tea." He motioned at a wooden chair. On a small side table was a cup next to a blue-white pot.

Quan reached and picked up the cup. "Thank you, sir." He took a small sip, still wary of the reason behind all the informality.

"Discipline and respect for military authority is very important for our success," Nguyen explained. "But we are people, also, and sometimes it is good to just be people instead of soldiers, lest we forget what it is we are fighting for. Do you know what we are fighting for, Quan?"

He cleared his throat and kicked his brain up a gear. A quiz? "We are fighting for freedom and to reunite our country and our people."

Nguyen smiled faintly. "That is the propaganda isn't it? That's what you have been taught to say to questions like mine, and it's true." He touched his own chest. "But in your heart, what are you fighting for?"

It seemed like an honest question from a man who wanted an honest answer. He searched his feelings. "I think I am fighting for my family, my wife, our village. The Americans need to be gone so we can return to a normal life."

Nguyen reached across and poured himself a cup of tea. "A reasonable answer, young man. I think I would give a similar answer. It is good to remember the propaganda lines. It is also good to remember one's heart. They may not say exactly the same words, but they are reaching for the same end."

Quan relaxed a little more, apparently having passed the quiz. "Thank you for those thoughts, sir. If I may be so bold, why have you asked me here this evening?"

Nguyen took a long drink from his cup. "Does the name Hon La mean anything to you?"

He knew almost nothing of the place, but it was a familiar name because of one thing. "Has something happened to my grandfather?"

Nguyen raised his eyebrows. "No, quite the contrary! You have already answered my next question. There are reports of, shall we say, an eccentric and influential old man who lives there. I was told that he is your grandfather and I was going to confirm that with you."

Quan was smiling now. "From what you have told me so far I would say it is likely to be him. He would definitely find a way to be running the show."

The old man, Ong Ngoai to Quan, his maternal grandfather, had moved away from the village several years earlier and unlike anyone Quan had ever known, he had done quite a bit of traveling. He had come back to visit the village a few times and Quan had fond memories of him.

"Here is the reason I am asking you these things," Nguyen explained. "A Chinese freighter has been unloading rice and other supplies in the anchorage off shore at Hon La. In spite of attacks by American ships and planes, there is a sizable stockpile built up which we have been authorized to take from. You have probably noticed that we are in need of food."

Quan's hand went instinctively to his stomach. From the inside and outside he felt the emptiness there.

"Since your grandfather is apparently someone of importance in that area, I thought it might be a good idea if you went along with the trucks to pick it up. There are probably too many commands and others who have their eyes on that rice. It certainly can't hurt our cause with the old man if you are there."

"I think I would like that, sir." Quan answered. "A change in my routine and a chance to see my grandfather. I'll do everything I can to see we get our share, or maybe more!"

Nguyen chuckled. "That's the spirit! It's not that far, but it will take a day or two by truck. As a result of the war the roads are very bad, I hear and there is danger from American planes and ships. You'll be leaving in the morning at 0600. Report here a few minutes before and I'll walk you out to the drivers.

Quan had ridden in a truck only a few times in his life, but even with his limited experience he was absolutely certain that the one he was now in had to be the noisiest, worst-riding one every made. It seemed to him that every piece of metal or glass in it rattled, vibrated or squeaked and there were a number of different whines and grinds from the engine and transmission.

They had set out early that morning and the roads had alternated between rough and non-existent. The sun was setting and the driver had just said they would be there soon. Quan leaned his head back and tried to rest, but mostly he was thinking of home and Lam, and wondering how his village's fields were faring. When they reached Hon La he would still be over a hundred miles from home, but maybe he could give a letter to his grandfather if he really was there. Maybe his grandfather could find a way to get it to the village or take it there himself if he was going there.

He awoke with a jump as the truck came to a halt in darkness and the engine stopped. Following the driver's lead, he stepped out and stood with the other three men, still trying to clear the sleep from his brain. The night was very quiet and the soft breeze carried hints that somewhere nearby the sea was swelling and breaking. After several seconds, five men appeared from the darkness and walked toward the group.

"How is the road?" the other driver asked.

One of the soldiers from the group took an extra step forward. "Not too bad right now. We just finished repairs on it again a couple of hours ago. The Americans usually don't start shooting again until later, but sometimes sooner." He shrugged.

Quan's driver looked up at the star-only sky. "At least there is no moon tonight."

The apparent leader of the group grunted a laugh. "That is good. This way you can be killed running off the road instead of the Americans blowing you up." All the men with him laughed at the familiar remark.

The drivers laughed too, but more nervously. "Let's get started," Quan's driver said. The four of them turned and made their way back to the trucks.

Quan, wide awake now, jumped up to his worn seat. "So, what is all this about the road?"

The driver began the irritating process of alternately pumping the accelerator and turning on the ignition while he explained. "We could have gone along the coast from the south but that road is often under attack. There is a road along the mountainside down to the village. There is one very sharp bend about halfway down that faces the ocean. Almost every day the American ships shell the area around the bend blocking the road with rubble or causing part of the roadway to slide down the mountain. Then almost every night our repair crews open it up again."

The truck's engine finally fired to life. Quan thought over what the driver had said and decided that the more he learned about the war the less sense it made. "So, right now the road is fixed again, but we might get shot at?"

The driver fiddled with the choke lever, then sat back upright, satisfied that the engine was running as well as it ever would. "At night they also do what is called harassment fire. They shoot at the bend in the road and other places along the road. Sometimes they don't shoot at all for a long time, sometimes they shoot every few minutes at the same place or at other places. You never know where or when."

"Why?"

"Because the freighter is unloading a lot of food and other supplies."

"Why don't they shoot at the freighter?" he asked.

"It is Chinese and they aren't at war with China. They also never shell the village because it's not a military target and it would look bad to the rest of the world if they were to do that just because they couldn't fire at the ship. So they just shoot at the sampans and the other boats unloading from the ship and at the road."

Quan shook his head and made a pained expression that clearly showed he thought the whole thing was absurd. "Do they ever hit anything?"

The man nodded. "The boats, but not all of them. It's not just the ships firing at the boats. Cobra helicopters also attack the boats during the day so a lot of the movement to and from the freighter is at night. During the day it's a good idea to stay off the road. Once in a while they hit a truck or something on the road, but they tell me we get a lot out of here. Enough talk for now. Hold on."

The driver put the truck into gear with a long grind and they bounced forward, over a small rise and down sharply onto the dark, waiting road.

TWENTY-EIGHT

Dear Cathy,

...And here's something that probably sounds disgusting. I've told you we can't make enough fresh water and we get some from unrep ships when we can. Well today is a new record. This will be the 9th day in a row with no showers. Great huh? Our noses are all dead, but just think what it would be like if a new guy came aboard. He wouldn't get seasick he'd get stink sick! Keep the scented letters coming!

Love,
Jeffs

"Hello, Grandfather."

The old man turned around slowly and a broad smile filled his leathery face. "Quan!"

They embraced for just a moment then parted, taking in long looks of each other. Quan was pleased that his maternal grandfather still looked so much like he remembered him, though he was more wrinkled. In fact, he was more wrinkled than anyone he could ever remember seeing. To those who knew him well, he seemed more weathered and worn than old.

"So, how have you been, Grandfather?"

Chien thought for a moment. "Well enough. It was just thirteen years ago that I moved away from the village and I have only returned a few times since. We have much to talk about." He scrutinized his grandson's clothing. "I see you have been serving our country. And I...I have been on more adventures than a sensible old man should have." He often said such things to please others. He would not have traded his experiences for the world. "I knew you arrived during the night with the trucks. How is duty at Dong Hoi?"

Quan folded his arms and studied the face before him. "You know where I have been stationed?"

The old man smiled slyly. "I know a lot of things. I do not usually have anything to do except go around being a wise old man and everyone likes to talk to me. I also know they are not over-feeding you. I was just about to fix my morning meal. Do you have time to join me?"

Quan nodded eagerly. He sat on a straw mat near the stove and a flood of good memories about his grandfather came to him. The old man's casual friendliness set him apart from most of the other older men in his life. He did not conform to the conventions of traditional Vietnamese culture. Had Quan known the terms, he would have referred to his grandfather as worldly and even westernized.

Even the house was quite unlike anything anyone would expect. It was situated just a few hundred feet from the water front where the boats from the freighter unloaded. It stood along one side of an old warehouse that had been built by the French in the early fifties. One wall was the stone and mortar of the warehouse. The front wall appeared to be the front door of some former building that had been left and then built around. It was made of wood and plaster with a small, square window to one side, which was nearly useless because of the scratched and yellowed glass. By Vietnamese standards it was a generous dwelling for one person--about eighteen by twenty-five feet.

The old man handed Quan a heaping bowl of rice topped with a few strips of dried fish—something he had seen only a handful of times since leaving home. While they ate, Quan looked around the dwelling at the strange mixture of Vietnamese, American, Chinese and haphazard wartime throw-together. A table and wooden chairs stood in one corner, a crude altar with candles took up the middle of the back wall, and near the table was a neat stack of mats and blankets. All in all it was a bit pretentious for an old peasant.

Quan said nothing until he had put several bites into his deprived stomach. "I think I must be confused about something. I thought Hon La was an island but we came here in trucks last night."

The old man smiled and pointed behind him. "Out that way is Hon La Island. It's very close. The place where the Chinese ship is anchored is called Hon La Anchorage. The area here near the beach is also called Hon La. All around here is Hon La." His face scrunched into something like a mischievous grin. "You know sometimes I ride a sampan out there to the freighter and back."

"You ride sampans out there? Aren't the Americans shooting at the boats?

"I've done it at night a few times. During the day attack helicopters are a little more of a problem. I just think they won't shoot at me." He shrugged and cackled a laugh.

Over the next couple of days Quan learned much about his grandfather, and about the war, as they walked around the village and talked. He was surprised to learn that his grandfather was a respected man in the village and seemed to be regarded as a mixture of wise old sage, learned teacher and mysterious eccentric. People came to him for advice, to verify the truth of the latest war rumors, or to just talk. What he did not learn was that his grandfather, Chien, was the leader of the group known as Seven.

TWENTY-NINE

War News

The Pentagon reported today that the USS Warrington, the United States Navy destroyer damaged by an explosion off the coast of North Vietnam in mid-July was likely a victim of one of our own mines. A powerful explosion lifted the stern of the destroyer several feet out of the water, causing extensive damage and slightly injuring two crewmen.

Several military ordinance experts were in agreement that the mine probably detonated several yards behind the ship after it passed over it. "That was a very powerful explosion," one of them was quoted as saying. "If it had gone off directly under the destroyer, we would have had many casualties and possibly one less ship in the fleet.

There was no official explanation of how the accident could have occurred. An unnamed source noted that "It is absurdly ironic that the only known casualty from our mining of the North Vietnam harbors has been one of our own ships."

Since leaving his home village all those years before, Chien had travelled and seen more than his family could ever imagine. He had seen a lot of people die, Vietnamese, French and Americans, and he had seen a lot of senseless destruction and bungled plans. The glorious defeat of the French at Diem Ben Phu had been eighteen years ago and all the killing and destruction had only led to more of the same.

In his travels he had talked with many people and seen many things. He had studied books and had learned history, geography and much about the war. He had read widely on many topics and had gained insight into much of what was going on around the world. Even though he was quite aware that he was getting too old to see much of the great big planet he had grown so aware of, he wanted to start anyway. He had outgrown his country and grown weary of the ravages of war. He did not want to die in Vietnam.

He was under no illusions about who were the good guys and the bad guys. He knew about communism and democracy and the various ways they were being put into practice around the world. He held no affections for the government in the north, but at least they were widely supported and would unify the country. He hated the regime in South Vietnam for carrying on a war that was butchering their people and he hated the Americans for supporting them and prolonging a fight they could not win.

So, he was planning to leave this land he worked so desperately hard for. He had already obtained permission from the captain and he would be leaving aboard the Chinese freighter when it set sail.

But he would be leaving with the knowledge that he had engineered a parting shot of huge consequence that would collect on a debt from long ago. For more than a year now, he had focused his hatred into a year of planning in a daring scheme that would strike a demoralizing blow against the U.S. military. At the same time, he would finally have the chance to avenge a wrong, one that he was never sure he would be able to, but his patience had paid off.

He knew it made no rational sense to take out his revenge on a ship. The ship was run by men and the men who ran her now had nothing to do with him. But he also knew that a ship was a little piece of her homeland and the homeland deserved everything it had coming.

In July 1953 the cease-fire was signed that ended the Korean War, or at least the fighting. In May, the next year, the French were defeated in Vietnam at Dien Bien Phu and began their military withdrawal from the country. During that time, the United States kept an active naval presence in the region and the *Rattano* was part of that presence for several months.

On a number of occasions the *Rattano* and other destroyers participated in operations to assist the French, the Vietnamese anti-Communist sympathizers or to gather information. These operations brought them into Vietnam territorial waters. There was little that Vietnam could do about it at the time and their protests to the United Nations were drowned out by Korean War aftermath and the growing cold war rhetoric between the West and the Soviet Union.

One of those operations was just off the coast from Quang Khe in North Vietnam. Under cover of darkness, the *Rattano* steamed slowly to within just eight hundred yards of the beach. Another couple of miles off shore, the cruiser *St. Paul* waited in case there were any problems that might require her additional firepower or other assistance. The mission was to evacuate a dozen men from the country. They were French Special Forces troops and several Vietnamese anti-Communist military officers.

Chien was on the shore watching through binoculars that gathered enough available moonlight for him to make out what was going on. Even though he had fought hard against the French he was not a fanatical supporter of the communist government in Hanoi. He and several of his fellow Viet Minh were on a mission of mercy this night.

Along with the boatload of French and Vietnamese soldiers, he had arranged for another boatload of twenty-five individuals to be picked up by the destroyer. The group was made up of several local civilian officials and their families who were probably going to be imprisoned or executed for their pro-France support. The government of France had unofficially agreed to take them in if they could somehow make their way to an American ship.

The first boat had reached the destroyer and was bringing people aboard. The boat with the civilian officials and their families was approaching from shore and still had a hundred yards to go. Suddenly from farther down the beach shooting began from what sounded like several rifles. Chien didn't know then who fired the shots, but he guessed it was another soldier or group who had discovered he was up to something.

The men on the destroyer apparently believed the shots were being fired from the boat and opened up with several machine guns. It was obvious after the initial volley that there were no further shots being fired at the *Rattano*, but the firing from the ship continued. Chien watched as the boat was ripped to shreds and the people in the water, alive and dead, were raked repeatedly with machine gun fire.

Less than a minute later the destroyer was underway and making good speed out to sea. Chien and his companions went out into the calm water in two other boats to look for survivors. They found none. Every single one of the twenty-five people for which he had arranged an escape were shot to death, drowned or just gone.

Five of those killed had been Chien's oldest daughter and oldest son, their spouses and his two year old grandson. He had never forgiven any of the people involved. Within a few days he found out who four of the men were who had fired the shots from the shore and arranged for them never to be seen again. That had been many years ago, but he had promised himself that he would someday bring his wrath upon the ship for the unnecessary killings.

THIRTY

War News - September 1972

The military announced today that Quang Tri City, after being lost to the invading North Vietnam Army at the beginning of May, was recaptured by South Vietnamese troops a few days ago on September 16th. It was the area of some of the most intense ground fighting as well as air and naval bombardment during the Easter Offensive. A South Vietnamese officer noted, "We have not recaptured a city. We have recaptured a piece of land that as far as the eye can see is strewn with rubble and corpses where a beautiful coastal city used to be."

Quan was seated in the truck watching the two drivers and his grandfather talk with the man in front of the entrance to the warehouse. It was located next to a building that was conspicuously marked as a hospital to stand out clearly on American reconnaissance photographs. In reality the "hospital" was a doctor's house with a few beds in the back used as officer quarters.

The man at the entrance of the warehouse was a North Vietnamese Army officer who was young and seemingly quite impressed with both his own importance and that of his job. The discussion had started off calmly enough as the drivers showed the young officer their papers. Quan's grandfather was familiar with the officer and they exchanged polite conversation while everything in the paperwork was checked out. The dialogue became slightly tense when the officer refused to let them take two truckloads of rice, but was still on the relatively polite, traditional Vietnamese level.

Suddenly, the old man was jumping up and down and directing a tirade of obscenities at the officer. He knew the drivers could not get away with such a thing so he had decided to take action himself. They both watched in frightened, but somewhat amused, amazement.

Even the helper from the other truck, who had not been all that friendly during their trip, came over and sat with Quan to watch the scene. "Some grandfather you have there," he observed. Both young men stifled laughter as they watched things unfold before them.

The old man lowered his voice some, but was still speaking loudly. He followed the officer into the warehouse and back out again, scolding as he walked just inches away. The officer said something back a couple of times, but mostly he was silent.

Finally, after about fifteen minutes, it was agreed that they would be allowed to fill one truck with sacks of rice and half fill the other. In lieu of the additional rice they would get a can of grease, two shovels, four bottles of Russian vodka, a mix of small arms ammunition and ten cartons of American cigarettes.

Later that afternoon, after loading the trucks, they took them to a small garage where they paid a portion of the vodka and cigarettes to have them locked up and guarded overnight. Then they walked the short distance back to his grandfather's house and began the celebration.

Quan learned of his grandfather's capacity and love for something the old man had first encountered in Haiphong and had later grown intimate with at the American base at Cam Rahn Bay—whiskey. Usually he saved it for special occasions and this night definitely fit his definition. Not only had he been able to spend time with his grandson after many years, but he had argued some badly needed food and supplies out of the pompous young officer that he thought such a pathetic fool. The old man rounded up a few of his friends, young and old, and soon there was plenty of food, music and storytelling.

Quan sipped a little of the whiskey and listened to the stories and reminiscences from his grandfather and the others. There was plenty of news about the war, or at least what they knew of it from their part of the world. Several men spoke of the Americans and Quan came to the conclusion that they were often just as illogical and disorganized as his own force.

Occasionally his grandfather would exchange knowing looks with him or direct comments his way so he would not feel left out. He even urged him to share his story about the attack by the destroyers and how his gun position had narrowly missed hitting one of them. It was a good story and everyone seemed sufficiently impressed.

At some point during the night's merriment, Quan rested his head where he had been sitting and fell asleep. Much later he suddenly awoke with a start, and as he sat up he discovered something about whiskey drinking as a formidable pain impacted the front of his head.

After several disoriented moments he began to realize there was light showing through the discolored glass of the small window bright enough that it had to be well into the morning. Pressing both thumbs into the inside corners of his eye sockets in a vain attempt to subdue his swiftly unfolding headache, he surveyed the room and found that his grandfather was missing.

He shuffled over to the old man that his grandfather had seemed the closest to. "Where is my grandfather?" he whispered. The old man opened his eyes and stared blankly. "Where is my grandfather?" Quan repeated.

The old man smiled widely and even chuckled softly. "Oh, he left some time ago to talk to the guards. He said he knew they were lonely and probably thirsty too. He took them some whiskey."

Quan looked puzzled. "What guards?"

"At the top of the road on the mountain. He took my bicycle."

Quan was no longer whispering. "Why did you let him do that? He's probably still drunk!" He winced as the pain in his head grew another step.

The Chinese man laughed softly. "There is something you should know about your grandfather, young man. Drunk or sober, he does what he pleases. Don't worry, he will be fine."

A few of the others had been awakened by the conversation and slowly followed behind Quan as he ran out the door. He ran across and down to the end of the dirt road where he had a clear view of the winding road on the face of the mountain. As he stopped and looked up he could see his grandfather on his way back down, just emerging from the first corner near the top of the road.

"There's that old man again, Captain." Lieutenant Wiffler held the binoculars up to his eyes as he spoke. "That guy is probably a messenger or something. Part of our mission here is to keep traffic off that road and he's traffic!" A few of the men on the bridge threw looks at each other and rolled their eyes as Wiffler ranted.

McHenry was studying the road through his own binoculars now. "An old man on a bicycle, Mr. Wiffler?"

He could feel some of the looks behind him and he knew what most of them thought of the pompous, snobbish officer. Nevertheless, technically he was right. Traffic was traffic and there was nothing else going on. They were calling him an old man because he just gave that impression, but from over four miles away it wasn't all that clear what his age was. Maybe he wasn't such an old man.

"Well, everyone over there ought to know better by now than to be out sightseeing on that road. It's time to close it again anyway. Since you're so anxious to hear those guns, Mr. Wiffler, they're all yours."

There were snickers from several men on the bridge watch, and an outright laugh from the gunnery chief who was out on the wing.

Lieutenant Wiffler had a strange look of satisfaction and child-like excitement as he leaned over and pressed the button to talk with gun plot.

"George, get out here," Jeffs called.

George hurried out of the signal shack and joined him at the railing just above the port wing.

"I think we're going to blow away some guy on a bicycle. The captain got all disgusted with Wiffler again and told him that if he was so anxious he could go ahead and close the road and take care of the bicycle rider while he was at it."

"Why?" George asked.

Jeffs shrugged. "Cause he's there?"

Suddenly the gun director, a structure just forward of the signal shack that looked somewhat like a small, gunless turret topped by a radar dish, came to life with a hydraulic whine and a quick turn toward the shore. A gunner's head popped out of the hatch on top wearing headphones and holding binoculars to his eyes. "I see him. He's just about to the hairpin, but we'll get him." Then he disappeared again just as suddenly.

Jeffs watched through the big-eyes as George used a pair of binoculars. The forward gun mount turned, and a few seconds later the renting concussion of the first shot shuddered the water all around the destroyer.

As Quan stood watching, he heard the hollow buzz of the shell as it headed for the mountain. As he realized what the sound was, he opened his mouth to yell to his grandfather, though yelling would do no good at this distance. At that same moment there was an explosion just above the road and fifty yards behind the old man, who now felt suddenly more sober and began pedaling faster.

Quan was yelling at his grandfather to pedal even faster. Many of the people around the village were now watching as well and shouting to others to watch. Another soft buzz of a shell passed overhead then it hit a ways above the road, but just even with the bicycle, sending a shower of dirt and rocks down onto the road.

Quan gasped as he saw his grandfather fall, but a second later he was up again and back on the bicycle. He was sure he would make it now. He just had to reach the corner ahead and he would be out of sight until he entered the edge of the village below.

Aboard the *Rattano* the settings were adjusted and another concussion fractured the air as a third shell was sent to the beach.

The men and women of the village, along with Quan, watched silently as another shell approached. No one watching on the ship or on the land would ever know just how incredibly accurate that round was. The tip of the shell struck the front wheel of the bicycle. Quan and the others looked on in awestruck horror as a sudden explosion instantly took the place of his grandfather.

Chief Neal, the gunnery chief, called out from the bridge wing. "Captain, that last shot took out the bicycle rider."

Captain McHenry took in the scene around him and slowly shook his head. "Great job, Mr. Wiffler. Send a few more over and close down that road again.

As he made his way nimbly down the inside ladder from the bridge he heard the barrage begin. He walked into his cabin, closed the door behind him and glanced around the small space, not quite sure just why he had entered. Getting off the bridge and away from Wiffler just seemed necessary. Killing a bicycle rider was no worse than a lot of other shit that went on in this war, he told himself. They were about to close the road again anyway and the rider was on the road. But he felt like he had let Wiffler take control of his ship for human target practice.

He reached into his desk and pulled out the bottle of Jack Daniel's and poured an inch into his glass. He watched the whiskey as he made it swirl and stepped to the porthole beside his bed. He looked out from the port side of the destroyer, the side away from the coast, and took several moments to take in the expanse of peaceful ocean before him.

"This is to you bicycle man." He raised his glass in a toast. "And to you, Mr. Wiffler, you arrogant shit head."

As if in salute, one of the five-inchers fired and McHenry downed the contents of his glass. For several more minutes he continued to silently gaze out over the expanse of calm sea.

Quan stood staring across the distance to where his grandfather had been less than a minute before. The dust was beginning to drift away in the breeze and settle from the half dozen rounds fired in quick succession and the rock slide that followed. He could hear the crowd that had gathered around him break into many agitated conversations. One group of men were planning to go up the road and hopefully retrieve his grandfather's body, or what was left of it. Some were still holding out hope that he had somehow escaped injury.

Out past the freighter he could see two ships. They seemed far away, too far away to be a threat. Why, he wondered, did an American ship use its guns to kill an old man on a bicycle? He would never understand that. At that moment he could not even cry, did not even want to. He turned and shuffled slowly back toward his grandfather's house, feeling a jumble of anger, hate and confusion.

Just like a gunslinger adding a notch to the handle of his six-shooter, the gunners on the *Rattano* painted a small red bicycle on the side of their gun director. Also like a gunslinger whose exploits grew while he traveled from one town to the next, the reputation of their already legendary guns had just been kicked up another step.

A report of the unlikely shooting was passed along from the *Rattano* by Teletype to be included in the gun line report. A day later it was communicated to all the ships on the gun line and various related commands as part of the daily Gun Damage Assessment. From there it was passed along by word of mouth all over the fleet. Three days later it was tagged onto the end of a newscast on Armed Forces Radio and the following week it was mentioned in an article in the Stars and Stripes newspaper. The focus of all of these reports had little to do with the bicycle rider. It was to illustrate how accurate naval gunfire could be.

To most people, the man on the bicycle was just another of the hundreds of thousands of Vietnamese killed in the war. To Quan he was the only grandfather he had ever known. To a few knowledgeable individuals he was one of seven. To the men aboard the *Rattano*, he was a curiosity. Just part of an absurd event of war. They had not the remotest inkling that they had any connection to him or that he had put into motion a chain of events that would place the ship and her crew in deadly peril

THIRTY-ONE

Dear Jeffs,

...I'm sure by now you've heard the news about the Olympics in Munich. It was so horrible. Israeli athletes were taken hostage and then nine of them were killed. I can't believe people do such things to each other. I'm so tired of you being gone. Stay safe. I miss you. I love you.

Love,
Cathy

The crew of the *Rattano* had not returned to Dong Hoi since their first night in the war. During that interval the area had been attacked numerous times by other groups of ships. None had taken any sizable hits, although several had been hit, or nearly, and there had been some light damage along with a few minor casualties.

It was nearly the end of September and their turn had come around again. Once again they would be participating in a night raid on Dong Hoi. There would be no spotting or observing required this time. Both Jeffs and George had been ordered to stay inside the signal shack during the action.

Two decks below them in Radio, it was the usual general quarters routine. In the main space, Leon was manning the sound powered phone circuit that connected with the signal bridge, CIC and the transmitter room just across the passageway from Radio. Shakes and another radiomen were manning the broadcast and network teletypes in the next space which was just a few feet away with an open door between. Chief Ross was helping duplicate some messages and distribute them to the various department and division boxes.

"Hey, Chief," Leon said. "Phil's across the passageway in the transmitter room. He said to let you know it's after midnight so he's only got twenty-two days left."

Ross smiled. "Tell him he's getting so short he's hard to see, but I can still find him if there's some work to be done."

Leon nodded and pressed the talk button on the mouthpiece hanging in front of him. "Phil, Chief says you're an ignorant maladroit."

Ross just smiled, shook his head and continued distributing the latest message as Leon listened to Phil's response in his headphones. The ship leaned to starboard and the deep, increasing vibrations told them they were increasing speed for the beginning of the attack. A few seconds later the first firings jarred the ship. "Here we go!" Ross shouted.

"Chief, Phil says thank you and Ryder up on the signal bridge says for you to quit making me talk this shit over the phone circuit."

Ross threw him a look. "Thanks, Thomsen. I'm writing all this down, you know."

Seconds later a deafening crack and accompanying concussion stunned all the men in the space. A smoky haze filled the air and it took several seconds for them to realize what had happened.

Shakes was the first one to speak. "Look at this!" He had been seated at a teletype. The bulkhead just behind it, where he had been facing just seconds before, now had a three-inch jagged hole in it right at his eye level. "I just bent down to pick up the paper! Jesus! Shit!"

For several more seconds, they did not realize what else had happened. The shell had gone right through the main space without exploding, passed through the door out to the passageway, leaving a similar hole there. Straight across the passageway was the small transmitter room.

Leon looked around then noticed the hole in the door. "Chief!"

Ross picked up his glasses and turned to where Leon was pointing. He stepped to the door and opened it. The door into the transmitter room had a matching hole. With Leon pushing just behind him, he opened that door and discovered the projectile had finished its journey inside the transmitter room. It had not been a large enough shell to cause any real structural damage to the ship, but the same could not be said for damage to human flesh.

As the other men crowded around the smoke-filled doorway, they became silent. There was nothing to be done. Radioman Third Class Philip Omata was quite dead. He was torn nearly in half at the chest with his shoulders and head leaning back at a grotesque angle between a smoking, ruined radio transmitter and a smoldering stack of cases of copy paper. His lower half was still seated on a low stool. All around the room were splattered pieces of flesh and bone and below him was a growing puddle of blood.

Chief Ross took another step into the room for a closer look. He let out a long sigh and a quiet, "Christ." He turned to his men. "Anybody else hurt?"

They all looked at themselves and each other.

Ross pushed his hair back. "Thomsen, plug yourself back in and tell CIC what happened here. Logan, get back on the broadcast. He turned again to survey the room and his dead man. "Poor son-of-a-bitch never knew what hit him."

The next morning a helicopter from the *Kitty Hawk* picked up a body bag from the *Rattano's* hangar deck. There was no need to return to port for repairs. A temporary patch was put on the inside and outside of the bulkhead behind the teletype and on the doors. The ruined radio transmitter was an old one that they only used for spare parts for another one just like it. The two other transmitters in the room suffered some superficial damage but were still working. The chief corpsman and the second class picked up all the tissue and fragments they could and placed them in the body bag with the remains of Phil Omata. Mercifully, they also cleaned up the puddles and splatters of blood so none of the radiomen would have to.

Over the next few days, the other members of the radio gang frequently saw Shakes staring at the patched hole behind the teletype, or standing in the transmitter room surveying the damage. All of them kept having thoughts about how the war had suddenly lashed out at them. Something that was supposed to only happen to other men had happened to one of them.

THIRTY-TWO

There is no safety in numbers, or in anything else.
—James Thurber

It was just past midnight, the first minutes of October. The night was almost cool compared to the day, but as usual, it would never quite get cool enough before dawn came again. The usual number of night firing missions was taking place and everything was routine. Up and down the gunline there were ships firing their guns, but there were also some just sitting, having finished their firing missions or waiting for one to begin.

Several miles north of the *Rattano*, the captain of the *Newport News* had just retired to his cabin after staying up late to oversee the first stages of the firing mission. They had fired at a variety of targets spread over a large area near the edge of Quang Tri City and several miles north near the DMZ. Now, though, everything had calmed down and only the number two eight-inch turret, just forward of the bridge, and one five-inch mount were active.

Inside number two gun turret on the *Newport News* the crew was fresh as any could be at just before 0100 hours. They had come on at midnight and the pace had been slow since then. Even the low keyed tempo would seem a flurry of activity to a novice. The constant flow of shells and powder canisters from the magazine up to the triple battery of powerful guns kept a number of men and machines busy. The 260 pound high explosive projectiles and the eighty-pound powder canisters were moved much of the way automatically after being loaded into hoists in the lower levels of the turret. The empty powder casings were automatically ejected onto the cluttered deck outside the gun mount after each thunderous firing.

Only a few of the men manning the system were actually gunners. As Lacy had explained in Subic, most of the jobs were manual and routine requiring little skill, so they were manned mostly by young seamen borrowed from various divisions around the ship. The average age of the turret crew was just nineteen years and three of them were only seventeen. Most of their thoughts were not on the assembly line of slaughter and destruction they were running. They were too far removed from their results to think about them most of the time. Many of the men were looking forward to going off duty in a few hours and enjoying a slow Sunday. A few, down in the magazine, were continuing a discussion begun before they came on duty concerning Miss September, who had just been torn off the calendar, and if she had been more of a favorite than the newly exposed Miss October.

Then a shell entered the system. Just an explosive projectile like all the others, but something inside was different, something minute, something poised. It had passed the x-ray inspection when it was manufactured. It had been stored in a pallet with other shells, transported on a truck with hundreds of other shells, journeyed the seas in the bowels of an ammunition ship with thousands of tons of explosives, powder and fuel. All the bumps and shocks of moving and loading and unloading had not bothered it.

But now that shell was pushed swiftly and smoothly into the gun, a powder canister was rammed in behind it and as the breech closed, that "something" could hold itself no longer. The minute, silent, unfeeling defect suddenly let loose the awesome destructiveness of the 260 pound high-explosive projectile inside the breech of the gun.

The explosion instantly detonated the powder canister behind it and several hundred pounds more in the hoists on their way up to the guns went off as well. The men in the top levels of the turret structure died instantly from the combined effects of the explosions and the superheated poisoned air. In a flash in the levels just below where the powder ignited, every inch of space was immediately filled with toxic smoke and instantaneously became a searing inferno. Anything flammable or alive was consumed. All of it happened in the span of one blink, one breath.

"Fire in gun turret two!" sounded throughout the ship. As the firefighting and damage control parties made their way to the incident, the powerful signal lights were trained onto the forward part of the great warship. The center gun barrel was cocked at a curious angle between its two companions. Smoke and flames from the exploded and burning powder surged from where the gun barrel and turret met and from the open doors on each side of the formidable structure. There was worry that the rising heat could set off more powder or the projectiles down in the magazine, causing a catastrophic eruption that would destroy the ship. The captain ordered the space flooded.

What was designed to be a sudden explosive destruction for an enemy had turned and invaded their own ship with fiery choking death. The lethal mix of chlorine, phosgene, cordite and other chemicals in the smoke rapidly spread to nearby compartments and passageways injuring many more men as they fought to save their ship and fellow crewmembers. Many of them would end up hospitalized with serious lung injuries and some would never fully recover their health.

After a while the process of blowers clearing the smoke and pumps dewatering the flooded spaces took place and the living could enter the gun turret spaces. Nineteen young men were dead. A twentieth would die within a day. Some had been the young men in the club in Subic just a few days before with Jeffs and Leon, drinking, laughing and enjoying the small break war had granted them.

A flurry of messages went out to the fleet and the other ships on the gun line where the duty was routine, predictable, safe.

The morning of October third, the *Newport News* entered Subic Bay. A few hundred yards astern of the wounded cruiser sailed the *Rattano*. The crews of both ships manned the rail at attention, not so absurdly this time, wearing their whites. As they had been each time before, they were a little less crisp, a little less white, a little more experienced than they had been on that morning in San Diego that seemed so long ago, but they still stood out impressively against the haze gray background of the warships.

The washed out sky seemed very low and the overcast looked as though it had been brushed on with water colors. News of the incident had reached all over the world and as the two warships neared the piers, shipyard workers and sailors stopped their duties to look on in respectful and curious silence.

Tugs pushed the cruiser into her berth. Captain McHenry, preferring to work without assistance, as usual, maneuvered the destroyer into her place across the pier.

Reporters crowded near the huge warship snapping photographs and describing the scene into tape recorders or writing furiously onto small note pads. Just one of the reporters had somehow heard about the death of a crew member aboard the *Rattano* and came aboard to ask questions.

Some of the men aboard the destroyer watched the scene unfold before them. Many noted to themselves, or to each other, that they could not remember such a media greeting for any ship before. If the cruiser had been returning from a successful mission or some other positive accomplishment from her duty in Vietnam the pier would have stood empty as usual. Except for a few bored line handlers, the ship would have been greeted by the silence of apathetic, mundane routine. The war, with all its death and destruction, was no longer news unless something extremely out of the ordinary happened.

Jeffs was seated on his rack, legs dangling over the side, already changed into his civilian clothes, waiting for liberty to be called. Leon was just finishing dressing. The two of them had talked little in the last few minutes.

Leon bent over to tie his shoe. "They sent a message just a little while ago with the final list of names. One more guy died. That makes twenty."

Jeffs took a long drag from his cigarette and blew the smoke out with a long sigh, watching it swirl around the light fixture in front of him. "Well, you haven't said shit for the last few minutes and now you won't even look at me while you tell me this. So let's hear it."

Leon raised up, folded his arm across his chest and looked directly at Jeffs. "Both of them, man" he said shakily. "That last guy who died was Lacy."

"Son of a bitch," Jeffs said quietly. He jumped down from his rack, and this time he yelled. "Shit! First Phil and now...what the hell is going on here? How old were they, twenty maybe? I can just see the letter they send to their families. 'Gee, we're awfully goddamn sorry. Your son died in the war, but the enemy didn't get him, we did!' How in the..."

He stopped, sighed and kicked the metal trash can hard into the side of the locker below the mirror. "Fuck!" Tears filled his eyes and he kicked the trash can again and watched it bounce up onto a bottom rack then he sat down next to it and said nothing.

Leon watched silently, moving aside to make room for the rebounding trash can, then he stepped over to Jeffs and put his arm on his shoulders. "Let's go."

That night, several men from the *Rattano* were gathered in a bar and dance club called The Old West. Shakes was making an effort to join in with the drinking and carousing as usual, but those who knew him could see that he wasn't quite himself. In fact, things were just a bit more subdued than normal and most of them were thinking that none of them were their usual selves.

Shakes just couldn't get the idea out of his mind of that shell passing right through the spot where his head had been a second before. Also working on his thoughts was the notion that the mighty hulking armored cruiser offered no safety either.

He turned to Jeffs and shouted over the music. "Couldn't get them from the outside so they got 'em from the inside."

Jeffs stared at him for a second. "Who?"

"They got Phil from the outside. But Lacy, Schultz, all those guys, they were safe. Couldn't get them from the outside so they got 'em from the inside."

The music was loud, but a couple of men nearby had picked up on what Shakes was saying and their eyes met Jeffs' with a curious look.

"What do you mean they got them?" Jeffs asked. "Who's they?"

Shakes just looked at him for a long time, and finally said. "They!" He swept his arm through the air. "The gods of war! Hell, I don't know. Whoever's cranking out bullets with names on them and..."

His words trailed off and he grabbed his beer and took a long swallow. He knew it didn't sound right when he said it, but he knew what he meant.

The plan to capture Beach Boy had been canceled after Chien's death. The whole idea had been the old man's to begin with and some of the other's had been a bit skeptical of the value of such a move. They were now armed with firsthand information about the layout of the ship from the team that had trained aboard the *Holliner*. The remaining details would be obtained without the unwanted attention that the disappearance of a sailor could bring.

THIRTY-THREE

Dear Cathy,

...Here's something you don't have to deal with. When we're eating on the mess deck in rough weather, if you leave the table for anything you have to remember to tell the guys sitting with you to watch your food tray. It was stormy and three times during lunch somebody's tray ended up on the deck. It's pretty funny if it's not you. Lots of clapping and cheering, but messy!...

Love,
Jeffs

Hong Kong, one of the busiest ports in the world. The illegal traffic alone amounted to more than most places handled legitimately. It was one of the great crossroads of the world and there was an electricity, an excitement that existed in and around the city. Unlike Subic, the U.S. Navy's presence here was a mere speck on the economic and cultural landscape. Here, a shipload of sailors on liberty added just a handful of visitors to the population of a thriving sprawling city.

Viewed from the harbor, the stacks and layers of signs, structures and roadways that covered the hillsides were both troubling and amazing in their complexity of styles, colors, sizes and shapes. It looked as though a thousand architects and planners had worked all at the same time, but separately from one another, and everywhere could be seen cranes and scaffolding to show that the mostly upward sprawl continued.

Jeffs and his companions stepped off the small taxi boat that had brought them to shore from the ship. Victoria Harbor was actually just a strip of ocean between the island of Hong Kong and Kowloon on the mainland peninsula, also part of the colony. The short ride over the choppy unrestrained sea was plenty long enough, even for a group of destroyer sailors.

He took a deep breath and looked around as the rest of them filtered out of the crowd from the tightly packed boat. "This is going to be great," he said aloud, trying to convince himself. He wanted desperately to step back from the *Newport News* tragedy, Phil Omata's death, the whole damn war. He just wanted to somehow have a good time for a while in spite of everything that had happened. He wanted things to go back to normal.

He gazed out across the harbor and was glad to see some water between himself and the *Rattano*. Anchored nearby was a World War II vintage LST that now belonged to the South Korean Navy. Moored at a pier were two British frigates and a New Zealand destroyer, and at a quay near them rested a Canadian corvette, another destroyer-like ship. The remainder of the harbor was a teeming conglomeration of hundreds of junks of various sizes and designs, all bobbing horribly as they hurried in every direction as though working their way through a teetering dancing maze.

Chief Ross walked by with two other chief petty officers and smiled and waved. He was wearing a ridiculous Hawaiian print shirt with bright red and white flowers that hung too large on him, but the broad grin on his face said that he was out to have a good time and didn't care how stylish he appeared. For him, the afternoon and evening would include a couple of guided tours, a couple of bars, a restaurant or two and some shopping. He was fond of telling some of his men that he could have twice as much fun in half the time because he had learned to pace himself. He also often told them that now that he was a little older, his brain was able to overrule his dick and he stayed out of trouble because of it.

Finally, Carlos Villegas, an electronics technician named Vandemere and Mike Gonzales the quartermaster, joined Jeffs, Leon, Shakes and George. They all got along well and had decided they wanted to see Hong Kong and not spend all their time sitting in bars, at least not right away.

George, as usual, was on the lookout for casinos or some way of betting on something. They went into the tourist information center that was just across the street, exchanged their currency for Hong Kong Dollars, picked up brochures and maps, and reassembled outside to begin their day of freedom.

Before the *Newport News* explosion and the death of Phil Omata, Hong Kong was a destination that promised some fun and entertainment. Jeffs' scratch from the shrapnel during their raid on Dong Hoi had been thought of by many of the crew as their glorious initiation into combat. But the deaths of twenty-one young sailors had been something altogether different. Hong Kong was now not just liberty, it was an escape from the reality that had reared up and slapped them across the face. It was the next oasis in their journey through the war. If they could just get to Hong Kong then they could go on to the next leg of that journey.

They had all been given some information about tours, about the city itself, and a list of do's and don'ts for military personnel to keep in mind as visiting Americans. Leon was intently looking over this information, pretending to ignore Jeffs. "It says here we can't start any fires, can't flirt with any old ladies, can't do impressions of old Chinese women just to piss off waiters and we can't fart in taxi cabs 'cause it's considered very rude."

"Really?" Gonzales said. Both he and Carlos began looking for the information on their list.

Jeffs just looked over to Leon and smiled while George made eyes like he was watching idiots.

"These two might be more fun than I thought," Jeffs said.

They headed into the city not quite knowing yet where they were going. They wandered along a busy thoroughfare feeling a little out of place and knowing they looked just like a bunch of American sailors. They walked by a park and stopped for a few minutes to watch a group of British men play cricket. Every time they thought they were beginning to understand the game, something would happen that they didn't understand.

A little later they rode a tram up an astonishingly steep hill because it was there, and it was cheap. At the top was a spectacular view of the harbor and much of the city. From here they could see that the hillsides were just as crowded as they appeared from below. Large areas showed no ground at all--just rooftops and walls built one against the other.

Freighters and tankers loaded and unloaded at places all around the channel with crowds of activity around each one like ants on a fallen cookie. Open areas of any size in the rough waters of the harbor were rare. A multitude of junks dashed over the water in every possible direction, seemingly headed for a group collision in a giant demolition derby.

George was busy clicking photographs. "Leslie loves this sightseeing stuff. I think it's partly because it shows her that I did do something besides sit in bars or gamble."

Jeffs smiled as he listened and took in the view. "Once in a while."

"We can set her straight on that if you want!" Leon offered.

On their way back to the station to take the tram back down the hill to the heart of the city, they ran across a small grocery store. They bought some soft drinks and sat on the edge of a grass area in front of the store to drink them.

An older British gentlemen was quite surprised when he walked out of the store into an excited group of young men who thrust a camera into his hands. He took a group picture as they stood in the middle of the quiet street, the only photograph ever taken of Jeffs, Leon, George and Shakes together. Then the old man reminisced for a time with them about his own days in the Royal Navy during World War II.

Later in the afternoon they somehow managed to stumble onto the fact that there was a British communications post in the middle of a very busy commercial area. It looked very out of place with its park-like layout of well-manicured lawns and shrubs meandering among the low buildings, all of them packaged in clean, white siding with green trim. The closest building was located among large trees, and instead of the chain-link fences and guarded gates that the four of them were used to, there stood just one small sign identifying it as a British Military Installation, and very politely suggesting that trespassers keep out.

Jeffs folded his arms and surveyed the sign and the landscaping. "Some base. You want to explore a little?"

Shakes was leafing through one of the brochures they had picked up at the dockside service building. "I think I saw something about this place.

Here it is." He ran his finger back and forth as he read it to himself. "It says here that American servicemen are welcome at their club."

They stood looking at each other for a few seconds, shrugged and followed Jeffs' lead up the stone path. They walked through an open double door and stopped just a few feet inside. To their left was a small bar. To the right the room opened up into a large, high-ceilinged rectangle. A few tables and chairs were scattered around, but most of them were stacked along one wall. The opposite wall was nearly all glass and outside shimmered a large swimming pool.

"Americans, I see," boomed a voice from the far corner.

They all jumped and turned toward the far end of the large room, where a kilted figure sat alone at a table. George cleared his throat. "Is this the club?"

"This is it!" the man confirmed in his Scottish accent. "You're welcome to use it."

With eerie suddenness, an old Chinese man appeared behind the bar. "Have a beer," the Scotsman continued. "It's good and it's cheap. But don't order a drink. Charlie Chan there will give you some weird British version and you'll think we're all stupid ass holes!"

They were surprised and pleased when they each paid less than a quarter for a cold pint of draft San Miguel. They scooted chairs over to the man's table.

"How did you know we were Americans?" Jeffs asked.

"Well, look at you!" he said it with an easy smile, then a laugh. "There is a great view of the harbor from the barracks. I saw your ship come in yesterday and I knew some of you would wander in here."

"What do you do here, man?" Leon asked.

"It's a communications post, but I don't do anything like that. I'm in the Scottish Militia. We guard the place, escort British dignitaries, stuff like that." He took a long drink from his beer. "I'm on duty right now, but there are no fucking duties that need doing!" He raised his glass and took another long swallow, finishing the beer and slamming the mug down with a broad grin."

They spent the afternoon at the club. As the beer and the conversation flowed freely, the Scotsman's uniform with its kilt, wide decorated sash and polished sword became a popular topic. The man was in his early thirties, tall and muscular with bright red hair. He had "been around" in a Scottish sort of way and the four Americans were highly entertained by his outlandish stories.

The tales from all the men got taller as the keg under the bar got lighter, and later they were joined by more kilted militia men and several young women, members of the British Army who did the communications work.

The educational high point of the day came toward nightfall. In answer to their day-long questioning, Jeffs and his friends finally learned what Scotsmen wear under their kilts. Three very drunk militia men lined up and lifted their kilts in unison to reveal, as one of the British women referred to them, "their punies."

The next day was a duty day for Leon and George. George was standing duty as a radioman during their time in Hong Kong so more of the radiomen could have time off. He knew the job well enough from his time in the Riverine Force on the Mekong where he served as signalmen and radiomen aboard the boat. He was not as familiar with all the equipment and procedures aboard the *Rattano*, but he always had a radioman with him.

After breakfast, Leon walked into Radio a little hung over and wishing he was still in bed. George and he would run the communication center of the ship until the next morning. Chief Ross had come up with the plan and the men had reluctantly gone along with it, though they had since come to appreciate it. Twenty-four hours was too long to stay on watch, but with two men trading shifts with one sleeping while the other took care of incoming Teletype traffic it worked out reasonably well. The amount of message traffic was normally much less while the ship was in port. If any equipment broke down or if too many messages were brought to be typed up and sent out or if any emergency messages were received that required the man on watch to leave the room to deliver it, then the sleeping half of the team would have to be awakened. The payoff was three days completely off between duty days to enjoy Hong Kong.

Leon half sat, half leaned, into the tall metal shelf opposite the row of teletypes, took a large swallow of coffee and lit a cigarette as he watched the noisy machine spit out a tiresome hundred words a minute.

The messages were sent out from several naval communications stations after being received from various other stations, commands and ships. Each message was addressed to the ship or station it was destined for. The communications station ran messages on several different radio frequencies at the same time, one after another, for all the addressees within its large area. Each ship or station then received all the messages being sent out on the "fleet broadcast" as it was called.

The glorious job this morning of reading at least the heading of each message to determine the addressees, had befallen Leon Thomsen. He rubbed his roughened eyeballs and looked at the sixth message in a row that had nothing to do with the *Rattano*.

"George, have you ever wondered how much fucking money is wasted just having us do this useless, horse's ass bullshit?"

George was sitting at the desk just around the corner from Leon. He had been appreciating that it had been slow and was reading the familiar labels on the communication equipment in front of him as he thought of nothing in particular, except getting to climb into his rack soon.

"Billions!" George answered. He started laughing as he said it. The question was the first thing Leon had uttered since walking into Radio. "You going to be able to stay awake back there? You look like hell."

Instead of answering, Leon just started making snoring noises just to see how much he could annoy George. He kept it up so long that George finally reached around the corner and threw a stapler at him.

A couple of minutes went by and Leon tore off a message addressed to them and brought it out to George.

"What've you got?"

"It says here that this South Vietnamese liaison officer is going to report aboard for temporary duty. Some Commander named Nguyen Chi Khiem. Anyway, it's an immediate so I gotta take it to the XO or the captain."

"When's he coming?"

Leon scanned the message. "Says sometime during the next couple of weeks."

"So why the hell is it an immediate priority?" George asked.

"See! That's the same stuff I always ask! Somewhere some dumb ass is just giving out random letters for these priorities."

George stood, stretched and yawned. "Go ahead, I can watch the broadcast for a couple of minutes."

Leon headed for the door but stopped and turned back as he opened it. "So, is that true that Vietnamese names are backwards? You know, the first name is last and the last name is their first name?"

"That's what I was always told," George answered. "I worked with a lot of Vietnamese on the Mekong. But some of them would fix it for us because they knew it was backwards to us. So they would tell us their name already turned around so we wouldn't get confused, except some of us who thought we knew what we were doing would turn it around again. So I finally figured out the best thing to do is just ask them what they want to be called."

Leon looked down at the message he was holding. "So we don't know if we call this guy Mr. Nguyen or Mr. Khiem. George, I want to be called Mr. Leon from now on, okay?"

"I think Mr. Dumb Shit sounds better," George said.

THIRTY-FOUR

Dear Jeffs,

...I was so happy when you called yesterday from Hong Kong! It was so great hearing your voice and being able to talk at least for a little while. We talked for a little less than 15 minutes. Wow, $8.00 a minute is going to be a huge phone bill, but I don't care. I'm sorry I cried a lot but it was such a surprise and I miss you so much. I'm glad I got to tell you my boss is a bitch. It felt good to say it to you instead of just writing it! I still can't believe what happened to Phil Omata! And then all those men on the Newport News. It's so sad and scary. It's been on the news every day. We're scared for you and for all of you over there. I'll write again tomorrow. Please be careful and be safe.

Love,
Cathy

After a few days in Hong Kong, the crew of the *Rattano* was on their way back to the war. Once again they would be putting in some time off the coast of Hon La. The time away from the war had been good for all of them. Jeffs was feeling that maybe he could put in his time, put the war behind him and just get through it the best he could. It was a nice thought, but it was to be one of the last times he would really believe it.

George's gaze shifted to the window behind Jeffs. "Hey, look out there."

Outside in the dark, a lone, bearded figure stood by the railing of the signal bridge. The inside of the signal shack was dimly lit by a small, red lamp. The lone man knew the two signalmen were watching, but he wasn't concerned about them. He knew them well enough to know that they appreciated the elegant ingenuity of his little project.

Jeffs smiled. "I guess Hughes still has his unbuilding project going."

Hughes reached into his left shirt pocket, which contained only nuts, and threw the contents overboard. The ship was moving at better than twenty knots. Between the wind, the rumble of the engines and the churning of the sea being pushed aside, there was more than enough commotion to cover up any small splashes that might be noted by the lookouts or some crew member who just happened to be passing by down on the main deck. One by one he emptied each of his various pockets of screws, bolts, nuts and miscellaneous into the dark sea. All told it represented the discards of three day's deconstruction.

"I hope the damn ship doesn't fall apart before we get back home," George commented.

"You've got to admire his originality," Jeffs said. "I wonder what even made him think of it. It sounds like something from a movie."

"We had something kind of weird at the Long Beach Naval Station," George said. "I was on temporary duty there for a few weeks. We had a phantom shitter."

Jeffs laughed out loud just from the sound of it. "What the hell's that?"

George was laughing now too as he remembered it. "Every night the guy on watch would find a big pile of shit in the doorway between the offices and the mess hall."

"Human?"

George nodded. "For about three weeks they'd find this pile around one or two in the morning. We started calling whoever it was the Phantom Shitter."

Jeffs was still laughing as he tried to ask questions. "So what happened? Did they ever catch him?"

"In fact, this other guy and I caught him. The captain posted us on a stakeout. Turned out to be to be the chaplain."

They were both laughing even harder. "The chaplain!" Jeffs shouted. "Did the devil make him do it?"

"I never heard," George gasped. "I couldn't believe it. He just walked up, dropped his pants and dropped a big load. Didn't even wipe for Christ's sake! Anyway, they sent him off to some psychiatrist or something and we never saw him again. Almost every place I've been there's been at least one guy who just seems to move on down the road in a different direction and never quite gets back." He tapped the side of his head.

Jeffs was standing trying to get his breath and wiping tears from his eyes. Suddenly, Hughes opened the door of the signal shack and stepped inside. Without a word he reached under his bulging shirt with both hands, gave an object to both Jeffs and George, then turned and left, closing the door behind him. George found himself holding a can of peanut butter with a can opener taped to it. Jeffs was holding a half a loaf of bread with a knife inside the wrapper.

"Bribery!" George said. "Good timing, too. Chow was that brown macaroni bullshit thing he makes."

Jeffs was impressed. "I've heard of hush money, but hush food?"

George gave a quick chuckle as he opened the can. They finished their peanut butter sandwich feast and lit up cigarettes.

After several silent minutes, Jeffs said, "I'm just so damn excited about going back to Hon La. Someday when my kids ask me what I did in the war, I can tell them I just cruised back and forth in front of a Chinese ship making faces at them and shooting at their toy boats."

The next day was Sunday and the lookout on the starboard bridge wing had just come on duty after eating a hurried breakfast. Sunrise would arrive in just a few minutes and the world had been lighting up quickly. Through his binoculars he was sweeping the area between the ship and the coast when he noticed a shape floating on the water about fifteen-hundred yards off. He brought the binoculars down and found he could just barely see something with the naked eye.

He brought the lenses to his eyes again and studied the object for few moments. Keeping the binoculars to his eyes he called out to the duty officer. "Mr. Kelsey, I think there's something out there, but I can't make out what it is." That wasn't quite true, but he was convinced his imagination was playing tricks on him.

Lieutenant Kelsey stepped out onto the wing. "What is it, Pucinni? Where?"

The lookout pointed with a free hand as he kept it in sight. "About a mile or a little less, I think. It's small, but I can't tell really. Might just be some debris of some sort."

Just as Lieutenant Kelsey brought it into view through his own binoculars the phone talker from inside the bridge called out. "Mr. Kelsey, the aft lookout reports an unknown sighting to starboard about a mile off."

Kelsey stepped back inside the bridge and reached up to the bitch box and pressed the CIC switch. "CIC, bridge. Any contacts to starboard, a mile or so?"

"Bridge, this is Chief Emory. We've had an intermittent blip for half the night in that direction. Never could confirm anything. Whatever it is, it's very small, if it's really there. Probably just some more fucking rice bags or some other crap."

"CIC, this is Lieutenant. Kelsey. No, there's something there, but you're right, it's small. The lookouts spotted something out there a few minutes ago. I'll keep you posted."

He turned to the junior officer on duty. "Go up to the signal bridge and get on the eyes and see if you can get a better look."

Jeffs was leaning out the window of the signal shack doing nothing in particular when he saw Ensign Davis, the division officer of the electronics technicians, come up the ladder from the bridge wing. He walked outside just as the officer grabbed hold of the big eyes on the starboard side. "Mr. Davis, what brings you way up here?"

"Hi Ryder, how ya doing? Well, everybody on the bridge and CIC says there's something out there, but nobody knows what the hell it is, so they sent me up to get a look." He was looking through the powerful big eyes now, scanning the general area of concern.

Jeffs stood to one side, just a bit behind him to figure out where he was talking about. Jeffs heard footsteps coming up the ladder from the ASROC deck and turned to see George making his way up from breakfast. He caught his eye and motioned him over to where he and Ensign Davis were standing.

"What's up?" George asked.

"The lookouts are seeing something out there," Jeffs explained.

George became suddenly more alert and glanced out over the sea between the ship and the coastline. "What do you mean, something?"

Jeffs shrugged as Mr. Davis straightened and turned to them. "Son-of-a-bitch," he said quietly. "You guys look through here and tell me what you see."

The two men looked at each other for a second, then Jeffs stepped forward to the eyes, bent down slightly and fit his face into the soft rubber cups. The figure floating in the small rubber raft was far enough away that Jeffs could not immediately identify who it was. But after the first few seconds of getting over the initial surprise of seeing anyone in a raft, he began to recognize that bald head and freckled face. He didn't understand how it could possibly be true.

"George, you flat out are not going to fucking believe me, but it's Shakes in a raft."

Jeffs straightened, looked out over the sea with his own eyes and began laughing.

George gave him an incredulous look as though he hadn't understood him. For a moment he thought the laughter meant it was some kind of a joke. Then he looked through the lenses. "Jesus H. Christ, it is Shakes! What the fuck is he doing?"

Ensign Davis was halfway down the ladder back to the bridge wing. "Wait 'till I tell 'em this!"

Lieutenant Kelsey's eyes widened and all the personnel on the bridge looked at each other in disbelief. "Mr. Davis, you've got the conn. I'm going down to tell the captain."

Radioman Third Class Bobby Dexter was feeling fine. The raft he was in was not one of the large life rafts from the ship, which would have been spotted much sooner and much easier. No, this was a small one that he had bought in Hong Kong, but it was doing well enough in the gently undulating swells. The day was a bit overcast, the sea was calm and he was sipping from a canned soda, feeling rather smug about his clean getaway, while he read the latest issue of the paperback series *The Executioner*. He was also wondering when they would notice he was gone, or if they could see him this far away. Wisely, he thought, he had chosen a bluish-green sort of color that probably wouldn't stand out too much.

He looked up from his book toward the ship, a couple of concerns gnawing at him again. He hadn't decided if he wanted them to see him or not, but he hadn't quite decided what he would do if they didn't come for him. Would he paddle back on his own? If they did send the boat out for him, would he go back or paddle toward shore until they gave up? With a shrug he went back to his book. Time enough for those questions later, he thought.

As he took another sip from his can of cola he noticed that his hand was barely trembling. "Look at that," he said out loud. "This little break in the routine must be doing me some good. I'm feeling fine!"

Several men had noticed that he'd been a little more subdued than usual lately. Shakes had noticed the change in himself too. He'd been doing a lot of thinking about things like how Lacy, Shultz and all those other guys on the cruiser had been killed by a damn accident, and how Phil Omata had been sitting and minding his own business behind a bulkhead and two doors. Those events had started him thinking of the war in a different way. It had always been kind of a lark to him before that. A see-the-world navy experience. They all knew they were killing the enemy, but that was far away and easy to put out of your mind.

Until now, he hadn't personally known anyone who had been killed in the war and it just got him to thinking about how fast things can change, how short life can be. He felt like he was losing himself and becoming just one of the crowd. That worried him and made him feel trapped and in danger. If bending over to pick up a sheet of paper was the only difference between living and dying then anything could happen. Hell, somebody else ducking down could kill you.

The notion had come to him that he had to do something really different, something to redefine his "self," something to show the war, to show God, to show himself that he wasn't just one of the guys who could be snuffed out without warning. He didn't know exactly what good this was going to do, and he couldn't put it into words to properly explain it to anyone, but it felt right and he felt relaxed and he felt safer. After all, he reasoned, how could the war possibly kill someone who had the fucking balls to do this?

THIRTY-FIVE

Dear Jeffs,

...I can't believe stuff keeps happening. There's a girl downstairs named Kristy. Her husband is in the navy and deployed on a destroyer in Vietnam. He was killed a few days ago! I don't know the details. Something blew up near the ship and injured a couple of other guys too. Remember that guy at the party telling us how safe and lucky you were being out on a ship? Well, lately it sure doesn't sound too safe. I'm so scared for you. Please, please be safe. I love you.

Love,
Cathy

Aboard the *Rattano*, things were not so fine. Captain McHenry was on the bridge trying to decide what to do about a pain-in-the-ass sailor who appeared to be out on some insane lark.

"You know, Mr. Kelsey, I have had men overboard a couple of times in my career. One of those was a young man who jumped in on purpose just because he was hot. It didn't seem to occur to him that since we were making better than 20 knots at the time that we might have to go back and get him. But this..." He gestured toward the coast "We're in a goddamn war and he decides to take a little raft ride in towards the enemy shoreline to sunbathe and catch up on his reading! Shit!"

He turned to the quartermaster. "Sid, how far is he from the edge of the minefield?"

The quartermaster consulted the charts spread out before him. "Well, Captain, as you know, since you and I don't trust that the bastards who mined this harbor necessarily knew what they were doing, we've been keeping a little extra distance. He's probably a good two-hundred yards from the edge of the mines. But, going by the figures we've been using just to be on the safe side, he's...well, let's just hope if he decides to go for a swim that he doesn't conk his head on one. You know what they say in situations like this?"

McHenry and the others nearby waited with expectant looks.

He gave a cackling laugh then shouted, "Remember the *Warrington*!"—a reference to the destroyer that had run into a U.S. mine.

"Jesus!" McHenry sighed. There were a couple of snickers from the other men on the bridge. McHenry was wishing someone else was captain at the moment so he could enjoy the show too.

He walked out onto the starboard wing again and called up to the signal bridge. "Ryder! Hays!" Chief Ross was up on the signal bridge now too and all three heads appeared at the railing. "Do any of you guys have any idea why Shakes would do something like this?"

"I don't know," Jeffs answered, "but he has been a little different lately. Ever since Phil was killed and the *Newport News* thing he's been, I don't know, quiet. A couple of days ago he was up here and he kept asking me about swimming and surfing. He was wondering how far it was to the beach. He was up here a long time just staring at the land. I didn't think too much about it at the time, but..." He spread his hands.

George spoke up. "Captain, he bought this little kiddy raft back in Hong Kong. I asked him why a couple of times and he never would give me a straight answer. I figured he was going to do something stupid with it back in Subic, not this!"

Jeffs, George and the rest of the crew watched and waited. "Here they come," Jeffs said.

"I guess they talked him into the boat," George said.

The motor whaleboat was the utility boat carried on all destroyers. When it left the ship it had carried Chief Ross, a supply clerk who many thought might be Shakes' best friend, the coxswain who drove the boat and a first class gunner's mate armed with an M-16. The other men in the boat all carried .45's. The boat now also carried Radioman Third Class Bobby Dexter and a toy raft. Chief Ross had fought off a rather strong urge to just shoot him when they got out to him.

"Look at that, George." Jeffs was waving as he spoke. "He's waving at us and he's got that big, stupid-ass grin of his plastered across his face."

George got up from the paperback book he was reading and stepped up to the railing next to Jeffs and started laughing. "I'll bet you my next check that dumb shit is going home. I'd sure like to hear what he tells the captain about why he left the ship." George sat back down to his book and chuckled every minute or two thinking about Shakes.

Jeffs had been quiet for a while. "You know, maybe Shakes has the right idea. We need to open up our minds here to new possibilities. This gives me a whole new perspective. For instance, I never thought of surfing around here, but maybe I should look into it."

Less than an hour later a helicopter from the *Guadalcanal* landed on the hangar deck of the destroyer. Two officers from the amphibious attack ship got off the chopper, took custody of Bobby Dexter, and accompanied him back to the much larger ship for an evaluation by the medical staff. No one aboard the *Rattano* saw him again until many years later back in civilian life.

Later that morning, Jeffs and Leon were seated at the forward edge of the signal bridge, leaning on the railing, legs dangling down just above the windows of the bridge. They were both reading a paperback book.

Leon looked up from his reading and surveyed the ocean around them. "You know what's good about the navy?"

"Nothing," Jeffs replied absently, still reading.

"No, man, besides that. There's one thing—Sunday. No regular work day duties. If you're not on watch you can sit around and read or goof off or whatever."

Jeffs looked up from his book. "I suppose you're right. It's been a pretty good day, and we had free entertainment provided by Shakes this morning. Still, I think I'll enjoy civilian Sundays just fine."

Leon smiled and shook his head. "How about Shakes? What the hell got into that boy?"

"Maybe he just wanted some attention." Jeffs offered.

Leon laughed more. "Well, he sure as hell got some attention."

Suddenly, the morning stillness was broken by a loud burst of firing from one of the .50 caliber machine guns. Jeffs and Leon gave each other wide-eyed looks, and ran to the starboard railing.

As they looked over the side, another burst sounded from the heavy machine gun. Both men looked out over the water expecting to see a small boat or some kind of threat from the enemy. They could see nothing unusual, but the gunner swung the gun a few degrees and fired another twenty rounds. McHenry and a couple of chiefs were standing next to the young man pointing to something out in the water. One of the chiefs was using binoculars.

Jeffs looked again and this time noticed some small objects floating a few hundred yards away. Then he saw that some were closer and soon realized that there were actually hundreds of them scattered over the calm surface of the sea. He tapped Leon's arm. "See all those?"

Leon nodded and whispered, "What are they?"

Jeffs looked harder at the closest ones. "They look like plastic or something. I don't know."

One of the chiefs was shooting now and the young gunner was standing to one side just below Jeffs. "Hey, Miller. What the hell are you shooting at?"

Miller looked uncomfortable. "Bags of rice," he muttered.

Jeffs and Leon looked blankly at each other, then back at Miller. "What?" Jeffs asked.

"Bags of rice," he repeated softly. "I guess we've been getting better at hitting their boats lately, so they are tying the bags of rice up in plastic and letting the current take them into the beach. Looks like the current didn't do what they expected."

Jeffs had a contemplative look on his face. "People are going to eat that stuff. Why are you shooting it?"

The young man shrugged. "Captain said to. I guess 'cause it's the same stuff we've been blowing up in the boats. Why should we let the bad guys eat it if we can help it? Chief said it's good target practice anyway."

Jeffs nodded slowly and stood up again next to Leon. "We're getting the rice before it gets us."

Leon leaned over the railing above the gunner. "Hey Miller!" he called out, purposely too loudly. "Chief Ross wants to know where the hell you were this morning when Shakes was out there? He could've used you!"

McHenry and the chief looked up at Leon and laughed hard. McHenry was choking and walked the few steps to the door into the bridge. He went inside and repeated what Leon had said for everyone on duty. He was immediately answered with a roar of laughter that could be heard on the signal bridge.

Jeffs slapped him on the back. "Good one, man. You even made the Captain laugh."

By now there were men lined up all along the railings along the starboard side of the ship. Below the machine gun a head stretched out looking up from on the main deck. "Hey, what are we shooting at?"

Miller was back on the gun and he was beginning to feel a little stupid as he realized more and more of the crew were now watching and wondering. "Rice, goddammit! Bags of rice!" As he pulled his cap down farther and fired another burst, on order from the chief, he looked every bit as dim as some of the crew had accused him of being in the past."

The sailor from below grinned broadly. "Rice? Shit!" He cupped his hands and yelled aft where the biggest crowd of onlookers had gathered. "Hey! They're shootin' bags of rice!"

Around him, several crew members were laughing, and a great hoot of laughter was heard along the ship as the news spread.

Now every time Miller fired the gun, men cheered and several began imitating him, pretending to hold a machine gun as their elbows and head flopped around like Jell-O. As the jeering continued, Miller became even more serious and intent on his task until even McHenry and the two chiefs had to stand back and smile more than a little.

After several minutes, Jeffs and Leon tired of the show and returned to their reading spots at the forward edge of the signal bridge. In the background the gunfire, shouting and laughter continued for some time. The sounds of a rice massacre.

THIRTY-SIX

The greater the power, the more dangerous the abuse.
-Edmund Burke

Admiral Loflin sat patiently while a young Lieutenant Dickson showed him the half-dozen photographs. He had come along with Lieutenant Commander Taylor from the Pacific Fleet Photo Reconnaissance Office.

"These were taken from two different high altitude fly-overs just one week ago on November 10th," Dickson explained. "At the docks here you can clearly see two boats that might be Styx missile boats tied up and another one out here just pulling in. The large shrouded launchers on each side should make them pretty easy to identify."

"I see," Loflin said. He picked up each photograph and studied it.

"As you know, Linebacker is suspended for now," Taylor said, referring to the name of the combined Navy and Air Force bombing of the far north that had been ongoing since May. "As of October 23rd there is a bombing halt in place north of the 20th parallel. Apparently this is a good will gesture to get North Vietnam to continue the Paris Peace Talks. Before this current bombing halt we really laid it to them in August and September, Admiral. Over 4,700 sorties last month. Bridges, rail lines, roads, traffic, everything. The boats were present a couple of times while sorties were flown in the area, but as you requested, this dock area is off limits."

Loflin was still studying the photographs. "Good, good. And I didn't request it, I ordered it."

"So right now, Admiral, nobody can hit that area without special authorization, but word is that if the Peace Talks don't progress well then a balls-out bombing campaign will happen and that will make it even harder to keep those boat facilities from being bombed."

The young lieutenant reached in pointing to the photos. "But that's the exact area on the recon photos that show *Styx* boats using those facilities. Don't you want those taken out?"

The man is irritating, Loflin thought. He looked up from the photograph and his eyes narrowed. "If those docks are bombed when some of the boats are not there, or if none of them are there, they won't come back and they'll be hiding all up and down the coast in every little river and jungle covered inlet they can find. They'll be harder than hell to find and even more dangerous."

Taylor spoke up. "We could put it on special targeting. No weapons released unless there are at least three boats, or four boats are there. Whatever you decide, sir."

Loflin sighed. "Do you have any photos of those facilities with more than three boats tied up?"

"No, Admiral, we don't," Commander Taylor answered.

"That's because they never put more than three of them there!" Loflin bellowed. "Now both of you listen up good! I want those boats and their facilities to be destroyed by the navy, the goddamn surface navy, the real navy! Yes, they're safe at the moment, but if bombing resumes and Haiphong is attacked, I don't want those docks touched! I don't care how you do it, but I'm the commander of the fucking 7th Fleet and I say we're going to take out these sons-of-bitches ourselves when we're damn good and ready! And when we do, we're going to take out those docks, any boats there, and all the damn boats sneaking around close by!"

"Sir," Taylor began, then cleared his throat. "If the Peace Talks are going well then the bombing halt will probably stay in place. So, you understand, as it is right now you won't be able to go after the boats either."

Loflin paced his office now as he resumed his ranting. "Of course I understand! But I've got plans in the works to do just that and I don't want them fucked up by any of this on again off again shit that's going on! You hear about those boats that came at the *News* and the *Rowan* in August? It was nighttime. Something like fifteen miles out they spotted several high speed surface targets. Those two ships fired over three-hundred rounds at those fucking boats! They finally hit one, they think! A couple of others were either hit or ran."

Taylor nodded. "They think they were *Styx* boats?"

Loflin sounded disgusted. "Who the hell knows? We've instructed all our ships to assume high speed surface craft to be possible missile boats. But look what they had to do? Over three-hundred goddamn rounds. Hell! You know, I wasn't born yesterday. Why do you think they made a run at those ships without firing?" He looked back and forth between the two men.

"To see how they'd react?" Taylor ventured.

"Exactly!" Loflin said. "They're testing us, and they just found out that the *Newport News*, with all her vaunted rapid firepower, took three-hundred shots to maybe hit one of 'em!"

He sighed and began looking over one of the photographs again. Flecks of saliva sprayed from his mouth as he spoke. "If I hear any flak about this I'm going to have both of you shipped off to the goddamn Aleutians! I don't care who you lie to, who you threaten, who you know or who you blow, but you keep those docks at Do Son off the target list even if Nixon decides to bomb the whole fucking country. Dismissed!"

The men left and Loflin was alone again with his thoughts and fears. His greatest fear, the one he never said aloud to anyone, was that the war would end before he had a chance to go after the missile boats.

THIRTY-SEVEN

War News – December 1972

The U.S. military announced that during the bombing campaign known as Operation Linebacker I, which ended at the end of October, U.S. warplanes flew more than 40,000 sorties and dropped over 125,000 tons of bombs and aided in disrupting North Vietnam's Easter Offensive.

It was only the first of December but Cathy Stone wanted a tree up right away and she planned to leave it up until Jeffs came home, no matter what month that turned out to be. She arranged the last bit of tinsel onto the head-high tree and walked outside to see how it looked in the window of the apartment. She gazed at the twinkling beauty of the window-framed tree and tears filled her eyes and streamed down her cheeks.

Arms folded, holding herself, she turned and walked slowly to the black iron railing. From there she could see the doors and front windows of most of the forty apartments in the complex. It was a common, even generic, southern California arrangement with twenty units downstairs and twenty upstairs arranged in a rectangle around an open courtyard with a pool. From her vantage point she looked down upon various pieces of plastic and aluminum furniture scattered around the perimeter of the pool deck.

She was pleased with her new home. Most of the other tenants were friendly enough and the older couple that managed the complex often checked in on her and treated her almost like a daughter. On Sundays they sometimes invited her for dinner and they always stopped to talk if business brought either one of them nearby. She liked everything about living there except being alone.

Now it was just her, but she knew that it would be the two of them at some point. November had come and gone and now there was no information being put out about when the *Rattano* might return.

Just three doors away lived the wife of a man aboard the ammunition ship *Vesuvius*. Cathy had developed a casual friendship with the woman. Her husband had originally been scheduled to come back in August and the ship was to begin a six month overhaul. She had been very pleased and happy that they would be spending Christmas together for the first time in three years. But, now, two extensions later, they thought he might be coming home in January.

Once, Cathy had tried to remember when she had first known there was even a place called Vietnam. She thought maybe in junior high school and as far as she could remember she had never heard of it except in the context of this war and she certainly did not feel caught up in some notable time in history.

For months there had been promises of truces and cease-fires, even victories that would "bring the boys home." But every promise had brought nothing but more promises from the peace talks in Paris. And every night as she watched the news, men, women, children, machines, buildings and hopes and dreams crumbled and died. She hated the war news, but she had to watch in case there was anything about his ship, or him, or just in case something happened.

For most of the time since Jeffs had left, the war news had never been about navy ships other than aircraft carriers. Whenever there were new casualties to report it was always ground forces or pilots. But Phil Omata's death and the *Newport News* tragedy had brought to the front of her awareness that, yes, something could happen to sailors on a ship.

She now followed a routine of going to bed with all the lights on. Something might happen in the darkness, but not with all the lights on she told herself. That was her new rule. As long as the lights were on then she could relax and sleep a little because nothing bad would happen, not even ten thousand miles away. Sure it was crazy, but she held onto the thought that as long as she knew it was crazy then it was all right.

In a place the locals called The Village by the Lone Hill, a young woman named An Ky Lam stood for a moment looking out across the rice paddies and plots of tea to the low hills to the southeast. Quan was somewhere on the other side of those hills. The complex of gun positions at Dong Hoi were unknown to her and Seven was just a vague myth, like it was to most everyone. Lam had never heard of a missile patrol boat or seen a navy destroyer, but there were some simple truths she did know. Living, just existing really, one day to the next was not what she had ever wanted, but there seemed to be no future in which to put any trust. But at the same time there was hope that someday, somehow, things would be better. Holding on to that belief was not easy, but she wanted to believe it and she knew it *should* be true. What she knew better than anything else in the world was Quan needed to come home before her swollen belly gave up the new life it was sheltering.

Shaking her head she came out of her thoughts and allowed herself a short, bitter laugh before returning to stirring the pot of rice cooking on the small stove. Her every waking minute was taken up with hoping, wondering, fearing about the war. The entire focus of her existence hinged on the notion that when Quan returned, their life would be normal again, although exactly what that meant was a mystery to her. If he would just come home she would have a chance to find out if the vision of the future she was constantly spinning in her head could come to be.

It was exhausting but Lam had decided that if she could fill up every day, every hour, every minute, every second with thoughts of her own version of how their life could be, then no other possibility could materialize.

⬇ THIRTY-EIGHT

War News – December 1972

It was announced that the Easter Offensive that began in April was largely defeated some weeks ago, although enemy forces remain in control of some areas south of the DMZ. A U.S. spokesman said estimates are that during the offensive, including ground fighting, bombing and shelling by U.S. ships, the North suffered an estimated 40,000 killed and 60,000 wounded in addition to losing half its tanks and artillery. An estimated 10,000 South Vietnamese soldiers died with 33,000 wounded. He added that these figures reflected the heaviest fighting of the entire war. When asked about American casualties during this period he declined to disclose the figures.

Quan had returned to his duty at Dong Hoi a few days after his grandfather had been killed. The next day he was again called to command headquarters. Along with Captain Nguyen was another man dressed in green khakis with North Vietnamese Navy insignia on his collar and hat.

The navy officer spoke first and bowed slightly in greeting. "Hello, Quan, I am Lieutenant Tai. I knew your grandfather. I was sorry to hear of his passing."

Quan returned the bow. "Thank you, sir."

"Please everyone be seated," Captain Nguyen instructed. "Quan, I want you to know that after Lieutenant Tai presents his information to you, the choice is yours. I will respect your decision whatever it is."

Quan looked first to one man and then the other with a confused and wary expression. "Thank you, sir."

"Let me go straight to the reasons why I am here," the stranger said. "I am going to divulge something to you that few people know, but I think I owe you a complete explanation. I want an understanding from you that what I am about to tell you is absolutely confidential and must be kept a secret."

"I understand, sir," Quan said, becoming more alarmed and curious by the second.

Lieutenant Tai nodded as he decided just how to present what he was about to say. "There is an American destroyer called the *Rattano*. It is known by many Americans, even by her own crew, as the *Rat*. That is the ship that killed your grandfather."

Quan looked surprised. "How do you know that?"

"We know. You know of the group known as Seven?"

Quan nodded. I've heard of them."

"I am speaking for Seven. Your grandfather was our leader. Without him there never would have been Seven. It was his idea to use this ship to punish the American navy.

"Seven?" Quan repeated. "My grandfather?"

"Yes," Tai said. "He was a great man. We have had plans in the making for a long time and we will see the fruits of our planning soon. I don't know the whole story, but a long time ago that ship killed five people very close to your grandfather."

Quan's eyes widened. "I know that story! The five people were his daughter and her husband, his son and his wife and their child. I was just a toddler and never knew them, but my family made sure that I knew I had aunts, uncles and a cousin." He was feeling less intimidated now that it seemed to be centered on something he knew about. "What did you mean about punishing this ship?" Quan asked."

"We are going to capture this ship. That is all I can tell you for now."

Quan cleared his throat, and tried to think of a proper response. He glanced at Captain Nguyen, whose mouth was still hanging open as he stared at Tai. "Why are you telling me this?" he finally asked.

"I am here to ask you if you would like to participate in this mission. We already have the skilled people for running the ship and its weapons, but we need additional soldiers in our boarding party for the initial attack and to secure the ship. Seven has instructed me to tell you that several of them are either from your village or nearby villages. They knew your grandfather as well, and they know of you. Revenge is not always the path to follow, but in this war, honor is in short supply. Avenging a loved one's death is an honorable path. Not only your grandfather's, but those in your family. You could help to continue what he did not live to see completed."

Quan took a deep breath. He was trying to think, but couldn't figure out how to go about even starting. "What if I say no?"

Tai shrugged. "Then I will leave and find others who will follow orders to do this."

Quan could feel a return to normal life slipping away from him. "Tell me more," he said.

THIRTY-NINE

War News - December 13, 1972

Peace negotiations in Paris collapsed once again after the United States presented a list of 69 changes demanded by President Thieu of South Vietnam.

Jeffs reached up and marked off another day on the calendar that was taped to the beam over his rack. The scheduled November return had passed and they were now well into December.

The guns had been hammering every few seconds for the last hour. The aft gun mount was further away from Ops compartment, but was still easily heard with each firing. The forward guns were just a few yards closer to the bow of the destroyer than the Ops compartment and the mess deck above.

He rolled to his side. Just a couple of other lights were on and several men who had mid watches coming up soon were sleeping. Somewhere across the compartment against the opposite bulkhead a guitar and harmonica were being taken through some easy blues riffs. In the far corner a group of men were lounging in several bottom racks, talking softly and occasionally stifling outbursts of laughter.

His attention was suddenly drawn to something missing. For perhaps thirty seconds there had been no firing. The others realized it too. The natural rhythm of their existence had been thrown off. A minute went by. Even the sounds from the mess deck quieted. Some nervous laughter sounded from the corner, a few non-musical strums from the guitar.

Then a sharp, metallic blow sounded from the forward mount, then another, and life resumed its proper tempo. The music was back from the blues duo, laughter and talking continued from the corner. On the mess deck the clatter started in again and a loud, "Hell's bells!" erupted from a game of pinochle. Later a break in the firing would be welcome. It was easier to get lost in the movie that would be shown on the mess deck when the screen wasn't jumping with each loud interruption.

Jeffs felt his stomach growl. He looked at his watch and figured that dinner was over and cleaned up. It was almost five hours until midnight rations or midrats which were usually leftovers and sandwich makings so the men going on mid watch or those coming off watch would have an opportunity to eat.

He wished now that he had eaten dinner, but he hadn't been hungry when he and George were relieved and had just come down to his rack to rest and think. He jumped down and put on his shoes, grabbed a candy bar and a pack of cigarettes from his locker and headed topside for some fresh air.

The sun was nearly onto the horizon and the calm, warm air was still thick with humidity. Three gunners were headed Jeff's way from the forward mount, lighting cigarettes and walking with a familiar, exhausted shuffle.

"Hey, Ryder, how ya doing?" one of them greeted with a giggle. "You look like shit."

"Thanks, Kopper. You're looking pretty sexy too. You guys done shooting?"

Kopper nodded. "For now, at least. I guess they're starting up again in a couple of hours. You can go on up there now if you want."

Jeffs turned, then turned back. "Hey, what were we shooting at anyway?"

The gunners looked at each other blankly and shrugged. "Who knows? Something about gun emplacements and bunkers, but they don't even tell us most of the time. Hey, earlier today they told us we hit a bathtub!"

Jeffs gave them a disbelieving look. The three men were laughing and nodding in agreement.

"Really, man!" Kopper continued. "Neal told us that the spotter reported a North Vietnamese squad had dragged a bathtub out of some building and set it up by a group of trees. I guess he had already seen several guys carrying water out to it and taking baths, so he zeroed us in on it and we scored a direct hit right when some poor bastard was taking a bath!"

Jeffs slowly shook his head and gave one short incredulous chuckle. All three gunners burst into renewed laughter and continued on their way aft.

The ship was sitting about two miles off shore waiting for the next shooting assignment that was scheduled to begin in a couple of hours. They were back near the DMZ again, but a few miles farther south.

He made his way forward on the steepening main deck almost to the pointed bow of the destroyer. The area around the gun mount was littered with empty powder casings.

He sat on a coil of mooring line and lit a cigarette. The ship was moving forward slowly now, about five knots, parallel to the beach and the soft breeze against his over-heated, humidified face felt soothing. About a mile away, another destroyer began firing toward some unseen target. Bicycles and bathtubs, he thought.

He watched as the puff of smoke issued from the guns in silence, then five seconds later the sharp report would reach him. The sun had disappeared below the horizon creating a multi-colored splash across the sky that was quite unlike any sunset he had ever seen before.

He took a last drag from his cigarette and flicked it over the side and watched it drop with a quick hiss into the South China Sea. He had been smoking more than ever lately and he had been telling himself that he would cut down once they got this can back to San Diego.

After firing just a few rounds, the other destroyer stopped shooting and made speed for the open ocean. The splashy sunset was quickly fading and Jeffs sat for a long time just watching the world darken and listening to the soft rippling below as the bow easily parted the sea. After a while the three gunners returned to clear the clutter they had left behind and Jeffs strolled the length of the main deck to the fantail.

By morning they would be in some other area of the gun line, a mile or two out to sea from another unfamiliar place name, but it wouldn't matter. Wherever it turned out to be it would feel and look the same. He gazed at the water softly churning out a trail that disappeared into the deepening dusk. He imagined everything that had happened being left behind along with the wake. But then he considered it awhile and it occurred to him that no matter how far it trailed off behind, the wake moved with them. It was always right there off the stern.

FORTY

War News – December 1972

The pentagon announced today that American troop withdrawal from Vietnam was completed at the end of November although there are still 16,000 Army advisors and administrators remaining to assist South Vietnam's military forces. A spokesman admitted that it was possible these army advisors may still be involved in combat situations alongside South Vietnamese troops.

The 1MC aboard the *Rattano* came to life with a buzz. "Now hear this. This is the captain speaking. I have some war news I want everyone to be aware of. A few hours ago our Commander in Chief, President Richard Nixon, ordered full scale bombing to proceed against military and strategic targets in and around the cities of Haiphong and Hanoi. Over the past couple of months these areas have been largely off limits to attack by the U.S. military in the hopes that the Paris Peace Talks would bring about an end to the war or a cease-fire. Apparently the United States government has reached an impasse with North Vietnam at the peace talks and in an effort to persuade the North Vietnam government to return to the bargaining table these attacks have been ordered. This is a massive bombing campaign to be carried out over a period of several days beginning December 18 by Air Force B-52's flying out of Thailand and Guam, Air Force F-111s, navy fighters from carriers *Enterprise, Saratoga, Oriskany, America* and *Ranger,* as well as a multitude of various Air Force and Navy support aircraft. All gun line units are being advised of the possibility of retaliatory attacks to be carried out by enemy aircraft or patrol surface craft. That is all. Carry on."

Jeffs and George were on duty on the signal bridge sitting in the stools in the shade of the shack, both windows slid open.

"Well, George, we wondered what was up with all these cans getting the Red Eye. Now we know. Let's fire one off just to see if the damn thing's working!" He lowered his voice. "Hey, it's the old man!" Both men hurried outside and met McHenry as he stepped away from the ladder.

"Take it easy, guys." McHenry sighed deeply. "Damn it's hot. Listen, you heard the announcement I just made. You know your shit on this Red Eye?"

They both nodded. "It's pretty simple. We trained Tinsley and Villegas on it too," George explained. "So, there's always someone on duty up here that's checked out on it."

McHenry nodded. "Chief Ross told me. There may be nothing to this, but you never know. Anyway, you guys may have to save our ass. And those rules of engagement? Here's McHenry's rules of engagement—if there is a MIG around close enough to see we're going to engage it. We're not going to wait and see what he might be up to."

"We're with you on that," Jeffs said. "We don't like the idea of giving the other guy the first swing."

"It's our new toy," George said. "We're up here going through the steps practicing with it all the time. We know our shit as good as we can without actually firing it."

"Great," McHenry said. "Get both the cases out of the shack and keep them lashed to the railing outside here. I want you to be able to open them up and get to them fast. Never know when you might need both." He was heading toward the ladder. "See you two later. Stay awake."

George looked uneasy. "Captain."

McHenry turned.

"We need to talk to you about something, sir." He lowered his voice. "Privately."

McHenry walked back to where they stood by the signal shack. "What's up?"

"It's about Commander Khiem," George said.

McHenry looked back and forth between the two. "Yeah?"

"What do you think of him?" Jeffs asked.

McHenry shrugged. "He's a liaison who is usually stationed in Yokosuka. Admiral Loflin knows him. He's been kind of quiet, keeps to himself. In fact I've barely seen him at all since he's been on board. The admiral wants him to get some shipboard experience. Why?"

"There's something about him, sir." George knew he had nothing much to offer. "I can't explain it. You know I was on the Mekong for a while?"

McHenry nodded.

"Well, I worked with a lot of Vietnamese during that time. There's something not right about him. He's up to something."

McHenry didn't say anything, but turned to Jeffs. "Any thoughts?"

Jeffs took a deep breath. "I don't have any background with Vietnamese like George, but I have experience with shady people. It's like he's trying to act like he's just making conversation, but he asks too many questions. I don't trust him."

McHenry folded his arms and said nothing for several moments. He didn't want to just brush off what they were saying. "What's he ask about?"

"Hell, everything," Jeffs answered. "How to get to the bridge from up here. Where your sea cabin is? How many men on bridge watch? Where the emergency radio equipment is stored? What flags do we fly during normal steaming? I don't even know what else."

"One more thing," George added. "Yesterday he was giving me a bunch of situations and asking what we would do and what signal flags would be flown. It was okay, but the last two things he asked really made me wonder. He wanted to know what flags we'd fly to show all our radio communication was out and what we'd fly to show we had captured vessels in tow."

McHenry made a face. "Captured vessels? Awfully specific stuff, huh? Did you tell him?"

"I told him I'd have to look it up," George said. "Then he told me what flags it would be. I looked it up later and he was right."

McHenry looked around, thinking. "Okay, keep this to yourself for now. Keep me posted on anything else he asks about and I'm going to see if I can keep a little closer watch on him. By the way, it seems the other cans all got one Red Eye launcher. Why'd we get two?"

"Well," Jeffs said, "the marine trainer mentioned they shipped way more Red Eye kits than they would need. I told him you wanted us to request two. So when they delivered them, they brought two aboard."

McHenry stared for several moments, flashed a quick smile, shook his head and left.

FORTY-ONE

Dear Quan,

..A soldier delivered one of your letters today! It was from two months ago. It was dirt stained and wrinkled and looked like it had been through a lot, but it made me so happy. I can hear so much bombing happening in the distance all the time, but we are still safe here. I long to see you again and be with you. I hope you are safe and well.

Love,
Lam

Fake Eggs had always been perceived as a little on the serious side, business-like and rarely quick to laugh. But something had been eating away at him since the ship's last visit to Subic that no one else knew about.

His parents, his wife and his children, as well as his extended family, had always been a source of pride for him. He gained a lot of satisfaction from the fact that their station in life was several notches above what many American servicemen thought of the average Filipino. For many years the United States had maintained a special arrangement allowing Filipino citizens to serve in the U.S. military. He and both of his brothers were in the United States Navy just as their father had been. Though not well-off at all by American standards, by Philippine standards they were solidly middle class, which was a definite minority in their poverty ridden country.

Lately they had been having trouble with his fifteen-year-old niece. She had taken to hanging around with gangs of teenagers, staying out late, wearing make-up and generally being as rebellious as possible toward anything having to do with the family.

Fake Eggs didn't often go into Olongapo City. When they were in port he usually traveled to a suburb of Manila to see his wife and parents. This last time, though, he had given in to some of the supply division crew members and gone into town with them.

In a club called "The 007" Fake Eggs saw his fifteen-year-old niece working. At first he wasn't sure it was her behind the eye shadow and dark lipstick, inside the mini-skirt and tube top. He kept watching her as she hustled drinks and more than once went upstairs, hand in hand with sailors, to the club's well-known twenty-five peso blow job floor. He finally confronted her later in the evening. After recovering from her initial surprise, she cursed him and ran into a back room.

Something happened to him that night. As he sat in the club he watched her and the other girls and the drunken sailors. Feelings he had not felt since 1944 came back to him. He had been a young boy during World War II when the Japanese military conquered and occupied the islands. He had seen firsthand the beatings, rapes and murders the population had been subjected to. He had seen Japanese soldiers force young girls into gang rapes and prostitution. That night, while he watched his niece playing the role of sex object for the American sailors, something inside him that had been asleep all these years rolled over and opened its eyes.

He hadn't told anyone about her, or about how much he was thinking back about life during World War II. He was too ashamed, too angry, too confused. That had been two weeks ago and he felt like it was getting more difficult every day to just be himself.

After breakfast, Jeffs, Leon and George once again stayed on the mess deck smoking. The three of them had all been on midwatch and there were no unreps or other interruptions scheduled to interfere with their upcoming sleep and they were all looking forward to sleeping until mid-afternoon.

Fake Eggs walked in busily from the serving line carrying several bundles of napkins that the mess cooks would be using to fill the holders.

"Hey, Fake Eggs," George called out. "Those hash browns were good." The cook stopped and stared, expecting some joke or put-down to follow. "Really, they were," George added genuinely.

The cook smiled. "Good. Now you guys hurry up. Work to do."

Leon raised his hand. "Check please."

Fake Eggs set the bundles on a table and gave Leon a serious look. "You just check yourself out of here."

Just then Chief Ross walked in eating a piece of bacon snatched from the line and just behind him came Lieutenant Commander Smith, the XO. "Hey, Fake Eggs, how you doing?" Smith greeted.

"Fine, sir," he answered.

"Say," Smith continued, "the stewards brought in some hash browns from your line this morning. They were awfully salty, weren't they?"

The cook turned and looked at George. Leon's eyes went wide and Jeffs sat smiling and waiting to see what would happen next. George just shrugged. His compliment had been sincere, but he instantly realized that nothing he could say at this point would be believed. He opened his mouth to try to say something, but instead he was struck by the bizarre situation and he laughed out loud.

Then Fake Eggs saw Ross eating bacon from his serving line and the thing inside that had rolled over and opened its eyes stood and would no longer be controlled. He screamed, "You fucking Japs!" and threw the bundle of napkins at George. It hit his uplifted elbow, broke open and showered their table with white.

Ross stuffed the rest of the bacon into his mouth. "Shit, not this again!"

The enraged cook ran past Smith, who just stared, and into the food serving area. A second later, Ross, who could see through the open doorway, yelled and jumped to one side as a wide-bladed knife twirled past him and struck the coffee machine, shattering the glass tubing above the spigot.

"Fucking Japs!" the cook screamed again.

Jeffs and the others at the table jumped to their feet. Ross yelled back at the cook, "You crazy shit, you could've killed me!"

Smith took a couple of tentative steps toward the serving line doorway just as Fake Eggs jumped through it holding a large carving knife with both hands. "You goddamn Jap bastards!" He took a step toward the XO and swung the knife at him.

Smith jumped back and Fake Eggs just held the knife at the ready. Smith slowly moved back a few steps and the cook seemed content to let him.

The mess cooks had called the bridge when the trouble began, and now two heads appeared around the edge of the serving line doorway just behind the cook. At the same time, just beyond Jeffs and the others, three crew members showed up at the doorway that led to the forward head and the chief's quarters. For several moments everyone concerned just watched and waited.

Smith backed away further to where Jeffs and his companions stood, just fifteen feet across the mess deck from the crazed cook. No one moved. Soft whispers could be heard from the two security parties that had been sent to the unfolding scene, and then the clicks and mechanical meshing sounds of two .45 automatics being loaded and chambered.

Suddenly, Fake Eggs sensed the two men behind him near the serving line. He shrieked and whirled around, letting the knife fly. It struck one of the men a glancing blow leaving a superficial cut across his cheek and left ear.

Jeffs, Leon and George hurdled over and around two tables and tackled the cook high and low, crashing to the deck with him. They were quickly joined by the others. With Jeffs and George each holding a leg, Chief Ross and Smith each holding an arm, and the members of the security parties either sitting on him or gripping some piece of his clothing, Fake Eggs was effectively immobilized. He struggled to twist away, screamed curses in Filipino and flopped his head from side to side spitting and trying to bite his captors. Finally the chief corpsman arrived and administered an injection that put the cook to sleep.

In the sudden silence that followed, Chief Ross was the first to speak. "That crazy son-of-a-bitch threw a knife at me!"

Smith let go of the arm he had been subduing and stood. "Damn, Chief, what the hell happened here?"

Ross shrugged and looked at George.

"Well, sir, I had just told him the hash browns were good and you walked in and told him they were too salty. He went nutso!" George chuckled as he spoke the last word.

Smith turned to Jeffs. "Ryder, that sound about right?"

Jeffs nodded. "Yes, sir. Also, the chief was eating bacon from the line and Leon had just asked Fake Eggs for the check, like in a restaurant, you know? So, I don't know. He just went ape shit!"

Smith looked down at the cook as some of the others laughed at Jeffs' explanation. "He sure as hell did. Okay, Doc, lock him up in sick bay. I want him restrained in case he wakes up thinking about those goddamn hash browns! Thanks everyone. Back to whatever you were doing before this happened." He pushed his fingers through his hair and let out a long sigh. "Jesus! Shakes and now this."

Later that day a helicopter from the *Kitty Hawk* flew the still drowsy cook back to the carrier with its more complete hospital facilities and staff. No one aboard the *Rattano* ever heard from Fake Eggs again. Presumably, he followed the same route into oblivion as Shakes and the Phantom Shitter.

Jeffs took off most of his clothes and climbed into his rack. "Well, we can finally get some sleep now," he commented. The three of them had spent awhile on the mess deck talking over Fake Egg's demise and letting their adrenaline levels return to normal.

"Damn this feels good," George called out as he scrunched himself under the sheet. "This is better than sex!"

Jeffs just laughed and rolled over onto his side, enjoying the sensation of sleep beginning to envelope him.

A moment later he felt a push against his shoulder. "Wake up, white boy."

Jeffs kept his eyes closed. "I'm not asleep, you mental case. Where'd you go anyway?"

"Up to Radio. Louie told me Chief wanted to see me. Guess what?"

"I don't care," Jeffs answered, eyes still closed.

Leon poked him again. "Yes you do. Chief just showed me some mail we got from the last unrep. The results of the third-class test finally came in."

Jeffs opened his eyes.

"Sorry to be the one to tell you this, but no more Seaman Ryder. You made Petty Officer Third Class four days ago."

Jeffs didn't want to awaken his brain, but smiled anyway. "No kidding? What about you?"

Leon smiled bigger. "I made it too. No more lousy shitty details and puny-assed paychecks!"

"Right," Jeffs said. His eyes opened wider. "Now we get lousy, shitty third class details and puny-assed checks!"

Leon undressed just as quickly as George had and rolled into his rack. Jeffs remained wide-eyed on his back for several minutes. He was glad something had gone right.

Cathy would be excited for him and happy because it meant more money for the two of them when they married, if that was still the plan. He was happy, or at least he knew that's how he should feel, but so much bad had happened in the last few weeks that he hadn't been expecting any good news and it had hit him off guard.

FORTY-TWO

Dear Cathy,

…My 21ˢᵗ birthday happened a couple days ago. I celebrated by carrying a bunch of ammunition we received from an unrep for about an hour and then I celebrated some more by standing a mid-watch in Radio while the ship fired the guns every few minutes. It was all very exciting. I'm pretty sure my next birthday will be better.

Love,
Jeffs

With their leader, Chien, now gone they were only six, but still referred to themselves as Seven to honor his memory. Also, though they had not actually discussed it, they were beginning to realize that this would be their last endeavor as a group. The boarding and capture of the *Rattano* had become an all-consuming project and had involved so many players that they were no longer confident of keeping their group secret beyond this mission. Moreover, if they succeeded, it would be so monumental that there would be no further purpose for their work. The war would either be over or their entire country would be wiped off the globe by an enraged United States.

Lieutenant Tai, the naval officer of the group, was now functioning as de facto leader. He was much younger than Chien, but he was now the oldest of the group and had been the closest to the old man. The mission being planned was mostly a naval affair and he had been personally involved in nearly all aspects of the planning.

At the moment he was meeting with two young naval officers. They didn't know exactly just who Tai was, but they knew that somehow this whole mission had something to do with Seven. They had the feeling that it was just a little out of the loop of being official since it wasn't coming to them through the usual channels, although it appeared to have the blessing of their immediate superiors.

"As you know, Khiem has been successful in feeding the right bits of information to Loflin," Bao reported. "Now we have one other piece in place."

Tai waited with an expectant look, and just a hint of a smile because there could be only one other piece to fall into place. "Yes?"

Bao continued. "Khiem has told us that Admiral Loflin has put together a mission that will send the *Rat* far north alone just as we had counted on. We don't have the last of the details yet, but we will soon enough.

Tai looked pleased. "Excellent. Now, you are quite sure that our thugs in Subic know to leave Beach Boy alone now? We have the information we need and we don't want to raise any sort of suspicion that could put the plan in jeopardy. Khiem will get the needed signaling information himself."

Bao nodded. "It is all taken care of. They were paid three hundred pesos anyway just to make sure they don't strike out on their own against him."

Tai turned his attention to the two young naval officers, both of them Styx missile boat Captains. "Gentlemen, you have been trusted with a great responsibility in this venture. You understand this must be kept under the utmost secrecy?"

"Yes, sir," they chorused. Then the senior of the two said, "We look forward to bringing honor to our navy against the Americans."

"One more thing," Bao said. "Through a Chinese supplier we have also secured the twenty Strella missiles. On the way back down the coast the destroyer will be well stocked with air defense."

Tai was pleased. "Very good, major. Everything certainly does seem to be falling into place for our success."

The boat captains were being promised a large payment for even a partially successful mission, but Tai and the rest of Seven regarded it as largely a suicide mission. If the *Rattano* was successfully captured then once the rest of the action started, no member of Seven could imagine a scenario that would allow the boats to escape by sea. Alternate plans were in place that involved making for shore then retreating on land, but these were viewed as unlikely long shots. Khiem had made his own plans to save himself no matter what happened to the others. He knew that the *Rattano* would eventually come under attack by the Americans after firing her torpedoes and opening up on every nearby ship with the five-inchers.

It was definitely looking to Tai as though Chien would finally have his revenge for his country and for his family. He was missing the old man and he was sorry that he was not here to enjoy how well the plan was coming together.

Both captains had their missile patrol boats tied up on each side of a small dock two miles up a river channel from Do Son. Their official headquarters was a waterfront area at Do Son, but they were rarely there and now that renewed bombing was taking place they never ventured out of protected waterways. This location up river was well hidden from the air by trees and foliage-filled netting draped between them. They were using two similar locations farther up river and two others on another channel a few miles down the coast. They were switching the only two Styx missile boats they possessed along with several other fast attack boats every day or two to avoid being targeted. The bombing from American B-52s and from fighter attack aircraft had been relentless and ongoing for days, but had not come close enough to their camouflaged positions to cause any damage.

Across from the docks under another row of overhanging trees floated four large motorized rafts. A hundred yards away on the opposite edge of the river channel was a strange looking structure built of bamboo, scrap plywood and cardboard. At first glance it appeared that a group of hut builders had taken off on some new design concept. But to the knowledgeable observer it might be recognized as a crude, bare-bones full size mockup of a destroyer from the fantail to the forward gun mount.

The main deck was at ground level with the makeshift superstructure rising up from there. It wasn't a perfect replica, of course, and it didn't need to be. It was merely a tool for learning the general layout of the vessel, but important doorways and hatches had been measured and located exactly where they existed on the *Rattano*.

Lined up in two ranks on the dock were twenty young men who would be running through drill after drill over the next few days until they could find their way around the ship with their eyes closed. One of the young men was Quan.

The two boat captains stood together on boat thirty-nine facing the assembled troops. They were known to the men only as Dao and Vu and they both intended to let their teams know little more than that.

"Good morning," Vu greeted from the deck of the boat, standing a few feet above the assembled group. "You have all been told the generalities of this mission over the last few days. Today we start working on the details, and there are plenty of them. To begin with, these are the two boats that will be participating in the final phase of the mission. You have all been told that you will be participating in a boarding and capture of an American destroyer. Several of you took part in a training exercise aboard another destroyer. I'm certain you have all been trying to guess why and I'm just as certain that none of you have guessed correctly. You will be participating in a historic event."

Dao took a few paces toward the stern of the boat as he began speaking. "The destroyer is going on a firing mission up a river. Your job will be to board it in the river. After it is secured it will be sailed back down to the river mouth. Two of you will join the crew of each boat. The rest of you will be staying aboard the destroyer and we will all be taking a little trip south."

The men looked around at each other with surprised looks and questions on their faces.

Dao turned and walked back toward the prow of the boat while he spoke. "Right here at the nose of each boat will be a tow cable. The cable will be immediately rigged to the stern of the destroyer to give the illusion that they have captured the two boats and are bringing them south. The destroyer will be flying colors to show their communications were knocked out in the attack and they are towing captured vessels. We will have control of the signal bridge and will be able to communicate the same diversion by flashing light to nearby ships. When we reach the northern end of the gun line, we will unleash these two missile boats as well as the *Rattano*'s guns and six torpedoes upon the American fleet. If we achieve the complete surprise we are counting on, we may be able to destroy or severely damage at least half a dozen ships, maybe more."

The men were turning back and forth and murmuring to each other about how surprising this sounded. Some of them were smiling, some were laughing, some were silently thinking and they were all feeling a sense of urgent fear beginning to take hold.

Vu resumed lecturing again. "Please, give us your attention!" The men quieted immediately. "Two of you, one on each boat, will be moving to the back of the boats after they are rigged to the tow cables."

He walked to the boat and gestured for them to come to the edge of the dock. "Step up here. Right here on each boat will be six pre-loaded Strella surface to air missiles. Eight more will be laid out in the hangar of the destroyer. They are a shoulder-fired weapon, very simple to operate and we will be training certain of you in how to operate them just in case our little deception is detected too soon."

He stepped over to the edge of the boat again facing them. "Now back to the initial boarding. You will be broken up into four teams of five men each. You will be approaching the ship in those large motorized rafts over there. Along with the five of you in each raft will be five technical people who will be manning the bridge, communication, engineering and weapons aboard the destroyer. It will be up to you twenty men to immediately take control of radio and the bridge to prevent any messages being sent and to secure the rest of the ship in a matter of five minutes. We will be showing you how to do that over the next few days. Make no mistake in your thinking. This is war and to achieve the capture and full control of the destroyer your job will include killing many members of the crew."

Dao stepped off the boat onto the dock. "You're going to be very busy the next few days learning all this and perfecting this mission. But keep this in mind--you will be making history. If we are successful, you will change the course of the war and forever change America, Vietnam and the world."

Quan listened to every word and still didn't know for sure if he was doing the right thing. So much of it felt right, necessary, even honorable. He knew it was dangerous beyond anything he had been involved in before. In fact he had done his best to just stop thinking about and just do it. Someone had to do it so he had decided that he would do the best he could, because what he really wanted was for all of it to be over so he could go home.

FORTY-THREE

War News – December 29, 1972

President Nixon announced today that North Vietnam has agreed to return the negotiating table in Paris to discuss the terms of a possible cease fire in the war. This follows a military campaign officially designated Linebacker II, which was a massive eleven day bombing of targets in and around the Hanoi and Haiphong area. The U.S. lost fifteen B-52s during the operation as well as a number of other navy and air force attack aircraft.

Polish the brass, the floors, the pipes on the urinals and the showerheads. Dust the bulkheads, the overheads, the tops of the light fixtures where nobody, especially a visiting officer, ever looks. Use some precious water and do some laundry so clean sheets can be seen, and smelled, on the enlisted men's racks. Clean up that damned condiment cabinet on the mess deck that the cockroaches keep breeding in, and spray, or *something*.

Leave the damn torches and surfboard up on the signal bridge because the admiral has heard about "surfs up" and wants a look. Get a haircut or stay out of sight, shine the war-scuffed shoes and get a damn shirt on, sailor. An admiral is coming aboard and, hell, there just might be a personnel inspection so he can see what fine looking marauders serve aboard the *Rat*.

This was a high-level visitor indeed. Vice-Admiral Tillman Loflin, Commander 7th Fleet. His accompanying entourage included three aides carrying pouches, two of his staff officers who worked in mission planning, a South Vietnamese SEAL or Hai Kich unit commander, Franklin DeMoorts, skipper of the *Holliner*, and Commodore William Gordan commander of Destroyer Squadron Seventeen.

Loflin was working to subdue his own very upbeat mood, but was still quick with a smile for every man he met on his way from the hangar deck down to the wardroom. There had been precious little publicity lately concerning the navy except what some considered the inhumane bombing of Haiphong over the Christmas holidays and the ulcer-inducing *Newport News* explosion in October.

Loflin was figuring to remedy some of that. With this one mission he could thumb his nose at the North Vietnamese by daring to send a ship so far into enemy territory, destroy *his* missile boats, as he was now referring to them, and gain the navy some much deserved positive media time. He knew there was the chance that the *Rat* would fall into some real trouble since he was making it known that she was available for bounty collection, but he was counting on McHenry's experience to most likely get them out of any situation. And he was still telling himself that the sacrifice of one ship, if it came to that, for the chance to go after the missile boats and save other ships was worth it.

The admiral and his entourage filed into the wardroom along with McHenry and the XO, Gil Smith. Loflin spotted Khiem, who was staying discreetly in the background, and stepped toward him with his hand extended. "Commander, good to see you again."

Khiem unsmilingly shook Loflin's hand. "Good to see you, Admiral."

Loflin, still holding Khiem's hand, turned his head to McHenry. "We miss Commander Khiem in Yokosuka. He behaving himself?" He just laughed at his own remark, not waiting for an answer.

McHenry eyed the two of them and thought again about what George and Jeffs had told him about Khiem.

There were introductions and handshakes all around and everyone began to position themselves around the large table and behind those already seated at it.

Loflin spoke up first to officially begin the briefing. "Welcome back to the gun line, Mac. Just in time for New Year's Eve!" He flashed his famous winning smile.

McHenry nodded politely. "Thanks, Admiral. Actually it's probably safer here than in Subic. Marcos and his martial law has everyone a little on edge. Along with that, it seems there are more hoodlums and diseases than ever."

"Yes, Marcos," Loflin echoed, referring to the dictatorial President of the Philippines. Privately he admired the man and wished he could run his fleet the same way. "He's a cunning little bastard, isn't he? Well, let's get down to business, gentlemen. Mr. Stimm from my staff has a brief introduction for you."

The lieutenant stood, cleared his throat and said nothing for several seconds. He'd been warned by Loflin that McHenry would not like what he was about to hear and he realized now that he wasn't sure just where to begin. "In a nutshell, your mission is to back three miles up the river in the early morning before dawn."

Loflin winced at the bungling awkwardness of this beginning.

"You will fire upon twelve designated targets. All together the firing sequences last about fifteen minutes, then you head back out to sea and that's it."

Stimm immediately felt like he had opened a can of worms that were now crawling all over him.

McHenry threw a quick look at his XO, who was already looking at him, then to Gordan. In that brief instant he saw on his friend's face that he was unable to help. It was McHenry and his XO against everyone else in the room. Making an effort to keep his tone calm and serious, he asked, "What river and what are we shooting at?"

Stimm picked up a folder and began leafing through it. "Let's see here. VC training areas, villages that harbor VC and North Vietnamese Regulars, a couple of weapons storage areas, an emergency air field, stuff like that."

McHenry reached for the folder. "May I?" Before Stimm could hand over his folder, another aide handed McHenry his own copy.

McHenry opened the folder, and repeated just as forcibly and just as calmly as he had the first time, "What river?"

Stimm cleared his throat once more. This was not going as he had imagined. "We're not sure, sir." The last word came out barely audible.

McHenry looked up from his folder and stared at the young officer with a look that begged for something reasonable to be uttered next.

Loflin could hold it no longer. "Mr. Stimm!" he bellowed. "What the fuck is wrong with you? Are you going to explain this properly or are we going to have to throw your ass overboard?"

"Oh, we know which river," Stimm corrected quickly. "It's just that we're not too sure about its name. The Red River splits off several branches where it flattens out of Hanoi into the Delta, and..."

McHenry stood suddenly and turned toward Loflin. His voice was no longer calm. "The Red River!? What the hell have you got me doing, sailing us right into Haiphong Harbor?"

Loflin had expected something like this. In fact, he would have been disappointed at anything less. "Relax, there's a lot more to hear."

Stimm continued as McHenry slowly seated himself, directing a look at DeMoorts. The lieutenant pointed to a map that McHenry was holding. "We've got good charts on it, but there's a lot of confusion of names in the area due to the large number of offshoots and channels. It's called different names by different people, so we've just given it our own name for now. We're calling it the Little Big Horn. The tides will be running high so you won't have any draft problems. Also a clear weather forecast and a high nearly full moon should made river navigation easier."

Loflin snickered as McHenry turned and looked at him with unsmiling seriousness. "Great name, huh, Mac?"

McHenry mustered his best sarcasm. "At least it's a good American name for once. Something we can pronounce instead of this Tra Bong and Mekong crap. Little Big Horn. Makes us feel right at home, just like Custer and his men riding into two-thousand Sioux warriors. You do remember they were all killed?"

"I knew you'd love it," Loflin added enthusiastically.

McHenry's sarcastic smile faded. "So, anyone with us on this?"

Stimm motioned to the man seated on his left. "Commander Ponce has some further information on that. He's been working closely with the intelligence people in Subic." Stimm seated himself, obviously relieved at relinquishing the spotlight.

Ponce was standing now and talking as he taped a map to the wall behind him. It showed roughly the northern half of North Vietnam.

"It obviously would not be wise to send more than one ship up the river channel and a companion ship sitting and waiting off the beach would be in more danger. The *Coral Sea* and the cruiser *Chicago* will be on station about forty miles off the coast. This shouldn't arouse any suspicion in the enemy. The *Coral Sea* has been in the area for some time now and from time to time other ships, including the *Chicago* have come up to join her. If there's any real trouble, fighters from the carrier are just five minutes away."

He handed out more papers to McHenry and Smith. "On the night of your raid, the *Chicago* will swing in a little closer just in case of any MIGs, and, of course, you have the Red Eye. To be honest, though, since Linebacker II, we're not too sure the North Vietnamese have any MIGs left to fly. You know the *Chicago* shot down a MIG on take-off a few months ago? It was thirteen miles away and they watched that sucker on their radar and hit him before he was out of sight of his own airfield."

McHenry nodded at the third version he had heard of the now familiar story that had made the ship famous all over the fleet. He knew part of it was true, he just didn't know which part. Privately he had wondered if the incident had been concocted just to make the destroyer captains feel more secure about their own lack of air defense.

He was looking through the contents of the folder, but he and Smith had exchanged more looks over the last minute or two. "How do I know what the hell I'm backing into?"

Loflin motioned to a Vietnamese officer. "This is Lieutenant Pham, commander of the South Vietnamese SEALS on this mission."

Pham stood. "Two of our SEAL teams, we call them the Hai Kich, will be inserted into the area several hours before your arrival. We have been trained over the years by some of your own best SEAL teams and we know our job. They'll secure the adjacent area and create a diversion or two away from the river channel during your firing. It's cut pretty deep so you've got some high banks with some decent cover on both sides. We will discuss the details later, but as planned for in the mission, our team will ride out of the river after the firing mission aboard the *Rattano*."

Loflin motioned to Khiem. "Our liaison officer, Commander Khiem, will work with the team leaders to see that everything is in place.

Khiem nodded and made a small wave, but said nothing.'

Loflin stood again. "Even though you won't be sailing into Haiphong as you suggested, it is pretty damn far north. It's several miles south of Haiphong proper, between there and the Hanoi channel entrance."

McHenry just nodded, thinking it was an insane idea. His eyes slid toward DeMoorts who was seated just two slots over from the admiral. Their eyes met for two seconds, then DeMoorts looked away and McHenry knew that he thought it was crazy too.

Loflin noticed the exchange and quickly continued the briefing. "Captain DeMoorts was brought in as a consultant on this and has reviewed the mission thoroughly with my team. I thought it was important to run it by a destroyer captain who was over here to see what kind of reaction we got. He made a couple of suggestions that we incorporated into our fine tuning and though he thinks it is a daring mission, he also thinks it's a sound one."

In truth he had made no suggestions and was only shown the final, unchanged plan a few days before in a meeting with the CNO staff to convince them to approve it.

DeMoorts cleared his throat and adjusted himself in his chair. "I think one of the real strengths of the mission is that you are the skipper, Mac. It is potentially a dangerous mission, but this is a war and sometimes things need doing even if they are not so safe. Also, nobody could argue that we shouldn't try something new to get this God-forsaken war off its ass. The Peace Talks are ready to resume, but we've heard that before. I believe that with help so close the risk to your ship and the crew are minimized."

"What about Styx boats?" McHenry asked.

"May not be any left, Mac," Loflin lied. "We bombed the shit out of Haiphong and the reports are that the whole population, including the military, are busy cleaning up the mess."

A lot had been made in the news about Nixon ordering massive bombing of North Vietnam during Christmas week. Loflin had heard and read reports that quoted pilots as saying so many places had been bombed that they had been running out of military targets during the last couple days of bombing.

Maybe, he thought, but he'd been keeping his eye on the porting facilities at Do Son. He knew that in spite of the many sorties flown against the area, there were still Styx boats operating from there and from an adjacent river channel that he would hit as well. Just as he had arranged, their main facilities had been missed.

McHenry folded his arms and considered DeMoorts for a moment. He still held his gaze on him as he spoke to Loflin. "Doesn't this mission violate the current bombing halt?"

He brought his eyes to the admiral on the last word. He wasn't quite sure what to make of DeMoort's role in the whole thing, but he was sure that, somehow, the man had gained something from Loflin for supporting the viability of the mission. Maybe it was motivation enough just to have the opportunity to send him up a river into North Vietnam.

Stimm answered McHenry's question for the admiral. "Special permission from CNO. It's been cleared through the Joint Chiefs."

"We sure this area isn't mined?" McHenry asked, then added sarcastically, "Getting blown up from the air doesn't really bother me, it's those pesky underwater explosions that piss me off."

"That's been taken care of," Loflin explained. "Mac, we chose you for several reasons. Your ship is just about the most reliable of any over here. You never break down. Those guns of yours have a reputation all over the damn navy. Hell, whenever the *Rat* comes up, the first thing I hear is how you guys picked off a bicycle rider from four miles away at Hon La or how on your first day on the line you walked twenty rounds down a line of trucks. This can's guns are a goddamn legend, Mac! We can show those pansy-ass fly boys there are still some good targets to go after. They missed plenty. You might be heading home soon and this can be your parting shot, not to mention a star on your own record. Maybe even a couple of silver eagles for your collar."

McHenry smiled. He knew better. Making rank at this point in his career was no longer a priority. Commander was a respectable enough rank to have attained and he had made up his mind to be content with it if he wasn't promoted again. "This is a very good ship. Some of it's luck, some of it isn't."

Loflin looked around at the other members of his party and chuckled knowingly. "We all agree that McHenry's Marauders are up to the task."

There's another reason I won't make captain, McHenry thought. "I'll take that as a compliment, Admiral. Now, about this mission. Has anyone else tried anything like this lately?"

Ponce, the intelligence officer, cleared his throat. "About five months ago was the last time we tried any river surprises, so it's not something they watch for that they would really expect. There's just not the same NVA presence in the area that there was previously. About three years ago we did try a river in this same area, but a little farther south. The ship took a few small hits but no casualties. There wasn't near the planning on that one. They just kind of threw it together on site and they only went up a few hundred yards."

McHenry nodded. "I remember that. The *Rupertus*, wasn't it?" Ponce nodded. "I hope the planning on this one is better."

Several of the officers began to empty the contents of their briefcases and pouches out onto the table to show him how thorough their planning really was.

Chief Ross absently reached up and punched in the four-digit code that allowed entry into Radio. Known only to him he had rewired the security device a few hours earlier so that any four digits could be used. He was sick of his radio crew always forgetting the code. He was holding the latest issue of *Popular Science* in his left hand, folded open to an article about so-called "stealth" aircraft designs that might someday make radar detection obsolete. When the buzzer sounded, he pushed open the door. Still reading, he stepped into the noisy communications center.

The rattily din of three Teletypes poured from the back room while in front of him a mimeograph machine clunked out copies of the latest message.

He looked up from his magazine. He was surprised to see that there were several radioman who were just coming off duty still there with the four who had just come on.

"Well, I'm glad I've got a few of you here," Ross said, "except for you Ryder. Why are you hanging around in here again? My God, we're going to have to make you a radioman. It's against regs you know, just like all the other times I told you. All these guys have top secret clearances which you need to work in this space. You don't have one of those."

"I stay out here in the main space," Jeffs said. "I don't go back in the crypto room with the Teletypes running and all that. Besides, Chief, you love me, remember? Leon is always hanging around up on the signal bridge. Can we make him a signalman?"

Ross looked at Leon, who was placing copies of messages into the various departmental boxes and pretending to ignore the conversation. "Good idea, Ryder. We can make both of you radio signalmen and you can stand back-to-back watches and just forget sleeping! Anyway, listen up. Several of you have been having to ring the buzzer again to come in because you can't remember the four digit code. Why is that? It's just four numbers. What if there's nobody who can let you in? It's supposed to be a security feature, not just buttons to play with. I changed it last week, remember? Who knows the new code? Maybe you'll win a prize."

Jeffs raised his hand. "3437."

The chief's eyes widened and he looked quickly from each man to the other. "Why the fuck does Ryder know it? You guys can't remember it and he's not even authorized to know it."

"What's the prize, Chief?" Jeffs asked.

Leon snorted a laughed while Logan and two others turned and pretended to busy themselves with paper on the desk.

Cassini, one of the radiomen, appeared in the doorway from the back room. "Chief, we're got a high priority coming in on the broadcast."

Ross hurried to the Teletype, not necessarily hoping that it was something interesting, which often meant some problem.

"Go see what it is," Jeffs urged Leon.

"Hell, it's nothing," Leon said sourly. "It's always nothing."

Ross returned shaking his head and slapping the paper that he had torn off the Teletype. "Really important shit, gentlemen. It seems that tomorrow, Senator Post and his entourage will be making surprise visits to several gun line ships by helicopter. Guess why?"

He waited with an expression of exaggerated anticipation. Jeffs and Leon looked at each other and shrugged.

Jeffs said, "He wants to see if we all know the code to get into Radio?"

Everyone laughed, even Ross. "No, goddammit! He is investigating reports of, and I quote, navy personnel being deprived of even minimal amounts of fresh water for upkeep of personal hygiene and cleanliness."

"Shit yeah!" Leon said. "We're going to bitch at a senator about the lack of water aboard ship. The captain won't mind, will he?"

"Not at all!" Ross agreed. He was reading the message over again to himself. "Well, anyway, it's an immediate and it's hot shit when congress is taking a look at what you're doing. Take it to the captain or Mr. Smith in the wardroom." He handed it to Jeffs. "Here's your fucking prize. Real radioman stuff."

Jeffs hesitated. "The admiral and everyone is in there."

"Doesn't matter," Ross answered. "It's gotta go."

"Okay." At least it was something to do he thought. He headed for the door with the message in hand. "They just have to initial it like when I take signals received to them, right?"

Leon and Ross both nodded and Jeffs headed out the door.

Officers were used to the daily comings and goings of the radiomen and signalmen. Jeffs had no apprehension about walking in on the briefing other than the fact that Admiral Loflin was one of the highest ranking officers in the United States Navy.

He knocked on the door of the wardroom and waited. An officer unknown to him from the admiral's staff opened the door. A few of the men in the room gave him a quick glance and returned their attention to the briefing. Most took no notice at all. Gil Smith was seated several feet inside the door and Jeffs held up the message when he looked his way.

Smith motioned him in and as Jeffs handed him the paper, he knelt down next to him and whispered in his ear, "This is a weird one, sir."

Smith whispered back. "So is this meeting. Did you ever see so many gold-plated turds in your life?"

Jeffs smiled and waited silently as he listened.

Loflin was speaking. "The thing I like about this is that it's going to be a surprising and demoralizing blow far north into enemy territory. You'll only be thirty miles below Haiphong and it'll make damn good press. We haven't had a good, glorified, daring news event for some time."

McHenry nodded and wished to God they had picked some other ship.

Jeffs felt his mouth hanging open and suddenly clamped his jaw shut. A rustle of paper against his chest brought his attention back from the scene before him. Smith had initialed the message and had been tapping against Jeffs' chest for several seconds.

He took the message and looked questioningly at his executive officer.

"Uh, are we...?" He gestured toward Loflin who was still talking beside the map."

Smith just nodded, but with a look that Jeffs immediately read as alarm. "We're taking this boat up a damn river right into North Vietnam," he whispered. "Like far north, up by Haiphong Harbor."

Jeffs surveyed the wardroom quickly, then turned and left. He closed the door softly behind him and leaned against the bulkhead in the empty passageway. His legs felt too heavy to move, but he forced them to start moving him back toward Radio.

When he got back to Radio he pushed the buzzer to be let in instead of punching in the code. Leon opened the door and Jeffs stepped inside and returned to the spot where he had been leaning on a file cabinet. After several moments he looked up and saw Leon, Ross and two other radiomen all silently staring at him.

Ross stepped closer. "What's the matter, Ryder? You look like you saw a ghost."

FORTY-FOUR

It doesn't make a damned bit of difference who wins the war to someone who's dead.—Joseph Heller

The last person to enter the wardroom of the guided missile cruiser *Oklahoma City* was Admiral Loflin. Already standing around the table were Captain Richardson of the *Oklahoma City*, the commander of destroyer squadron seventeen, William Gordan, and Franklin DeMoorts, Captain of the *Holliner*. Loflin had moved his flag to the cruiser two weeks before just for this mission. He wanted to be sure he got a firsthand look as his personally planned scheme unfolded.

Loflin's original plan had been to be aboard the *Newport News* where he would watch her come alive and he would feel and hear the overwhelming, spectacular violence as her eight-inch guns were unleashed against the missile boat facilities and adjacent river channels where they knew the boats were operating and hiding. The mere thought of the experience made his whole body come alive with anticipation in a way that could only be described as sexual. However, the *News* left for home on the east coast at the end of November, even though he had tried unsuccessfully to stop its departure, so he was forced to settle for the *Oklahoma City*. He told himself it would still be a satisfying experience but he considered the ship to be several steps below the mighty gun cruiser.

The *Oklahoma City* was a light cruiser that had been converted to a guided missile cruiser. The surface-to-air missile launcher was in the after part of the ship where gun mounts used to be. Just forward of the bridge the cruiser still retained one triple mount of six inch guns and a double mount of five inch guns.

"Good morning, gentlemen," Loflin greeted. "Let's get started, shall we."

On the table before each of them was a folder stamped TOP SECRET. Inside each folder were twenty pages detailing the operation, along with several more pages that neither Captain McHenry nor anyone else aboard the *Rattano* knew about.

Loflin remained standing while the others seated themselves. "As you already know, at 0600 hours tomorrow the destroyer *Rattano* will begin Operation Little Big Horn. However, the report in front of you gives a great deal more insight as to why this mission is taking place and why we brought the *Okie City* up here yesterday."

Each of the men present opened their folders as the admiral continued. "Please turn to page nine. In August the *News*, *Kitty Hawk*, *Robison* and *Rowan* sank a couple of patrol boats and hit some areas around Cat Bi and Do Son and came under some real enemy fire. By the way, I understand that raid made all the newspapers and TV news. Everyone got a big kick out of us going right up to Haiphong like that. Anyway, as you all know we have yet to deal with these missile boats. They've been moving the fuckers all over to keep us from hitting them and only sparingly using the facilities at Do Son. If they know how to use those boats they're sure as hell going to get themselves a ship."

The three men exchanged uncomfortable looks. "Admiral," Captain Richardson interrupted. "I'm just now seeing this and haven't had a chance to read it all, but right here it calls for hitting Do Son. We've still got a bombing halt in force, don't we?"

"That's exactly right," Loflin said, "but who knows what the hell the bullshit of the day will be tomorrow or next week. Anyway, stay with me on this, Captain and it'll all come together for you. We think there's a good chance that one or two of those boats will be operating in the area and go after the *Rat* when she comes out of that river."

He pointed to the map of the Haiphong area that hung on the wall behind him. "I want those goddamn boats. They're a threat to every ship over here and they seem to be getting ready to make their move. We're going to take them out! When they come after the *Rat*, we're going to sink them and then were going to blow the shit out of Cat Bi and Do Son and all the nearby river inlets where more of them are hiding."

He was trembling noticeably. "We're going to make that raid in August look like a Red Cross delivery. The whole area is fucked up from the Christmas bombings. With air cover from the *Coral Sea* we're going to steam the *Okie City*, and the *Holliner* and the *Wilson* right up to the beach and light up the place and the adjacent inlets. We're going to cause so much fucking damage that they won't know where to ever start figuring out what's left! We are going to save the navy from the humiliation of an attack from these goddamn boats!"

He suddenly realized how excited he had become and stopped talking.

There were several moments of awkward silence before Gordan cleared his throat and spoke. "Admiral, this is all fine with me, and I think we should hit those targets, but what about the bombing halt? As a matter of fact, the *Rat* isn't supposed to be shelling anything up there either."

Loflin sat down, poured himself some iced tea then pointed at DeMoorts to answer.

"We received a message from CNO a few hours ago. Basically, it says that since the bombing halt a few days ago, there have been, as usual, numerous incidents of stepped-up activity by the North. In view of this, CNO has gotten authorization through the Joint Chiefs to go ahead with this mission. They're calling it a limited action in response to cease-fire violations to demonstrate to the north that we are serious about enforcing a cease-fire. We are authorized to attack the shore targets only if the *Rat* comes under direct attack."

Gordan glanced back and forth between Loflin and DeMoorts. He knew he had purposely been left out of the loop in the planning of this. "Well, Admiral, I hope that South Vietnamese SEAL team does a damn good job of securing that river. Otherwise, it's pretty certain they're going to come under some kind of attack, wouldn't you say?"

"There's one possibility we haven't discussed here," said Captain Richardson. "What if the *Rat* is hit hard and disabled or sunk?"

"They have all the air and sea support they could possibly need just minutes away," Loflin answered.

"What about Mac?" Gordan pressed. "He doesn't know he's being set up. Shouldn't we at least warn him about possible boats operating in that area?"

"Mr. Gordan!" Loflin stood again, glaring at the squadron commander. "You're letting your friendship with Mac run your emotions. I don't think 'set up' is a fair description of what's going on here. Those are viable targets he's after, boats or no boats, and his penetration this far north is a necessary military and morale blow."

Loflin, of course, knew that "set up" was a dead accurate description of the situation.

Gordan backed off his tone a bit, but continued to stand up for the destroyer's plight. "You're right about Mac being a good skipper, and the *Rat's* got a hell of a reputation in this part of the world, but I just think he should be kept fully apprised. You said yourself these boats are dangerous and we are talking about almost three-hundred lives aboard that ship that we are placing in harm's way. There could be some serious consequences if anything goes wrong."

Loflin opened his mouth to answer, but Richardson interrupted, hoping to take some heat off Gordan. "May I, sir?"

Loflin gave a quick nod. He and Richardson had discussed it at length already.

"CNO agreed. He doesn't want them to be used as bait, but he also cannot justify meeting up with missile boats as a part of the mission as an excuse to circumvent the bombing halt. As the *Rat* nears the end of her firing mission and begins heading back out of that river, we'll radio them about the possibility of boats in the area. When he comes out of that river, Mac will be ready for anything. Air help won't be far off and we won't be pulling any surprises at that point."

"Any further questions, gentlemen?" This was Loflin's usual signal that there were to be no further questions. He stared at Gordan, daring him to speak. "We'll meet back in here at 0500 hours. Make sure your CIC and Weps officers are here. We'll be contacting the air boss on the *Coral Sea* as well so they'll know to be ready if we need them. See you in a few hours, gentlemen."

Even though he had no authorization to do so, Loflin had ordered all air patrols over the gulf to stand down for a few hours until told to resume normal operations. He rightly figured that by the time anybody with any authority caught on to what he was doing it would be too late to make any difference. He had even gone so far as to meet with the air boss aboard the Coral Sea. The man owed him a favor and Loflin had managed to buy some down time for the launch catapult aboard the carrier right around the time the *Rattano* would be exiting the river as well as no aircraft being in the air. Loflin had done everything he could to ensure that one of his ships would be engaging and hopefully destroying the missile boats and not any "fly boys" as he usually referred to them.

Typically the northern Tonkin Gulf was bristling with fighters and patrol aircraft in the air constantly guarding against any MIGS attempting to mount an attack against U.S. aircraft carriers or other vessels. At the present time, all that extra protection had been taken away and it was just a lone destroyer sailing far north deep into enemy waters.

FORTY-FIVE

Dear Mom and Dad,

I haven't written as much as I should. I have received ten of your letters but some were over a month after you mailed them. I have decorated the signal shack with a surf board and tiki torches and the captain likes it. We're kind of famous with the ships we get fuel and supplies from at sea. They send us "surf's up" greetings. Since it's December now I guess we won't be back in November! Soon though I hope.

Love,
Jeffs

Jeffs took off his helmet and rubbed the top of his sweat-soaked head. "George, this is getting to be like a real war."

George just grunted in reply. "Just what I needed, another damn river."

It was 0430 hours and they would be approaching the river mouth in ninety minutes. They were already deep into North Vietnamese waters and the crew was at battle stations. That afternoon they had all been issued helmets, and not just those men working outside stations as on earlier raids.

Now as each man felt the unfamiliar weight of the steel shell they also felt the weight of the coming action. Bridge personnel and men working outside stations had also donned their required flak jackets. The machine guns just aft of both bridge wings were manned by a gunner and an assistant with two thousand rounds of ammunition. In a little while, three groups of four men each would take up positions on the torpedo deck, the fantail and the hangar deck armed with M-16's. They would also be armed with ear plugs to deaden the hammering of the guns that would be firing right beside some of them. Unfortunately they would not be armed with the knowledge that a boarding party awaited them with their deaths as its first objective.

In preparation for this mission, special aircraft had been electronically jamming radars all along the North Vietnam coast at irregular intervals for a week. It was not known for sure just how effective this effort was, but also working in favor of the *Rattano* and her crew was the fact that the recent massive bombings had thrown the operations of the North Vietnamese military into various degrees of disarray.

Loflin and his mission planners hoped that even if a radar operator picked up that lone blip so far north he would doubt himself and his equipment into inaction or by the time the right message got to the right command it would be too late. It was also hoped that the two-vessel squadrons of fast attack patrol boats that had been motoring about the area for the last several weeks were not all Styx boats with the means to blow the destroyer right out of the water. They needn't have worried.

It had cost Seven more than all the bounties they had ever paid out combined, but there would be no premature attacks by any patrol boats or MIGs this night. A clear path had been opened up for the *Rattano*. Between the group's efforts and Loflin's arrangements, the destroyer and her crew were actually going to be quite safe until they reached their river.

Aboard the *Rat*, the 1MC clicked on. "This is the captain speaking. The preparations for this mission have gone very smoothly and I thank you all for that. In about forty-five minutes we'll be beginning our river excursion. We'll be backing in about three miles and then waiting for a few minutes before we start our firing sequences. I don't think I need to remind any of you that this is a dangerous mission. For some reason we've drawn the most difficult assignment last. Remember to keep doors and hatches secured, no lights outside and no loud noises or talking topside once we begin backing in."

McHenry paused for a moment and wiped the sweat from his forehead. He felt he should say more before such a dangerous operation. His eyes scanned the shelf before him and he remembered the large blue bible that rested on the end of the shelf, a book he had not opened for some time.

He pulled it down and laid it in front of the microphone before him. He leafed through it for a passage he knew, then resumed speaking. "We don't have a chaplain on board, as you know, and I'm not too good at making prayers, but I think I have something here that will express something for all of us.

He held the book upright on the desk top and moved a little closer to the microphone.

"The Lord is my shepherd, I shall not want;

He makes me lie down in green pastures.

He leads me beside still waters, he restores my soul.

He leads me in paths of righteousness for his name's sake.

Though I walk through the valley of the shadow of death, I fear no evil; for though art with me;

Thy rod and thy staff, they comfort me."

Here and there around the ship there had been a few nervous laughs as he began reading the passage, but mostly it was quiet. After a few moments of silence, McHenry said quietly, "Carry on."

He leaned back in his chair staring at the now dead microphone. A knock sounded at his door and Gil Smith walked in. McHenry swiveled his chair around and faced his executive officer. "Too dramatic?"

"I'd say you sobered a few minds out there. Sure can't hurt." Smith leaned back against the door and considered his skipper for a moment. "Tell me, now that we're almost there, what are your latest thoughts on this mission?"

McHenry sat against the edge of his desk and folded his arms. "The same thing we've already talked about. Too risky and not very necessary. I suppose it'll hurt the North Vietnamese if we blow up enough good stuff, but if eleven days of bombing by hundreds of B-52s didn't do it what the hell are we going to do? I think we must be after something more important than they're telling us."

Smith nodded. "Loflin gives me the creeps. Anyway, I was looking over the maps again. Do you realize that we'll only be sixty miles from Hanoi? I guess there really shouldn't be any trouble with a SEAL team going in ahead of us, but it makes me nervous backing this thing up a river this far north."

McHenry chuckled. "Good, it should."

The phone buzzed. Smith picked it up. "XO. Very well, thanks." He replaced the receiver. "That was Don on the bridge. We got a message from the *Coral Sea*. She's on station forty-three miles out. The *Oklahoma City* along with the *Holliner* and the *Wilson* are formed up just a few miles farther in."

McHenry stood. "Hope we don't need any of them. I'm heading up to the bridge."

"So what's the latest on Khiem?" Smith asked.

McHenry sighed. "Good question. I've noticed him getting quieter and quieter the closer we got to this little deal. He barely talks to anyone, always makes himself kind of scarce. Wil says Loflin and Khiem work together regularly. He doesn't seem like anyone to be concerned about, but I think I am anyway. That reminds me, the code word for the outside security people is Geronimo. Might as well stick to our damn Indian theme."

Smith looked puzzled. "Code word?"

"Well, I started thinking," McHenry explained. "We're on a river way into enemy territory and I just want all our bases covered. I don't think I trust anybody that had anything to do with this, beginning with Admiral Loflin and good old DeMoorts." He turned toward the door again.

"So, what's the code word for?" Smith asked.

McHenry turned. "Not exactly sure but this isn't a real SEAL team, it's a Vietnamese team. I don't care what they say, it ain't the same thing and I don't know if I can trust this situation. Our guys on deck know we've got friendlies out there and at some point we're picking them up. If there's some trouble on that river I don't want them being hesitant 'because they're worrying about shooting at the wrong guys. Weps has been working with them for the past couple of days. They've each got a bag of ammo clips. If I pass the word, it's shoot to kill, and if that damn Vietnamese SEAL team is still out there they better just duck."

"It's better being on this thing than one of those river patrol boats you've told me about, isn't it?" Jeffs' tone was hopeful.

George took a deep breath and let it out slowly as he gazed out the window of the signal shack into the darkness. "I don't know. We're on a damn big target and I keep thinking we can only go two directions on that river, up and back. I doubt it's wide enough to turn around and even if we could it would take a while. Those river patrol boats I was on could go from a dead stop to thirty knots in just a few seconds. Man, it felt like a hundred when they were wide open, and we all told ourselves we were too damn quick to hit."

He turned away from the window to Jeffs. "We used to call the boat a piece of shit, but tonight I'd rather be back on that piece of shit than sitting on this one." He folded his arms and turned back to staring out at the darkness.

Jeffs watched him for a moment then stepped outside for some air and a cigarette. He walked to the front edge of the signal bridge and managed to shield the cigarette enough from the wind to get it lit. He rested his left foot on the bottom railing and watched over the bow of the destroyer. They were doing better than twenty-five knots and if he turned aft he could just make out the white water as it churned out a wake, the wake he'd lately observed was always right behind them. They were headed straight in toward the coast and would be slowing soon for their entrance into the river mouth.

Far to the north he could see a few scattered lights on the horizon about where he guessed would be the southern end of the Haiphong area. Those lights were enemy lights and he did not want to be close enough to know they were there. The ship was running under darkened conditions and the glow of his cigarette cupped under his hand was technically a violation of that condition, but he felt like they must be able to see the destroyer. Somehow the North Vietnamese must know a dangerous intruder was in their midst, he thought.

"What the hell am I doing here?" he whispered aloud. "I should be on the coast of California not the goddamn coast of North Vietnam." The soft glow of his cigarette suddenly seemed too bright and it was making his mouth even dryer. He reached down and placed it under his shoe and twisted it into the deck.

Breathing deeply he gazed around at the stars and the rising moon and let the wind tangle his hair. That sense of adventure he felt when they were heading across the Pacific seemed like a long ago, naive concept. In its place right now he was finding a trapped panicky, sensation that seemed to be coming from somewhere deep in his chest, and he was doing his best to keep it under control. At the moment he only cared about himself and Cathy and he wasn't just wishing for the familiar return to normal life. All he wanted right then was to get through the next few hours alive and well.

The ship slowed and his attention returned from the star dotted blackness. He heard a heavy click from one of the machine guns as the gunner locked the ammunition belt into place.

William Gordan had decided to stay aboard the *Oklahoma City* during the mission rather than returning to the *Holliner* to just wait. This was where Admiral Loflin was and this would be the command center, although unless there was some sort of emergency there would be little in the way of communication.

There were twelve firing sequences. As each one was completed there would be just a one word count passed over the secure voice radio circuit.

Captain DeMoorts had left the *Holliner* in the capable hands of his XO and elected to sit out the mission aboard the cruiser as well.

DeMoorts and Loflin had been up in CIC and on the bridge for most of the evening, but Gordan could only take the two of them in small doses and had been passing the last hour or so just reading and trying to relax in the small cabin that had been provided to him as a squadron commander.

He was lying on top of the blanket on his rack and had drifted from reading to thinking again about the *Rat's* impending mission. He checked his watch. The destroyer would be making the approach to the river mouth in a few minutes.

Gordan swung out of the lower rack and made his way through the deserted officers-country passage to the wardroom to grab something to eat before returning to the nerve center of the ship to wait out the mission with the others. No other personnel were about and he was surprised to find someone sitting on the sofa in the wardroom eating a sandwich and reading a magazine.

The South Vietnamese officer looked up. "Good evening sir."

Gordan recognized him as the SEAL commander who had been at the briefing aboard the *Rattano*. "Good evening. Lieutenant Pham, isn't it?"

Pham smiled. "You have a good memory Commodore."

On the counter the stewards had left a platter of sliced cheese and cold cuts along with bread and the usual condiments. Gordan began putting together a sandwich. "I didn't realize you were aboard, lieutenant. Been hiding?"

Pham chuckled. "No, I came over on a launch a few hours ago. I have been on the *Coral Sea* for the last several days with my two Hai Kich teams seeing to all the details. But now that they don't need us, I decided to watch the mission progress from here."

Gordan nodded as he continued his sandwich building, then stopped and stared at Pham. "I heard there were three replacement teams going in instead of the original two. I thought you were still going in with them though. They don't need you?"

Pham's eyes narrowed. "No, they don't need us, the teams. Something about the mission being changed to an offshore firing. I don't understand what replacement teams you're referring to. There are no replacement teams."

The knife he was using clattered into the sink and Gordan ran out of the wardroom, down the passageway and up three decks to the bridge. It took a few moments for his eyes to adjust to the darkened conditions. The only light was a dim red glow from the chart table and another near the captain's chair where Richardson, the skipper of the cruiser, was seated. Admiral Loflin was standing next to him.

Gordan walked up to the two men. "Admiral, I was just talking to Lieutenant Pham. I think there's a problem. We need to talk."

Loflin looked annoyed. "What's the problem?"

"Let's step out where we can discuss this."

They stepped out into the passageway. It too was lit only by a few red lights.

"Pham told me his SEAL teams were called off the mission."

"Calm yourself, Mr. Gordan. That's correct. Their command decided to make a change. There was some kind of conflict in their schedule. Rather than his Alpha and Bravo teams they switched it to the X-ray, Yankee and Tango teams. Three teams instead of two. Everything's just fine."

Gordan shook his head emphatically. "His two teams are sitting aboard the *Coral Sea* right now. He was told there was a change in the mission and they didn't need the river secured."

Loflin scowled. "They're having some confusion, but the reason doesn't matter. His two teams are off, the other teams are on. That's it. I just talked with Khiem yesterday. All the arrangements are set."

"Are you sure about that, Admiral? Let's go talk with Pham. He's down in the wardroom."

FORTY-SIX

Dear Jeffs,

...I promised I would write every day. I haven't quite kept that promise but almost. I feel like I am getting more afraid every day and all I can think about is how badly I need you to come home. They keep saying this war is about to be over, but it's still killing people. I'm sorry if I sound depressing. I love you. Please be safe. Please be careful. I love you.

Love,
Cathy

Every small squeak of a door, scrape of a shoe, hum of a vent and every muffled cough or whisper seemed impossibly loud to the men aboard the *Rattano*. The river banks had been slowly sliding by in reverse for what seemed like an eternity. At intervals along the way they were signaled by dim red blinking lights from the SEAL team to show them both that the banks were secured and to help them keep to the center of the channel. It would be more than an hour before the real dawn would come, and nobody, including Jeffs felt very secure about what the sun would shine down upon when it arrived. The mission had been timed so they would be departing the river channel in the predawn light. With McHenry's agreement, it was decided to give the destroyer the advantage of some light rather than running blind.

Captain McHenry sat in his usual high-perched chair for a moment and drew hard on his nearly dead pipe to re-light it. He covered the bowl with both hands to conceal the glow, but he knew by now that it really mattered little. Anyone close enough to notice his pipe would surely not have missed four-hundred feet of metal festooned with guns and masts gliding by on the moonlit river.

He was thinking that everything was going well enough so far. It was a wide, gentle curve back down river, so a quick escape would present no real navigational problems, but the river channel was shallow, even with the high tide promised by Admiral Loflin, so if he did have to leave in a hurry, the furious churning of the twin screws so close to the river bottom would probably cause a vibration through the entire ship that would feel like all hell breaking loose. He had come to know that, for whatever reason, she was one of those ships that would put out for her captain and crew. McHenry hoped that if he did break anything they could keep running long enough to at least clear the river mouth and wait for help.

"George!" Jeffs said in a loud whisper. "We've still got fifteen minutes to just sit here and wait. Why they doing this to us?"

Before George could answer, the door of the signal shack opened and Seymore, one of the gunners, stepped in. "Hi guys, how we doing?" He was whispering too.

"Just great!" Jeffs hissed. "We were just talking about how we'd like to come here again sometime."

Seymore was too nervous to fully appreciate Jeffs' sarcasm. He just looked at him as though he had not really heard him and threw a quick smile. "Anyway, here. Mr. Smith said to make sure at least one man in each space was armed. You guys are in a topside area so you each get one."

He handed them each a belt with a .45 in the holster. "There's two full clips in each pouch. Gotta go. Later man." He stepped through the doorway and was just about to close the door when it opened again and his head thrust back inside. "Sure hope you guys don't need those things. By the way, Mr. Smith says load 'em and be careful so you don't shoot each other in the ass. His words exactly." Seymore managed a smile then left with a silent wave.

Jeffs took one of the clips from his belt and shoved it into the handle of the gun with a hard metallic finality. George did the same and looked at the gun as he held it in his right hand with the bearing of someone who not only knew how to use it but had used it before.

Jeffs lifted his weapon and considered the weight of it. He had fired one only once before and that had been just a few shots at the shooting range in boot camp. He thought about how it would be and he looked out at the darkness, wondering if someone was looking back."

"This is stupid," George said, just above a whisper. "They aren't going to walk up to us and let us pick them off. If anything they'll just blow the hell out of us with mortars or something."

"I was afraid of that," Jeffs said. He holstered the .45 and looked outside again. "Or maybe fucking MIGs, huh?'

George just nodded.

The horizon to the east could be vaguely distinguished by the dim glow behind it. He looked to the steep river bank again and thought that he could now make out a few dark shapes in the moonlight along the water's edge, but it was still too dark to be sure that it wasn't his adrenaline fueled imagination. The ship had slowed nearly to a stop.

Leon's battle station was in Radio manning the phone circuit that connected with the signal bridge and one of the phone talkers in CIC. For lack of anything else to occupy him he was also watching the broadcast Teletype droning out its infinite messages. Along with him were six other radiomen. Two were typing messages to be sent later, one was running copies of incoming messages and distributing them to their respective departmental boxes, and two were sitting around talking and arguing about what was going on outside after the guns stopped.

Ross was overseeing all of this as he thumbed through the latest issue of *Playboy*. The battle dress and the fact that the first class radioman, an Idaho Okie named Stokes, was armed with a .45 did lend a certain seriousness to their collective attitude that hadn't often been evident before.

Leon's attention grew as the Teletype began building the next message. It was a FLASH priority, a rarity amid the droning onslaught of routineness, and it was addressed only to them.

FM COMSEVENTHFLT

TO USS RATTANO

S E C R E T

PATROL SURFACE CRAFT ACTIVE IN YOUR
AREA. POSSIBLE STYX MISSILE BOATS. ALERT
RADAR OPERATORS AND ALL LOOKOUTS TO
BE ESPECIALLY COGNIZANT OF APPROACHING
SURFACE CRAFT. EXERCISE CAUTION WHEN
DEPARTING RIVER MOUTH. RECOMMEND
PROCEED DUE WEST TO CLEAR NORTH
VIETNAM TERRITORIAL WATERS ASAP. BOATS
MOST LIKELY NORTH OF YOUR POSITION BUT
UNCONFIRMED AT THIS TIME. AIR SUPPORT
FROM CORAL SEA STANDING BY JUST MINUTES
FROM YOUR POSITION.

"Damn!" Leon declared. The others all stopped and looked at him. He tore off the message and walked around the corner to Chief Ross and set it down on top of the photo he was studying.

Ross read it and whistled. "I'll take it." He handed the magazine to Leon and hurried out the door.

Leon pressed the button on the phone that hung on his chest. "Hey, sigs."

"Fort Apache here," Jeffs answered. "And in case you're wondering, no, nobody's shooting at us yet."

"Terrific," Leon said quickly. "Listen, you'll be hearing from the bridge in a minute. We just got a flash message. Patrol boats out there. Missile boats maybe."

Jeffs was sitting on the stool at the desk of the signal shack. George had his back to him standing just outside the window watching the river bank. "George."

George turned and leaned through the window just as the "bitch box" came to life. "Sigs, bridge."

He held down the switch. "Sigs."

"Hays, this is the XO. We just got a message here. Possible missile boats in our area. When we head out of here keep your eyes peeled. Also, the captain says to have that Red Eye ready for whatever else might pop up. Don't fire at anything until you hear from us. The *Coral Sea* might have planes coming to us."

"Aye aye, sir." George let go of the switch and turned to Jeffs.

"That's what I was going to tell you. Leon called from Radio."

FORTY-SEVEN

If war were a living beast, then a fondness for chaotic, pointless, unexpected death would certainly be one of its most prominent characteristics.

Jeffs had envisioned a river something like the pictures he had seen of the Amazon or Congo--thick, tangled rain forest reaching to the water's edge with the high jungle canopy behind and looming overhead. But this river was much different.

At its mouth, more than a thousand yards wide, thick stands of mixed bamboo and Asian oaks marked the opening into the coastline. Here, nearly three miles up the gradually curving waterway, it had narrowed to just a couple hundred yards on each side of the ship. Here, where the ship would be slowing to a stop in just a few more feet, stood bare levees built up more than fifteen feet on each side of the river. Some that had stood without being disturbed for some time were sprouting new green, and here and there were stands of trees and undergrowth, but nothing like the rain forest he had envisioned. So far, though, all Jeffs knew for sure was it was dark.

Suddenly the two forward guns fired, catching both Jeffs and George completely by surprise. Flashless powder was being used and for a couple of seconds the two men were not sure what had caused their instant sensory overload. They both jumped and then just stared at each other in the near darkness.

"Goddammit!" George finally blurted out.

Another blast jarred the ship. "I guess we don't need to whisper anymore!" Jeffs yelled.

The aft gun mount came to life as well and both men gripped their side arms and watched intently out the windows, still wondering who was looking back.

On both shores, forty men waited in their rafts. Two rafts on each bank with ten men in each raft. All of them had the reflective tape red X on the front of their uniforms, their ticket for getting aboard the destroyer and being well on their way to capturing it before they were found out.

Along with them, down at the water's edge, and above them up on the levee and on the other side, more men waited, more than a hundred all told. If things went wrong too soon, they were to open up on the ship with everything they had. This was mostly small arms and a couple of light machine guns, but there was also a single forty-millimeter Bofors gun. Originally designed for anti-aircraft use, it was also very effective for ground attack.

This particular one had seen duty on a river patrol boat at one time. Now it was mounted on the back of a flatbed truck. The projectiles it fired were just over an inch and a half in diameter. It was not a large caliber weapon made for destroying a ship and sinking it but just a nice powerful gun for punching it full of holes and shredding its crew and everything else inside it to pieces at just over a hundred rounds a minute. If the *Rat* couldn't be captured then she was going to be punished.

As they had been trained, the men in the rafts waited until the destroyer began its shelling. They were counting on the noise and distraction of the ship's guns to work in their favor. Now that the first few firings had taken place, Quan and the others made all their last minute checks and prepared to push off from shore.

"This is Commodore Gordan. Call Captain Richardson and Captain DeMoorts to come to the wardroom immediately." He replaced the handset and turned back to Pham and Loflin.

"Lieutenant Pham," Loflin said. "I think there must be some mistake."

"No, sir," Pham repeated. He was becoming more agitated by the second and talking faster which was causing his English to carry more of an accent. "I talked with Commander Khiem and I confirmed it with my command. We were called off the mission and the reason given was that it had changed to an off shore bombardment."

He took a step toward Gordan and riveted a look to him. "There are no X-ray, Yankee or Tango teams!"

"Are you sure about that?" Loflin asked.

Richardson and DeMoorts walked into the wardroom.

"Yes!" Pham snapped. "I am the senior team commander of the Hai Kich! I know where all of them are and what they are doing! My two teams are on the *Coral Sea*, Admiral, and there is nobody on your river!"

Loflin looked suddenly sick as he tried to piece together what was happening.

"Did I hear that right?" Richardson demanded. "No SEAL team on the river?"

DeMoorts' eyes locked with Loflin's. "Oh, Jesus!"

Gordan was desperately trying figure out what was happening. "So, Khiem told you the mission was changed and canceled your team?"

"Yes," Pham repeated.

He turned his attention to Loflin. "Khiem told you that replacement SEAL teams would be taking over the mission."

Loflin was now breathing quickly and running his hand through his hair. "Yes," he managed to answer. His lips were puffing out with each breath and he was looking wildly around the room as though he could find some answer. "What the hell is Khiem doing?"

"Wait!" Gordan barked, looking back and forth between Pham and DeMoorts. "That SEAL training aboard the *Holliner* a couple of months ago in DaNang."

"That was canceled," Pham snapped. "I took that message myself."

"No, it wasn't!" Gordan said. "Captain DeMoorts?"

DeMoorts felt like he'd been sucked into a black whirlpool. "Oh, shit. Oh, Jesus. They were practicing boarding a destroyer!" He turned to Pham, his voice trembling. "If you were canceled then who the hell was on my ship?"

"You better talk to Khiem," Pham answered. "He changed that training exercise as well."

Gordan pounded the table with his fist. "Goddammit! They were practicing boarding a destroyer! Can you see what's going on here, Admiral? We've been had!"

Loflin's face was quickly changing to greyish red. "Khiem!" He was bellowing at the top of his lungs now. "Khiem, what the fuck have you done?"

"You and your goddamn mission!" Gordan shouted at Loflin. "Mac is expecting to pick up that SEAL team and ride them out of there! They won't have to fight their way on, they're going to be invited aboard!"

"Then what?" DeMoorts asked. "What are they going to do?"

"Shit!" Gordan shouted. He stepped to the door. "We have to call Mac, let him know what's up and get him some air support in case those damn Styx boats are around."

"Hold on!" Richardson said, a pained expression coming over him. "*Coral Sea* radioed just before I came down here. They have no planes up. They have some problem with the steam plant for the catapults. They said maybe twenty minutes before they could launch again. Since the bombing halt, *Midway* and *America* have left and gone into port in Subic and Yokosuka. The *Coral Sea* is it."

"*Coral Sea* is free to launch when they are able but I ordered all other regular air patrols over the gulf to stand down until further notice from me," Loflin said. "That includes *Coral Sea*. They have nothing up now either until they can launch. My orders."

There was a moment of stunned silence.

"Admiral I want you to order all area air patrols back up right now," Gordan said.

Loflin raised his chin defiantly. "No, I won't do that. In fact I've ordered everything grounded until I say different! It takes a while for the idiots out there to question an order from the fucking Commander of the 7th Fleet! Everything will be grounded long enough. I don't want those flyboys going after those boats! Those are our targets and..." His voice trailed off. "Missile boats! That's it, that's it! There's a bounty on the *Rat*. They're going to take it over so they can sink it."

"A bounty?" Gordan stepped toward Loflin. "How do you know that?"

"Khiem," Loflin whispered.

"Isn't Khiem on the *Rat*?" Gordan asked.

"Yes! That bastard set me up!" Loflin's eyes were almost comically wide open. "This mission was to attract the attention of the North Vietnamese so they would send missile boats after her and we could go after the fucking Styx boats! He set me up!"

Gordan stepped up and grabbed Loflin's lapels with both hands. "You goddamn lunatic! You set up Mac and every sailor on that ship! How dare you send a destroyer out as bait!"

He let go of Loflin and pointed angrily at DeMoorts. "And you helped him with this." He hurried to the door again while he spoke.

"Captain Richardson, let's go. We have to call Mac."

FORTY-EIGHT

Sooner or later, everyone sits down to a banquet of consequences.
— *Robert Louis Stevenson*

On the bridge of the *Rattano*, Captain McHenry had just read the message brought to him by Chief Ross. "Mr. Wiffler, call the aft gun turret. Chief Neal is back there somewhere. Have him report to the bridge on the double. Mr. Owens too."

He then turned to the sailor manning the phone circuit to CIC. "Ruiz, tell Mr. Smith to report to the bridge on the double.

McHenry met Smith at the doorway onto the bridge and motioned him to the red-lit passageway at the top of the ladder that separated the bridge and CIC and read him the message.

"So," McHenry said. "You and I have been kicking this mission back and forth wondering why it didn't feel right. Why is air support still standing by? If they know there are boats out there, how come they haven't sent out air cover all ready?"

"Bait!" Smith said. "It seems so obvious now."

"It sure as hell does," McHenry agreed. "We've been sent up this fucking river on our own to draw those boats out of hiding." He sighed. "Shit!"

Lieutenant Owens, the weapons officer, came up the ladder followed by Chief Neal. McHenry spoke quickly and calmly. "Okay, here's the situation. We just got a flash message from Admiral Loflin. We've got missile boats out there, maybe. In a few minutes we'll be busting out of this river and clearing the coastline. So, if CIC spots surface contacts, what's our next move?"

Their conversation was interrupted every few seconds by the hammering of the ship's guns as the firing sequences continued.

"If they're within, say, six miles or so then we'll have to take them on," Owens offered. "If we can get both mounts pointed at them, then we just might make a quick score. At least if we can scare the shit out of them maybe they'll take off."

McHenry nodded. "Chief, how's our ammo?"

"I checked before I came up here." He pulled a small piece of paper from his shirt pocket. "Aft, we've got just under four-hundred, forward we're down to two-eighty."

"Good enough," McHenry said. "Another question. Will we know if they fire a missile?"

"We should see a flash and, if it's light enough, a smoke trail," Owens answered. "I don't think they'll fire from more than ten miles out. I guess they could but, I don't know." He shrugged.

"And if they fire on us?" McHenry looked from one man to the other.

Owens took a deep breath. "Try some hard turns and hope it misses. Try the chaff rockets at the last few seconds and hope the missile chases the chaff cloud. Maybe just fire all the five-inchers we can at it and hope for a hit. Try the Red Eye but with it coming straight at us that probably wouldn't work. The *Okie City* has missiles but she's too far away. Mac, we're not really made for this."

McHenry was silent for a bit. "Okay, here's what we're going to do. It's pretty shallow right here, but it gets deeper before we reach the river mouth. We're coming out of this river moving as fast as I think I can get away with due east. If we've got far off contacts to the north then we're going to make a hard right south, try to keep some distance and hope like hell we get air support. If we've got them closer or to the south, then we'll keep due east and go at them with all the guns. Hopefully those damn boats are somewhere else minding their own business."

"Speaking of air cover," Owens asked, "how come we don't have it right now?" He looked back and forth between McHenry and Smith.

McHenry answered. "It seems Admiral Loflin has put us all out here to see what we might attract."

Owen's eyes went wide. "You gotta be kidding me." Both men shook their heads slowly.

Lieutenant Wiffler stepped into the passageway from the bridge. "Captain, Commodore Gordan on the secure voice circuit. Says it's an emergency."

McHenry turned to Smith. "I'm canceling the last two firing sequences. Call up to the signal bridge and have them signal the SEAL team aboard right now. We're getting the hell out of here."

McHenry made his way back into the bridge and picked up the red handset. "McHenry here, over."

"Listen, Mac, this is Wil. *Coral Sea* is no help for a few minutes. Fixing the catapult. Air patrols over the gulf are all grounded right now. The SEAL team is a fake. I repeat, the SEAL team is a fake. They intend to board and capture your vessel. Khiem is in on it somehow. Take all available measures to repel boarders and get the hell off that river!"

McHenry could feel his chest pounding and he said nothing for what seemed like too long. "Christ, Wil! Do what you can." He replaced the red handset. "Mr. Wiffler, all ahead one third."

He grabbed the 1MC microphone to announce throughout the ship. "This is the captain speaking. This is no drill. Standby to repel boarders! I repeat, standby to repel boarders! The SEAL team coming aboard is enemy soldiers. Security teams, Geronimo! Geronimo!"

McHenry felt his mind racing, but he struggled to think as clearly and quickly as he could to save his ship and his crew. He reached up to the bitch box. "Sigs, bridge. You guys seen Khiem?"

"Negative," Jeffs answered.

"If you see Commander Khiem, place him in custody, put an armed man covering him. If he resists or tries to escape, shoot him. Understood?"

"Understood, Captain," Jeffs answered.

At that moment, gunfire erupted seemingly from everywhere. The rafts were alongside and the first men were just making their way onto the main deck near the stern, but had been cut down immediately by fire from the team on the hangar deck just above. More men were pouring over the side and some made it onto the main deck. Now the security teams were exchanging fire with the boarders in the rafts and with several who had made it aboard.

McHenry pressed the button for Gun Plot and yelled his orders over the din of gunfire. "This is the captain. Tell the gunners to train the forward guns to port and the aft guns to starboard and begin firing at both riverbanks as fast as they can. Alternating single barrels. Just point and shoot just above the water! If it's too close for the shells to explode I don't care. I just want to disrupt whatever's going on out there and scare the shit out of them. Got that?"

"Aye aye, Captain!"

Seconds later, McHenry watched from the bridge as the forward mount turned, lowered its guns and fired. At the same time he heard the aft guns come to life. All the while the crackle of automatic weapons fire was filling the air as the crew fought off the boarders and began exchanging fire with soldiers along the river banks.

The Hai Kich plan was in shambles. Fourteen of the Hai Kich had been killed and several more seriously wounded. The nine men who had made it onto the destroyer alive were now cut off from the rest of the teams who were still in the rafts. Several others had fallen into the river uninjured, but were now being left behind. The ship had reached just over eight knots and the men maneuvering the rafts were now contending with a moving ship. Two of the men were hanging from the side of the ship by the lower lifeline as bullets hit all around them.

On the signal bridge, George had decided that the thin metal walls of the shack offered little protection. Jeffs, George and Villegas had thrown themselves to the deck outside, trying to stay as flat as possible and at the same time watch for anyone coming up the ladders. They were all facing a different direction holding a .45 at arm's length and trying to stay as watchful as possible amid the commotion of small arms fire and the ship's guns blasting away at the shore.

The deeper bark of both .50 caliber machine guns started up, ordered by McHenry to start raking the riverbanks and the water with bursts of fire. He didn't know exactly what he was dealing with and decided to shoot first and find out later.

Khiem was making his way to the signal bridge, the "high ground" from which he was to oversee the final stages of the capture before he would swim to shore to save himself from the suicidal climax of the plan. Instead he had seen the attack plan fall apart in a matter of seconds and now he was in the midst of a ferocious battle that had erupted all around him. He reached the top of the ladder in a crouch and fell flat, facing Jeffs just six feet in front of him.

Jeffs, lying flat on the deck, brought his .45 straight out in front of him and held it steady with both hands. "Commander Khiem!" he yelled over the sound of the gunfire. "Captain McHenry has ordered us to take you into custody!"

George spun around and was facing Khiem as well from farther back, his gun also leveled at the officer.

Suddenly, right behind Khiem, a Vietnamese soldier jumped up to the top of the ladder at the aft edge of the signal bridge, spraying rounds from his AK-47. Jeffs and George both flinched as bullets ricocheted all round them and off the walls of the shack. Amazingly they were not hit, but Khiem rose, stumbled a few steps forward, falling against the door and into the signal shack. George fired at him, hitting him in the knee just as he fell through the doorway.

At the same time, Jeffs fired three quick shots at the gunman, hitting him in the chest and knocking him back down the ladder.

Jeffs and George looked at each other, wide-eyed as the cataclysm of gunfire continued. Every few seconds the ship's five-inch guns shattered the air and the machine guns continued their intermittent bursts of fire. They could hear the pings and dull thuds of bullets striking the mast above them and the superstructure all around them.

Khiem pulled a nine-millimeter pistol from his waistband, at the same time pulling up his left pants leg to examine his wounded knee. It was too dark to see well inside the shack, but he determined that, although painful, it was mainly a flesh wound just beneath his kneecap.

Then he looked around, gasping for breath lying on the deck inside the shack, and realized he had escaped the gunfire outside but thrown himself right into a dead end he'd have to fight his way back out of.

On the bridge a lookout was hit and killed instantly. Three members of the topside security teams had been hit and two others killed. The boarders in the rafts that were not shredded by fire from the *Rattano* had retreated. On the main deck lay five of the attackers either dead or dying.

Another was at the bottom of the ladder on the ASROC deck, killed by the combined effects of Jeffs' bullets and the fall.

There was one remaining surviving boarder. Quan was huddled against the aft gun turret just out of sight of any crew members. His rifle was in his lap. His knees were drawn up against his chest with his face buried between them and his hands were pressed hard against his ears. Just a few feet above his head, two five-inch guns were discharging every few seconds. Each time he could feel the heat from the blast and his body was being slammed by the concussion. He was afraid to look up, afraid to move his hands, afraid to move at all.

All over the ship, bullets were striking the hull and the outside of the superstructure. Men on the bridge were crouching and ducking as gunfire shattered several of the windows and ricocheted off various objects. One of the lookouts lay dead out on the port bridge wing, shot through the throat. Another bridge lookout had been struck in the shoulder and sat in a corner while others attended to him. Outside, gunfire had damaged several of the radar and communication antennas.

"Take her up to twelve knots!" McHenry ordered.

The light had grown considerably over the last few minutes and, although it was still twenty minutes until sunrise, they could now easily make out the banks of the river.

Jeffs was still lying flat on the deck, but had scooted around to the forward side of the shack just under the main mast where there were no windows to stay out of Khiem's sight.

McHenry, was crouching behind the waist high bulkhead of the bridge wing. Suddenly new, loud and sustained firing started up as the 40 millimeter Bofors gun opened up on the opposite side of the destroyer. The operator intended to keep firing until his two hundred rounds were used up. At the present rate of fire, that would take less than ninety seconds.

The gunner did not need to swing the heavy mounted gun. He was able to just move it up and down while he fired so as to hit the hull and the superstructure while the destroyer slid by. Several shells tore through the fragile spots in the hull and into the mess deck, killing one member of a damage control party stationed there and tearing up tables and chairs. More shells struck the bridge, destroying the quartermaster's table and sending shrapnel throughout the space. Somehow no one was seriously injured, though several men, including McHenry, were left bleeding from minor flesh wounds.

CIC and Radio sustained more than ten hits between the two of them. Several radar stations were destroyed and two men killed in CIC. In Radio, Chief Ross suffered some deep shrapnel wounds in his legs and all four working Teletypes were destroyed along with the cryptography equipment that allowed them to receive the fleet broadcast as well as several receivers and a transmitter. The space was filled with smoke, everyone had minor shrapnel cuts but they all escaped any serious injuries.

And so it would have continued for another minute, the two-pound projectiles slamming into the ship, exploding and ripping apart metal and flesh. But the machine gunner on the port side of the ship, Gunners Mate Third Class Miller, of rice massacre fame, spotted the gun at the top of the levee, about level with his position just fifty yards away. He opened up with a long burst from the heavy machine gun, killing the gunner, both men on his crew and damaging the ammunition feeding mechanism.

The last two rounds fired from the Bofors gun tore into the signal shack. Their explosive charge was relatively small, but the sheer destructiveness of the projectile ripping into its target could cause just as much damage as the shrapnel. Both of the rounds tore through the port side of the signal shack leaving jagged punctures. The force of the impacts broke out all three windows and buckled two corners of the square structure, but it was still standing basically intact.

Inside, Commander Khiem was now quite dead having been shredded and mangled by the fire of his own forces.

The gunfire from the banks was fading as the *Rattano* increased her speed to twelve knots, leaving behind the area where the riverbank forces had concentrated.

George rose and looked through the window into the shack.

"He's deader than shit, man."

Jeffs sighed. "Good, the fucker!" He reached up and wiped blood from his cheek. "Damn, not again."

George leaned down and peered at his face in the growing light. "Looks pretty small. Feel around. You bleeding anywhere else?"

Jeffs checked himself out. "No, I think I'm okay."

In the chaos of the last couple of minutes, they had forgotten about

Villegas. Jeffs looked over at him now, just a few feet away. He was lying with his back to them, his helmet knocked sideways with a large chunk of his brain showing. The pool of blood around his head had run several feet across the deck and up against the signal shack.

"Villegas is dead," Jeffs reported matter-of-factly.

George took a deep shaky breath. "I know. He was right there with us. It could've been any of us."

FORTY-NINE

Power does not corrupt. Fear corrupts... perhaps the fear of a loss of power.
– John Steinbeck

The *Rattano* was still seaworthy enough and running strong, but she had taken some serious drilling. Most of the windows across the front of the bridge were either broken or missing altogether. They could send and receive messages by voice only, and only on the open high frequency radio circuit, which meant anyone listening on that frequency could hear their unencrypted communication. There were thirty-nine holes in the hull or superstructure where the 40mm shells had penetrated.

Fortunately for the crew, the gunners manning the 40mm gun were using an aged, mismatched assortment of ammunition. Some of it was armor piercing and penetrated clear through the superstructure before exploding on the other side of the ship. Some of the regular anti-aircraft rounds did not detonate at all, but still tore through whatever or whomever was in their path. As destructive as it was, it could've been much worse.

Captain McHenry was still crouched low out on the bridge wing. "Cease firing!" he yelled into the bridge.

The word was passed and the dawn fell strangely silent. There was now no gunfire of any kind where just a minute before had been an anarchy of bullets striking, men screaming and shouting, and the successive concussions of the ship's main batteries unleashing on the river bank.

He rose up and looked around. Right in front of him was a ladder up to the signal bridge. He climbed up far enough to see over. "Hays!"

George turned. "Ryder and I are fine. He's bleeding a little again, but it's just that damn head of his. Khiem's dead. It sounded like they were firing a forty at us. Tore the shit out of the shack and Khiem. Villegas is dead too."

McHenry shook his head angrily. "Okay, get that Red Eye ready, both of them, and stand by. I don't know what the hell else is going to happen, but maybe there's missile boats out there. Probably MIG's, UFO's and who knows what the hell else. Shit!"

Jeffs looked over. "Captain, you know your face is bleeding?"

McHenry wiped his cheek and looked at the smear on his hand. "Yeah, I think we all are down here. I'm okay."

McHenry climbed back down and walked onto the bridge to survey the carnage. "Is that Gonzales out there?"

Sid, the quartermaster nodded. "He's dead, Captain."

"Get him in here and cover him up." The XO walked in from CIC. "Gil, we gotta find out how hurt we are."

"I'm on it," he answered.

"Captain." It was the phone talker. "Radio says all you have is the open voice circuit on the gray handset."

He reached up and grabbed the handset. "Capital this is Custer, over."

"Capital here. Good to hear your voice, Mac."

"Well, it was bad. Don't have damage reports yet, but I know we've got some killed. They shot the hell out of us. Boarders repelled. Khiem's dead. We're underway. Over."

"We're working on getting some planes up to you, but *Coral Sea* is still the closest. They say they can launch in minutes. You want to wait on the river until they send help?"

"Negative!" McHenry replied. "We're getting the hell out of here now. I'll get back to you, Wil. Out."

Smith was back and forth on two sound-powered phones and the intercom writing hurriedly on a small notebook while contacting every part of the destroyer he could.

McHenry surveyed the damage to his bridge while he waited to hear about the rest of the ship. "Jackson, get a broom or rags or something and get some of this glass off the top of things."

The XO put down the phones. "Okay, here's the picture. Engine room and both gun turrets are fine. The mess deck, Radio and CIC took some pretty bad damage and the radar dish on the gun director is knocked out. The outside security teams have three dead, one signalman dead, one sonarman, one radarman, two damage control parties have one dead each, plus Gonzales here. That's nine known dead. So far we've got another ten or so with serious wounds and just about every division had a few minor cuts and scrapes, but most of those can wait on medical attention."

He flipped the page on his notebook. "There's six enemy dead on board and one prisoner. Teams are checking to make sure there's nobody else. No gun director like I said but we can still point and shoot and we can still maneuver and make good power. Communications is limited and we've got no surface radar. The antenna is shot up. When we bust out of this river we won't know about any surface craft except what we can see visually"

McHenry took a deep breath and sighed. "Mr. Wiffler, use the men from topside security and get the bodies moved into the hangar. Help the wounded that can be moved to sick bay or the passageway just outside it. Gil, call Chief Spencer. He's got the damage control party on the mess deck. Have him and his party meet Mr. Wiffler on the fantail on the double. Mr. Wiffler, see to it that all gets done ASAP. We've only got a few minutes and we may be back into it. As soon as you're done tell those security guys to report to their regular battle stations."

Lieutenant Wiffler answered a quick, "Aye, Captain," and hurried from the bridge.

McHenry gazed to where Petty Officer Mike Gonzales had been moved inside and covered with a blanket. "Get a couple of CIC guys in here for extra lookouts." He stepped out onto the port bridge wing and shouted to Miller and his ammo man. "Stay ready. We may have some patrol boats coming up."

He hurried across to the starboard wing and told the machine gunner there the same thing, then looking upwards he bellowed, "Sigs!"

Jeffs' face appeared over the railing. "Sir?"

"Keep those two men on the big eyes and the rest of you keep a sharp lookout too. I want to know immediately if anyone sees anything."

"Yes, sir," Jeffs answered.

"Both those Red Eyes all set?"

"Yes, sir!"

"Hays, you listening?" George's head appeared alongside Jeffs'.

"You guys don't fire unless we tell you but have them ready. We've got friendlies coming in, at least I fucking hope we do. I think they'd frown on being shot down."

George nodded. "Right, Captain."

McHenry looked back into the bridge. "Let's try seventeen knots, Mr. Simons. Keep us in the middle of the channel."

He looked up again to Jeffs and George. "Time for the war paint. Run up the Marauders flag. We still have the torches?"

"Somehow they are still standing," Jeffs said.

"Good," McHenry said. "If they still work, light 'em up."

Jeffs responded with a quick, admiring nod. "Aye aye, Captain."

Five minutes later the river widened considerably and ahead could be seen the stands of trees on either side of the river mouth that marked the end of the river and the beginning of the sea. The sun was about to break the horizon and there was enough light to see well.

The dead and wounded had been moved and Lieutenant Wiffler was back on the bridge. The weapons gang was alert to the impending threat, the gun mount crews were ready. Two extra lookouts were posted on the bridge wings and two others were watching forward from inside the bridge. Because of the broken windows it was just as windy inside as out.

Two other signalmen were manning the big eyes while Jeffs and George stood at the forward railing just above the bridge. Both of them were leaning on the metal, watching intently into the wind and the near-dawn, hoping to see nothing but clear sea. It was beginning to look more like the sea than a river now with the swells pushing against the river current. Even though it was causing more vibration than he liked from the still too-shallow river bottom, McHenry was holding at seventeen knots.

"You know, I'm starting to have a little better feeling about this." George called out against the wind. "I think we've got better than a fifty-fifty chance of making it out of here alive. I'll bet you twenty bucks we make it."

Jeffs stared hard at George trying to decide if he was kidding or not. "You're on, you stupid bastard. If we don't make it, I'll never have to pay up!"

He extended his hand and they shook on the deal. They returned to their vigil at the railing.

The long tail of Jeffs' headband was blowing out from under the back of his helmet. He was feeling better too with the wind in his face and the panorama of the widening river opening up into the sea. "This is better having a little breathing room!" Jeffs yelled against the increasing wind.

George just nodded and kept watching. His old river senses were on full alert and his whole body, every bit of his being, knew something more was out there.

The southward area of tree-covered land was coming up on the starboard bow just a thousand yards ahead. Gil Smith was in and out of CIC keeping a close eye on air radar contacts. McHenry was out on the port wing, the side he felt sure the boats would be coming from, but he had paced through the bridge several times from one side to the other over the last few minutes. He had alerted the helmsman twice in anticipation of the hard turn he felt sure he would be making in a matter of a minute or two.

FIFTY

My Dearest Lam,

…I received a letter from you today! At least I know you have received at least one of mine. I have been moved to a different duty, at least for a while and I do not know if I will be returning to Dong Hoi. I don't think you will receive this letter for some time so I want to tell you that I am doing something very dangerous but necessary. If I see you ever again or if I don't, know that I love you with all my heart.

Love,
Quan

The captains of the two missile boats had chosen this spot to conceal their vessels against the backdrop of the tree-covered cape while they awaited the arrival of the destroyer to continue the next phase of the mission. They were most concerned about being spotted from the air before the arrival of the ship. They had heard the firing from up river, but were unaware that anything had gone wrong with the capture.

From their vantage point three miles away they reasoned that all the small arms and machine gun fire was just part of the takeover, though they had been a little surprised by the destroyer firing its five-inchers at that point. They had not seriously considered the possibility of the plan not working. It all seemed so well designed and so unforeseen by the Americans that they just expected everything would proceed as planned.

The rumble of their idling engines masked any sounds that may have alerted them to the present threat coming out of the river toward them.

They decided it was time to take another look up river. If everything was on schedule, they would soon see the captured ship slowly emerging from the bend about a mile and a half up river. Vu had his binoculars ready to check that the flags were flying, signaling that radio communications were out. This was his signal that all was ready, as well as a delaying tactic for American ships and planes as they proceeded down the coast to their destiny. As they circled out slowly from the shoreline foliage into the river mouth, the captains and crews of the two boats were shocked then panic-stricken at the sight of the destroyer cutting through the water from upriver, just over a thousand yards away and bearing down on them.

Incredulous, Vu brought the binoculars to his eyes. He couldn't make out the pirate or the rat at this angle, but he knew the single large crimson flag was not the right signal. And he didn't know what to make of the two tails of flames streaming out from atop the super structure.

Suddenly, Chomsky, the signalman watching through the starboard big eyes, was pointing and yelling. "Boats! Boats!"

At the same instant two bridge lookouts also began shouting. Jeffs and George jumped a few steps to that side of the railing so they could hear anything directed their way. McHenry appeared just below them, having run through from the other wing.

George yelled, "Get down!"

They both flopped onto the deck. Jeffs caught his helmet just before it rolled under the railing. He quickly plopped it back on his head and fastened it in place.

The machine gun on the starboard side began firing while a confusion of shouts sounded from the bridge as orders were barked to phone talkers and into headsets.

The forward gun mount turned slightly, leveled both guns and fired with a hot concussion that Jeffs felt hard on his stomach through the metal deck. Two splashes shot up just in front of the boat. The other boat captain hit the throttles and disappeared around the cape as the guns fired again at the nearest boat and missed.

The guns fired a third time just as the boat was about to accelerate seaward. Both shells slammed into it just above the aft main deck into the side of the missile launcher. There was a large explosion and a cheer sounded from the men on the bridge just as another enormous detonation of the eleven-hundred pound missile warhead convulsed the air and water all around. Jeffs and George buried their faces in their arms as debris splattered the ship.

Below, on the bridge, Lieutenant Owens, the weapons officer, ran in from CIC. "Captain, stay on the other boat! He's too close to use his missiles against us. When we come around that point we have to chase him and hit him hard before he gets enough distance to turn and fire on us!"

"Got it!" McHenry answered. He reached up and clicked on the 1MC. "This is the captain. We've just destroyed one North Vietnamese missile patrol boat and we're chasing another. Stand by for some hard maneuvering and a hell of a fight!"

He hung up the microphone. "Helmsman, stand by for a hard right rudder on my command!" He reached up to the bitch box and punched a button. "Radio, Captain! Still just the open voice circuit?"

Leon answered, "Yes, sir. Looks like that's all we're going to have."

McHenry grabbed the gray handset again. "Capital, Custer. Over."

On the bridge of the cruiser, Admiral Loflin watched silently as he slumped on a stool.

"This is Capital," Wil Gordan answered, switching onto speaker so the others could hear. "*Coral Sea* is about to launch."

"It's about time!" McHenry shouted. "Damn near ran over two missile boats at the river mouth. One destroyed, pursuing the second boat to engage before it can return fire. A little help would be appreciated!"

He started to break off contact, but returned the handset to his mouth. "By the way, you can tell Admiral Loflin and his whore DeMoorts that I've got at least nine dead sailors and a ship full of holes. Out!"

He slammed down the handset and shouted out two orders. "Helm, hard over starboard now! Mr. Simons, order us to flank speed."

McHenry knew he was cutting it close, but decided against taking a quick look at the navigation charts, that were laid open just a few feet from him, which he doubted were updated anyway,. "Sid, how am I doing?"

Sid, McHenry's senior quartermaster, was good and he knew his captain was good. Holding on to his table to stay on his feet, he answered,

"Captain, at this speed even if we don't clear the mud we might just plow right over it and end up okay."

McHenry was hurrying out to the wing, but called over his shoulder, "If I run us aground at least we won't have endure an investigation. They'll just blow us up!"

Up on the signal bridge, Jeffs and George were standing again, holding onto the railing with white knuckled tightness as the destroyer leaned hard into its sharp turn. They had cleared the cape and could see the missile boat throwing up white water already over a mile ahead and doing forty knots on a line taking it at an angle away from the coastline. The *Rattano* was rotating out of its turn and still spooling its way up to thirty-four knots as McHenry set it on a course directly behind the boat.

"Jeez, George, we're going to chase the damn thing!"

They were both shouting above the wind noise. "They can't fire behind," George explained. "They'll have to get a little distance and turn to get a radar lock on us to get a missile off!"

The forward guns interrupted their wind-whipped conversation with a double salvo. A few seconds later there was another and then another. They watched as splashes burst up all around the speeding boat, but it continued unharmed. This was going to take the collective talent, experience and luck of the *Rattano's* gunners.

But just then, some of that luck left them. For the first time since 1955 during a training exercise, the warship's guns let her crew down. The first class gunner pulled the red trigger and...nothing. No metallic thunder. No quick, hammer-blow concussion. Nothing.

He drew back his hand and stared for a second. "Son-of-a-bitch," he muttered, then reached up and punched a button. "Bridge, forward turret. Hot gun. I repeat, hot gun. Both barrels did not fire."

The three officers, two chiefs and five other enlisted men on the bridge all looked at each other and then at McHenry. In the heavily damaged CIC, just seconds later, a phone talker relayed the problem aloud to Gil Smith, and everyone looked silently to their executive officer for the answer to the unspoken, "Now what?"

On the bridge, McHenry felt like his brain was trying to think of too many things at once. Since the *Newport News* incident, and other less serious ones aboard a couple of destroyers, there had been several directives ordering that "hot gun" situations were to be handled by abandoning the gun turret until a later time when a limited number of men would attempt to unload or re-fire the gun. Directive or no directive, McHenry reasoned that in this situation there was going to be a much larger explosion if that boat was not stopped.

He reached up to the box. "Attempt to fire the guns again."

A few seconds later the gunner called again. "Nothing, sir."

McHenry looked out over the gun mount, over the bow to the speeding missile boat. "Clear both breeches, throw both shells and powder canisters overboard, reload and re-fire. Hurry it up, Hepner. We're about to be in deep shit here!"

He turned to watch from the row of broken windows that ran the length of the front face of the bridge. A few feet above him, Jeffs and George were listening to the commotion on the bridge and watching too. They saw Chief Neal running forward along the main deck to the turret. The bridge was silent. CIC was silent. The wind and vibration of the driving ship was mere background noise. They watched and waited, knowing that if the guns did fire it would scare the hell out of them. They watched them dump the shells and canisters overboard.

Several seconds later, Neal's voice came over the speaker on the bridge. "No luck, Captain. The guns won't fire. It could be awhile to find out why. Could be some damage from all the hits we took."

McHenry ran out to the starboard wing just below Jeffs and George and scanned the sky. "Where are those damn planes?" he muttered.

Smith came onto the bridge again from CIC and called out to him. "Captain, two planes from *Coral Sea* coming at us hot, but they're still two and a half minutes out! Owens says the boat might have just about enough distance to try a wide turn and launch."

McHenry nodded. The destroyer was pitching and plowing through swells just hard enough that he knew they would never get much past thirty knots if that.

Chief Neal appeared beside him out of breath. "Well, Chief, Mr. Owens says they've got enough distance to launch. What do you say? How long until that bastard turns and launches?"

"Depends on what kind of balls he's got, sir! He can get better target homing with more distance and a little more time. He could try it with incomplete radar info and go ahead and launch. A couple miles might be enough according to the literature but…" He shrugged. "We could hang a hard left and start firing with the aft guns."

McHenry had considered that move already, but he didn't want to be the one to give the boat captain the extra distance he needed. "Not yet. If he starts a turn then maybe we can turn at the same time and beat him to the punch!"

Just above McHenry and Neal, George felt a slap on his back. He turned and found Jeffs holding the Red Eye launcher in both hands raised above his head, a foot of white headband whipping in the wind from beneath his helmet. The expression on his face showed the beginnings of a dead serious grin. Neither of them said a word.

George turned and leaned over the railing. "Captain!"

McHenry looked up. Jeffs held up the launcher with an expectant look. McHenry turned and watched the boat as it continued to pull farther ahead. He looked up at Jeffs and George again.

Chief Neal was pointing. "There he goes, Captain! Looks like the start of a wide sweeping turn. Probably wants to keep up his speed and distance as much as possible instead of stopping to launch."

McHenry glanced at his watch. Over a minute and a half until help arrived. It wouldn't take that boat a minute and a half to get off a missile. He pointed up at Jeffs and George. "Go for it now!"

He stuck his head back through the doorway. "Ryder's going to fire a Red Eye at the boat! If you've been saving any prayers, say 'em now. Maybe that war paint of his will come through for us."

The phone talker immediately relayed that information to CIC. Within ten seconds, other phone talkers at their battle stations throughout the ship had relayed the information to most of the crew.

Jeffs stepped back and gestured with the launcher at George. George shook his head. "You thought of it, man! Let's do it! Bet you a hundred bucks you miss!"

Jeffs shouldered the weapon and saw that the boat was beginning a sweeping arc that would bring it around toward them. "We have two launchers ready to go!" George yelled from behind him. "As soon as you fire, drop it. I'll hand you the other one. It'll be all set. It's faster than putting a new missile tube on the first one."

Jeffs was already aiming. His mind was focused. He locked onto the boat with his eyes and pulled the trigger.

A sharp, loud whoosh sounded as the missile left the tube, and a fraction of a second later it ignited past the speed of sound with a high-pitched shriek. He dropped the launcher. No one, least of all Jeffs, knew if the aircraft-intended missile would even respond to the heat of the boat or do enough damage if it did.

The exhaust trail rose slightly, veered to the right of the speeding boat, then suddenly dove straight onto it scoring a direct hit at the stern. There was a bright flash and flames shot up briefly, but the boat was still moving just as fast and it was halfway through the turn that would point it at the *Rattano*.

He had already shouldered the second launcher. "Hit it!" George barked. Jeffs fired again. This missile followed nearly the same course, then it too suddenly dove straight into the flames ignited by the first shot. There was another bright flash and the boat lost power so suddenly that the top of the bow plowed into the water as it dropped and it came to a powerless stop, smoke beginning to pour from the stern. The bow had not yet come around toward the destroyer.

McHenry yelled at the bridge crew. "Ryder got it with a goddamn Red Eye! Ryder nailed the boat!"

The phone talker immediately relayed the incredible news to the others on his circuit.

Jeffs and George both stumbled against the railing and into each other as the ship slowed and turned seaward so the aft guns could finish off the boat. George grabbed Jeffs and he dropped the empty launcher. "You did it!" He wrapped his arms around him, then backed away and shook him by the shoulders. "You did it!"

Jeffs felt shaky, but managed to return a weak smile. "We did it."

The aft gun mount came to life and fired four single shots just a few seconds apart. All hit near the boat but missed.

CIC had been tracking the approaching fighter, and the men on the bridge had listened as the approach was relayed to their speaker, but everyone jumped anyway as the first A-6 tumultuously appeared on the scene. It screamed in just two hundred feet above the water from the port side and fired a missile at the boat from just over the bow of the *Rattano*.

It, too, scored a direct hit, but this time one of the boat's missile warheads was detonated and a gigantic explosion launched flaming shards of the formerly feared patrol craft high into the air and out in every direction.

Cheers sounded from all around the ship.

The two signalman couldn't stop smiling at each other. Jeffs poked George in the chest. "You owe me a hundred bucks, and I'm not paying you the twenty for making it out of this mess alive."

Aboard the *Oklahoma City* as McHenry and the A-6 pilot radioed in, Admiral Loflin briefly rallied from his stricken state. He now had confirmation of the excuse he needed for his attack. His mission was a success after all, he reasoned. "So it worked! Our next step is to call the bridge and set a course for Do Son."

"Admiral!" Wil Gordan shouted. "You are to stand down. There will be no attack on Do Son or anywhere else. This ship is going nowhere except to render aid to the *Rat* and her crew. In just a couple of minutes I am contacting CINCPAC by secure voice and teletype advising them of why I have relieved you of your present duties. Also I am ordering your Deputy Commander, Rear Admiral Parker, to restore air patrols over the gulf immediately and informing him that he is temporarily Commander 7th Fleet. You want to call this a mutiny, Admiral, you go right ahead."

Loflin looked around at the others and was met with silent stares.

Gordan turned to DeMoorts. "Captain, you are ordered to stay aboard until we put into port. Your executive officer will assume temporary command of the *Holliner* until further notice."

"Captain Richardson," Gordan continued. "See to it that Admiral Loflin is confined to his cabin and post two guards. Also he is to have no access to any communication whatsoever until approved by me."

The *Rattano* now had an umbrella of air cover and the crew was taken off of battle stations. She was steaming south east away from the coast at just twenty knots toward a rendezvous point with the cruiser.

Jeffs and Leon met on the ASROC deck, just outside Radio. "I hear Hughes is dead," Jeffs said.

"No more taking apart the ship," Leon said. "Another guy was killed in CIC too. Forgot his name. Your buddy Mikey was killed on the bridge."

"I heard," Jeffs said. He slowly shook his head and sighed. "How's Chief?"

"He'll be okay," Leon said. "They bandaged up both his ankles after they pulled some shrapnel out of him. Just cuts, I guess. He's walking around on one crutch. Man, they shot the hell out of Radio. Reminded me of when Phil was killed. We were all looking around expecting to find somebody dead again."

"Maybe Shakes left just in time," Jeffs observed.

While they talked they walked to the open end of the hangar and looked in. Two gunners were stationed with M-16's slung on their shoulders. A row of body bags were laid side by side along the forward end of the hangar.

Between the two sentries sat Quan. His wrists and ankles were handcuffed together. He looked up. Jeffs and Quan stared at each other for a few moments. Jeffs was struck by how young the man looked, and by an unsettling feeling that they somehow recognized each other.

Jeffs and Leon hung around for a while longer. Other crew members found their way there as well, out on the hangar deck, talking over the day's events, reminiscing about the guys in the bags, wondering about the prisoner.

✔
FIFTY-ONE

January 1973

I have asked for this radio and television time tonight for the purpose of announcing that we today have concluded an agreement to end the war and bring peace with honor in Vietnam and in Southeast Asia.

--President Richard Nixon

When they reached the rendezvous point, helicopters from the *Coral Sea* took the bodies and the more seriously wounded men back to their extensive medical facilities. A few of the less seriously wounded that just needed some first aid and rest before returning to duty in a day or two were taken to the medical department on the *Oklahoma City* where they had more beds and more room than the destroyer.

On the way back to Subic, the deck crew made some repairs to the exterior of the ship with sheet metal and rivets. That and some matching haze grey paint pretty well hid from the rest of the world just how shot up the old gunslinger actually was.

In Subic more repairs were completed. Some communication and radar equipment was replaced as well as the windows across the face of the bridge. All in all enough work was done to get the ship on her way across the Pacific. After just a seven day turn around, the *Rattano* and her crew were on their way east, back to the real world.

There was great interest in Quan at first as the only prisoner from the attack. He was questioned aboard the carrier by Pham and others and a few days later he was flown to Yokosuka where a CIA team interrogated him. All concerned quickly concluded he was nothing more than a low level foot soldier and knew practically nothing about the planning or people involved in the attack. He was held for a couple of weeks while they decided what to do with him. During those two weeks some political and military maneuvering by members of Seven and their friends was taking place. One day he was abruptly released to a team of North Vietnamese "officials" and flown to Hanoi. A few days later he was driven to his home where, with a sizeable payment in his pocket, he was reunited with Lam and his three-month-old son. The incredible good fortune of the Village by the Lone Hill had continued and he was able to begin doing what he could to try to rebuild his longed for normal life.

The on-again, off-again Paris Peace Talks were grabbing most of the media attention and this time they finally followed through. Somewhere between Midway and Hawaii the men of the *Rattano* learned that the cease-fire agreement, the agreement that would end the war for the United States, but not for Vietnam, so many times promised then taken away, would be signed in a few days.

The world never heard much of anything about the perilous river raid. It was, after all, the result of deception, betrayal and a delusional conspiracy perpetrated by a fleet commander, which was not the kind of press the navy wanted. Officially the navy played down the casualties and the damage to the ship. There was a quiet investigation into the whole operation in which Captain McHenry criticized the lack of air cover that left his ship unnecessarily in harm's way. He also managed to use the word bait more than once. This, along with some supporting testimony from Wil Gordan and the captain of the *Oklahoma City*, persuaded the navy to relieve Admiral Loflin of his command for cause, force him to retire immediately and reduce his rank one star down to rear admiral.

But, as he sometimes told old friends later, "Retirement pay for an admiral, no matter how many stars, is pretty fucking good."

Franklin DeMoorts was transferred to a dead end shore assignment and never commanded another vessel. After a couple of discouraging years as second in command of a supply facility in Long Beach, California he retired, still a commander.

Captain McHenry, regarded "McHenry's Marauders" as the finest crew he had ever sailed with, and he made a point of staying in contact with some of them, including Jeffs Ryder, Leon Thomsen and George Hays. He was not surprised when none of their well-deserved glory materialized for saving their ship and each other. He did, however, retire as a captain.

There was a small article on page four of a San Diego newspaper and a similar one in Stars and Stripes. Neither of them had most of the details correct although one of them did mention the name of a signalman who fired a missile as Jeff Ryder, not Jeffs. But it was all lost in the big end-of-the-war news. Besides, the world was sick of the war and nobody was in the mood to write much about any Vietnam heroics.

For several years afterward whenever the *Rat* or McHenry's Marauders was mentioned, more than a few heads turned and former crewmen drew admiring looks and questions. Word of the river raid and other exploits got around in navy circles, though it was difficult to figure which versions to believe of the several that were being circulated. Some thought the whole thing was some sort of myth.

One of the stories circulating was the line of twenty-seven trucks destroyed in sequence in a single firing mission. Then there were the three bicycle riders destroyed on that road at Hon La on three different days. The one most often repeated was about the two missile boats that ambushed her at the mouth of a river way up in Indian Country not far from Haiphong. Some said she destroyed one boat, evaded the missile fired from the other, and finally stopped the second boat with a shot fired by some signalman with a Red Eye anti-aircraft missile. The part that people most often doubted was the Red Eye shot.

After President Nixon announced on January 23rd that the peace agreement was indeed about to become a reality, the mood aboard the *Rattano* was subdued. The men wanted to be glad that the "end" had come, and they were, but in a way that they hadn't quite figured out yet, they felt cheated.

They had made a personal investment of time, fear, sweat, ingenuity, courage and the lives of some of their shipmates. As more details of the peace agreement were made known, it became clear that everyone was just quitting. The Vietnam War had ground itself down and now at last it was truly going to be over. It had taken too long, but it had finally died of sad, futile, terminal irrationality.

Their way back from Vietnam had been the same islands and endless stretches of open sea as on the way over. The routineness of everyday tasks on the way back seemed easier, less toiling, but it was also less purposeful. Their quest was over.

There were, however, two events that made the return trip a memorable one. The first was an affirmation of the accomplishments of every man aboard the *Rattano*. In Pearl Harbor there was a ceremony on the pier next to the ship. The press was kept away, of course. The entire crew was awarded the Navy Unit Commendation and the Combat Action Ribbon for their operations in Vietnam. The presentations were made by Admiral Elmo Zumwalt, Chief of Naval Operations and Commodore William Gordan, Commander Destroyer Squadron Seventeen. Fifty-eight crew members were awarded the Purple Heart, ten of them posthumously. All the members of the security team that fought off the attackers were awarded the bronze star along with Miller, the machine gunner who had silenced the Bofors gun that was tearing up the ship.

In addition, George and Jeffs were awarded the Silver Star for their action in crippling the enemy patrol boat and very probably saving the ship and the lives of many of her crew.

Both men had reveled in the attention directed their way since the incident, and enjoyed more of it at the ceremony. They were still surprised at how many men who they never really knew before, now greeted them with genuine courtesy, some of it bordering on reverence.

The second event occurred just the next night after leaving Hawaii. For many of the men aboard the destroyer it made the entire dreadful experience of serving with Lieutenant Wiffler worthwhile. It was also a fitting tribute to the memory of Radarman Danny Hughes and the artistry of his ship deconstruction project.

Fake Eggs had been replaced by another Filipino cook. He knew his business, was making food that the crew liked and they had accepted him as one of them. His name was also a difficult one for Americans so the crew had taken to calling him New Cook. That evening, New Cook served a new chili on rice concoction that he had prepared once before that the crew enjoyed. This night, though, the heads throughout the ship had become quite busy by 2100 hours due to an apparent overdose of chili powder and other "secret ingredients" in the recipe.

The officers' heads were also full, so Mr. Wiffler, newly promoted to Lieutenant Commander, wisely decided that just this once he would lower himself and slip into the aft, main deck crew's head, the largest one aboard the ship.

He was alarmed to find all eight stalls occupied, but relieved that he was the next in line. Within a couple of minutes he had a stall to himself. The stalls were grouped four on one bulkhead and four on the opposite bulkhead with a row of sinks in between. This particular head was one of the more civilized ones on the ship and each stall had doors.

As Mr. Wiffler took his seat, the two men across from each other, both at the end of their row of stalls, stood to buckle their belts and leave. At that exact moment the ship took a bit of a roll and both men stumbled against the partition between themselves and the neighboring stall. Not big clumsy stumbles, just a pair of small, off-balance bumps. The kind than happened all the time. Someone later commented that if Hughes was watching down on the crew that night he must have been jumping up and down, clapping and laughing.

The partitions of all eight stalls, along with their occupants, gave way in sequence like dominoes. Amid all the cussing and yelling, the occupants of the two stalls at the far end, Lieutenant Commander Wiffler and a radioman by the name of Leon Thomsen, were knocked off their perches by the falling partitions, fell against the sheet metal bulkhead, which also gave way, and spilled out into the main passageway. The cause seemed to be an extensive lack of screws and rivets holding everything together.

Leon, of course, made sure he told the story to as many of the crew as possible, describing in detail the look on Mr. Wiffler's face as he lay, pants down, bare-assed in the passageway.

FIFTY-TWO

...There has been a lot of talk the last few days about certain members of this crew being heroes. I would not take that away from them, but I would like to add that every member of this crew, in his own way, became a hero that day. During the months of this deployment, you all became a genuine part of the ship and because of that we were able to fight as though the ship had been brought to life by its crew. I am honored to have served with and been the captain of a group of men who were proud to call themselves McHenry's Marauders.
--James McHenry, speaking at the awards ceremony in Pearl Harbor

Five miles away shimmered the lights of the city, the bay and the surrounding hills. Those who knew where to look amid the multitude of illuminations could pick out the lighthouse near the harbor entrance, just two miles away, the bridge that arched over the bay to Coronado, the tower at Lindbergh Field.

The ships had run ahead of schedule and, though it seemed entirely unsuitable even to the two captains, they were to sit at anchor overnight and arrive at their scheduled morning homecoming time. Many of the men were purposely busying themselves below decks with reading or playing cards as though they were still making their way back across the Pacific.

After a few short hours of restless sleep, Jeffs dressed in the darkness of the compartment and made his way back up to the signal bridge. The clean dungaree pants and work shirt were still a pleasant novelty. Since leaving Subic, the steady steaming had allowed the ship to maintain a comfortable water supply. Jeffs had even skipped a shower and gone to sleep once because it was the third night in a row they had been allowed showers.

He zipped his faded work jacket as he stepped out onto the ASROC deck. The change from the mostly warm tropical humidity of Southeast Asia to midwinter in the states felt drastic, even in San Diego. The sun had not cleared the mountains yet, but it was light enough to see well. The lights of the city had extinguished down to just a few leftovers.

George was standing at the railing on the signal bridge smoking a cigarette and watching the city come to life. He smiled as Jeffs appeared at the top of the ladder. "Can't sleep?"

"Not much," he answered. "I keep waking up so I figured I'd just get the hell up." He lit a cigarette too.

George gestured toward the city. "Can you believe this? We're actually home."

Jeffs took in a deep breath of the cool air. "I don't know if I believe it or not. It seems like we've been gone a long damn time."

The two of them stood in silence for a few minutes before Jeffs said, "Remember up here watching the morning come on that river?"

George answered with a nod, thinking that it too seemed like a long time ago. It had been less than a month. "We've been in a different time, Jeffs." He sounded like he was talking mostly to himself. "I think maybe time is going faster now. It felt like that before too." His voice trailed off.

Jeffs looked at him, but didn't ask. He turned and saw Chief Ross approaching, dictionary under his left arm. "Hey, Chief, got a word in there for this day?"

"Greetings and salutations, men. As a matter of fact, Ryder, I do." He walked to them with a slight limp, rested the dictionary on the top of the railing and opened it to a place he already had marked. Jeffs and George stood on each side of him. Ross ran his finger down the page. It was light enough to read. "Here it is. The word for this day is sublime."

He looked at both men and they just waited. He chuckled. "I underlined the parts that apply. 'Lofty, grand or exalted. Tending to inspire awe usually because of elevated quality; as of beauty, nobility or grandeur. That, gentlemen, is what this day is all about."

Jeffs and George had nothing to add. They just smiled a little and nodded in agreement.

A dull, coastal morning overcast hung all around them, but to the east, behind the city, it was clear with the near dawn. A bright speck appeared where the hilltops met the sky, then moved quickly toward forming a sphere.

Jeffs said quietly, "Here comes the sun."

The three of them, along with many others who were on duty stations or had made their way topside, watched in worship-like silence as their sublime day of return came upon them.

As they passed the buoy marking the inner harbor channel, the ship slowed to just eight knots, the speed they were required to maintain through the long curve of the harbor that would take them the length of the city's waterfront to the 32nd Street Naval Station. They were really home now, but it would be an unbearably long forty-five minutes before they would tie up at the pier, still eight miles away. Several hundred yards behind them sailed the *Wilson*, the guided-missile destroyer that had made the trip over with them in July, and a crew with their own tales to tell.

Jeffs watched as the end of the green-shrouded peninsula called Point Loma slid by, rising high on the port side. They sailed slowly past the busy airport, the old sailing ships turned into floating museums for four dollars a peek, the tankers and freighters from around the planet. Black, green, white, blue hulls, and everywhere the rust invaded, apparently winning the battle in places. Fishing vessels and pleasure boats of endless types and sizes littered the docks along Harbor Drive. The concrete quay walls where cargo was given and taken displayed graffiti records of years of passing sailors and bored teenagers.

The bridge connecting San Diego with Coronado loomed larger and finally passed overhead, two-hundred feet high, alive with speeding metal and rubber on its back, sixty cents round trip.

Every pair of eyes on the destroyer took in all these details and gloried in their return to civilization and home.

But for many of them there was also the beginnings of a notion that no matter how wonderful it all was, the anticipation was maybe a bit greater than the realization of it. It was, after all, just a return to the normal, predictable, regular routines of life.

They had been warriors aboard a ship of war. They had known the adrenaline-pumped fear, the excitement, the craziness, the camaraderie, the gut-wrenching highs and lows of war. For weeks and months on end they had lived with the thunderous hammering of naval guns sending a final total of over nineteen-thousand rounds to the enemy. A few times they had seriously considered that they might die in the middle of the night on the dark sea, or trapped in a river too far north, or at dawn while they chased a boat that held the seeds of their annihilation.

They had been bestowed with honors from their country for these accomplishments, and now they were back to their longed-for normal life. It was beginning to dawn on them that everything they had been through seemed so damned out of place here. Already they were beginning to wonder if it all meant anything back here.

Jeffs was at his customary vantage point at the forward railing of the signal bridge, along with Leon, George and several others who had come up for the view. Unlike the Marauders of just a month ago, they all had proper haircuts and complete regulation uniforms. Their required dress blues for the transit through the harbor hadn't seen the light of day in quite some time and they were just a little heavier than before with the weight of those new medals and ribbons.

He watched intently as the ship began a turn that started them towards their berth between piers four and five. He could faintly hear the music of the band, then the crowd came into view. More than three-hundred people were gathered along the expanse between the piers. Balloons and welcome signs bobbed above the throng. The *Rattano* was only a quarter mile from her destination, but it would still be almost fifteen minutes of maneuvering before they were moored. The yelling and waving began from both sides of the closing distance and for now, at least, the doubts and worries of the returning warriors were put aside.

Jeffs felt George move closer to him as they both watched the crowd growing closer by agonizing inches. "Jeffs, uh, this coming home stuff won't be exactly what you think." He sounded a bit nervous.

Jeffs looked at him. "What do I think?"

"Hell, we all think the same thing," George answered. "How great it's going to be to get our old ladies in the sack again, how the kids won't bother us no matter how much racket and fighting goes on, how getting home is going to make everything fucking just right again."

Jeffs nodded. "Is that what you think too?"

He shrugged. "I guess so, but really I should know better." He studied his companion's face for a moment, then chuckled lecherously. "Hey, don't worry, it'll be great to get her in bed again. But, listen, it won't make everything right again. Somehow, it will never be quite the same as it was. They won't understand."

"They?"

"Nobody, everybody," George said. "Not Cathy, not your parents, and especially not old buddies back home who were never in the war. You want to tell them what it was like and how important it was to you and how in a strange way, you were really living, really alive. But you're trying to tell them and you start to realize it's not coming out the way you feel. It's like trying to explain a dream. You'll start seeing in their faces that most of them just don't get it. They'll never understand how bad it was, or how goddamn good it was."

Jeffs scanned the crowd, then turned to George. "Is that how it was before?"

George nodded. "And you know what? In a funny kind of way, they're right. You're not the same, and they aren't either."

He stopped talking while they took in some of the growing noise from the crowd and the band.

"That time I spent on the Mekong was my first time over. After I'd been back for a few weeks I ran into one of the guys from the boat. We had a few beers and talked about what it was like to be home again and all that shit. He said something I'll never forget. He said that when you come back from the war, any war, you leave a little bit of yourself there, and it its place you bring back a little piece of the war. What do you think of that? I thought it sounded like just some weird bullshit at first, but the more I thought about it the more I thought he was right."

George didn't know what else to say and was thinking he had said too much too late. "Anyway, I thought maybe it would help if I clued you in a little, seeing as how we're big shittin' war heroes now."

Jeffs snorted a laugh and put his arm across his shoulders. "So, you've got three pieces of yourself over there now."

George smiled just a little. "I guess so. Hey, last night I was thinking that if this war is really over, this will be the first time since I've been in the navy that the Vietnam War hasn't been going."

Leon had stayed out of their conversation, but he'd been taking it all in. "Don't worry, brother. Those generals and admirals and politicians in Washington are already cooking up some dumb ass thing to keep us all busy."

They looked around at each other and something told them he was probably right.

"You know, I wasn't going to say anything," Jeffs said, "but I got this strange feeling out of nowhere last night. I was up on the bow having a smoke when I got this idea that it would be easier to go back than to go home." His voice trailed off. Saying it sounded even worse to him than thinking it. He turned to George with a long serious look before he spoke again. "We were important over there, weren't we?"

George gave him a look of approval and a nod. "Damn straight, buddy. We were all important as hell."

Flanked by his two best friends in the world, Jeffs searched the waving, shouting, screaming mass of people, but his mind kept being pulled to other thoughts. He realized that for the last couple of weeks he hadn't been thinking of much of anything except getting home. He was counting on that to take care of everything. He could already see that George was right and it just wasn't going to happen that way.

In the years to come the feeling that the crew had experienced when they learned of the peace agreement would be tucked away most of the time. Jeffs, and thousands like him, had given up a time in their lives, a young time, and had allowed themselves to live in danger and to kill for what they were told was a greater good.

They would watch on television as the prisoners of war came home, some of them, at least. Later they would watch as the last few desperate souls escaped from Saigon as the city fell to the invading North Vietnamese. There would forever be a twinge when they heard the name Ho Chi Minh City. For them it would always be Saigon.

He remembered twenty young men on a cruiser, all dead by malfunction. He remembered ten members of their own crew who would never come home and of five others still recovering in hospitals. And he remembered how they had all fought so hard for their lives and for each other and for the ship.

That look that passed between himself and the prisoner, Quan, came to him again. He had wondered many times over the last few months about the enemy who had fought against them, and about the nameless, faceless people who must have been there somewhere on the other end whenever the ship sent its projectiles soaring. Quan had been that face. He wondered if he had been that face for Quan.

On top of everything else, he still couldn't figure how two nations who barely knew each other, barely recognized each other, could still find reason enough to lay waste to a region and its inhabitants.

Thoughts of Cathy returned him to the present commotion and he realized he was looking straight into her face, now only fifty yards away. She was in a frenzy of waving and when he finally waved back at her she dropped her arms and began to cry and smile in that same curious way she had done nine months before.

In a little while he would hold her and they would work to know each other again. Little by little he would come to understand better what George had tried to explain to him. He had survived, and the war was now a part of his past, which made it a part of him.

Life would go on, and life would have some bad times and some good times. Whenever he remembered younger days, times when life was fuller, more carefree and more dangerous, and deeds were daring, he would think back to that time and no matter how many years passed, sometimes it would feel just like yesterday.

FIFTY-THREE

In war, there are no unwounded soldiers. — José Narosky

Present day— Santa Cruz, California

The undulating swells and sea breezes always reminded him of other days, other times, other places. The surf this day was nothing to brag about, but he was enjoying being out on the water.

Just like George had told him, and just like he had found out himself over the years, normal life wasn't like starting up where he had left off. The surfing these days was going well enough, but the experience wasn't the same as when he was younger and never had been in all those years since returning from the war. There had just never been the same exhilaration as before. It wasn't bad, and he couldn't really say what had changed, but it was different. Sometimes he would smile a little and admit that at this point he was just older. Other times he wondered if he was weighed down more than he knew by that piece of the war he came back with.

He was quietly proud of his board and he actually thought it worked pretty well, but it did bring its share of comments. He had made no effort to hide where two small holes, two very large holes and a long jagged split had been patched and sanded. It was common for surfers to adorn their boards with elaborate designs. Jeffs had decided he liked the design this one had developed on its own. The only adornment was a small painting near the nose of the board of a cartoonish, snarling rat wearing a sailor hat.

Every now and then when he was unloading the board from the top of his car or carrying it down to the beach or back, he was asked what had happened to it. He always answered, "War paint."

THE END

ABOUT THE AUTHOR

Brian Lehman spent four years in the U.S. Navy from 1971-1975 working as a radioman. He was stationed aboard a destroyer, an LST and a guided missile destroyer, each one for about a year. After his honorable discharge he went back to college with the goal of becoming an elementary school teacher. He earned a bachelor's and a master's degree and spent thirty-two years teaching 4th grade a few years and mostly 5th grade. He currently lives in Phoenix, Arizona with his wife Julie and two dogs—a corgi and a miniature dachshund named Scratch and Sniff. He has written two other novels which are not military oriented and hopes to see them published in the future. He plays guitar a little and he is a pretty decent cook.